P9-BYG-178

PINO

Dear Reader,

Thank you so much for reading my novels. From *Virtue* to *Vice* and the five *V* romances in between, each one is very special to me, and it meant so much to know that you found them so too. I particularly enjoyed writing the story of the accident-prone Juliana and her Duke of Redmayne and feel this passionate pair are a fitting finale to my *V* books. Coming up next are the Charm Bracelet romances, a set of love stories encircled by the magic of an heirloom bracelet. Look for *The Diamond Slipper* in early 1997. I hope you'll find this tale of a forced bride, a reluctant hero, and a jeweled charm as deliciously romantic as I do. Until then, please do enter the seductive world of *Vice*. . . .

Warmest wishes,

Jane Feather

Also by Jane Feather:

Vanity

Violet

Valentine

Velvet

Vixen

Virtue

And coming soon:
The Diamond Slipper

VICE

JANE FEATHER

Bantam Books

New York   Toronto   London   Sydney   Auckland

VICE

A Bantam Book / June 1996

All rights reserved.
Copyright © 1996 by Jane Feather.
Cover art copyright © 1996 by Alan Ayers.
Insert art copyright © 1996 by Pino Dangelico.
No part of this book may be reproduced or transmitted in any form or by
any means, electronic or mechanical, including photocopying, recording, or
by any information storage and retrieval system, without permission in
writing from the publisher.
For information address: Bantam Books.

If you purchased this book without a cover you should be aware that
this book is stolen property. It was reported as "unsold and destroyed"
to the publisher and neither the author nor the publisher has received
any payment for this "stripped book."

ISBN 0-553-57249-0

Published simultaneously in the United States and Canada

Bantam Books are published by Bantam Books, a division of Bantam
Doubleday Dell Publishing Group, Inc. Its trademark, consisting of the words
"Bantam Books" and the portrayal of a rooster, is Registered in U.S. Patent
and Trademark Office and in other countries. Marca Registrada. Bantam
Books, 1540 Broadway, New York, New York 10036.

PRINTED IN THE UNITED STATES OF AMERICA

OPM   0 9 8 7 6 5 4 3 2 1

Dedication

This one, *finally,* is for Jim. Always my inspiration. Always—well nearly always—the soul of patience. Always a rock of support and reassurance. Always my love.

VICE

Prologue

London—1750

I do not have such a piece at present, Your Grace."

"I didn't imagine you would, madam. But I assume you could procure one." Tarquin, third Duke of Redmayne, bent to inhale the fragrance of a rose in a deep bowl on the table at his side.

"Such specific requirements will not be simple to furnish," Mrs. Dennison mused from behind her painted fan.

A smile flickered over the duke's lean countenance. "You and Mr. Dennison will find the reward matches the effort, Elizabeth."

His hostess glanced over her fan and her eyes twinkled. "La, Duke, you know how I hate to discuss terms . . . so vulgar."

"Very vulgar," he agreed smoothly. "However, it must be the genuine article, madam. I have no interest in counterfeit maidenhead, however fresh the piece might appear."

Elizabeth Dennison looked wounded. "How could you suggest such a thing, Your Grace?"

The duke's smile broadened, but he shook his head slightly and drew a lapis lazuli snuffbox from the deep pocket of his full-skirted velvet coat. There was silence in the sunny parlor as he took a leisurely pinch, closed the box, and replaced it before dusting his nose with a lace-trimmed handkerchief.

"Is the piece to be for Your Grace's own use, may I ask?" the lady inquired a trifle hesitantly. One could never be certain with the Duke of Redmayne where he drew the line between useful inquiry and impertinence.

"You may assume when you go about the search that she will be for my exclusive use." The duke rose to his feet. "That way we can be certain she will meet the most exacting of standards."

"I trust you will find that all of our ladies meet the highest standards, sir." There was a note of reproof in her voice as Mistress Dennison rose in a rustle of silk. "My husband and I pride ourselves on the quality of our house." She pulled the bell rope.

"Had I believed otherwise, Elizabeth, I wouldn't have sought your help," the duke said gently, picking up his gloves and cane from the console table.

Mistress Dennison looked somewhat mollified. "I shall put inquiries in train immediately, Your Grace."

"Keep me informed of your progress. I give you good day, madam." Her visitor bowed courteously, but there was a glint in his hooded gray eyes that his hostess, sweeping him a low curtsy, found vaguely discomfiting. But it was a familiar sensation when doing business with the Duke of Redmayne, and she was not alone in feeling it.

She turned with an assumption of brisk assurance to the flunky who'd appeared in answer to the bell. "His Grace is leaving."

"Madam, your most obedient . . . ," the duke murmured with another bow. He followed the flunky from the room, into the hall. There was a hush over the house in the sunlit morning, the maids creeping about their business as if anxious not to disturb the sleepers above stairs—those whose business was conducted at night and who took their well-earned rest in the daylight.

The smile faded from Mistress Dennison's countenance as the door closed behind her visitor. The duke's commission would not be easy to fulfill. A piece still in possession of her maidenhood, who could be coerced into obeying the duke's dictates.

Virgins could be discovered easily enough . . . innocent country girls arriving friendless in the big city were ten a penny. But one who would have a reason to agree to the duke's dictates . . .

And not the dictates customary in this kind of contract, as the duke had been at pains to emphasize. He wanted no common whore, because he had a most uncommon use for her. He hadn't elaborated on that use.

Elizabeth Dennison shrugged her plump, creamy shoulders. She would put the situation to Richard. Her husband and business partner could be relied upon to come up with a plan of campaign. One didn't disoblige a client as wealthy and powerful as Tarquin, Duke of Redmayne.

Chapter 1

❧

Juliana was suffocating. Her husband was making no attempt to protect her from the full force of his weight as he huffed and puffed, red-faced and bleary-eyed with wedding drink. She was perfectly resigned to this consummation and indeed was quite well-disposed toward Sir John, for all his advanced years and physical bulk, but it occurred to her that if she didn't alert him to her predicament in some way, she was going to expire beneath him.

Her nose was squashed against the mountainous chest and her throat was closing. She couldn't think clearly enough to work out what was happening to the rest of her body, but judging by John's oaths and struggles, matters were not proceeding properly. Black spots began to dance before her eyes, and her chest heaved in a desperate fight to draw air into her lungs. Panicked now, she flailed her arms to either side of her imprisoned body, and then her left hand closed over the smooth brass handle of the bed warmer.

With an instinctive desperation she raised the object and brought it down on her husband's shoulders. It was not a hard blow and was intended simply to bring him back to his senses, but it seemed to have the opposite effect.

Sir John's glazed eyes widened as he stared at the wall

behind her head, his panting mouth fell open; then, with a curious sigh like air escaping from a deflated balloon, he collapsed upon her.

If she thought he'd been heavy before, he was now a deadweight, and Juliana shoved and pushed, calling his name repeatedly, trying to wake him up.

If she'd been panicked before, she was now terrified. She tried to call out, but her voice was muffled by his body and lost in the thickly embroidered brocade bed curtains. There was no way anyone could hear her behind the firmly latched oak door. The household was asleep, and George had passed out after his third bottle of port on the couch in the library. Not that she could have endured being found here in this mortifying exposure by her loathsome stepson.

Juliana wriggled like an eel, her body slick with the sweat of effort; then, finally, she managed to draw up her knees and obtain sufficient leverage to free her legs. Digging her heels into the mattress, she heaved with her arms and shoulders, and John rolled sideways just enough for her to squiggle out before he flopped back again.

Slowly she stood up and gazed down at him, her hand over her mouth, her eyes wide with shock. She bent over him.

"John?" Tentatively, she touched his shoulder, shook him lightly. "John?"

There was no sound, and his face was buried in the pillows. She turned his head. His sightless eyes stared up at her.

"Sweet Jesus, have mercy!" Juliana whispered, stepping back from the corpse. She had killed her husband!

Dazed and incredulous, she stood by the bed, listening to the nighttime sounds of the house: the ticking clocks, the creaking floorboards, the wind rattling open casements. No sounds of human life.

Dear God, it was her cursed clumsiness again! Why, oh why did everything she ever did always come out wrong?

She had to waken someone. But what would they say? The round mark of the bed warmer stood out on the dead man's back. She must have hit him harder than she'd intended. But, of course, that was inevitable given her blunder-headed, accident-prone nature.

Sick with horror, she touched the bed warmer and found it still very hot. She'd struck and killed her husband with a burning object.

George would waste no time. He would listen to no reasonable explanations. He would accuse her publicly as he'd done privately that morning of gold digging. Of marrying a man old enough to be her grandfather just for his money. He'd accuse her of manipulating his father's besotted affections and then arranging his death so she'd be free and clear with all that had been allotted to her in the marriage settlements. Property that George believed was his and his alone.

It was petty treason for a woman to kill her husband. Just as it was for a servant to kill his master. If she was convicted, they would burn her at the stake.

Juliana backed farther away from the bed, pushing aside the bed curtains, rushing to the window, where she stood drawing deep gulps of the warm night air, enlivened by a faint sea breeze from the Solent. *They would burn her at the stake*.

She'd seen it happen once, outside Winchester jail. Mistress Goadsby had been convicted of killing her husband when he'd fallen down the stairs. She'd said he'd been drunk and had been beating her and he'd tripped and fallen. She'd stood in the dock with the bruises still on her face. But they'd tied her to the stake, hanged her, and set fire to her.

Juliana had been little more than a child at the time, but the image had haunted her over the years . . . the smell of burning flesh embedded in her nostrils. Nausea swamped her, and she ran back to the bed, dragging the chamber pot from beneath, vomiting violently.

Perhaps the magistrates would believe that John had died of natural causes in the midst of his exertions . . . but there was that mark on his back. He couldn't have put that there himself.

And George would see it. A stepmother convicted of murdering her husband couldn't inherit. The marriage settlements would be nullified, and George would have what he wanted.

Juliana didn't know how long she sat on the floor, hunched over the chamber pot, but gradually the sweat dried on her forehead and her mind cleared.

She had to leave. There was no one there to speak for her . . . to speak against the facts before their eyes. Her guardian had negotiated the marriage settlements, ensuring, of course, that he, too, benefited from the arrangements. He had then thankfully washed his hands of one who had been nothing but a troublesome charge from the first moment his orphaned infant niece had been delivered into his arms. There was no one else remotely interested in her.

She stood up, thrust the chamber pot back beneath the bed with her foot, and took stock. The stagecoach for London stopped at the Rose and Crown in Winchester at four o'clock in the morning. She could walk the ten miles to Winchester across the fields and be there in plenty of time. By the time the household awoke, or George emerged from his stupor, she would be far away.

They would pursue her, but she could lose herself easily in London. She just had to ensure she wouldn't draw attention to herself at the Rose and Crown.

Averting her eyes from the bed, Juliana went to the armoire, newly filled with her trousseau. But she'd secreted a pair of holland britches and a linen shirt. In this costume she'd escaped Forsett Towers on the frequent occasions when life had become more than usually unpleasant under the rule of her guardian's wife. No one had ever discovered the disguise, or the various places where she'd roamed. Of course, she'd paid the price on her return, but Lady Forsett's hazel switch had seemed but a small price to pay for those precious hours of freedom.

She dressed rapidly, pulling on stockings and boots, twisting her flame-red hair into a knot on top of her head, tucking telltale strands under a woolen cap pulled down low over her ears.

She needed money. Enough for her coach fare and a few nights' lodging until she could find work. But she wouldn't take anything that would be missed. Nothing that would brand her as a thief as well as a murderess.

Why she should concern herself about such a hair-splitting issue Juliana couldn't imagine, but her mind seemed to be working on its own, making decisions, discarding possibilities with all the efficiency of an automaton.

She took four sovereigns from the cache in the dresser drawer. She had watched John empty his pockets . . . hours ago, it seemed—after the revelers had finally left the bedroom door and taken their jovial obscenities out of the house, leaving the newlyweds to themselves.

John had been almost too drunk to stand upright. She could see him now, swaying as he poured the contents of his pocket into the drawer—his bloodshot blue eyes gleaming with excitement, his habitually red face now a deep crimson.

Tears suddenly clogged her throat as she slipped the still-unfamiliar wedding ring from her finger. John had always been kind to her in an avuncular way. She'd been more than willing to accept marriage to him as a way of escaping her guardian's house. More than willing until she realized she'd have to contend with George . . . malicious, jealous, lusting George. But it had been too late to back away then. She dropped the ring into the drawer with the remaining sovereigns. The gold circlet winked at her, its glow diffused through her tears.

Resolutely, Juliana closed the drawer and turned back to the cheval glass to check her reflection. Her disguise had never been intended to fool people close at hand, and as she examined herself, she realized that the linen shirt did nothing to disguise the rich swell of her bosom; and the curve of her hips was emphasized by the britches.

She took a heavy winter cloak from the armoire and swathed herself. It hid the bumps and the curves, but it was still far from satisfactory. However, the light would be bad at that hour of the morning, and with luck there'd be other passengers on the waybill, so she could make herself inconspicuous.

She tiptoed to the bedroom door, glancing at the closed bed curtains. She felt as if she should make some acknowledgment of the dead man. It seemed wrong to be running from his deathbed. And yet she could think of nothing else to do. For a minute she thought hard about the man whom she'd known for a bare three months. She remembered his kindnesses. And then she put him from her. John Ridge had been sixty-five years old. He'd had three wives. And he'd died quickly, painlessly . . . a death for which she had been responsible.

Juliana let herself out of the bedchamber and crept along the pitch-dark corridor, her fingers brushing the walls to guide her. At the head of the stairs she paused. The hall below was dark, but not as black as the corridor behind her. Faint moonlight filtered through the diamond panes of the mullioned windows.

Her eyes darted to the library door. It was firmly closed. She sped down the stairs, tiptoed to the door, and placed her ear against the oak. Her heart hammered in her chest, and she wondered why she was lingering, listening to the rumbling, drunken snores from within. But hearing them made her feel safer.

She turned to leave, and her foot caught in the fringe of the worn Elizabethan carpet. She went flying, grabbed at a table leg to save herself, and fell to her knees: a copper jug of hollyhocks overbalanced as the table rocked, and crashed to the stone-flagged floor.

She remained where she was on her knees, listening to the echo resound to the beamed ceiling and then slowly fade into the night. It had been a sound to wake the dead.

But nothing happened. No shouts, no running feet . . .

and most miraculously of all, no change in the stertorous breathing from the library.

Juliana picked herself up, swearing under her breath. It was her feet again. They were the bane of her life, too big and with a mind of their own.

She crept with exaggerated care toward the back regions of the house and let herself out of the kitchen door. Outside all was quiet. The house behind her slept. The house that should have been her home—her refuge from the erratic twists and turns of a life that had brought her little happiness thus far.

Juliana shrugged. Like a stray cat who had long ago learned to walk alone, she faced the haphazard future with uncomplaining resignation. As she crossed the kitchen yard, making for the orchard and the fields beyond, the church clock struck midnight.

Her seventeenth birthday was over. A day she'd begun as a bride and ended as a widow and a murderess.

"I give you good day, cousin," a voice slurred from the depths of an armchair as the Duke of Redmayne entered the library of his house on Albermarle Street.

"To what do I owe this pleasure, Lucien?" the duke inquired in bland tones, although a flicker of disgust crossed his face. "Escaping your creditors? Or are you simply paying me a courtesy visit?"

"Lud, such sarcasm, cousin." Lucien Courtney rose to his feet and surveyed with a mocking insouciance his cousin and the man who'd entered close behind him. "Well, well, and if it isn't our dear Reverend Courtney as well. What an embarrassment of relatives. How d'ye do, dear boy."

"Well enough," the other man responded easily. He was soberly dressed in gray, with a plain white neck cloth, in startling contrast to the duke's peacock-blue satin coat, with its gold frogged buttons and deep embroidered cuffs. But the physical resemblance to the duke was startling: the same aquiline nose and deep-set gray eyes, the same thin, well-shaped mouth, the same cleft chin. However, there the resemblance ended. Whereas Quentin Courtney regarded the world and its vagaries with the gentle and genuine sympathy of a devout man of the cloth, his half brother Tarquin, the Duke of Redmayne, saw his fellow man through the sharp and disillusioned eyes of the cynic.

"So what brings you to the fleshpots?" Lucien inquired with a sneer. "I thought you'd become an important official in some country bishop's diocese."

"Canon of Melchester Cathedral," Quentin said coolly. "I'm on my bishop's business with the Archbishop of Canterbury at the moment."

"Oh, aren't we rising far, fast, and holy," Lucien declared with a curled lip. Quentin ignored the statement.

"May I offer you some refreshment, Lucien?" Tarquin strolled to the decanters on the sideboard. "Oh, but I see you've already taken care of yourself," he added, noting the brandy goblet in the younger man's hand. "You don't think it's a little early in the morning for cognac?"

"Dear boy, I haven't been to bed as yet," Lucien said with a yawn. "Far as I'm concerned, this is a nightcap." He put down the glass and strolled to the door, somewhat unsteadily. "You don't object to putting me up for a few nights?"

"How should I?" returned Tarquin with a sardonically raised eyebrow.

"Fact is, my own house is under siege," Lucien declared, leaning against the door and fumbling in his pocket for his snuffbox. "Damned creditors and bailiffs bangin' at the door at all hours of the day and night. Man can't get a decent night's rest."

"And what are you going to sell to satisfy them this time?" the duke asked, pouring madeira for himself and his brother.

"Have to be Edgecombe," Lucien said, taking a pinch of snuff. He sighed with exaggerated heaviness. "Terrible thing. But I can't see what else to do . . . unless, of course, you could see your way to helpin' a relative out."

His pale-brown eyes, burning in their deep sockets like the last embers of a dying fire, suddenly sharpened, and he regarded his cousin with sly knowledge. He smiled as he saw the telltale muscle twitch in Tarquin's jaw as he fought to control his anger.

"Well," he said carelessly. "We'll discuss it later . . . when I've had some sleep. Dinner, perhaps?"

"Get out of here," Tarquin said, turning his back.

Lucien's chuckle hung in the air as the door closed behind him.

"There's going to be little enough left of Edgecombe for poor Godfrey to inherit," Quentin said, sipping his wine. "Since Lucien gained his majority a mere six months ago, he's run through a fortune that would keep most men in luxury for a lifetime."

"I'll not stand by and see him sell Edgecombe," Tarquin stated almost without expression. "And neither will I stand by and see what remnants are left pass into the hands of Lucien's pitiful cousin."

"I fail to see how you can stop it," Quentin said in some surprise. "I know poor Godfrey has no more wits than an infant, but he's still Lucien's legitimate heir."

"He would be if Lucien left no heir of his own," the duke pointed out, casually riffling through the pages of the *Gazette*.

"Well, we all know that's an impossibility," Quentin declared, stating what he had always believed to be an immutable fact. "And Lucien's free of your rein now; there's little you can do to control him."

"Aye, and he never ceases to taunt me with it," Tarquin responded. "But it'll be a rainy day in hell, my friend, when Lucien Courtney gets the better of me." He looked up and met his half brother's gaze.

Quentin felt a little shiver prickle his spine at this soft-spoken declaration. He knew Tarquin as no one else did. He knew the softer side of an apparently unbending nature;

he knew his half brother's vulnerabilities; he knew that the hard cynicism Tarquin presented to the world was a defense learned in his youth against those who would use the friendship of a future duke for their own ambitions.

Quentin also knew not to underestimate the Duke of Redmayne's ruthlessness in getting what he wanted. He asked simply "What are you going to do?"

Tarquin drained his glass. He smiled, but it was not a humorous smile. "It's time our little cousin took himself a wife and set up his nursery," he said. "That should settle the matter of an heir to Edgecombe."

Quentin stared at him as if he'd taken leave of his senses. "No one's going to marry Lucien, even if he was prepared to marry. He's riddled with the pox, and the only women who figure on his agenda of pleasure are whores from the stews prepared to play the lad."

"True. But how long do you think he has to live?" Tarquin inquired almost casually. "You only have to look at him. He's burned out with debauchery and the clap. I'd give him maybe six months . . . a year at the outside."

Quentin said nothing, but his gaze remained unwaveringly on his brother's countenance.

"He knows it, too," Tarquin continued. "He's living each day as if it's his last. He doesn't give a damn what happens to Edgecombe or the Courtney fortune. Why should he? But I intend to ensure that Edgecombe, at the very least, passes intact into competent hands."

Quentin looked horrified. "In the name of pity, Tarquin! You couldn't condemn a woman to share his bed, even if he'd take her into it. It would be a death sentence."

"Listen well, dear brother. It's perfectly simple."

Chapter 2

B y the time the stagecoach lumbered into the yard of the Bell in Wood Street, Cheapside, Juliana had almost forgotten there was a world outside the cramped interior and the company of her six fellow passengers. At five miles an hour, with an enforced stop at sunset because neither coachman nor passengers would travel the highways after dark, it had taken over twenty-four hours to accomplish the seventy miles between Winchester and London. Juliana, like the rest of the passengers, had sat up in the taproom of the coaching inn during the night stop. Despite the discomfort of the hard wooden settles, it was a welcome change from the bone-racking jolting of the iron wheels over the unpaved roads.

They set off again, just before dawn, and it was soon after seven in the morning when she alighted from the coach for the last time. She stood in the yard of the Bell, arching the small of her back against her hands in an effort to get the cricks out. The York coach had also just arrived and was disgorging its blinking, exhausted passengers. The June air was already warm, heavy with city smells, and she wrinkled her nose at the pervading odor of rotting garbage in the kennels, manure piled in the narrow cobbled lanes.

"Ye got a box up 'ere, lad?"

It took Juliana a moment to realize the coachman's question was addressed to her. She was still huddled in her cloak, her cap pulled down over her ears as it had been throughout the journey. She turned to the man sitting atop the coach, unlashing the passenger's baggage.

"No, nothing, thank you."

"Long ways to travel with not so much as a cloak bag," the man remarked curiously.

Juliana merely nodded and set off to the inn doorway. She felt as if she'd traveled not just a long way but into another world . . . another life. What it would bring her and what she would make of it were the only questions of any interest.

She entered the dark paneled taproom, where a scullery maid was slopping a bucket of water over the grubby flagstones. Juliana skipped over a dirty stream that threatened to swamp her feet, caught her foot on the edge of the bucket, and grabbed at the counter to save herself. Stable again, she nodded cheerfully to the girl.

"I give you good morning."

The girl sniffed and looked as if it was far from a good morning. She was scrawny and pale, her hair almost painfully scraped back from her forehead into a lank and greasy pigtail. "Ye want summat t'eat?"

"If you please," Juliana responded with undiluted cheerfulness. She perched on a high stool at the counter and looked around. The comparison with the country inns with which she was familiar was not favorable. Where she was used to fresh flowers and bunches of dried herbs, polished brass and waxed wood, this place was dark, dirty, and reeked of stale beer and the cesspit. And the people had a wary, hostile air.

The innkeeper loomed out of the dimness behind the counter. "What can I get ye?" The question was courteous enough, but his tone was surly and his eyes bloodshot.

"Eggs and toast and tea, if you please, sir. I've just come off the York stage." Juliana essayed a smile.

The man peered at her suspiciously in the gloom, and she drew the cloak tighter about her.

"I'll see yer coin first," he said.

Juliana reached into her pocket and drew out a shilling. She slapped it onto the counter and glared at him, her jade-green eyes suddenly ablaze.

The innkeeper drew back almost involuntarily from the heat of that anger. He palmed the coin, gave her another searching look, and snapped at the still-mopping scullery maid, "Ellie, get into the kitchen and bring the gentleman 'is eggs an' toast."

The maid dumped her mop into the bucket with a rough impatience that sent water slurping over the rim and, sighing heavily, marched behind the counter into the kitchen.

The innkeeper's pale, bloodshot eyes narrowed slyly. "A tankard of ale, young sir?"

"No, just tea, thank you."

His crafty glance ran over her swathed figure. "Tea'll maudle yer belly, lad. It's a drink fit only fer women. Didn't nobody teach ye to take ale with yer breakfast?"

Juliana accepted that her disguise was not convincing, but it had served its purpose thus far. She was certain no one had thought twice about her at the Rose and Crown in Winchester, and as far as the innkeeper was concerned, she'd just alighted from the York stage—almost as far from Winchester as it was possible to be this side of the Scottish border.

"I'm looking for lodging and work," she said casually, confirming his suspicions by default. "D'you know of anything around here?"

The man stroked his chin thoughtfully. "Well, now, I just might be able to think of summat. Let's see what ye've got under that cap."

Juliana shrugged and pulled off her cap. "I fail to see what my hair has to do with getting a job."

Ellie came back with the breakfast at this point and

gawped as the fiery mass, released from the confines of the cap, tumbled loose from its pins.

" 'Ere, what ye doin' dressed like a lad?" She thumped the plate in front of Juliana.

"It makes traveling easier," Juliana responded, dipping her toast into her egg. "And could I have my tea, please?"

"Oh, 'oity-toity, an't we?" Ellie said. "I'll bet yer no better than ye ought t' be."

" 'Old yer tongue and fetch the tea, girl,'" the innkeeper ordered, threatening her with the back of his hand.

Ellie ducked, sniffed, and ran off to the kitchen.

"So jest what's a lady doin', then, wanderin' the streets dressed like a lad?" he inquired with a careless air, polishing a dingy pewter tankard on his sleeve.

Juliana hungrily wiped up the last of her egg yolk with her toast and put down her fork. "I'm looking for work, as I told you."

"Ye speaks like a lady," he persisted. "Ladies don't look fer work 'ereabouts."

"Ladies down on their luck might." She poured tea from the pot Ellie had plumped down at her elbow, put the pot down again, and, as she moved her arm, caught the fold of her cloak on the spout. The pot rocked and clattered on the counter, but she managed to extricate her garment without too much spillage.

"Aye. I suppose they might," the innkeeper agreed, watching her struggles with the teapot.

"So do you know of anything?"

"Reckon I might. Just bide 'ere a while an' I'll see what I can do."

"Thank you." She smiled radiantly, and he blinked his little eyes, then stomped off into the nether regions, leaving Juliana alone with her tea.

In the kitchen he summoned a potboy, scrubbing greasy pans in a wooden tub beside the door. "Eh, you, lad. Take yerself to Russell Street in Covent Garden. Mr. Dennison's 'ouse. You tell Mistress Dennison that Josh Bute from the Bell might 'ave summat of interest. Got that?"

"Aye, sir, Mr. Bute," the boy said, tugging a forelock with a wet and greasy hand. "Right away, sir." He scampered off, and Mr. Bute stood for a minute rubbing his hands together. The Dennisons paid a handsome commission for a good piece, and there was something indefinable about the one sitting in his taproom that convinced the innkeeper he'd found a prime article for that very exacting couple.

Nodding to himself, he returned to the taproom. "I reckon I can do summat fer ye, miss," he said with a smile that he considered jovial but that reminded Juliana of a toothless, rabid dog.

"What kind of work?" she asked.

"Oh, good, clean work, miss," he assured her. "Jest as long as ye can please Mistress Dennison, ye'll be all set up."

"Is it live-in work?"

"Oh, aye, miss, that it is," he returned, drawing a tankard of ale for himself. "Genteel, live-in work. Jest the thing fer a young lady on 'er own. Mistress Dennison takes care of 'er girls." He wiped the froth off his mouth with the back of his hand and smiled his rabid smile.

Juliana frowned. It all seemed remarkably convenient, quick and easy. Too much so. Then she shrugged. She had nothing to lose by waiting to meet this Mistress Dennison, and if she *was* looking for a parlor maid or even a skivvy, then it would give her a start.

"Should I go to her?"

"Bless you, no. Mistress Dennison will come 'ere," he said, drawing another tankard of ale.

"Then I'll sit in the inglenook." Juliana yawned deeply. "I'll take a nap while I'm waiting."

"Right y'are," Mr. Bute said indifferently, but his eyes remained on her until she'd curled up on the wooden settle in the deep inglenook, her cheek pillowed on her hand. Her eyes closed almost immediately.

Mr. Bute sucked at his toothless gums with a slurp of satisfaction. She'd be no trouble until Mistress Dennison arrived. But he remained in the taproom, nevertheless, keeping a weather eye on the sleeping figure, until, two hours later, he heard the rattle of wheels in the stable yard and the sounds of bustle in the passageway outside.

He hastened from behind his counter and greeted his visitor with a deep bow.

"So what have you for me, Bute?" the lady demanded, tapping a high-heeled shoe of pink silk edged with silver lace. "It's devilish early in the morning for making calls, so I trust I'm not on a fool's errand."

"I trust not, madam," the innkeeper said with another bow, his nose almost brushing his knees. "The girl says she's off the York stage."

"Well, where is she?" Elizabeth plied her fan, her nose wrinkling slightly at the stale, unsavory air now embellished with the scent of boiling cabbage.

"In the taproom, madam." The innkeeper held open the door and the lady swished past, deftly twitching aside the hoop of her green satin skirts.

"In the inglenook," Mr. Bute said softly, pointing.

Mistress Dennison crossed the room, her step light, a speculative gleam in her eyes. She stood looking down at the sleeping figure wrapped in the cloak. Her assessing gaze took in the tumbled richness of the flame-red hair, the creamy pallor of her skin, the shape of the full, relaxed mouth, the dusting of freckles across the bridge of a strongly defined nose.

Not pretty, Mistress Dennison decided with an expert's eye. Too strongly featured for true prettiness. But her hair was magnificent. And there were many gentlemen who preferred something a little out of the ordinary. What in the world was she doing dressed in those clothes? What did she have to hide? Something, for sure. And if she should prove to be a maid . . .

Elizabeth's beautiful eyes narrowed abruptly. A virgin with something to hide . . .

She bent over Juliana and shook her shoulder. "My dear, it's time you woke up."

Juliana swam upward from the depths of a dreamless

sleep. She opened her eyes and blinked up at the face hovering over her. A lovely face: smiling red lips, kind blue eyes. It was not a face she knew, and for a moment she was completely disoriented.

The woman touched her shoulder again. "My dear, I am Mistress Dennison."

Memory rushed back. Juliana sat up on the settle, swinging her legs over the edge. Beside this radiant creature in rich satin, with a dainty lace cap perched atop dark-brown curls, she felt all grubby elbows and knees. She tucked her feet beneath the settle in the hope that they would stay out of mischief and hastily tried to push her hair back into its pins.

"Mine host seemed to think you might be looking for a parlor maid, ma'am," she began.

"My dear, forgive me, but you don't speak like one accustomed to service," Mistress Dennison said bluntly, taking a seat pushed forward by the eager Mr. Bute. "I understand you traveled on the York stage."

Juliana nodded, but Elizabeth's gaze sharpened. She was too well versed in the ways of the world to be fooled by an inexperienced liar. Besides, this girl had no hint of Yorkshire in her accent.

"Where is your home?"

Juliana pushed the last pin back into her hair. "Is it necessary for you to know that, ma'am?"

Elizabeth leaned over and placed her gloved hand over Juliana's. "Not if you don't wish to tell me, child. But your name and your age, perhaps?"

"Juliana Ri— Beresford," she corrected hastily. They would be looking for Juliana Ridge. "I am just past seventeen, ma'am."

The lady nodded. She hadn't missed the slip. "Well, why don't you come with me, my dear? You need rest and refreshment, and clothes." She rose in a satin rustle, smiling invitingly.

"But . . . but what work would you have me do,

madam?" Juliana was beginning to feel bewildered. Things were happening too fast.

"We'll discuss that when you've refreshed yourself, child." Mistress Dennison drew her to her feet. "My carriage is outside, and it's but a short ride to my house."

Juliana had a single sovereign left from her little hoard. It might buy her food and lodging of a sort for a day or two. But she was hopelessly inexperienced in this alarming city world, and to turn down the protection and hospitality of this charming, kind-eyed woman would be foolish. So she smiled her acceptance and followed her benefactress out of the inn and inside a light town carriage drawn by two dappled horses.

"Now, my dear," Mistress Dennison said confidingly, "why don't you tell me all about it? I can assure you I've heard every story imaginable, and there's little in the world that could surprise or shock me."

Juliana leaned her head against the pale-blue velvet cushions, her tired gaze swimming as she looked across at the gently smiling face. It occurred to her that the only other person who had ever smiled at her with such kindly interest had been Sir John Ridge. Tears welled in her eyes, and she blinked them away.

"My poor child, what has happened to you?" Elizabeth said, leaning over to take her hands. "You may trust me."

Why? But the question was a little niggle in the back of Juliana's mind. The temptation to take someone into her confidence, someone who knew the ways of the world, was overwhelming. If she didn't identify herself or where she came from, she could still keep the essentials of her secret. Still protect herself from the long reach of the law.

"It's a strange story, ma'am," she began.

If Your Grace would do me the inestimable honor of paying a visit to Russell Street this evening, I believe I might have something of interest to show you.

Your obedient servant,
Elizabeth Dennison

The Duke of Redmayne examined the missive, his expression quite impassive. Then he glanced up at the footman. "Is the messenger still here?"

"Yes, Your Grace. He was to wait for an answer."

Tarquin nodded and strolled to the secretaire, where he drew a sheet of vellum toward him, dipped a quill into the inkstand, and scrawled two lines. He sanded the sheet and folded it.

"Give this to the messenger, Roberts." He dropped it onto the silver salver held by the footman, who bowed himself out.

"So what was that about?" Quentin inquired, looking up from his book.

"I doubt you really want to know," the duke said with a half smile. "It concerns a matter that doesn't have your approval, my friend."

"Oh." Quentin's usually benign expression darkened. "Not that business with Lucien and a wife?"

"Precisely, dear boy. Precisely. Sherry?" Tarquin held up the decanter, one eyebrow raised inquiringly.

"Thank you." Quentin tossed his book aside and stood up. "You're really set on this diabolical scheme?"

"Most certainly." The duke handed his brother a glass. "And why should you call it diabolical, Quentin?" There was a gently mocking light in his eyes, an amused curve to his mouth.

"Because it is," Quentin said shortly. "How will you protect the girl from Lucien? Supposing he decides to exercise his marital rights?"

"Oh, you may safely leave that to me," Tarquin said.

"I don't like it." Quentin scowled into his glass.

"You've made that very clear." Smiling, Tarquin patted his brother's sober-suited shoulder. "But you don't care for most of my schemes."

"No, and I wish the devil I knew why I care for *you*,"

the other man said almost bitterly. "You're an ungodly man, Tarquin. Positively Mephistophelian."

Tarquin sat down, crossing one elegantly shod foot over the other. He frowned down at the sparkle of diamonds in the shoe buckles, musing, "I wonder if jeweled buckles aren't becoming a trifle outré. I noticed Stanhope wearing some very handsome plain silver ones at the levee the other morning. . . . But, then, I doubt that's a topic that interests you, either, Quentin."

"No, I can't say that it does." Quentin cast a cursory glance down at his own sturdy black leather shoes with their plain metal buckles. "And don't change the subject, Tarquin."

"I beg your pardon, I thought we'd reached an amiable conclusion." Tarquin sipped his sherry.

"Will you give up this scheme?"

"No, brother dear."

"Then there's nothing more to be said."

"Precisely. As I said, we have drawn the topic to an amiable conclusion." The duke stood up in one graceful movement, placing his glass on the table. "Don't fret, Quentin. It will only give you frown lines."

"And don't play the fop with me," Quentin declared with more passion than he usually showed. "I'm not fooled by your games, Tarquin."

His brother paused at the door, a slight smile on his lips. "No, thank God, you're not. Don't ever be so, if you love me, brother."

The door closed behind him and Quentin drained his glass. He'd known his half brother for thirty years. He remembered Tarquin's rage and disillusion as a boy of fifteen, betrayed because he wouldn't buy the friendship of his peers. He remembered the desperation when a year or two later the young man had discovered that the woman he loved with such fervor was interested only in what she could gain from being the mistress of the Duke of Redmayne.

Quentin knew how vitally important the family's heritage was to the third Duke of Redmayne. Tarquin had been brought up as the eldest son and heir to an old title and vast estates. He would uphold the family pride and honor to his dying day.

And Lucien was threatening that pride. For as long as he'd been Tarquin's ward, the duke had managed to keep control of the reins, but now he had no say in the way their cousin conducted his own life or managed his fortune and estates. Quentin understood all this, yet he still couldn't accept Tarquin's demonic scheme to save Edgecombe. Tarquin would come out the winner, of course, at whatever cost.

But surely there had to be another way. Quentin picked up his book again, seeking solace in Plutarch's *Parallel Lives*. He hoped the archbishop would take his time over the business that had brought Quentin to London. Someone needed to keep a steadying eye on events at Albermarle Street. Sometimes Tarquin would listen to Quentin and could be persuaded to modify his more far-reaching schemes. Quentin loved his half brother dearly. He had hero-worshiped him through their childhood. But he couldn't close his eyes to the darker side of Tarquin's nature.

"Ah, Your Grace, you are come." Elizabeth rose and curtsied as the duke was shown into her private salon.

"But of course, ma'am. With such incentive, how could I possibly stay away?" He withdrew an enameled snuffbox from his pocket and took a pinch. Mistress Dennison couldn't help but notice that the delicate gold and ivory of the snuffbox exactly matched His Grace's silk coat, waistcoat, and britches.

"Do you wish to see her now, Your Grace?"

"I am all eagerness, madam."

"Come this way, sir." Elizabeth led her guest out of the parlor. It was evening and the house was awake. Two young women in lace negligees sauntered casually down the corridor. They curtsied to the mistress of the house, who greeted them with a smile, before passing on.

A footman bearing a tray with champagne and two glasses and a platter of oysters knocked on a door at the end of the passage.

"The evening is starting early," the duke remarked.

"It often does, my lord," Elizabeth said complacently. "I understand His Royal Highness will be visiting us later."

"Alas, poor Fred," murmured the duke. The bumbling Frederick Louis, Prince of Wales, whose addiction to women was a society joke, was a regular visitor to the Dennisons' harem.

Elizabeth led him up a narrow flight of stairs at the rear of the corridor. It was a route unknown to the duke, and he raised an eyebrow as he followed the swaying, rich crimson hoop ahead of him.

"This is a private passage, Your Grace," Elizabeth explained as they turned down a narrow corridor. "You will understand its purpose in a minute."

She stopped outside a door at the end of the passage and softly opened it, standing aside to permit the duke entrance. He stepped past her into a narrow wardrobe, lit only by the candle in the sconce in the passage behind him.

"In the wall, Your Grace," Elizabeth whispered.

He looked and saw it immediately. Two round peepholes, at eye level and spaced for a pair of eyes.

Wondering if all Mistress Dennison's rooms provided opportunity for the voyeur, the duke stepped up to the peepholes. He looked into a candlelit chamber. He could see a dimity-hung poster bed, matching curtains billowing at an open window, a washstand with a flowered porcelain jug and ewer. It was a bedroom like many in this house.

But it contained a girl. She stood at the open window, idly brushing her hair. The candlelight caught the flames in the glowing tresses as she pulled the brush through with strong, rhythmic strokes. She wore a loose chamber robe that fell open as she turned back to the room.

He glimpsed firm, full breasts, a white belly, a hint of

tangled red hair below. Then she moved out of sight. He
waited, his eyes focusing hard on the part of the room he
could see. She came back into view. With a leisurely
movement she threw off the chamber robe, tossing it over
an ottoman at the foot of the bed.

The duke neither stirred nor made a sound. Behind him
Elizabeth waited anxiously, hoping that he was seeing
something worth seeing.

Tarquin looked steadily at the tall figure, noting the generous curve of hip, the fullness of her breasts that accentuated the slenderness of her torso, the tiny waist. He noted
the whiteness of her skin against the startling flames of her
hair. She moved toward the bed, and he noted the flare of
her hips, the smooth roundness of her buttocks, the long
sweep of thigh.

She raised one knee, resting it on the bed, then suddenly
glanced over her shoulder. For a minute she appeared to be
looking directly at him, her eyes meeting his. Those eyes
were the color of jade, deep and glowing, wide-spaced
beneath the uncompromisingly straight line of her dark
brows. Her eyelashes, dark and as straight as her brows,
swept down and up as she blinked tiredly. Then she
yawned, covering her mouth with the back of her hand,
and climbed into bed.

Leaning over, she blew out the candle.

The Duke of Redmayne moved out of the wardrobe,
back into the light of the passage. He turned to face the
expectant Mistress Dennison.

"Is she a maid?"

"I am certain of it, Your Grace."

"Can she be bought?"

"I believe so."

"Then let us talk terms, Elizabeth."

Chapter 3

Juliana awoke to a bright dawn. Always an early riser, she came awake without intervening drowsiness and sat up immediately, gazing about the chamber. It was small but comfortable, well furnished, although not luxuriously so. The bed hangings and curtains were of starched dimity; simple hooked rugs were scattered on the waxed oak floor, cheerful cretonne cushions piled on the chaise longue.

It felt comfortingly familiar, similar to her bedchamber at Forsett Towers. But the sounds coming from the street outside bore no relation to the high cry of the peacocks strutting on the mansion's lawns or the clarion call of the roosters on the home farm.

She flung aside the bedcovers and stood up, stretching with a sigh of pleasure, then padded to the window. Drawing aside the curtains, she looked down into a narrow street crowded with wagons and drays, piled high with country produce. Raucous barrow boys pushed their way through the throng, heading for Covent Garden at the end of the street. Two disheveled young men in evening dress stumbled out of a tavern across the street and stood blinking in the daylight. A woman in a grubby red petticoat hitched up to show her calves, with torn, tawdry lace at her low neckline, sidled up to them, an insinuating smile on her face, and drew down the neck of her dress to bare her breasts.

One of the men grabbed her with a loud laugh and pressed his mouth against hers, holding her roughly by the head. Then he pushed her from him, still laughing, and the two men staggered toward the Strand. The whore picked herself up from the gutter, swearing and shaking her fist. Then she twitched the tawdry lace into position, shook out her skirts, and set off toward the market.

Fascinated, Juliana stared down at the scene below her window. Even Winchester on market day wasn't this lively.

Filled with the energy of curiosity and excitement, Juliana ran to the armoire. She took out the simple muslin gown and cotton shift that her benefactress had insisted on giving her when they'd arrived at the house the previous morning. Juliana had accepted the garments because of their very simplicity. The gown was the kind a well-looked-after serving maid might wear on Sundays.

She threw the shift over her head and stepped into the gown, hooking it up, fastening a muslin fichu discreetly at the neck. She thrust her bare feet into a pair of leather slippers, also provided by Mistress Dennison; splashed water from the ewer onto her face; brushed her hair, pinning it roughly in a knot on top of her head; and was out of the door and running down the wide staircase to the hall within ten minutes of waking.

The front door was open to the street, and a maid was on her hands and knees polishing the parquet. Juliana had seen little of the house the previous day. After changing her clothes she'd spent the rest of the time with Mistress Dennison in her private parlor. She'd dined there alone and retired early, too overwhelmed by the strangeness and excitements of the day following the fatigue of the journey to examine her position or her surroundings too closely.

Now, however, she was refreshed and clear-headed, and she looked around her with interest. Double doors stood open to the right of the hall, revealing a long, elegant salon. From what she could see, the furniture, apart from some deep, inviting sofas and plump ottomans, was all dainty gilt and elaborately carved wood, the carpet richly embroidered, the draperies and upholstery emerald-green velvet. The scent of tobacco and wine lingered in the air, fighting with the fragrance of fresh roses and potpourri from the bowls scattered on every surface.

Juliana could see a footman and a maid polishing the furniture in the salon, but apart from this activity the house seemed to lie under a curious hush. It was like a stage set, she thought. All ready and waiting for the players. The atmosphere wasn't like a private house at all, more like a hotel.

With a slightly puzzled frown she approached the maid polishing the floor. But before she could reach her, a voice said softly but with great authority, "And where d'ye think y'are off to, missie?"

She spun round, startled, not having heard footsteps behind her. A burly man in scarlet livery with a powdered wig, impressive gold braid and frogging on his coat, and a heavy gold watch chain slung across his broad chest surveyed her, hands on his hips.

"I was about to go for a walk," Juliana said, unconsciously tipping her chin, her expression challenging. "If it's any business of yours."

A strange little sound came from the maid still busily polishing on her hands and knees a few feet away. Juliana glanced quickly at her, but the girl's head was down, and she seemed to be putting even more effort into her work. Juliana looked back at the liveried butler, or so she assumed him to be.

He was surveying her with an air of incredulity. "It seems ye've a lot to learn about this 'ere establishment, missie," he declared. "And lesson number one: My name is Garston. *Mr.* Garston, to you, or just plain *sir*. And everything you do is my business."

Her eyes threw green fire at him. "My good man, the only person who's entitled to question my movements in this house is Mistress Dennison. Now, if you'll excuse me,

I'm going for a walk." She tried to step past him toward the door, but he moved his considerable bulk to block her way.

"Doors is closed, missie." He sounded amused rather than annoyed by her defiance.

"They are not!" she stated. "The door is wide-open to the street."

"Doors is closed to the ladies of the 'ouse, missie, until I says so," he said stolidly, folding his arms and regarding her with an amused smile.

What was this? Juliana stared up at him, for the moment nonplussed. As she tried to order her thoughts, a burst of laughter came from the open front door as two women entered the hall, followed by a footman. They were in evening dress, dominoes over their wide-hooped gowns, black loo masks over their eyes.

"Lud, but that was a night and a half," one of them pronounced, plying her fan vigorously. "Such a pair of swordsmen, I do declare, Lilly!"

The other woman went into a renewed peal of laughter and unfastened her mask. "That Lord Bingley, I dareswear, would have been all cut and thrust for another hour if I hadn't near swooned with exhaustion. . . . Oh, Mr. Garston, would you be so good as to send a salt bath to my room? I'm in sore need."

"Immediately, Miss Lilly." He bowed. "I gather you and Miss Emma 'ad a good night. Mr. and Mistress Dennison will be right 'appy to 'ear it."

"La, good enough, Mr. Garston." Miss Emma yawned. "But a tankard of milk punch won't come amiss."

"I'll order it straightway, miss. You go along up and leave it to me." Mr. Garston sounded positively avuncular now as he beamed at the two yawning young women.

Juliana was staring with unabashed curiosity. They were both very pretty, richly gowned, elaborately coiffed, but they were so thickly painted and powdered, it was hard to tell their ages. They were certainly young, but how young she couldn't decide.

"Lud, and who have we here?" Miss Lilly said, catching sight of Juliana behind the stolid figure of Mr. Garston. She regarded her with interest, taking in the simple gown and the roughly pinned hair. "A new servant?"

"I don't believe so, miss," Garston said with a meaningful nod. "But Mistress Dennison 'asn't made clear to me quite what 'er plans are fer the young lady."

"Oh?" Miss Emma examined Juliana with a raised eyebrow. Then she shrugged. "Well, I daresay we'll find out soon enough. Come, Lilly, I'm dead on my feet."

The two wafted up the stairs, chattering like magpies, leaving Juliana uneasy, annoyed, and exceedingly puzzled.

"Now, then, missie, you cut along to yer chamber," Mr. Garston said. "Ring the bell, there, and the maid'll come to ye. Anythin' ye wants, she can provide. I daresay Mistress Dennison will be seein' you when she rises."

"And what time's that?" Juliana debated whether she could duck past him and reach the door before he could catch her.

"Noontime," he said. "That's when she 'as visitors in 'er chamber, while she's dressing. But she'll not be ready fer ye much 'afore dinner." As if guessing her thoughts, he turned to the open door and banged it closed.

Juliana stood frowning. It seemed she was a prisoner. And what kind of woman was it who had visitors in her bedchamber while she was dressing for the day?

There didn't seem much she could do about the situation at present, so, thoughtfully, she returned upstairs to the peace of her own chamber to consider the situation. She couldn't be kept there against her will indefinitely, and Mistress Dennison had so far given no indication of wishing to do so.

The maid who answered the bell seemed tongue-tied, capable of little more than a curtsy and a murmured "Yes, miss" to all conversational sallies. She either couldn't or wouldn't answer direct questions about Mistress Dennison's establishment, and when she left, Juliana found her appetite for her breakfast tray had diminished considerably under her growing unease.

When a few minutes later she heard the key turn in the lock outside, she started from her chair, raced across the room to try the door, and found it locked. For ten minutes she banged on the door and called at the top of her voice. But she could hear nothing in the passage outside.

She ran to the window and gazed at the street three floors down. There were no handholds in the brickwork, no convenient wisteria or creepers. The windows on the floor below had small wrought-iron balconies, but Juliana couldn't imagine dropping safely onto one of them from the narrow sill outside her own chamber. She contemplated calling to the passersby in the street, but what could she say? That she was a prisoner? Who would take any notice? They'd assume she was an errant servant, locked in her garret for some peccadillo. No one would involve themselves in the domestic affairs of another householder.

Juliana flopped onto the chaise longue, nibbling at a fingernail, her brows drawn together in a fierce frown. It was her own fault for trusting a kind-seeming face. Just another piece of clumsiness, really. Tripping over her feet and stumbling headlong into something nasty. But there was nothing she could do until someone chose to explain matters to her and she fully understood the pickle she was in.

But the morning wore slowly onward, and it was early afternoon before the key turned again in the lock and the door opened to admit the little maid.

"Mistress is waitin' on ye in the small salon, miss." She curtsied. "If ye'd be pleased to come wi' me."

"It's about time," Juliana said, sweeping past the girl, who scurried after her, ducking ahead so she could precede her along the corridor, down a flight of stairs to a pair of double doors at the head of the main staircase.

The girl flung open the doors, announcing in shrill tones, "Miss is 'ere, madam."

A smiling Mistress Dennison rose from her chair. "My dear, I do apologize for the locked door," she said, coming forward with her hands outstretched to take Juliana's. "But after your little escapade this morning, I was so afraid you would run away before I'd had a chance to explain matters to you. Now, do say you forgive me." She grasped the girl's hands and smiled winningly.

Juliana could see no treachery in the wide blue eyes, could hear no devious undertone in the smooth and gentle voice. But she withdrew her hands firmly, although not discourteously, and said, "Madam, I find it hard to forgive something I don't understand. Had you asked me to remain within doors, of course I would have done so, after your kindness yesterday."

Elizabeth regarded her quizzically. "Would you?" Then she nodded. "Yes, perhaps you would have. Living in town makes one so suspicious, I'm afraid. One forgets the ingenuousness of the country girl."

She sat down on a velvet chaise longue and patted the seat beside her. "Do sit down, my dear. I have a proposition for you."

"A proposition?" Juliana sat down. "I am willing to work, madam, as I made clear yesterday. If you have work for me, then of course I shall be most grateful."

"Well, I don't know whether you would describe my proposition as work precisely," the lady said with a judicious little frown. "But I suppose it is work of a certain kind."

Juliana looked around the room. It was smaller and more intimate than the salon downstairs, its opulent, elegant furnishings seeming to invite the sensual pleasures of idleness.

"Madam, is this establishment a bawdy house?" She asked the question to which she'd already guessed the answer during her long hours of cogitation.

"Indeed not." Mistress Dennison drew herself up on the chaise, looking distinctly put out. "We have only the most select company in our salons, and our young ladies take their places in the best circles of society."

"I see," Juliana said aridly. "A high-class bawdy house."

Mistress Dennison abruptly lost some of her smiling

good humor. "Now, don't be foolish and missish, child. You have barely a penny to your name. You are being pursued for the murder of your husband. You are cast upon the town with neither friend nor fortune. I am offering you both friendship and the means to make your fortune."

"I am not interested in whoredom, madam." Juliana rose from the chaise. "If you will return my clothes, I will leave here as I came. I'm grateful for your hospitality and will willingly pay for it by working in your kitchens if you wish it."

"Don't be absurd!" Mistress Dennison seized Juliana's hands, examining the long fingers, the soft skin. "You've never done a day's manual work in your life, I'll lay any odds."

"I am perfectly ready to begin now." She pulled her hands free with an angry gesture. "I'm no milksop, Mistress Dennison. And I'm not in the least interested in harlotry. So if you'll excuse me—"

"Perhaps I can be a little more persuasive."

Juliana spun around at the soft drawl. A man stepped through a crimson velvet curtain at the end of the room, and she glimpsed a small chamber behind him. He wore riding britches and a deep-cuffed black coat edged with silver lace. A single diamond winked from the folds of his starched white stock.

He stood against the curtain, negligently taking a pinch of snuff. All the while his gray eyes rested on her face, and Juliana had the uncomfortable fancy that he was seeing into her soul, was seeing much more than she had ever revealed to anyone.

"Who are *you*?" she demanded, her voice sounding raw. She cleared her throat and took a step back toward the double doors behind her.

"Don't run away," the newcomer said gently. He dropped the silver snuffbox into his pocket. "There's no need to be alarmed, as Mistress Dennison will assure you."

"No, indeed not, my dear. This is His Grace the Duke

of Redmayne," Elizabeth said, placing an arresting hand on Juliana's arm. "He has a proposition to put to you."

"I have told you, I am not in the least interested in your propositions," Juliana declared, her voice shaking with anger. She flung Mistress Dennison's hand from her. "I no more care whether they come from a duke or a night-soil collector." She turned on her heel and made for the door, thus missing the startled look in His Grace's eyes.

Annoyance chased astonishment across the cool gray surface, to be banished by interest and a reluctant admiration. The duke, accustomed to fawning obsequiousness, was surprised that he found such cavalier dismissal of his rank somewhat amusing. But his reaction didn't sound in his voice.

"The penalty for murdering a husband is death at the stake, I believe."

Juliana stopped at the duke's low, considering drawl. Her hand on the door was suddenly slippery with sweat, and the blood pounded in her temples. Slowly she turned back to the room, and her great green eyes, living coals in her deathly pale complexion, fixed accusingly upon Mistress Dennison. "You broke my confidence."

"My dear, it's for the best," Elizabeth said. "You'll see what a wonderful opportunity this is, if you'll only listen to His Grace. I know a hundred girls who'd give their eyes for such an opportunity. A life of luxury, of—"

"Allow me to lay out the benefits and rewards, madam." The duke spoke with open amusement now, and the cleft in his chin deepened as his lips quirked in a tiny smile. "It seems the young lady requires a deal of persuasion."

"Persuasion . . . blackmail, you mean," Juliana snapped. "You would hold that over my head?"

"If I must, my dear, yes," the duke said in tones of the utmost reason. "But I trust you'll agree to accept my proposition simply because it's a solution to your problems, will not be too arduous for you, I believe, and will solve a major difficulty for myself."

Juliana turned the porcelain handle of the door. All she

had to do was push it, race across the hall and out into the street. But if she left the house in the clothes given her by Mistress Dennison, her erstwhile benefactress could set up a hue and cry and accuse her of theft. She wouldn't get far in those crowded streets once the cry went up. They'd hang her for theft. They'd burn her for petty treason.

"Elizabeth, would you leave us, please?" The duke's soft, courteous tones broke through the desperate maelstrom of Juliana's thoughts.

Her hand dropped from the doorknob. She was caught in the trap that she'd sprung herself with that foolish burst of confidence yesterday. There was nothing to be gained at this point by fighting the gin. Like a snared rabbit, she'd simply chew off her own foot.

She stepped away from the door as Elizabeth billowed across the room.

"Listen well to His Grace, my dear," Mistress Dennison instructed, patting Juliana's cheek. "And don't show him such a long face. Lud, child, you should be dancing for joy. When I think what's being offered—"

"Thank you, madam." There was a touch of frost in the duke's interruption, and a tinge of natural color augmented the rouge on Elizabeth's smooth cheek.

She curtsied to the duke, cast another look, half warning, half encouragement, at Juliana, and expertly swung her wide hoop sideways as she passed through the door.

"Close it."

Juliana found herself obeying the quiet instruction. Slowly she turned back to face the room. The Duke of Redmayne had moved to stand beside one of the balconied windows overlooking the street. A ray of sunlight caught an auburn glint in his hair, tied at his nape with a silver ribbon.

"Come here, child." A white, slender-fingered hand beckoned her.

"I am no child." Juliana remained where she was, her back to the door, her hands behind her, still clutching the doorknob as if it were a lifeline.

"Seventeen from the perspective of thirty-two has a certain youthfulness," he said, smiling suddenly. The smile transformed his face, set the gray eyes asparkle, softened the distinctive features, showed her a full set of even white teeth.

"What else do you know of me, sir?" she inquired, refusing to respond to that smile, refusing to move from her position.

"That you are called Juliana Beresford . . . although I expect that's a false name," he added musingly. "Is it?"

"If it is, you wouldn't expect me to tell you," she snapped.

"No. True enough," he conceded, reaching for the bell-pull over the chimney piece. "Do you care for ratafia?"

"No," Juliana responded bluntly, deciding it was time to take the initiative. "I detest it."

The duke chuckled. "Sherry, perhaps?"

"I drink only champagne," Juliana declared with a careless shrug, moving away from the door. She brushed at her skirt with an air of lofty dismissal, and her fingertips caught a delicate porcelain figurine on a side table, sending it toppling to the carpet.

"A plague on it!" she swore, dropping to her knees, momentarily forgetting all else but this familiar, potential disaster. "Pray God, I haven't broken it. . . . Ah, no, it seems intact . . . not a crack."

She held the figurine up to the light, her fingers tracing the surface. "I dareswear it's a monstrous expensive piece. I'd not have knocked it over otherwise." She set the figurine on the table again and stepped swiftly away from the danger zone.

The duke regarded these maneuvers with some astonishment. "Are you in the habit of destroying expensive articles?"

"It's my cursed clumsiness," Juliana explained with a sigh, watching the figurine warily to make sure it didn't decide to tumble again.

Any response her companion might have made was curtailed by the arrival of Mr. Garston in response to the bell.

"Champagne for the lady, Garston," the duke ordered blandly. "Claret for myself. The forty-three, if you have it."

"I believe so, Your Grace." Garston bowed himself out.

Juliana, annoyed that her clumsiness had distracted her at a moment when she'd felt she was regaining some measure of self-possession in this frightful situation, remained silent. The duke seemed perfectly content with that state of affairs. He strolled to a bookshelf and gave great attention to the gilded spines of the volumes it contained until Garston returned with the wine.

"Leave it with me, Garston." He waved the man away and deftly eased the cork from the neck of the champagne bottle. "I trust this will find favor, ma'am." He poured a glass and took it to Juliana, still standing motionless by the table.

Juliana had but once tasted champagne, and that on her wedding day. She was accustomed to small beer and the occasional glass of claret. But with the bravado of before, she took the glass and sipped, nodding her approval.

The duke poured a glass of claret for himself, then said gently, "If you would take a seat, ma'am, I might also do so."

It was such an unlooked-for courtesy in the circumstances that Juliana found herself sitting down without further thought. The duke bowed and took a chair opposite her sofa.

Tarquin took the scent of his wine and examined the still figure. She reminded him of a hart at bay, radiating a kind of desperate courage that nevertheless acknowledged the grim reality of its position. Her eyes met his scrutiny without blinking, the firm chin tilted, the wide, full mouth taut. There was something uncompromising about Juliana Beresford, from the tip of that flaming head of hair to the toes of her long feet. The image of her naked body rose unbidden in his mind. His eyes narrowed as his languid gaze slid over her, remembering the voluptuous quality of her nudity, the smooth white skin in startling contrast to the glowing hair.

"If you insist upon making this proposition, my lord duke, I wish you would do so." Juliana spoke suddenly, breaking the intensity of a silence that had been having the strangest effect upon her. Her skin was tingling all over, her nipples pricking against her laced bodice, and she had to fight against the urge to drop her eyes from that languid and yet curiously penetrating gray scrutiny.

"By all means," he said, taking a sip of his wine. "But I must first ask you a question. Are you still virgin?"

Juliana felt the color drain from her face. She stared at him in disbelief. "What business is that of yours?"

"It's very much my business," the duke said evenly. "Whether or not I make this proposition depends upon your answer."

"I will not answer such a question," Juliana declared from a realm of outrage beyond anger.

"My dear, you must. If you wish to spare yourself the inconvenience of examination," he said in the same level tones. "Mistress Dennison will discover the answer for herself, if you will not tell me."

Juliana shook her head, beyond words.

He rose from his chair and crossed the small space between them. Bending over her, he took her chin between finger and thumb and tilted her face to meet his steady gaze. "Juliana, you told Mistress Dennison that your husband died before your marriage was consummated. Is that the truth?"

"Why would I say it if it wasn't?" Somehow she still managed to sound unyielding, even as she yielded the answer because she knew she had no choice but to do so.

He held her chin for a long moment as she glared up at him, wishing she had a knife. She imagined plunging it into his chest as he stood so close to her she could smell his skin, and a faint hint of the dried lavender that had been strewn among his fresh-washed linen.

Then he released her with a little nod. "I believe you."

"Oh, you do me too much honor, sir," she said, her voice shaking with fury. Springing to her feet, she drove her fist into his belly with all the force she could muster.

He doubled over with a gasp of pain, but as she turned to run, he grabbed her and held on even as he fought for breath.

Juliana struggled to free her wrist from a grip like steel. She raised a leg to kick him, but he swung sideways so her foot met only his thigh.

"Be still!" he gasped through clenched teeth. "Hell and the devil, girl!" He jerked her wrist hard and finally she stopped fighting.

Slowly Tarquin straightened up as the pain receded and he could breathe again. "Hair as hot as the fires of hell goes with the devil's own temper, I suppose," he said, and to Juliana's astonishment his mouth quirked in a rueful smile, although he still held her wrist tightly. "I must bear that in mind in future."

"What do you want of me?" Juliana demanded. An overwhelming sense of helplessness began to eat away at her, challenging bravado; and even as she tried to fight it, she recognized the futility of the struggle.

"Quite simply, child, I wish you to marry my cousin, Viscount Edgecombe." He released her wrist as he said this and calmly straightened his coat and the disordered lace ruffles at his cuffs.

"You want me to do *what*?"

"I believe you heard me." He strolled away from her to refill his wineglass. "More champagne, perhaps?"

Juliana shook her head. She'd barely touched what was in her glass. "I don't understand."

The duke turned back to face her. He sipped his wine reflectively. "I need a wife for my cousin, Lucien. A wife who will bear a child, an heir to the Edgecombe estate and title.

"The present heir is, to put it kindly, somewhat slow-witted. Oh, he's a nice enough soul but could no more pull

Edgecombe out of the mire into which Lucien has plunged it than he could read a page of Livy. Lucien is dismembering Edgecombe. I intend to put a stop to that. And I intend to ensure that his heir is my ward."

He smiled, but it had none of the pleasant quality of his earlier smiles. "I shall thus have twenty-one years to put Edgecombe back together again . . . to repair the damage Lucien has done—as much as anything, I believe, to spite me."

"Why can't your cousin find his own wife?" she asked, staring incredulously.

"Well, I suspect he might find it difficult," the duke said, turning his signet ring on his finger with a considering air. "Lucien is not a pleasant man. No ordinary female of the right breeding would choose to wed him."

Juliana wondered if she was going mad. At the very least she had clearly stumbled among lunatics. Vicious, twisted lunatics.

"You . . . you want a *brood mare*!" she exclaimed. "You would blackmail me into yielding my body as a vehicle for your cousin's progeny, because no self-respecting woman would take on the job! You're . . . you're treating me like a bitch to be put to a stud."

Tarquin frowned. "Your choice of words is a trifle inelegant, my dear. I'm offering a marriage that comes with a title and what remains of a substantial fortune. My cousin doesn't have long to live, hence the urgency of the matter. However, I'm certain you'll be released from his admittedly undesirable company within a twelvemonth. I'll ensure, of course, that you're well looked after in your widowhood. And, of course, not a word of your unfortunate history will be passed on."

He sipped his wine. When she still gazed at him, dumbstruck, he continued: "Your secret will be buried with me and the Dennisons. No one will ever connect Lady Edgecombe with Juliana . . . whoever-you-were." His hand moved through the air in a careless gesture. "You will be safe, prosperous, and set up for life."

Juliana drained her champagne glass. Then she threw the glass into the fireplace. Her face was bloodless, her eyes jade stones, her voice low and bitter as aloes. "And to gain such safety . . . such rewards . . . I must simply bear the child of an undesirable invalid with one foot in the—"

"Ah, no, not precisely." The duke held up one hand, arresting her in midsentence. "You will not bear Lucien's child, my dear Juliana. You will bear mine."

Chapter 4

I cannot imagine how we can help you, Sir George." Sir Brian Forsett offered his guest a chilly smile. "Juliana ceased to be our responsibility as soon as she passed into the legal control of her husband. Your father's unfortunate death leaves his widow her own mistress, in the absence of any instructions to the contrary in Sir John's will."

"And it leaves you, sir, holding her jointure in trust for her," snapped Sir George Ridge. He was in his late twenties, a corpulent, red-faced man, with hands like ham hocks. The son of his father, physically if not in character, he was the despair of his tailors, who recognized that all their skill and all their client's coin would never make an elegant figure of him.

"That is so," Sir Brian said in his customarily austere tones.

When he offered no expansion, his choleric guest began to pace the library from window to desk, muttering to himself, dabbing with his handkerchief at the rolls of sweating flesh oozing over his stock. "But it's iniquitous that it should be so," he stated finally. "Your ward has murdered my father. She runs away, and you still hold her jointure—a substantial part of my inheritance, I tell you, sir—in trust for her. I say again, sir, she is a murderess!"

"That, if I might say so, is a matter for the court," Sir Brian said, his nose twitching slightly with distaste. The warmth of the summer afternoon was having a malodorous effect on his visitor.

"I tell you again, sir, she is a murderess!" Sir George repeated, his nostrils flaring. "I saw the mark on my father's back. If she was not responsible for his death, why would she run away?"

Sir Brian shrugged his thin shoulders. "My dear sir, Juliana has always been a mystery. But until she is found, there is nothing we can do to alter the current situation."

"A murderess cannot inherit her victim's estate." Sir George slammed a fist on the desk, and his host drew back with a well-bred frown.

"Her children can, however," he reminded the angry young man. "She may be with child, sir. Her husband died in such circumstances as to imply that . . ." He paused, took a pinch of snuff, and concluded delicately, "As to imply that the marriage had been consummated."

His visitor stared in dismay. Such a thought had clearly never entered his mind. "It couldn't be." But his voice lacked conviction.

"Why not?" gently inquired his host. "You, after all, are proof that your father was not impotent. Of course, we may never know about Juliana. One would have to find her first."

"And if we don't find her, then it will take seven years to have her declared legally dead. Seven years when you will hold her jointure in trust and I will be unable to lay hands on half my land."

Sir Brian merely raised an eyebrow. He'd negotiated his ward's marriage settlement with the cold, calculated pleasure of a man who was never bested in a business deal. Bluff and kindly Sir John Ridge, heading into his dotage utterly infatuated with the sixteen-year-old Juliana, hadn't stood a chance against the needle wits of his acquisitive opponent. Juliana's benefit had been a mere sideline for Sir Brian in the general pleasures of running rings around the slow-witted and obsessed Ridge.

"Well, how are we to find her?" Sir George flung himself onto a sofa, scowling fiercely.

"I suggest we leave that to the constables," Sir Brian stated.

"And just how much do you think that lazy gaggle of poxed curs will bestir themselves?"

Sir Brian shrugged again. "If you have a better idea . . ."

"Oh, indeed I do!" Sir George sprang to his feet with an oath. "I'll go after the damned girl myself. And I'll bring her back to face the magistrates if it's the last thing I do."

"I commend your resolution, sir." Sir Brian rose and moved toward the door, gently encouraging his guest's departure. "Do, I beg you, keep me informed of your progress."

Sir George glared at him. There was only form politeness in Sir Brian Forsett's tone. The longer Juliana remained at large and in hiding, the longer Forsett would have to manage her jointure as he chose. It didn't take much imagination to understand that he would prove expert at diverting revenues from the trust into his own pocket.

"Oh, Sir George . . . pray accept my condolences. . . . Such a terrible tragedy." The crisp tones of Lady Amelia Forsett preceded the lady as she entered the library through the open terrace doors.

A tall woman of haughty demeanor, she sketched a curtsy. George, intimidated despite his anger, bowed low in return. Lady Forsett's clear pale-blue eyes assessed him and seemed to find him wanting. A chilly smile touched the corners of her mouth. "I trust I haven't interrupted your business with my husband."

"Not at all, my dear," Sir Brian reassured smoothly. "Sir George was just leaving." He pulled the bell rope.

Amelia curtsied again, and George, thus dismissed, found himself moving backward out of the library under the escort of a footman who seemed to have appeared out of thin air.

"What did that lumpen oaf want?" Amelia came straight to the point as the door closed behind their guest.

"As far as I can gather, he wishes to consign Juliana to the hangman with all dispatch, so that he can reclaim that part of his inheritance that formed her jointure."

"Dear me," murmured Lady Forsett. "What vulgar haste. His father is but three days in his own grave."

"The entire business is utterly distasteful," her husband said. "Of all the farcical—"

"Typical of Juliana," his wife interrupted, her thin lips pursing. "Such a clumsy, inconsiderate creature."

"Yes, but where *is* she?" Sir Brian interrupted with a familiar note of irritation. "Why would she run away? She couldn't possibly have been responsible for the man's death." He cast his wife an inquiring look. "Could she?"

"Who's to say?" Lady Forsett shook her head. "She's always been a wild and troublesome girl."

"With an immoderate temper," her husband put in, frowning. "But I find it hard to believe she could have deliberately—"

"Oh, not deliberately, no," Lady Forsett interrupted. "But you know how she's always doing the most inconvenient and inconsiderate things quite by accident. And if she flew off the handle . . ."

"Quite." Sir Brian chewed his lower lip, still frowning. "The whole business already bids fair to becoming the county scandal of the decade. If it comes to court, it will be hideous."

"Let us hope she isn't found," his wife said bluntly. "Then it will die down soon enough. If we don't search diligently for her, who else would bother?"

"George Ridge."

"Ahh . . . of course." Lady Forsett tidied up a tumbling pile of leather-bound volumes on a side table.

"But I doubt he has the wit to succeed," her husband said. "He's no brighter than his oaf of a father."

"Juliana, on the other hand—"

"Is as quick-witted as they come," Sir Brian finished for her with an arid smile. "If she doesn't wish to be found, I'll wager it'll take more than George Ridge to catch her."

George Ridge was still scowling as he rode out of the stable yard at Forsett Towers. His mount was a raw-boned gray, as ugly-tempered as his master, and he tossed his head violently, curling his lips back over the cruel curb bit. When his rider slashed his flank with his crop, the horse threw back his head with a high-pitched whinny, reared, and took off down the uneven gravel driveway as if pursued by Lucifer's pitchfork-carrying devils.

George had received even less satisfaction from the Forsetts than he'd expected. He cursed Sir Brian for an arrogant, nose-in-the-air meddler who hadn't the decency even to offer to assist in the search for his ungovernable, murdering, fugitive erstwhile ward.

Juliana. George pulled back on the reins as he turned the horse out of the gate and onto the lane. *Juliana.* Her image filled his internal vision in a hot, red surge of lust. He licked his lips. He'd lusted after her ever since he'd first seen her on the arm of his besotted, drooling father. His father's massive bulk had made her seem small as she walked beside him, but it couldn't disguise the voluptuous swell of her bosom beneath her demure bodice, the swing of her curving hips beneath the simple country gown that Lady Forsett insisted she wear.

Her hair had excited him as much as the hints of her body. A blazing, unruly mass of springing curls that seemed to promise an uninhibited and passionate nature. At first she'd been friendly, smiling at him, her green eyes warm, but then he'd made his mistake and yielded to the prompting of the lascivious dreams that swirled through his nights. He had attempted to kiss her, and she'd nearly scratched his eyes out. From then on her gaze had been cool and suspicious, her voice had lost its rich current of merriment, become distant and dismissive.

George's lust had not diminished, but anger and resentment had added a malevolent fuel. Now he saw his father's bride as the usurper. A twisting, manipulating bitch who had ensnared Sir John Ridge in his dotage with the promises of her youthful body. And in exchange for those promises she had been rewarded with the dower house in perpetuity, together with two thousand acres of prime land and all revenues accruing from its thick forests and tenant farms.

George had listened to his father's measured explanations for giving away George's inheritance. He had protested, but to no avail. Sir Brian Forsett had been adamant that these were the only terms on which he would agree to his ward's becoming Lady Ridge. And Sir John had been willing to agree to anything in order to have that sweet young body in his bed.

He'd had his wish, and it had killed him. George cut savagely at his horse's flanks. Juliana had disappeared, leaving her former guardian in possession of her jointure. And George was left with only half of his rightful inheritance.

But if he could find her, then her crime would disqualify her from her inheritance. Unless she was with child. If she pleaded her belly, they wouldn't sentence her to death. And her child would inherit the jointure. On the other hand, if she was to be married to Sir George Ridge—the grieving young widow wedded so appropriately to her late husband's son—then it wouldn't matter if she was with child or not. Everything would return to the Ridge family, and he, George, would have Juliana in his own bed.

Would she agree? He put spur to his horse, setting him at a high bramble hedge. The horse soared over, teeth bared in a yellow grimace, eyes rolling, and landed with a jolt on the far side.

George cursed the animal's clumsiness and jerked back on the curb rein. Juliana would agree because she would have no choice. In exchange he would swear that his father's death was accidental. No one would question George Ridge's interpretation of such an embarrassing incident. The story would be the joke of the county for months, and everyone would understand that a fat old man, drunk after his wedding, couldn't keep pace on his wedding night with a fresh filly of barely seventeen.

Juliana would agree. But first he had to find her.

He swung his mount to the right and headed for Winchester. She had to have left the area. And the only way to do that was by carriage or on horseback. No horses had been taken from the stables at Ridge Hall. But the stage-coaches departed from Winchester in the very early morning. He would inquire at the Rose and Crown, and he would post notices around the city just in case a wagoner or carter had taken up a lone woman in the middle of the night.

Juliana spent her next three days in the house on Russell Street in relative isolation, talking only to Bella, the maid who attended her and brought her meals. Her memory of the moments in the salon immediately after the duke's infamous proposition was vague. She had been devastated by outrage, rendered speechless; not trusting herself to remain in his company, she'd fled the room. No one had come after her, and no one had mentioned the matter to her again. Her chamber door was no longer locked, but on the one occasion she had ventured down to the hall, Mr. Garston had appeared out of nowhere and asked her in tones that brooked no argument to return to her chamber. She had been provided with everything she'd asked for: books, writing and drawing materials. But she was still unmistakably a prisoner in this topsy-turvy establishment that slept all day and awoke at night.

She would lie abed throughout the night listening to the strains of music from the salons, the bursts of feminine laughter, the sonorous male voices on the stairs, the chink of china and glass. Rich aromas from the kitchens wafted beneath her door, and she would entertain herself trying to identify the delicacies from which they emanated. Her own fare was the plain and plentiful food she assumed was served in the kitchens, but clearly the clients and the working ladies of the house dined very differently.

She would doze lightly throughout the night, usually falling deeply asleep at dawn as the door knocker finally ceased its banging and the sounds of merriment faded. As the sky lightened, she would hear voices in the corridor outside, soft and weary women's voices, the occasional chuckle, and once the sound of heart-wrenching weeping. The weeper had been comforted by a murmur of women, and then Mistress Dennison's voice had broken into the whisperings. Kindly but firm. Juliana had listened as she'd dispatched the women to their beds and taken the weeper away with her.

Apart from apprehension, which she fought to keep under control, Juliana's main complaint was boredom. She was accustomed to an active existence, and by the third day being penned in her chamber was becoming insupportable. She had asked no questions, made no demands for her freedom, stubborn pride insisting that she not give her captors the satisfaction of seeing her dismay. She would show them that she could wait them out, and when they saw she was adamant, then they would release her.

But on the early afternoon of the fourth day things changed. The little maid appeared in Juliana's chamber with her arms full of silk and lace.

"Y'are to dine downstairs, miss," she said, beaming over the gauzy, colorful armful. "And then be presented in the drawing room." She opened her arms, and her burdens toppled to the bed. "See what a beautiful gown Mistress Dennison 'as 'ad fashioned for ye." She shook out the folds of jade-green silk and held it up for Juliana's inspection.

"Take it away, Bella," Juliana instructed. Her heart was jumping in her breast, but she thought her voice sounded reassuringly curt and firm.

"Eh, miss, I can't do that." Bella stopped admiring the

gown in her hands and stared at Juliana. "Mistress Dennison 'ad it made up specially for ye. It wasn't ready till this
morning, so ye've been kept up 'ere. But now y'are all set."
She turned enthusiastically to the pile of material on the
bed. "See . . . fresh linen, two petticoats, silk stockings,
and look at these pretty slippers. Real silver buckles, I'll lay
odds, miss! Mistress Dennison 'as only the best fer 'er
girls." She held out a pair of dainty apple-green silk shoes
with high heels.

Juliana took them in a kind of trance, measuring the heel
with her finger. Her feet were unruly enough when they
were flat on the ground; what they would get up to in
these shoes didn't bear thinking of.

She dropped them onto the floor. "Would you inform
Mistress Dennison that I have no intention of wearing
these clothes or of being presented . . . or, indeed, of
anything at all."

Bella looked aghast. "But, miss—"

"But nothing," Juliana said brusquely. "Now, deliver
my message . . . and take these harlot's garments away
with you." She gestured disdainfully to the bed.

"Oh, no, miss, I dursn't." Bella dropped a curtsy and
scuttled from the room.

Juliana sat down on the window seat, ignored her
pounding heart, folded her hands in her lap, and awaited
developments.

They came with the arrival of both Dennisons within
ten minutes. Elizabeth, resplendent in a gown of tangerine
silk over a sky-blue petticoat, sailed into the room, followed by a tall gentleman clad in a suit of canary-yellow
taffeta, his hair powdered and curled.

Juliana, reasoning that she had nothing to lose by showing courtesy, rose and curtsied, but her eyes were sharply
assessing as they rested on her visitors. She had never met
Richard Dennison but guessed his identity from Bella's de-
scriptions.

"Now, what nonsense is this, child?" Elizabeth came
straight to the point, sounding annoyed.

"I might ask the same of you, madam," Juliana said evenly. Her mind raced. Could they force her into prostitution? Could they have her raped and ruined, so she'd have nothing further to lose? Her skin was clammy, but her voice remained steady, and she kept her eyes firmly fixed on the Dennisons.

"There's no need for discourtesy, my dear." Richard Dennison's voice was deep and mild, but the tone was belied by his keenly penetrating eyes. He stepped up to the bed. "Do you find fault with the gown . . . or the linen?"

"They are the garments of a harlot, sir. I am not a harlot."

"Oh, for goodness' sake, girl!" exclaimed Elizabeth. "This gown is the dernier cri at court. Everything here is of the best quality and design."

"I thank you for your kindness, ma'am, but I will not take your charity."

"This is not *my* gift, child, but—" She stopped abruptly as her husband coughed behind his hand, his eyes darting a warning.

Juliana bit her lip. If the clothes were not the gift of the Dennisons, then there was only one explanation. "I beg you will inform His Grace, the Duke of Redmayne, that I have no need of *his* charity either."

"Why do you keep prating of charity, child?" demanded Richard. "You are being asked to perform a service in exchange for our hospitality and His Grace's generosity."

"A service I will *not* perform," she stated, astonished at how firm she sounded when her knees were quaking like a blancmange and her palms were slippery with sweat. "I am not a whore."

"As I understand it, His Grace is offering to make you a viscountess . . . a far cry from a whore," Mr. Dennison observed aridly.

"There is a buyer and a seller, sir. I see no difference."

"Obstinate ingrate," declared Mistress Dennison. "His

Grace insisted you should have time to reconsider his offer without persuasion, but—"

"Madam!" Juliana interrupted passionately. "I ask only to be allowed to leave this house unmolested. If you will return my original garments, I will go as I came and be no trouble to anyone. Why would you keep me here against my will?"

"Because it is our considered opinion, my girl, that you don't know what's good for you," Richard said. "How long do you think you'll last on the streets? You have no idea how to go on in London. You have no money, no friends, no protection of any sort. In this house you have been offered all that and more. In exchange we ask only that you put on those clothes and come downstairs to dinner."

Juliana felt the ground slipping beneath her feet as some of her assurance left her. Everything they said was true. She'd seen enough from her window to know that a sheltered life among county aristocracy had ill equipped her for the life of an indigent girl in London.

"Bella said I was to be presented in the drawing room," she said. "I believe I know what that means."

"I believe you do not," Richard said crisply. "No demands will be made of you except for your company. You will not be required to entertain, except perhaps to play a little music and converse as in any civilized drawing room."

"And the Duke of Redmayne . . . ?" she asked, hesitantly now.

Mr. Dennison shrugged easily. "My dear, the duke's business is not ours. It lies with you, and he will deal directly with you. Mistress Dennison and I ask only that you dine with the other members of this household and take tea in the drawing room."

"And if I refuse?"

A look of exasperation crossed Mr. Dennison's face, but he held up a hand as his wife seemed about to remonstrate. "I think you know better than to do so," he said. "You are in need of a safe haven, and you have one here. But it seems reasonable to ask that you obey the rules of the house."

Juliana turned away, defeated. The threat was clear enough. It wouldn't take the magistrates long to discover her true identity once they were told her story. The landlord of the Bell in Wood Street would remember that the Winchester coach had arrived at the same time as the York stage. Piecing together the rest would be easy for them.

"Come, my dear." Mistress Dennison's voice was soft and cajoling. She laid a gentle hand on Juliana's arm. "I'll ring for Bella and she'll help you to dress. The gown will set off your eyes and hair to perfection, I promise you."

"That is hardly an incentive in these circumstances, ma'am," Juliana said dryly, but she turned back to the room. "If you are determined to have my maidenhead, then it seems there's little I can do to prevent it."

"Don't be so untrusting," Elizabeth scolded, patting her arm. "My husband and I will force nothing upon you. Your business lies with the Duke of Redmayne, and you may negotiate with him however you please."

Juliana's eyes narrowed. "You would have me believe that you have no interest, financial or otherwise, in the duke's plans for me? Forgive me, ma'am, if I doubt that. A procuress expects to be paid, I'm sure."

"What a stubborn, ill-tempered chit it is, to be sure," Elizabeth declared to her husband. "I wish His Grace joy of her." She tossed her elaborately coiffed head in disgust and sailed from the room, followed by Richard.

Perhaps it was unwise to alienate those two on whom her present comfort and security depended, Juliana reflected with a rueful grimace. She went over to the bed and began to examine the garments. There was an apple-green quilted petticoat to pair with the jade-green gown, an underpetticoat and chemise of embroidered lawn, silk stockings and garters, a pair of ruffled engageantes to slip over her forearms, and those ridiculous shoes.

She sat on the bed and slipped one cotton-stockinged foot into a shoe. It fitted perfectly. Presumably they'd used her boots as a model. Her feet were so big, they couldn't have guessed the size with this accuracy. She extended her foot, examining the shoe with her head on one side. It did make her foot look uncharacteristically elegant. But could she walk on it? She slipped on the other shoe, then gingerly stood up. Equally gingerly, she took a step and swayed precariously. The shoes pinched now most dreadfully, squashing her toes and making her insteps ache.

"Oh, miss, aren't they pretty?" Bella cried from the door as she bustled in, bearing a jug of steaming hot water. "Would ye care for a bath afore dinner? I could 'ave a footman bring up a tub."

Juliana sat down again and kicked off the shoes. Her last bath had been on her wedding morning. Maybe it would be as well to prepare herself for whatever the evening was going to bring. Like a sacrificial virgin, she thought with an unlooked-for glimmer of amusement. Her sense of humor was frequently misplaced and had in the past involved her in as much trouble as her unruly feet. But in present circumstances, she reflected, it could hardly make things worse.

"Yes, please, Bella."

"I could make up an 'enna rinse fer your hair, if'n ye'd like it," Bella continued. "It'll give it a powerful shine. Miss Deborah uses it when she 'as an evening with Lord Bridgeworth. Not that 'er 'air's as pretty as your'n. Quite dull it is, next to your'n." She beamed as if she took special pride in Juliana's superiority in this field.

"I use vinegar at home," Juliana said.

"Oh, but 'enna's a powerful lot better fer yer color, miss."

In for a penny, in for a pound. "Very well. Whatever you think Bella."

Looking mightily pleased, Bella whisked herself out of the room, and Juliana returned her attention to the garments on the bed. It was true that they were in the first style of elegance. Lady Forsett had pored over the periodicals and patterns of London style and had all her clothes

made up in Winchester to the latest specifications, although
Juliana assumed that since the periodicals and patterns had
been at least six months old by the time they'd reached
Winchester, they were probably unmodish by court standards. Not that she'd expressed this opinion to her guardian's wife.

Lady Forsett had insisted that Juliana herself wear only
the simplest country clothes suitable to a schoolgirl who
had no business in the drawing room. She had softened a
little over the wedding dress and trousseau, but Juliana had
been well aware that the garments had deliberately been
made up to outmoded patterns. Lady Forsett had said quite
bluntly that Juliana would have no need of a truly fashionable wardrobe married to Sir John Ridge. He was a wealthy
man, certainly, but not sufficiently refined to be received
by the leaders of county society.

But that wardrobe had been left behind with her dead
husband. Her britches and shirt had disappeared. The only
clothes she had were those on her back and now these
luscious, rippling, rustling silks and lawns. Juliana couldn't
help but be seduced by the delicious image of herself
dressed in such finery.

Bella returned with a footman and the boot boy, labor-
ing with copper jugs of steaming water and a wooden hip
bath. The footman and the lad bowed deferentially to Juliana as they left, and she began to feel that her position in
the house had insidiously changed.

"Everyone's very excited, miss, that ye'll be joining the
ladies tonight," Bella confided, pouring water into the tub.
"Mr. Garston says as 'ow y'are already promised to a great
patron. Everyone's very curious to meet ye."

It occurred to Juliana as she stripped off her clothes that
while she had been kept in isolation above stairs, the entire
household had been free to speculate on her position.
Somehow she'd assumed that her lack of interest in them
would be reciprocated. Not so, apparently.

She said nothing, however, stepping into the tub and
lowering herself into the steaming water with a sigh of

pleasure. She was unaccustomed to the services of a maid, Lady Forsett considering them unnecessary, but she soon discovered that Bella was as experienced as she was enthusiastic. In fifteen minutes Juliana was sitting on the ottoman while Bella vigorously dried her henna-rinsed hair.

"There y'are, miss, what did I tell you?" Bella held up a hand mirror as she took the towel from Juliana's head. "Glowin' like the sunrise."

Juliana ran her hands through the damp, springy curls until they stood out around her head like a sunburst. "But what are we to do with it now, Bella?" she inquired with a grin. "It's always been completely unmanageable after it's been washed."

"Mr. Dennison said as 'ow I was to leave it loose, miss. I'm to thread a velvet ribbon through it."

Juliana frowned. Mr. Dennison's voice, it seemed, penetrated into the intimate corners of his whores' bedchambers. She wouldn't have found Mistress Dennison's sartorial instructions offensive, she decided, but her husband's were quite a different matter. She would be obeying the orders of a pimp. But perhaps they were orders from the Duke of Redmayne, relayed through Mr. Dennison. If so, she had even less inclination to obey them.

"I shall pin it up myself," she declared, twitching the towel from Bella's slackened grip. She ignored the maid's protestations and roughly finished toweling the damp curls.

"Mr. Dennison was most particular, miss," Bella said, twisting her work-roughened hands in her apron.

"How I wear my hair is no business of his . . . or, indeed, anyone's." She tossed the towel to the floor and shook her head vigorously like a dog coming in from the rain. "There, now if I brush it carefully and use plenty of pins, I might be able to subdue it."

Bella, still looking very unhappy, handed her the new chemise and carefully unrolled the stockings. Juliana put them on and stepped into the underpetticoat. She glanced at herself in the cheval glass and decided that her wildly tangled ringlets resembled Medusa's snakes. Maybe she

should leave them just as they were—unbrushed and un-
pinned. It ought to be enough to cause even the Duke of
Redmayne to have second thoughts.

She glanced with distaste at the brocade stays Bella was
holding but turned her back so the maid could lace her.
She associated the restrictive garment with long, miserable
days when Lady Forsett had decreed she should be laced as
tightly as she could bear. It was supposed to have improved
both her bearing and her conduct, but it had only made
her more defiant.

She stood with her hands at her nipped-in waist, watching in the glass as Bella tied the tapes of the wide whalebone hoop. Juliana had never before worn anything but the
most modest frame. Now she took a step, watching the
hoop sway around her hips. It felt very cumbersome, and
the prospect of maneuvering herself on those impossibly
high heels struck her as laughable.

She stepped into the quilted overpetticoat, and Bella
dropped the jade-green gown over her head, hooking it at
the back. Juliana slipped the ruffled engageantes over her
hands, pushing them up to her elbows, where they met the
flounces sewn to the fitted sleeves of the gown. She slipped
her feet into the shoes and took a hesitant step.

Then she took another look at herself in the mirror. Her
eyes widened in astonishment. Apart from her disordered
hair, she didn't look in the least like herself. The stays
pushed up her breasts so that they swelled invitingly over
the décolletage of her gown, and the wide, swaying hoop
emphasized the smallness of her waist. The costume gave
her figure an air of enticing maturity that she found thoroughly disconcerting, although she was aware of a pleasurable prickle of excitement beneath the disquiet.

But did she look like a harlot? She put her head on one
side and considered the question. The answer was definitely
no. She looked like a woman of fashion. There was something indefinable about the gown that set it apart from
Lady Forsett's London imitations—a touch of elegance in
the fit or the style that could not be imitated.

"Oh, miss, ye look lovely," Bella said, darting around her, twitching at ruffles, adjusting the opening of the gown over the petticoat. "Now, if'n ye'd jest let me do yer 'air," she added wistfully, picking up a green velvet ribbon that exactly matched the gown.

"No, thank you, Bella. I'll do it myself." Juliana picked up the hairbrush from the dresser. She tugged it through the tangled curls until they fell in some semblance of order onto her shoulders, then twisted them into a knot on top of her head, thrusting pins into the flaming mass with reckless abandon. She felt like a hedgehog at the end, and wisps still escaped from the knot. She knew that within five minutes the whole thing would begin to tumble of its own volition and she'd be spending the evening adjusting pins in a desperate and finally futile attempt to keep it in place; but she stubbornly decided that she'd rather do that than obey the instructions of Richard Dennison or the duke.

"Will ye wear the ribbon as a collarette, miss?" Bella was still holding the velvet ribbon. "It would set off the neck of the gown."

Juliana acquiesced, and the maid looked somewhat happier as she pinned the ribbon around Juliana's throat. The deep green accentuated the whiteness of her skin, the slenderness of her neck, and drew the eye down to the swell of her breasts.

" 'Ere's yer fan, miss." Bella proffered a chicken-skin fan.

Juliana opened it and examined the delicate pattern of painted apple-green leaves. Someone had gone to a great deal of trouble to assemble this outfit.

"I'll show ye to the dining room, miss." Bella ran to the door, opening it wide. "Dinner's at four and it's almost five past."

Juliana snapped the fan closed and essayed a step. She realized immediately that her usual swinging stride from the hip was impossible with the hoop and the shoes. She was required to take mincing little steps, the hoop swinging gracefully around her. She could handle the little steps, she decided, so long as she didn't lose her balance and fall in a disorderly heap with her skirts thrown up around her head. Not that it would be the first time.

"I'm ready," she said grimly. "Lead on, Bella."

Chapter 5

Bella pranced ahead of Juliana, down the curving staircase to the front hall. Juliana proceeded much more slowly, one hand resting with apparent negligence on the banister, although in fact her fingers were curled over it as if it were a lifeline.

Mr. Garston came forward with a stately tread as she reached the bottom of the stairs. To her astonishment he bowed. " 'Ow nice to see you downstairs, miss. If ye'd care to follow me."

Her circumstances had definitely altered in the last hours. Juliana merely inclined her head and followed him to a pair of double doors at the rear of the hall. He flung them open and announced in ringing accents, "Miss Juliana."

"Ah, my dear, welcome." Elizabeth Dennison was all affability, as if the altercation in Juliana's bedchamber had never occurred. "Oh, yes, how very fetching that gown is. The color is perfect, isn't it, ladies?" She came toward her, extending her hands in welcome. "Let me present you to our little family."

Taking Juliana's hand warmly, she drew her forward to the oval table where ten young women stood at their chairs. She recognized Lilly and Emma from the encounter in the hall on her first day. Names and faces of the others blended with the speed of the introduction, but she managed to mark Deborah and take note of her hair. Bella was right that it didn't have the sparking vitality of her own. For some reason the recognition was satisfying. Juliana began to wonder what was happening to her. She rarely gave a passing thought to her appearance, and yet here she was, examining the other girls as if they were some sort of rivals. Rivals for what?

Lord of hell! She was beginning to think like a whore. It must be something to do with the atmosphere in the house.

She curtsied politely to each woman, receiving a similar salute in return, and she was aware that she was being assessed as shrewdly as she was assessing them.

"Sit down, my dears." Elizabeth waved a hand around the table. "Now we're all assembled, there's no need to stand on ceremony. Juliana, take your place beside Mr. Dennison."

The seat of honor? Juliana took the chair to Richard's right. He drew it out for her and bowed her into it as if she were indeed the guest of honor.

A footman moved around the table filling wineglasses. "Will you taste the partridge, Juliana?" Lilly inquired, deftly carving the breast of a bird on a platter before her.

Juliana noticed that most of the girls were occupied with one of the serving platters, filleting carp swimming in parsley butter, carving ducks, pigeons, and partridges.

"Are you skilled at carving, Juliana?" inquired Richard. "We consider it a necessary domestic art for a well-educated young lady of fashion."

For a whore? Juliana was tempted to ask, but she managed not to. It was not appropriate to insult her fellow diners even if she was engaged in a conflict with their keepers. "My guardian's wife also considered it necessary," she said neutrally. The fact that she could no more carve a bird elegantly than she could sew a straight seam was neither here nor there. She was well versed in the principles of both, just too ham-fisted to do either skillfully.

She took a sip of wine and listened to the conversation. The women in their rich gowns chattered like so many bright-plumaged birds. They all seemed to be in the greatest good humor, told jokes, discussed both their customers and the prospects of other women who'd left the house for secure establishments with some member of the nobility.

Juliana said nothing, and no one tried to draw her into the conversation, but she was aware of sidelong glances as they talked, as if they were assessing her reactions. She wondered whether this display of conviviality had been put on for her benefit . . . whether they'd been instructed to try to persuade her that they led charming, amusing lives under the Dennisons' roof and had only the brightest of futures to look forward to. If so, it was making not a dent in her prejudice and did nothing to relieve her suspicion and apprehension.

Richard Dennison also said little, leaving it up to his wife to direct the conversation. But Juliana felt his eyes were everywhere, and she noticed that some of the girls would hesitate in their speech if they felt him looking their way. Their whoremaster clearly exerted a powerful influence.

She could find no fault with the dinner, though. The first course was removed with a second course of plover's eggs, quail, savory tarts, Rhenish cream, a basket of pastries, and syllabub. Juliana quashed her apprehension for the time being and ate with considerable appetite, remembering how she had sat in her chamber trying to identify the various toothsome aromas wafting from the kitchens. Boiled beef and pudding, steak-and-kidney pie, stewed fish, were all very well for filling one's belly, but they did little to titillate the palate.

Eventually, Mistress Dennison rose to her feet. "Come, ladies, let us withdraw. Our friends will be arriving soon. Lilly, dear, you should touch up your rouge. Mary, there's a tiny smudge of sauce on your sleeve. Go to your maid and have it sponged off. There's nothing more off-putting to a gentleman than a slovenly appearance."

Involuntarily, Juliana's hands went to her hair, escaping from its pins as she'd known it would.

"Did Bella not tell you we wished you to leave your hair loose?" inquired Richard, still seated at the table as the ladies rose around him. He poured port into his glass and glanced up at Juliana.

"Yes, but I prefer it like this," she responded evenly. There was an almost imperceptible indrawing of breath in the room.

"You must learn to subdue your own preferences in such matters to those of the gentlemen, my dear," Elizabeth said gently. "It was a most specific request that you leave it loose this evening."

"No one's preferences have more weight than my own, madam," Juliana replied, her throat closing as her heart thundered in her ears. She would not submit to them without a fight.

To her astonishment Elizabeth merely smiled. "I dareswear that that will change quite soon. Come."

Juliana followed them out of the dining room and into the long salon she'd peeped into that first morning. It was candlelit with tall wax tapers, although the evening sun still shone through the windows. There were flowers on every surface, the scent of lavender and beeswax in the air. A long sideboard carried decanters, bottles, and glasses; there was both tea and coffee on the low table before the sofa, where Mistress Dennison immediately took her seat. The girls ranged themselves around her, took teacups, and sat down. An air of expectancy hung in the room.

Juliana refused tea and walked over to a window over-looking the street. Behind her the murmur of voices, the soft chuckles, filled the air. She heard Lilly and Mary return and Mistress Dennison approve of their adjustments. Someone began to play the harpsichord.

Along the street strolled two gentlemen coming toward the house. They swung their canes as they talked, and their sword hilts showed beneath their full-skirted velvet coats. When they reached the house, they turned up the steps. The front door knocker sounded. A whisper of tension rustled around the room. The girl on the harpsichord continued to play, the others shifted on their chairs, rearranged their skirts, opened fans, glanced casually toward the door as they waited to see who their first guests would be.

"Lord Bridgeworth and Sir Ambrose Belton," Mr. Garston announced.

Mistress Dennison rose and curtsied; the other women followed suit, except for Juliana, who drew back against the embroidered damask curtains. Deborah and a pale, fair girl she remembered as Rosamund fluttered toward the two gentlemen. Juliana recalled that Bella had said Lord Bridgeworth was Deborah's particular gentleman. Presumably Sir Ambrose and Rosamund made a similar pair.

The door knocker sounded again and a party of six gentlemen were announced. Juliana drew even farther back into the shadows, watching the scene as she nervously pushed loosening ringlets back into their pins. One of the new arrivals caught sight of her and bent to say something to Mistress Dennison. Juliana distinctly heard "His Grace of Redmayne" in amid Elizabeth's reply. Then Elizabeth turned with a smile and beckoned.

"Juliana, Viscount Amberstock wishes to be acquainted with you."

It seemed she had little choice. Juliana moved reluctantly from the semiconcealment of the curtains and crossed the room, taking tiny steps, feeling as insecure on the high heels as a baby who was just learning to walk.

"Redmayne's a lucky dog," the viscount boomed, taking her hand and raising it to his lips as he bowed with a lavish flourish. Juliana curtsied in silence, averting her eyes.

"Good God, ma'am, is the wench too shy to speak?" the viscount exclaimed to his hostess.

"Far from it," Elizabeth replied calmly. "Juliana has a very ready tongue when it suits her."

"But it belongs to Redmayne, what?" The viscount

laughed merrily at this risqué sally. "Ah, well, the rest of us must pine." He dropped Juliana's hand. She curtsied demurely and returned to her place by the window.

"You will annoy Mistress Dennison if you remain apart in this way." Emma spoke softly as she drifted casually up to Juliana in a mist of pink spider gauze.

"I find that a matter of indifference."

"You won't if they become really angered with you," Emma said, frowning. "They look after us very well, but they expect cooperation. It's hardly unreasonable."

Juliana met Emma's frowning regard and read both curiosity and a desire to be helpful in her dark-brown eyes. "But I am here against my will," she explained. "I see no reason why I should cooperate. I wish simply to be allowed to leave."

"But, my dear, you don't know what you're saying!" Emma protested. "There are bawds and whoremasters out there who will take every farthing you earn in exchange for the right to ply your trade in a shack in the Piazza. They charge five shillings for a used gown and shawl, and they'll squeeze the last drop of blood from your veins for the wine and spirits that you must have for the customers. If you refuse, or can't pay, then they'll throw you into the Fleet or the Marshalsea and you'll never be released."

Juliana stared at her, both horrified and fascinated. "But I have no intention of becoming a whore," she said at last. "Not here, nor anywhere."

Emma's frown deepened. "But what else is there for any of us?" She gestured around the room. "We live in the lap of luxury. Our clients are noblemen, discriminating, considerate . . . for the most part," she added. "And if you play your cards right, you could find a keeper who'll treat you well and provide for your future."

"But I'm not here because I wish to be," Juliana tried again.

Emma shrugged. "Are any of us, dear? But we count our blessings. You should do the same, or you'll find yourself lying under the bushes in St. James's Park every night. Believe me, I know. . . . Oh, here's Lord Farquar." With a little trill of delight—that may or may not have been feigned Emma hastened across the room toward an elderly man in a snuff-sprinkled scarlet coat.

Five minutes later Garston announced the Duke of Redmayne. Juliana's stomach dropped to her feet. She turned away from the room and stared out into the gathering dusk on Russell Street.

Tarquin stood in the doorway for a minute and took a leisurely pinch of snuff. His eyes roamed the room, rested on the averted figure in green by the window. Her hair blazed in a ray of the sinking sun. He couldn't see her face, but there was a rigidity to the sloping white shoulders. As he watched, a ringlet sprang loose from its pins and cascaded down the slender column of her neck. She remained immobile.

He strolled across the room to his hostess. "Elizabeth, charming as always." He bowed over her hand. "And the ladies . . . a garden of delights." He raised his quizzing glass and surveyed the attendant damsels, who curtsied as his gaze swept over them.

Elizabeth glanced pointedly over her shoulder to Juliana before raising an expressively questioning eyebrow. His Grace shook his head and sat down beside her on the sofa. "Leave her for the moment."

"She is as obstinate as ever, Your Grace," Elizabeth said in a low voice, passing him a cup of tea.

"But I see that you persuaded her to dress and come downstairs."

"With difficulty."

"Mmm." The duke sipped his tea. "You were obliged to coerce her?"

"To point out the realities of her situation, rather."

The duke nodded. "Well, I'm glad she's not stupid enough to ignore those realities."

"Oh, I don't believe Miss Juliana is in the least stupid," Mistress Dennison declared. "She has a tongue like a razor."

The duke smiled and laid his cup on the table. "If you'll excuse me, madam, I'll go and make my salutations." He rose and strolled across to the window.

Juliana felt his approach. Her spine prickled. A thick strand of hair worked its way loose from the knot and slid inexorably down her neck. Automatically her hands went to her head.

"Allow me." His voice at her shoulder was deep and dark, and although she'd been expecting him, she jumped visibly. "Did I startle you?" he inquired gently. "Curious . . . I could have sworn you knew I was here." His hands put hers aside and moved through her hair.

It took Juliana a moment to realize that he was removing the pins. "No!" she exclaimed, reaching for his hands. "I will not wear it loose."

"Your hair seems to have a different idea," he commented, capturing both her wrists in one hand. "It really seems to have a mind of its own, my dear Juliana." His free hand continued its work, and the fiery mass fell to her shoulders. "There, now, I find that infinitely more desirable."

"I am not in the least interested in what you find desirable, Your Grace." She tugged at her imprisoned wrists and they were immediately released.

"Oh, I hope to change that," he responded, smiling as his hands on her shoulders turned her to face him. "You look ready to thrust a dagger into my heart!"

"I would like to twist it like a corkscrew in your gut," she declared in a savage undertone. "I would carve my initials on your belly and watch you hanged, drawn, and quartered! And I would laugh at your agonies." She brushed her hands together with the air of a task well completed as she delivered the coup de grâce, her eyes sparking with triumph as if she really had disposed of him in such an utterly satisfying fashion.

Tarquin laughed. "What a fierce child you are, *mignonne*."

"*No child!*" she hissed, twitching herself out of his grasp.

"If you think I'm no more than an inexperienced simpleton to be twisted to your design like a straw, I tell you, sir, you quite mistake the matter!"

"I fear we're drawing attention to ourselves," he said. "Come, let us go somewhere private, and you may rail at me to your heart's content."

Juliana, aware that a curious hush had fallen over the room, glanced around. Eyes were swiftly averted and the buzz of conversation was immediately renewed.

"Come," he repeated, offering his arm.

"I will go nowhere with you."

"Come," he repeated, and a hint of flint lay beneath the smiling good humor in the deep-set gray eyes. As she still hesitated, he took her hand and tucked it into his arm, advising softly, "You have nothing to lose by behaving with good grace, my dear, and everything to gain."

Juliana could see no way out. All around her she saw men whose faces reflected the lascivious greed of those hungry for flesh. She could scream and create a scene, but she'd meet no sympathy or support from either the buyers or the sellers in this whorehouse masquerading as a softly lit, gracious salon. No one here would have any sympathy for a recalcitrant harlot.

Could she break free and run? But even supposing she could get past Garston and the burly footmen in the hall, where would she go? Dressed as she was, she could hardly lose herself in the narrow, twisting alleys around Covent Garden.

Her only chance was to appeal to the Duke of Redmayne's finer nature—Supposing he had one. Putting his back up wouldn't help.

In silence she allowed him to escort her from the salon. Covertly curious glances followed them. Richard Dennison was crossing the hall to the salon as they stepped through the double doors.

"Your Grace." He bowed low. His gaze flicked over Juliana, and he nodded as he noted her loosened hair. He smiled at her. "You will show His Grace all the hospitality of this house, Juliana."

"Were I a member of this household, sir, I should feel obliged to do so," Juliana retorted.

Richard's mouth tightened with annoyance. Tarquin chuckled, thinking he'd rarely met a creature with so much spirit. "I give you good evening, Dennison." He bore Juliana up the stairs and into the small parlor where she'd first met him.

Once inside, he released her arm, closed the door, and pulled the bell rope. "As I recall, you drink only champagne."

Juliana shook her head. That was a pretense that had little point now. "Not really."

"Ahh." He nodded. "You were attempting to put me in my place, I daresay."

"Is that possible?"

That made him laugh again. "No, my dear, I doubt it. What shall the footman bring for you?"

"Nothing, thank you."

"As you please." He asked the footman for claret, then stood behind an armchair, one long white hand resting on the back, his eyes on Juliana. She stood by the fireplace, staring down into the empty grate.

There was a quality to her that Tarquin found moving. A vulnerability that went hand in hand with the fierce determination to hold her own against all the odds. She was not in the least beautiful, he thought. She had an unruly, ungainly quirk that denied conventional beauty. But then he remembered her naked body, and his flesh stirred at the memory. No, not beautiful, but a man would have to be but half a man not to find her desirable. By the same token, she would be safe from Lucien. Her body was too voluptuous to appeal to him.

Suddenly she flung herself into a chair and kicked off her shoes with such vigor that one of them landed on a console table. The candlestick shook violently under the impact, and hot wax splashed onto the polished surface.

"A plague on the damnable things!" Juliana bent to massage her feet with a groan. "How could anyone wear such instruments of torture?"

"Most women manage without difficulty," he observed, much amused at this abrupt change of demeanor. Her hair obscured her expression as she bent over her feet, but he could imagine the disgusted curl of her lip, the flash of irritation in her eyes. Strange, he thought, that after only two meetings he could picture her reactions so accurately.

She looked up, shaking her hair away from her face, and he saw he'd been exactly right. "I don't give a damn what other women manage! I find them insupportable." She extended one foot, flexing it to stretch the cramped arch.

"Practice makes perfect," Tarquin said, taking the discarded shoe off the console table. He picked up the other one that had come to rest in the coal scuttle. He blew coal dust from the pale silk, murmuring, "What cavalier treatment for a fifty-guinea pair of shoes."

So he *had* paid for them. Juliana leaned back in her chair and said carelessly, "I'm sure they won't go to waste, Your Grace. There must be harlots aplenty eager to accept such gifts."

"That might be so," he agreed judiciously. "If women with feet this size were easy to find."

The return of the footman with the claret gave Juliana the opportunity to bite her tongue on an undignified retort. When the man had left, she was prepared to launch her appeal to the duke's finer feelings.

"My lord duke," she began, getting to her feet, standing very straight and still. "I must beg you to cease this persecution. I cannot do what you ask. It's preposterous . . . it's barbaric that you should demand such a thing of someone you know has no protection and no friends. There must be women who would be willing . . . eager, even . . . to enter such a contract. But I'm not of their number. Please, I beg you, let me leave this place unmolested."

Almost every woman Tarquin could think of in Juliana's situation would leap at what he was offering—wealth, position, security. The girl was either a simpleton or *very* unusual. He kept his thoughts to himself, however, remarking, "Somehow, I have the impression that pleading is foreign to your nature, *mignonne*." He took a sip of his claret. "That little speech lacked a certain ring of conviction."

"Oh, be damned to you for a Judasly rogue!" Juliana cried. "Base whoreson! Stinking gutter sweeping. If you think you can bend me to your will, then I tell you, you have never been more mistaken in your entire misbegotten existence!"

She leaped across the space separating them, tripped over the hem of her gown, grabbed at a chair to right herself, and turned on him, shaking her hair out of her eyes, her fingers curled into claws, her teeth bared, her eyes spitting hatred.

Tarquin took a hasty step back. Abruptly he lost the desire to laugh. Miss Juliana didn't take kindly to mockery. "Very well." He held up his hands in a placating gesture. "I ask your pardon for being so flippant. Sit down again, and we'll begin anew."

Juliana stopped. A hectic flush mantled her usually creamy cheeks, and her bosom rose and fell in a violent rhythm as she struggled to control herself. "You are the son of a gutter bitch," she said with low-voiced savagery.

Tarquin raised his eyebrows. Enough was enough. He said nothing until her flush had died and her erratic breathing had slowed; then he asked coolly, "Have you finished roundly abusing me?"

"There's no abuse I can inflict on you, my lord duke, to equal that which you would inflict upon me," she said bitterly.

"I have no intention of abusing you. Sit down before the room disintegrates in your cyclone and take a glass of claret."

The deliberately bored tone was deflating. Juliana sat down and accepted the glass of wine he brought her. The outburst had drained her, leaving her hovering on the brink of hopelessness. "Why won't you find someone else?" she asked wearily.

Tarquin sat down opposite her. "Because, my dear, you are a perfect choice." He began to tick off on his fingers. "You have the necessary breeding to appear as Lucien's wife without causing raised eyebrows. And you have both the breeding and certain qualities that I believe will make you a good mother to my child. And, finally, you need what I am offering in exchange. Safety, a good position, financial security. And most of all, Juliana, independence."

"Independence?" She raised a disbelieving eyebrow. "And how does that square with being a brood mare?"

Tarquin stood up and went to refill his glass. The girl was not a simpleton, but he was beginning to wonder whether, unusual or no, she was worth the time and the trouble he was expending. There were other women, as she so rightly pointed out. Women who'd jump at what he was offering. He turned back and examined her in silence, reflectively sipping his claret.

She was sitting back again, her eyes closed, her hair living fire around her pale face. The deep cleft between her breasts drew his eye. There was something intriguing as well as unusual about her. Her defiant resistance was such a novel challenge, he found it irresistible. He wanted to know what made her so unexpected, so out of the common way. What soil had she grown in? Maybe he was being a fool, but his blood sang with the conviction that Miss Juliana was definitely worth the time and the trouble to persuade.

He put his glass down and came over to her. Bending, he took her hands and drew her to her feet. "Let me show you something."

Juliana opened her mouth in protest and then gasped as his mouth closed over hers. His hands were in her hair, holding her head steady, and his lips were firm and pliant on hers. His tongue ran over her mouth, darting into the corners in a warm, playful caress that for a moment took her breath away. She was enclosed in a red darkness, all her senses focused on her mouth, on the taste and feel of his. Her lips parted at the delicate pressure, and his tongue slid inside, moving sinuously, exploring her mouth, filling her mouth with sweetness, sending hot surges of confused longing from her head to her toes.

Slowly he drew back and smiled down into her startled face, his fingers still curled in her hair. "That was what I wanted to show you."

"You . . . you ravished me!"

Tarquin threw his head back and laughed. "Not so, *mignonne*. I made you a promise." He moved one hand to cup her cheek, his thumb stroking her reddened mouth.

Juliana stared up at him, and he read the confusion, the dismay, and the excitement in her eyes.

"I promised you that what happens between us will bring you only pleasure. Nothing will happen to you, Juliana, that you don't wholeheartedly agree to."

"Then let me go," she begged, recognizing with quiet desperation that if she was compelled to remain, then Tarquin, Duke of Redmayne, would defeat her. She had yielded to his kiss. She hadn't fought him. Sweet heaven, she'd opened her mouth for his tongue without a moment's hesitation.

"No, you must remain in this house—that I insist upon."

Slowly Juliana crossed the room and picked up her discarded shoes. Sitting down, she slipped her feet into them. She knew he would see it as a symbolic gesture of acceptance, but at the moment she was too dispirited for further fighting.

She rose as slowly and walked to the door. "I beg leave to bid you good night, my lord duke." She curtsied formally, her voice low and expressionless.

"You have leave," he responded with a smile. "We will begin anew tomorrow."

Chapter 6

> ⤜⧓⤛

Y ou want me to take a wife!" Lucien threw back his head on a shout of derisive laughter that disintegrated into a violent fit of coughing.

Tarquin waited impassively as his cousin fought for sobbing breaths, his chest rattling, a sheen of perspiration gathering on his pale, sallow complexion.

"By God, Tarquin, I do believe you've finally lost your wits!" Lucien managed at last, falling back into his chair. He was clearly exhausted, but he still grinned, a gleam of malevolent interest in the dark, burning sockets of his eyes.

"I doubt that," the duke said calmly. He filled a glass with cognac and handed it to his cousin.

Lucien drained it in one gulp and sighed. "That's better. Eases the tightness." He patted his chest and extended his glass. "Another, dear fellow, if you please."

Tarquin glanced at the clock on the mantel. It was ten in the morning. Then he shrugged and refilled the viscount's glass. "Are you able to listen to me now?"

"Oh, by all means . . . by all means," Lucien assured him, still grinning. "Why else would I obey your summons so promptly? Amuse me, dear boy. I'm in sore need of entertainment."

Tarquin sat down and regarded his cousin in silence for a

minute. His expression was dispassionate, showing no sign of the deep disgust he felt for this wreck of a young man who had willfully cast away every advantage of birth, breeding, and fortune, pursuing a course of self-destruction and depravity that considered no indulgence or activity too vile.

Sometimes Tarquin wondered why Lucien had turned out as he had. Sometimes he wondered if he, as the boy's guardian, bore any responsibility. He'd tried to be an elder brother to Lucien, to provide an understanding and steadying influence in his life, but Lucien had always evaded him in some way. He'd always been dislikable, defeating even Quentin's determination to see the good in him.

"Your passion for little boys has become something of a family liability," he observed, withdrawing a Sevres snuffbox from his pocket. "That rather nasty business with the Dalton boy seems to have become common knowledge."

Lucien had ceased to look amused. His expression was sullen and wary. "It was all hushed up quite satisfactorily."

Tarquin shook his head. "Apparently not." He took a pinch of snuff and replaced the box before continuing. "If you wish to continue with your present lifestyle in London, you need to protect yourself from further whispers. A charge against you would inevitably mean your exile . . . unless, of course, you were prepared to hang for your preferences."

Lucien glowered. "You're making mountains out of molehills, cousin."

"Am I?" The duke raised an eyebrow. "Read this." He drew a broadsheet out of his waistcoat pocket and tossed it across. "That story on the front has been providing entertaining gossip in every coffeehouse in town. Remarkable likeness, I think. The artist has a fine eye for caricature."

Lucien read the story, his scowl deepening. The artist's caricature of himself was as lewd and suggestive as the scurrilous description of an incident in the Lady Chapel involving a nobleman and an altar boy at St. Paul's Cathedral.

"Who wrote this?" He hurled the sheet to the floor. "I'll have his ears pinned to the pillory."

"Certainly. If you want everyone to know who you are," the duke observed, bending to pick up the sheet. He shook his head, marveling, "It really is a remarkably good likeness. A stroke of genius."

Lucien tore savagely at his thumbnail with his teeth. "A plague on him! Just let me find out who he is, and I'll run him through."

"Not, I trust, in the back," Tarquin said, his voice mild but his eyes snapping contempt.

Lucien flushed a dark, mottled crimson. "That never happened."

"Of course not," Tarquin said in silken tones. "Never let it be said that an Edgecombe would put his sword into a man's back."

Lucien sprang to his feet. "Accuse me of that again, Redmayne, and I'll meet you at Barnes Common."

"No, I don't think so," Tarquin responded, his lip curling. "I've no intention of committing murder."

"You think you could—"

"Yes!" the duke interrupted, his voice now sharp and penetrating. "Yes, I would kill you, Lucien, with swords or pistols, and you know it. Now, stop sparring with me and sit down."

Lucien flung himself into the chair again and spat a piece of thumbnail onto the carpet.

"I lost interest long ago in trying to persuade you to choose another way of life," Tarquin said. "You are a vicious reprobate and a pederast, but I'll not have you bringing public dishonor on the family name. Which is what will happen if the parent of some other altar boy decides to bring charges against you. Take a wife and be discreet. The rumors and the scandals will die immediately." He tapped the broadsheet with a finger.

Lucien's eyes narrowed. "You're not foolin' me, Redmayne. You wouldn't give a damn if they hanged me, except for the blot on the family escutcheon." He smiled, looking very pleased with himself as if he'd just successfully performed a complex intellectual exercise.

"So?" Tarquin raised an eyebrow.

"So . . . why should I do what you want, cousin?"

"Because I'll make it worth your while."

A crafty gleam appeared now in Lucien's pale-brown eyes. "Oh, really? Do go on, dear boy."

"I'll take your creditors off your back," the duke said. "And I'll keep you in funds. In exchange you will marry a woman of my choosing, and you will both reside under this roof. That shouldn't trouble you, since Edgecombe House is in such disrepair at the present, and it will relieve you of the burden of maintaining a household."

"A woman of *your* choosing!" Lucien stared at him. "Why can't I choose my own?"

"Because no one remotely suitable would take you."

Lucien scowled again. "And just whom do you have in mind? Some ancient antidote, I suppose. A spinster who'll take anything."

"You flatter yourself," the duke said dryly. "No woman, however desperate, would willingly agree to be shackled to you, Edgecombe. The woman I have in mind will do my bidding. It is as simple as that. You don't need to concern yourself about her. You will have separate quarters and you will leave her strictly alone in private. In public, of course, you will be seen to have a young wife of good breeding. It should provide you with a satisfactory public facade."

Lucien stared at him. "Do your bidding! Gad, Tarquin, what kind of devil are you? What hold do you have over this woman to compel her in such a matter?"

"That's no concern of yours."

Lucien stood up and went to refill his glass at the sideboard. He tossed the contents down his throat and refilled the glass. "All my expenses . . . all my debts . . . ?" he queried.

"All of them."

"And you'll not be prating at me every minute?"

"I have no interest in your affairs."

"Well, well." He sipped his brandy. "I never thought to see the day the Duke of Redmayne begged *me* for a favor."

Tarquin's expression didn't alter.

"I have very expensive habits," Lucien mused. He glanced slyly at the duke, who again showed no reaction. "I've been known to drop ten thousand guineas at faro in an evening." Again no reaction. "Of course, you're rich as Croesus, we all know that. I daresay you can afford to support me. I wouldn't like to bankrupt you, cousin." He grinned.

"You won't."

"And this woman . . . ? When do I see her?"

"At the altar."

"Oh, that's going too far, Tarquin! You expect me to trot along to church like the veritable lamb to the slaughter without so much as a peek at the woman?"

"Yes."

"And what does she say about it? Doesn't she want to see her bridegroom?"

"It doesn't matter what she wants."

Lucien took a turn around the room. He hated it when his cousin offered him only these flat responses. It made him feel like a schoolboy. But then again . . . the thought of Tarquin's funding Lucien's lifestyle despite his unconcealed contempt and loathing brought a smile to the viscount's lips. Tarquin would squirm at every bank draft he signed, but he wouldn't go back on his word. And he had set no limits on Lucien's expenditure.

And to live here, in the lap of well-ordered luxury. His own house barely ran at all. He could rarely keep servants beyond a month. Something always happened to send them racing for the door without even asking for a character. But here he could indulge himself to his heart's content, live as wild and reckless as he pleased, all at his cousin's expense.

It was a delicious thought. In exchange he simply had to go through the motions of a marriage ceremony to some unknown woman. He'd never have to have anything to do with her. He had nothing to lose and everything to gain.

"Very well, dear boy, I daresay I could oblige you in this."

"You overwhelm me, Edgecombe." Tarquin rose to his feet. "Now, if you'll excuse me, I have another appointment."

"Go to it, dear fellow, go to it. I'll just sip a little more of this excellent cognac." He rubbed his hands. "You have such a magnificent cellar, I can hardly wait to sample it. . . . Oh, Quentin, my dear . . . ." He turned at the opening of the door and greeted his cousin with a flourishing bow. "Guess what. I'm to take a wife . . . settle down and become respectable. What d'you think of that, eh?"

Quentin shot his half brother a look more in sorrow than in anger. "So you are proceeding with this, Tarquin."

"I am."

"And my wife and I will be taking up residence under Tarquin's roof," Lucien continued. "More suitable for the young lady . . . more comfortable. So you'll be seeing a lot of us, my dear Quentin."

Quentin sighed heavily. "How delightful."

"How un-Christian of you to sound so doubtful," scolded Lucien, upending the decanter into his glass. "Seems to be empty." He pulled the bell rope.

"Good day, Lucien." Abruptly Tarquin strode to the door. "Quentin, did you wish to see me?"

"No," his brother said. "It would only be a waste of breath."

"My poor brother!" Tarquin smiled and patted his shoulder. "Don't despair of me. This is not going to turn out as badly as you think."

"I wish I could believe that." Quentin turned to follow Tarquin from the library. Lucien's chuckle rang unpleasantly in his ears.

"Last Friday, you say?" Joshua Bute pulled his left ear, regarding his customer with a benign attention that belied his shrewd, cunning calculations.

"Friday or possibly Saturday," George Ridge said, raising his tankard to his lips and taking a deep, thirsty gulp of ale. "Off the Winchester coach."

"A young lady . . . unattended?" Joshua pulled harder at his ear. "Can't say I did see such a one, guv. A'course, the York stage comes in at the same time. Quite a bustle it is 'ereabouts."

George leaned heavily on the stained counter of the taproom. Gold glinted between his thick fingers as he spun a guinea onto the countertop. "Maybe this might refresh your memory."

Joshua regarded the guinea thoughtfully. "Well, per'aps ye could describe the young person agin?"

"Red hair, green eyes," George repeated impatiently. "You couldn't mistake her hair. Like a forest fire, all flaming around her face. Pale face . . . very pale . . . deep-green eyes . . . tall for a woman."

"Ah." Joshua nodded thoughtfully. "I'll jest go an' ask in the kitchen. Mebbe one of the lads saw such a one in the yard, alightin' from the coach."

He trundled off into the kitchen, and George cursed under his breath. The Rose and Crown in Winchester had been no help. They couldn't remember who was on the waybill for either Friday or Saturday. The scullery maid thought she remembered a lad boarding on the Friday, but the information had been elicited after the outlay of several sixpences, and George couldn't be sure whether it was a true recollection. Anyway, a lad didn't fit the description of the voluptuous Juliana.

He loosened the top button of his waistcoat and fanned his face with his hand. A bluebottle buzzed over a round of runny Stilton on the counter. His only other companion was an elderly man in the inglenook, smoking a churchwarden pipe, alternately spitting into the sawdust at his feet and blowing foam off the top of his ale.

The sounds of the city came in through the open door, together with the smells. George was no stranger to the farmyard, but the rank odor of decaying offal and excre-

ment in the midday sun was enough to put a man off his
dinner. A wagon rattled by on its iron wheels, and a barrow
boy bellowed his wares. A woman screamed. There was the
ugly sound of a violent blow on soft flesh. A dog barked
shrilly. A child wailed.

George resisted the country boy's urge to cover his ears.
The noise and the bustle made him nervous and irritable,
but he was going to have to get used to it if he was to find
Juliana. He was convinced she was in the city somewhere.
It was the only logical place for her. There was nowhere for
her to hide in the countryside, and she would never escape
detection in Winchester or any of the smaller towns. Her
story was by now on every tongue.

"Well, seems like y'are in luck, sir." Beaming, Joshua
emerged from the kitchen.

"Well?" George couldn't keep the eagerness from his
voice or countenance.

"Seems like one of the lads saw a young person summat
like what ye described." Joshua's eyes were fixed on the
guinea still lying on the counter. George pushed it across to
him. The innkeeper pocketed it.

" 'E didn't rightly know which stage she come off, guv.
But it could've been the Winchester coach."

"And where did she go?"

Joshua pulled his ear again. " 'E couldn't rightly say, Yer
'Onor. She disappeared outta the yard with all the other
folk."

Dead end. Or was it? George frowned in the dim, dusty,
stale-smelling taproom. At least he knew now that she was
in London, and that she'd arrived in Cheapside. Someone
would remember her. As far as he knew, she had no
money. It appeared that she'd taken nothing from the
house . . . a fact that mightily puzzled the constables and
the magistrates. Why would a murderess not complete the
crime with robbery? It made no sense.

"What was she wearing?"

Joshua's little eyes sharpened. "I dunno, guv. The lad

couldn't rightly say. It was early mornin'. Not much light. An' the yard was a mad'ouse at that time o' day. Always is."

George's frown increased. "Bring me a bottle of burgundy," he demanded suddenly. "And I presume you can furnish a mutton chop."

"Aye, guv. A fine mutton chop, some boiled potatoes, an' a few greens, if'n ye'd like." Joshua beamed. "An' there's a nice piece o' Stilton, too." He slapped at the bluebottle, squashing it with the palm of his hand. "I'll fetch up the burgundy."

He went off, and George walked over to the open door. It was hot and sultry, and he wiped his forehead with his handkerchief. He had to find lodgings and then a printer. Reaching into his inside pocket, he drew out a sheet of paper. He unfolded it and examined its message with a critical frown. It should do the trick. He would have twenty or so printed; then he could hire a couple of street urchins for a penny to post the bills around the area. A reward of five guineas should jog someone's memory.

" 'Ere y'are, sir. Me finest burgundy," Joshua announced. He drew the cork and poured two glasses. "Don't mind if I joins ye, guv? Yer 'ealth, sir." He raised his glass and drank. Everything was very satisfactory. He had a guinea in his pocket from this gent, and there'd be at least another coming from Mistress Dennison when his message reached her. In fact, he could probably count on two from that quarter. She was bound to be interested in this gentleman and his curiosity about her latest acquisition. Not to mention the fact that the girl hadn't come off the York stage, as she'd maintained, but from Winchester. It was all most intriguing. And bound to be lucrative.

Joshua refilled their glasses and beamed at his customer.

Chapter 7

❧

"Juliana, do you care to come for a walk with us?" Miss Deborah popped her head around Juliana's door. "Lucy and I are going to the milliner's. I have to match some rose-pink ribbon. Do come."

"I have the impression I'm not permitted to leave the house," Juliana said. It was noon on the day after her presentation in the drawing room, and she hadn't stirred from her chamber since parting from the Duke of Redmayne. The house had been quiet as usual throughout the morning, but in the last hour it had come to life, and Juliana had sat in her room waiting for something to happen.

"Oh, but Mistress Dennison told me to ask you," Deborah said in genuine surprise. "She said an airing would do you good."

"I see." Juliana rose. This was an unexpected turn of events. She had expected to be more, rather than less, confined after her conduct the previous evening. "How kind of her. Then let's go."

Deborah looked a little askance at Juliana's dress. She was back in the simple servant's muslin. "Should you perhaps change?"

Juliana shrugged. "That might be a little difficult, since I have nothing but what I'm wearing and the gown I wore last night."

Deborah was clearly nonplussed, but before she could say anything, Bella bobbed up beside her in the doorway. "Mistress sent me up with this gown, miss, fer yer walk. I'nt it pretty?" She held up a gown of bronze silk. "An' there's a shawl of Indian silk to go with it."

"Oh, how lovely." Deborah felt the gown with an expert touch. "The finest silk, Juliana." She sighed enviously. "His Grace must have spent a pretty penny. Bridgeworth is generous enough, of course, but I often have to remind him. And it's so uncomfortable to have to do that, don't you agree?" She looked inquiringly at Juliana, who was hard-pressed to find a response that wouldn't offend Deborah but that would express the truth.

"I haven't yet found myself in that position," she said vaguely, taking the gown from Bella. The silk flowed through her hands like water. She glanced toward the open window. The sun poured through. How long had it been since she'd been outside? Days and days. She was in London, and she'd seen nothing of it but the yard of the Bell in Cheapside, and the street beneath this window. If she had to take the duke's gown to leave her prison, then so be it.

"Help me, Bella."

Deborah perched on the end of the bed as Bella eagerly helped Juliana into the underpetticoat and hoop she'd worn the previous evening before dropping the bronze silk gown over her head. " 'Ow shall I do yer 'air, miss?"

"It's more subdued today," Juliana said, unable to hide the uplift of her spirits at the thought of being out in the sunshine. "If you pin it up securely, it should stay in place."

Bella did as asked, then arranged the shawl of delicate cream silk over Juliana's shoulders. She stepped back, nodding her approval. Juliana examined herself in the glass. The bronze was a clever complement to her own coloring. Again she reflected that someone knew exactly what would flatter her. Did the Duke of Redmayne make the decisions?

Or did he provide the money and leave the choice to Mistress Dennison?

Panic fluttered suddenly in her belly as a sense of helplessness washed over her. Every day the trap grew tighter. Every day she grew less confident of her own power to determine her destiny. Every day she grew insidiously more resigned.

A thrush trilling at the open window, the warmth of the sun on the back of her neck, sent the black wave into retreat. She was going out for a walk on a beautiful summer morning, and nothing should destroy her pleasure in such a prospect.

"Come, Deborah, let's go." She pranced through the door, thankful that no one had made objection to the comfortable leather slippers she still wore.

Lucy was waiting for them in the hall. "That's such a pretty gown," she said a little enviously as Juliana bounced exuberantly down the stairs. "Those pleats at the back are all the rage."

"Yes, and see the way the train falls," Deborah said. "It's the most elegant thing. I must ask Minnie to make up that bolt of purple tabby in the same style."

Juliana was too anxious to reach the door to pay any heed to this conversation. Mr. Garston opened it for her, with a bow and an indulgent smile. "Enjoy your walk, miss."

"Oh, I intend to," she said, stepping past him, lifting her face to the sun and closing her eyes with a sigh of pleasure.

"Ah, Miss Juliana. What perfect timing."

Her eyes snapped open at the suave tones of the Duke of Redmayne. He stood at the bottom of the front steps, one gloved hand resting on the wrought-iron banister, a quizzical gleam in his eye.

"Perfect timing for what?" She waited for her pleasure in the morning to dissipate, but it didn't. Instead there was the strangest fizz of excitement in her belly; her face warmed, and her lips prickled as if anticipating the touch of his mouth on hers.

"I was coming to take you out for a drive," he said. "And I find you quite ready for me."

"You're mistaken, sir. I'm engaged to these ladies." She gestured to Lucy and Deborah, who both swept the duke a curtsy, a salutation that Juliana had omitted.

"They will excuse you," Tarquin said.

"Yes, of course, Juliana," Deborah said hastily.

"But I have no wish to be excused."

"I give you good day, ladies. Enjoy your walk." Tarquin bowed to Deborah and Lucy and stood aside to let them pass him on the step. As Juliana made to follow them, he laid a hand on her arm. "You will much prefer to drive with me, Juliana."

Juliana's skin burned where he touched her, and the fizzing excitement spread through her body as if she had champagne in her veins. She looked up at him, bewildered agitation flaring in her eyes. Tarquin smiled, then lightly brushed her lips with his own.

"You're very rewarding to dress, *mignonne*. Not many women could wear such a color without looking sallow and drab."

"So you did choose it?"

"Most certainly. I've been much entertained in designing your wardrobe. I trust it will all meet with your approval when you see it."

Juliana looked wildly up and down the street as if hoping to see some escape route, some knight in shining armor galloping to her rescue. But she met only the indifferent glances of grooms, barrow boys, fishwives, hurrying about their business.

"Come, my horses are getting restless." The duke tucked Juliana's hand into his arm and firmly ushered her across the street to where a light, open phaeton stood, drawn by a pair of handsome chestnuts. A groom jumped from the driver's seat and placed a footstep for them.

Juliana hesitated. The duke's hands went to her waist, lifting her clear off her feet and into the carriage. "You seem remarkably dozy this morning," he observed, step-

ping lightly up behind her. "Perhaps you slept poorly." He
sat down and took up the reins. "Grimes, you may go back
to Albermarle Street."

The groom touched his forelock and set off at a loping
pace down the street toward the Strand.

"Now, where would you like to go?" the duke inquired
affably. "Is there something particular you'd like to see?
Westminster, perhaps? The Houses of Parliament? Hyde
Park? The lions in the Exchange?"

Juliana contemplated a sullen silence and then abandoned the idea. It would be cutting off her nose to spite
her face. "All of them," she said promptly.

Tarquin nodded. "Your wish is my command, ma'am."

Juliana cut him a sharp sideways look. "I didn't think
you were a liar, my lord duke."

He merely smiled. "We'll drive around Covent Garden
first. You'll find it of some interest, I believe."

Juliana understood what he meant as soon as they turned
the corner of Russell Street and she finally saw what was
hidden from her window. The colonnaded Piazza was
thronged with men and women of every class and occupa-
tion. Dandies lounged with painted whores on their arms;
fashionably dressed women, accompanied by footmen,
paraded the cobbles, inviting custom as obviously as their
less fortunate sisters who leaned in the doorways of
wooden shacks and coffeehouses, beckoning with grubby
fingers, lifting ragged petticoats to display a knee or plump
thigh. Barrow boys and journeymen carrying baskets of
bread and pies on their heads threaded their way through
the produce sellers shouting their wares.

Juliana stared in fascinated disgust at the prints displayed
on a kiosk on the corner of Russell Street. The duke followed her eye and observed casually, "Obscenity sells well
in the Garden. Obscenity and flesh," he added. "The two
tend to go together." He gestured with his whip. "The
hummums and the bagnios over there do a thriving trade in
steam and sweat . . . and flesh, of course."

Juliana could think of nothing to say. She continued to

gaze around her, engrossed by the scene even as she was repelled by it.

"The Dennisons' young ladies do not frequent the Piazza. You're more likely to see them at court than here," the duke continued. Juliana stared at a couple standing against the wall of one of the bagnios. Then, abruptly, she averted her eyes, a crimson flush spreading over her cheeks.

"Yes, privacy is not a particularly valued commodity around here," her companion observed. "You could see the same in St. James's Park after dark . . . under every bush, against every tree."

Juliana remembered Emma's warning about lying under the bushes in St. James's Park. Her skin crawled. She wanted to ask him to take her out of this place, but she knew he had a reason for bringing her here, and she wouldn't give him the satisfaction of showing her dismay.

They turned onto Long Acre, and as they approached St. Martin-in-the-Fields, the duke slowed his horses. A ragged group of children were gathered around the church steps. Three elderly women walked among them, examining them, paying particular attention to the little girls. Some they dismissed with a wave; others they gestured to stand aside.

"What are they doing?" Juliana couldn't help asking the question.

"The children are for hire . . . some of them for sale," her companion told her nonchalantly. "The bawds are picking the ones that might appeal to their customers' particular fancies."

Juliana gripped her hands tightly in her lap and stared straight ahead.

"If they're hired, they'll get a decent meal and earn a few shillings," the duke continued in the same tone. "Of course, most of their earnings will go to whoever put them up for hire in the first place."

"How interesting, my lord duke." Juliana found her voice as she finally understood the point to this little tour of London's underbelly. Unless she was much mistaken, the Duke of Redmayne was showing her what life was like for the unprotected.

Tarquin turned the phaeton onto the Strand. He maintained a flow of informative chat as he drove her through St. James's Park and along Piccadilly, and Juliana was soon seduced by the other sights of London: the lavish shop fronts, the town carriages, the horsemen, the sedan chairs. Ladies carrying small dogs promenaded along the wide street, greeting acquaintances with shrill little cries of delight, exchanging curtsies and kisses. They were followed by powdered footmen in elaborate liveries and, in most cases, small liveried pages loaded with bandboxes and parcels.

Juliana began to relax. The streets in this part of London were cleaner, the cesspit stench not so powerful, the buildings tall and gracious, with glass windows glinting in the sunlight, shining brass door knockers, white honed steps. This was the London she'd imagined from the sheltered Hampshire countryside. Impressive and wealthy, and full of elegant people.

The duke drew up before a double-fronted mansion on Albermarle Street. The front door opened immediately, and the groom he'd sent home at Covent Garden came running down the steps. The duke descended and reached up a hand to Juliana.

"You will wish for some refreshment," he said pleasantly.

Juliana remained where she was. "What is this place?"

"My house. Be pleased to alight." The touch of flint she'd heard before laced the pleasant tones. Juliana glanced up the street, then down at the groom, who was staring impassively ahead. What choice did she have?

She gave the duke her hand and stepped out of the carriage. "Good girl," he said with an approving smile, and she wanted to kick him. Instead she twitched her hand out of his and marched up the steps to the open front door, leaving him to follow.

A footman bowed as she swept past him into a marble-tiled hall. Juliana forgot her anger and apprehension for a moment as she gazed around, taking in the delicate plaster molding on the high ceiling, the massive chandeliers, the dainty gilt furniture, the graceful sweep of the horseshoe staircase. Forsett Towers, where she'd grown up, was a substantial gentleman's residence, but this house was in a different class altogether.

"Bring refreshment to the morning room," the duke instructed over his shoulder, slipping an arm around Juliana's waist and sweeping her ahead of him toward the stairs. "Tea, lemonade, cakes for the lady. Sherry for myself."

"I imagine your servants are accustomed to your entertaining unchaperoned ladies," Juliana stated frigidly as she was borne up the stairs with such dexterity that her feet merely skimmed the ground.

"I have no idea whether they are or not," the duke responded. "They're paid to do my bidding, that's all that concerns me." He opened a door onto a small parlor, sunny and cheerful with yellow silk wallpaper and an Aubusson carpet. "I have it in mind that this should be your own private parlor. Do you think you would care for it?" A hand in the small of her back propelled her forward even as she wondered if she'd heard him aright.

"It's pleasant and quiet, overlooking the garden at the back," he continued, gesturing to the window. "If you wished to change the decor, then, of course, you must do whatever pleases you."

Juliana told herself that this was some dream . . . some ghastly, twisted nightmare that would all fall apart in a moment like a broken jigsaw puzzle. But he'd turned back to her and was smiling as he took her hands and drew her toward him. Her eyes fixed on his mouth, thin but so beautifully sculpted. There was amusement and understanding in the deep-set gray eyes, and something else—a flicker of desire that set her blood frothing again. And then she was lost in the warmth and scent of his skin as his mouth took hers, without hesitation, with assertion. And she was responding in the same way, without will or thought. His

mouth still on hers, he ran a fingertip over the rich swell of
her breasts above her décolletage. She moaned against his
lips, and when his finger slid into the deep valley between
her breasts, her stomach contracted violently with a wild
hunger that she couldn't put words to. Instead she pressed
herself against him, a deep, primitive triumph flowing
through her as she felt his hardness rising against her belly.

A tap at the door broke the charmed circle, and Juliana
jumped back with a little cry of alarm. She turned away,
blushing, her hand covering her tingling lips, as the footman placed a tray on the sideboard and asked the duke if
there was anything else he needed. Tarquin responded as
coolly as if nothing untoward had happened in the last
minutes. Juliana, vividly remembering the feel of his erection pushing so urgently against her couldn't believe he
could sound so matter-of-fact. She was relatively hazy
about male anatomy, but surely such a manifestation
couldn't be comfortably ignored.

She jumped when his hand touched her shoulder. Spinning round, she saw that the room was now empty. Tarquin laughed at her startled expression. "*Mignonne,* you are
delightful." He caressed her mouth with his forefinger. "I
do believe we are going to enjoy ourselves."

"*No!*" she cried, finding her voice at last. "No. I won't
let you do this to me." She flung herself away from him
just as the door opened without ceremony.

"The footman said you were in here, Tarquin, I wanted
. . . Oh, I do beg your pardon." Quentin's eyes ran over
Juliana in one quick, all-encompassing assessment. "I didn't
realize you had company," he said steadily. "Catlett should
have told me."

"Allow me to present Miss Juliana Beresford, as she likes
to be known." Tarquin took her hand, drawing her forward. "Juliana, this is my half brother, Lord Quentin
Courtney. I'm sure you'll be getting to know him quite
well."

Juliana was too flustered for a moment to do more than
stare at the new arrival. Then she realized that he was bow-

ing to her, and hastily she curtsied. "I give you good day, my lord."

Quentin surveyed her gravely, and she felt her blush deepen. She wondered if her lips were marked by the duke's kiss, if this man could detect something on her, something that would give away the shameless arousal that still pulsed in her belly. Was there an aura? A scent, perhaps? Unable to bear his gaze any longer, she turned away.

"Is it fair to the poor child to bring her here unchaperoned, Tarquin?" Quentin's voice was harshly reproving. "If she was seen on the street, her reputation will be compromised."

A flicker of hope sprang into Juliana's disordered mind. Perhaps in this mad world she had found a champion. "My lord, His Grace does not believe I have a reputation that could be compromised," she said in a low, plaintive voice. Slowly she turned and raised her eyes to the somber-suited man, noting the strong physical resemblance between the two men. "Are you perhaps a man of the cloth?" she asked, guessing from his dark, modestly cut coat and plain starched stock.

"I am, child." Quentin took a step toward her, but suddenly she flung herself to the floor at his feet, clasping his knees with a sob.

"Oh, sir, save me. Please, I beg you, don't let the duke have his wicked way with me." Ignoring the strange, strangled sound from the duke standing behind her, she burst into wrenching sobs.

"Oh, hush, child. Hush. Pray don't distress yourself so." Quentin bent to lift her to her feet. "Tarquin, this has got to stop! I won't permit this to go one step further." He stroked Juliana's bent head and handed her his handkerchief. "Dry your eyes, my dear. You have nothing to fear in this house."

Juliana took the handkerchief with a mumble and buried her face in the starched folds, every muscle strained to sense how the duke was reacting.

"Tarquin?" Quentin demanded. "You must let her go."

"Certainly."

Juliana's head shot up at this. She regretted it immediately when the duke caught her chin and turned her face toward him. "That was quite a performance, *mignonne,* I congratulate you. Real tears, too." He smudged the track of a tear on her cheek with his thumb. "Not many, but a respectable showing."

"Oh, you are loathsome!" she whispered, tugging her head free. "Let me go."

"But of course." He strode to the door and opened it. "You're free to go where you wish . . . except, of course, back to Russell Street. Mistress Dennison will have no incentive to continue to provide you with hospitality."

Juliana stared, uncomprehending. Was he really going to permit her to walk out of the house after everything that had been said?

"You may keep the clothes you have on your back, since the ones you arrived in appear to have been mislaid," he continued with an amiable smile that gave no hint of his inner uncertainty. Would she call his bluff? Or had he judged her correctly? Impulsive and yet far from irrational. Stubbornly defiant and yet clearheaded and intelligent.

Juliana looked down at her bronze silk gown, the fringe of the silk shawl. Where could she possibly go in such finery? She couldn't hire herself out as a servant dressed like this.

"Forgive me," he said gently, "but I grow weary holding the door for you."

Juliana walked past him, drawing her skirts aside. She marched down the stairs. The footman opened the door for her, and she stepped out into the street.

In the morning room Quentin turned on his half brother, rare anger snapping in his eyes. "How dare you treat her like that!"

"She's free to go. I won't keep her against her will. D'you care for sherry?"

"No," Quentin said shortly. "What's she to do now?"

"I really don't know." Tarquin poured himself a glass of

sherry. "She must have had a plan when she arrived in town. I imagine she'll put it into effect now."

Quentin went uneasily to the window, but it looked out over the back of the house, and he could see nothing of the street. "I'll go after her," he said. "Offer her money, at least. She's so young to be let loose on the city."

"My sentiments exactly, dear boy." Tarquin sipped his sherry, regarding his brother with narrowed eyes. "Far too young. And far too innocent."

"Gad, Tarquin, but you're a cold bastard," Quentin said as if he'd never spent three years in a seminary. "But if you'll do nothing for her, *I* will." He marched to the door just as it opened again.

Juliana stood there. Her eyes were on Tarquin. "Where am I to go?" she asked. "What am I to do?"

"Wherever and whatever you wish," he responded, but his voice had lost its hardness.

"You know what will happen to me. That's why you showed me all those things this morning, isn't it?" Her face was paler than ever, the dusting of freckles across the bridge of her nose standing out in harsh relief. Her eyes burned like green fire.

"My dear girl, you have no need to worry. I will give you some money and you can go home, back to your family." Quentin fumbled in his pockets.

Juliana shook her head. "Thank you, my lord. You are very kind, but you see I cannot go home, as the duke well knows. He also knows that I have no real choice but to do what His Grace demands."

Chapter 8

~~~

"Mistress Dennison asks that Your Grace would do 'er the honor of waitin' upon her." Mr. Garston bowed low, delivering this message as the Duke of Redmayne ushered Juliana into the hall at Russell Street half an hour later. "If you can spare the time, Your Grace."

"Certainly," Tarquin said. "I wish to speak with her anyway." He turned to Juliana. "Stay within doors. You'll be sent for shortly." He strode up the stairs without a backward glance.

"Looks like you and 'Is Grace 'ave come to some arrangement," Mr. Garston observed with a benign smile. "Lucky girl. A right proper gent is 'Is Grace. 'E'll see you right." He pinched her cheek. "Such a long face, missie. There's no call fer that. The other young ladies will be green with envy, you mark my words."

"Then I wish one of them would take my place," Juliana said wanly. She turned restlessly back to the front door, still open behind her.

"Now, now, missie. You 'eard what 'Is Grace said." Mr. Garston moved his large bulk with surprising speed to close the door. "Y'are to stay within doors till yer sent for."

Like a slave obeying her master, Juliana thought, still stunned by the magnitude of what she'd agreed to. She heard Emma's voice in the drawing room, followed by a giggle, and then a chorus of laughing voices.

They sounded so lighthearted. How could they accept this degrading servitude so cheerfully? Perhaps they could teach her a valuable lesson in resignation. Juliana went into the drawing room.

"Oh, Juliana, come and sit down." She was greeted with warmth and enthusiasm by the trio of women sitting heads together on the sofa, leafing through a pattern magazine. "You've been driving with the duke. Has he formalized his offer for you yet?"

"What do you mean . . . formalized?" Juliana perched on the arm of a chair.

"Oh, he has to make arrangements with the Dennisons. They draw up contracts if someone wants us exclusively," Rosamund explained. "Will you stay here, or will the duke set you up somewhere on your own? I don't think I'd like that myself, it would be so lonely." Her plump, pretty face beamed contentedly as she squeezed Emma's arm beside her.

"I am to marry the duke's cousin, Viscount Edgecombe," Juliana said flatly. She couldn't bring herself to tell them of the other half of the arrangement.

"Marriage!" gasped Emma. "Oh, my dear Juliana. How wonderful for you. You'll be set for life."

"So long as it's not a Fleet wedding," Lilly said darkly. "D'you remember Molly Petrie? She left Mother Needham's to marry Lord Liverton, only he took her to a marriage shop instead. And when he'd had enough of her, he threw her out with just the clothes on her back. And she ended up sleeping under the stalls in Covent Garden and taking anyone who'd give her a penny for gin."

"What's a Fleet wedding?" Juliana asked, curiosity finally penetrating her stunned trance.

"Oh, it's when they get an unfrocked preacher to perform the ceremony. There's marriage shops all around the Fleet," Lilly told her. "It's not a proper marriage, although sometimes the girl doesn't know it . . . like poor Molly."

"But that's dreadful!" Juliana exclaimed. "Wicked. It's evil to trick a woman like that."

Emma shrugged. "Of course it is. But men don't care. They do what they want. And there's not much any of us can do to stop 'em."

Juliana frowned fiercely, her straight brows almost meeting. "If you all got together and refused to be treated badly, then they'd have to change their behavior."

Lilly laughed indulgently. "My dear Juliana, don't be a simpleton. For every one of us who refused to give them what they wanted, there'd be half a dozen eager to take our place."

"It's not as if treating whores badly is a crime," Rosamund pointed out. "I mean, you couldn't go to a magistrate and lay a charge or anything."

"No, the magistrates are too busy persecuting us," Emma declared in disgust. "It's hard to earn any kind of a living if you're not in a respectable house. The others are always being raided, and the girls find themselves making a trip to Bridewell at the cart's arse."

Men and women whipped at the cart's tail through the streets of Winchester for vagrancy or disorderly behavior was a common enough sight, but Juliana had never expected to find herself in a world where such punishment was accepted as an occupational hazard. "I still think that if everyone protested, something would change."

"Brave talk, but you're new to the game, Juliana," Lilly said. "Wait for six months and see how brave you are then."

"If she's to be properly married to a viscount, she won't have to become accustomed," Rosamund pointed out. "But why is the duke procuring you for his cousin? It seems very peculiar."

"You'd best try to find out if this cousin wants anything special," Emma said. "Sometimes they have to have whores because respectable women won't do what they want. But he might want something bad . . . something hurtful. You want to be sure you know what you're getting into."

She couldn't tell these women that she was being black-mailed and that whatever the duke and his cousin wanted of her, she'd be obliged to provide. She couldn't tell them that all her brave protestations about making a stand and forcing a change in their conditions of service were so much posturing. She was as firmly caught as any one of them, with no more power to alter her destiny at this point than a pinned butterfly.

" 'Is Grace bids you join 'im and Mistress Dennison in the small salon, Miss Juliana," Mr. Garston spoke from the doorway.

Bids, not asks. Juliana rose. She had no choice but to do His Grace's bidding.

Outside the door to the small salon, she hesitated. She should knock. Then, with a little tilt of her chin, Juliana decided to make one small gesture. She threw open the door and stepped into the room.

"Oh, there you are, Juliana." Elizabeth looked startled.

"Not a surprise, madam, surely. I understood you had asked to see me."

Tarquin's lips twitched. Miss Juliana seemed to have recovered her spirit. He stood up and came over to her. "Come and sit down, *mignonne*." Taking her hand, he brushed it with his lips, then deliberately and very lightly kissed her mouth.

It seemed a casual greeting, but Juliana understood it for what it was. A public statement of possession. A shiver ran up her spine, and she looked away.

"My dear, someone has been inquiring for you at the Bell," Mistress Dennison said. "Do you know who it could be?"

Juliana's blood ran cold. They had traced her to London. She shook her head.

"This gentleman seemed convinced you had come from Winchester, not York," the duke said gently. He raised an eyebrow as he met her gaze. "He described you rather accurately. But perhaps you have a twin somewhere."

"Don't play with me, my lord duke," Juliana said

fiercely. "I have no intention of denying that I got off the Winchester coach. What point would there be at this stage?"

"None whatsoever," he agreed, taking a seat opposite her. "So who would be searching for you . . . apart from the constables?"

"My guardian, Sir Brian Forsett, perhaps."

"I understand this was a young man," Elizabeth said. "Somewhat corpulent and a little . . . well, rustic, according to Mr. Bute."

"George," Juliana said flatly. "But why would he bother to find me? It's a case of good riddance, I would have thought. For everyone," she added almost in an undertone.

Tarquin's gaze sharpened, resting on her face. He watched the flicker of hurt in the green eyes, the momentary soft quiver of the full mouth. To his astonishment he wanted to take her in his arms and comfort her.

Only with one other woman had he had such an urge. Pamela Cartwright. How flattered he'd been when the beautiful Pamela had chosen him, a naive youth, over the sophisticated men-about-town, the wealthy roués, the powerful politicians, who clustered at her feet. And how long it had taken him to understand that she was interested only in his fortune. He'd bought every kiss, every caress, and convinced himself that she gave him love in return. He'd trusted her with his innermost feelings, had stripped himself bare for her, and she had trampled on his youthful passions, his burgeoning sensitivity.

But that was in the past, and he was no longer an idealistic young fool.

"Come, now," he said briskly. "You can't imagine that you can disappear off the face of the earth without some member of your family looking for you."

"I don't see why not," Juliana said. "My guardian and his wife were delighted to wash their hands of me. They'll be in no rush to find me, particularly when I'm supposed to be a murderess. They're more likely to disown me."

Her tone was matter-of-fact, but Tarquin saw the hurt

that still flickered in her eyes, still tremored slightly on her mouth, and he caught a glimpse of the lonely, unloved child she'd been.

"This George," Elizabeth prompted, bringing the duke sharply back to the issue at hand. "Is he a member of your family?"

"My husband's son," Juliana said. "Sir George, I suppose he is, now that John's dead. He probably wants to find me so he can get the marriage settlements back. He was furious at the conditions of my jointure."

"Ahh," said Tarquin. "Money. That's a powerful motivation. How clever is he, in your opinion?"

"Thick as a block," Juliana said. "But he's as vicious as a terrier when he gets an idea in his head. He won't let go."

"Well, I daresay we can put him off the scent," the duke declared. "As the wife of Viscount Edgecombe, you'll be beyond the reach of some country bumpkin."

"But not beyond the reach of the Duke of Redmayne," she flashed.

Tarquin regarded her wryly and in silence for a minute while she stared back at him, refusing to drop her eyes. Then he turned back to Elizabeth. "If you'd send for Mr. Copplethwaite, madam, we can complete the formalities. The sooner Juliana is established, the safer she will be."

"Established as what, might I ask?" To Juliana's annoyance her voice shook slightly. "Am I to be married by an unfrocked priest in a marriage shop?"

"Now, who could have put such an absurd and insulting idea in your head?" demanded Tarquin, genuinely startled.

"Such an ungrateful creature, she is," Elizabeth declared, glaring reproachfully at Juliana. "To be so ungracious when she's being offered such an opportunity."

"Oh, spare me your pious hypocrisies, madam!" Juliana leaped to her feet. "I am being compelled into prostitution, so pray let us call a spade a spade." She spun on her heel and stalked to the door. Unfortunately, the dramatic effect of her exit was somewhat diminished when her skirt caught in the door as she slammed it behind her and she was obliged to open it again to release herself.

The Duke of Redmayne took a leisurely pinch of snuff. "I foresee a somewhat turbulent few months," he observed. "But I expect I shall find it interesting, at the very least." He rose to his feet. "I'll return this evening. I don't wish Juliana to keep company with the other girls today, I'm inclined to think she's listened enough to their tales and gossip. She should keep to her chamber for the rest of the day. I would find her there alone when I come."

"And the lawyer, sir?" Elizabeth walked to the door with him.

"Instruct Copplethwaite to call upon me in Albermarle Street as soon as the contracts have been drawn up to your satisfaction," he said. "I will then procure a special license. The marriage should take place without delay. . . . Oh, and reassure the child about the marriage, will you? I won't have her believing I would play her false."

"I cannot imagine how she could have thought such a thing." Elizabeth curtsied at the door.

"Neither can I," he responded aridly. "Good day, ma'am." He bowed and strode down the stairs, leaving Elizabeth at the top, looking both thoughtful and annoyed, before she turned and made her way upstairs to Juliana's chamber.

Juliana had discarded her hoop and was struggling with the laces of her corset when Mistress Dennison entered. "You should summon Bella to help you," Elizabeth said.

"I am accustomed to looking after myself," Juliana responded, gyrating impatiently as she tugged at a recalcitrant knot. It came undone, and with a sigh of relief she pulled the garment from her, tossing it onto the bed. "Did you wish to speak with me, ma'am?"

"His Grace bids you remain in your chamber," Elizabeth said.

Juliana sat on the bed in her shift and underpetticoat. "Why?"

"His Grace was most distressed that you should have

heard tales of the marriage shops," Mistress Dennison said.
"He prefers that you hear no more of such nonsense."

"Oh?" Juliana raised an eyebrow. "So it's nonsense, is it,
ma'am? They were making it up?"

"No," Elizabeth responded. "It does happen, but girls
who form contracts from this house are in no danger of
such a deception. And His Grace of Redmayne is a man of
honor."

"Pshaw!" Juliana declared disgustedly. "What he's proposing is hardly *honorable*, ma'am."

"Oh, I despair of you, girl." Elizabeth threw up her
hands. "I won't argue with you further. Do I have your
word that you'll remain in this room until His Grace re-
turns? Or must I turn the key?"

"I'll not leave," Juliana said, falling back onto the bed
and closing her eyes. "It makes no difference to me
whether you lock me in or not. I'm a prisoner either way."

Elizabeth snorted and marched out, closing the door
with a snap behind her.

As she lay on the bed, Juliana conjured up the image of
the Duke of Redmayne. He was a powerful man, one
clearly accustomed to getting his own way in everything.
And he'd made it clear from the very beginning that he
intended to have his own way in this.

She wondered how she would have reacted if he'd put
the proposition to her in another way. If he'd *asked* her if
she'd agree to it instead of threatening blackmail from the
first moment.

If it had been put to her differently, she might have
found the proposition almost enticing. If it had been suggested as a partnership that benefited them both, she might
well have considered it. It could be no worse a fate than
lying night after night beneath John Ridge, bearing his
children. . . .

Unconsciously, she moved her hands over her body outlined beneath the thin shift. That strange effervescence was
coursing through her again. A jubilant, exhilarated sense of
anticipation. The Duke of Redmayne was an arrogant ty-

rant, but when he touched her, her body took off on some weird flight of fancy over which her mind had no control. She could enjoy that, if she decided to. She could enjoy the Duke of Redmayne, if she decided to. But she didn't have to let him know that.

A slow smile curved her mouth.

After Juliana's solitary dinner Bella came in, her habitual beam on her round face. "Mistress sent ye up a right pretty chamber robe, miss." She shook out the delicate cambric folds of a white lace-trimmed wrapper. "Shall you put it on?"

Juliana took the garment from her. It was an exquisite froth of lace and ruffles, embroidered with tiny cream daisies. Another of the duke's sartorial inspirations?

"It's for when the duke visits ye," Bella said, confirming this unspoken assumption. "I'm to 'elp you get ready for 'im."

"Now?" Despite her earlier resolutions, Juliana's blood began to speed and her heart banged against her ribs. It was too soon. She wasn't prepared.

" 'Is Grace will be along after tea," Bella said. "Mistress said as 'ow I was to show ye about perfume an' what kind of refreshments the gentlemen like." She put a small vial on the dresser. "We jest dabs this be'ind yer ears, and knees, an' between yer breasts. Some gentlemen care fer it in other places, too, but I daresay 'Is Grace will tell you what 'e wants. They usually does." She smiled and nodded reassuringly. "Miss Rosamund 'ad a gentleman once what liked it between 'er toes. He liked to suck 'em." Bella giggled. "She said it tickled summat chronic. But she couldn't laugh in case 'e got upset."

Bella matter-of-factly began to remove Juliana's shift and petticoat. Juliana was for the moment speechless as she absorbed the maid's informative chatter. She'd heard similar discussions about adorning a prize pig for auction at the summer fair.

"I wonder if'n we should put a little rouge on yer nipples," Bella mused. "I don't know as 'ow 'Is Grace would like it. Lots of 'em do." She poured hot water into the basin and dipped a washcloth in. "I'll jest wash ye a bit. Freshen ye up a bit. Very fussy Mistress Dennison is about cleanliness in this 'ouse. We don't 'ave no need of mercury treatments or Dr. Leakey's pills 'ere."

"What are they for?" Juliana was prompted out of her stunned silence by this.

"For the clap a'course," Bella said in surprise. "Don't ye know about the pox?"

"Not intimately," Juliana said aridly. "But I imagine it's an occupational hazard, like the cart's arse and Bridewell."

The sarcasm missed Bella completely as she plied the washcloth over Juliana's naked body. "Oh, our ladies don't worry about that, miss," she said. "This is a respectable 'ouse. Only the best customers and the freshest pieces. We don't dabble in the market. Don't get no raids 'ere."

"You relieve my mind." Juliana gave herself up to Bella's attentions. The girl clearly knew what she was about when it came to preparing a harlot for a customer. She patted Juliana dry, then dabbed perfume behind her ears, at her throat, on her wrists, and behind her knees.

"What about the rouge, then, miss?" Bella opened an alabaster pot and dipped a finger in. "Jest a touch." Her finger approached Juliana's breast.

Juliana jumped back. "No," she said, revolted. "There are some things I'll endure, but that's not one of them."

Bella looked disappointed, but she wiped her finger clean on the washcloth. "What about paintin' yer toenails? Lots of the gentlemen likes that."

"No," Juliana declared. "No paint, no powder, no rouge. Just pass me that robe."

Bella hastened to fetch the chamber robe and slipped it over Juliana's shoulders. It fell in soft folds to her bare feet, caressing her sweetly fragrant skin. Bella fastened the fringed embroidered girdle at her waist and adjusted the high ruffled neckline.

"Oh, that's so demure, miss," she said in awe. "Doesn't show nothin' of you at all. I wonder what 'Is Grace fancies, then? Some men like the girls to dress as schoolgirls . . . and that Lord Tartleton likes 'em dressed like a nun." She shook her head wisely. "None so strange as gentlemen."

Juliana examined herself in the mirror. *Demure* was certainly the word, and yet not quite. The material was so fine that her skin glowed pink beneath, and when she moved, the gown flowed over her, revealing the shapes and shadows of her body. It was a most seductive garment.

Lord of hell, she was beginning to think like a whore! She took several steps around the room, feeling the sensuous swish of the robe, inhaling her scent as her skin warmed the fragrance. A bud of excitement grew in her belly, little rivulets of fire darting into her loins.

"Yer 'air, miss." Bella flourished the hairbrush. "I'll brush it fer you."

Juliana sat down on the ottoman, her head drooping beneath Bella's strong, rhythmic strokes. Her hair crackled, springing out from beneath the brush with a life of its own. It seemed to fill the room with color. She watched in the mirror as the candle's glow caught each vibrant strand.

"Will I thread the ribbon through it?" Bella laid down the brush and took up an ivory silk ribbon. Juliana nodded. She hadn't the will to make small, pointless gestures of independence tonight. They could prepare her for the duke's bed however they thought best. She had enough to do with mental preparation.

She watched as Bella fastened the ribbon around her forehead so that her hair was caught and held at the top but poured out in a river of fire beneath, framing her face and cascading onto the white cambric of her robe. "I look like some virgin shepherdess," she murmured. For some reason the thought set her eyes alight with the excitement that was blooming in her belly.

"All innocent like," Bella agreed. "I expect that's what 'Is Grace fancies this evening."

"Do the gentlemen always make their preferences known beforehand?"

"Not always." Bella began to tidy up the dresser. "Sometimes the ladies 'ave to change all of a sudden like, if a gentleman 'as a change of fancy. I 'elps them, then. Me an' Minnie." She gathered up the basin, ewer, and washcloth. "I'll get rid of these, miss. Then I'll bring in the refreshments."

Juliana went to the window after the maid had bustled out. Dusk was falling, and the riotous sounds from the Piazza came clear on the still and sultry air. There was music, a fife and drums, rising above the general cacophony. In the street below a blind harpist sat on a box, plucking his strings mournfully in competition with a shoeblack who was hailing potential customers in a shrill singsong.

She was watching for the Duke of Redmayne. But even as she watched, she wondered if perhaps he was already in the house. The door knocker had been sounding for the last hour, and the customary evening buzz was in the air. Hurried footsteps, giggles, rushed whispers, came from outside her door as the girls returned to their chambers for some minor repair. She hadn't yet heard a male voice, but presumably they were still drinking tea and conversing in the drawing room as if this mansion on Russell Street was a conventional, fashionable household.

" 'Ere we are, then." Bella staggered in under the weight of a laden tray. She was followed by a flunky bearing a tray with bottles and glasses. He set the tray on a low table before the empty grate and studiously avoided looking at Juliana in her robe of seduction. Presumably that was a rule of the house, she thought. He turned and left, again without acknowledgment, and Bella began to lay out covered dishes on the table.

"Now, 'Is Grace is partial to the claret," she instructed. "It's the right year, Mr. Garston says, so we won't 'ave to worry about that. Now, there's lemonade for you. The girls don't usually drink when they 'ave a gentleman. But there's a wine glass if the duke wants ye to join 'im." She

examined the table, tapping her finger against her teeth.
"Now, there's lobster patties, an' a little salad of sparrowgrass. 'Is Grace is right partial to sparrowgrass, dressed with
a little oil an' vinegar."

Juliana was not particularly fond of asparagus, and lobster
brought her out in spots, but of course her own wishes
were of no importance. There was also a bowl of strawber-
ries and a basket of sweetmeats that in other circumstances
might have enticed her; however, she was feeling too sick
with nerves to contemplate eating anything.

"Now, is that everything?" Bella counted on her fingers
as she inspected the room in minute detail. "There's fresh
'ot water in the jug on the washstand. Should I turn down
the bed, or will ye do it, miss? It's 'ard to know what'd be
best. Some gentlemen likes to feel that they're bein' seduced and don't want to come into the room and see it all
ready, like. But others don't care to waste time."

"Leave it as it is," Juliana said, knowing that she could
not sit and wait for the duke beside a turned-down bed.

"Right y'are then." Bella took one last look at Juliana,
made a final adjustment to a ruffle at the sleeve of the white
robe, then dropped a little curtsy. "If ye needs anythin',
miss, jest pull the bell. I'll knock 'afore I comes in."

"Thank you, Bella." Juliana managed a smile.

"A'course I'll come to ye as soon as 'Is Grace leaves."
The girl stood with her hand on the door. "Ye'll be
wantin' a salt bath then, I daresay, bein' a maid an' all. An' I
expect ye'll be glad of a mug of 'ot milk an' rum." With a
quick smile she whisked herself out of the room, closing
the door behind her.

Juliana stood in the middle of the chamber, arms crossed
convulsively over her breasts. A salt bath! So matter-of-fact.
How many virgins had Bella prepared for the loss of their
maidenheads? And then it occurred to her that losing one's
virginity in this knowledgeable, comforting, female-cen-
tered house was infinitely preferable to being bedded to Sir
John Ridge, carried to the bridal chamber amid a chorus of
obscene jokes from drunken male wedding guests who had

abandoned her to her fate at the chamber door. She'd known very little about what was in store for her. Lady Forsett had not thought fit to prepare her husband's ward for her wedding night. She knew a little more now, but not much.

The door opened as she stood there. Her hands fell to her sides, sweat trickling down her rib cage. The Duke of Redmayne quietly closed the door behind him. He turned to Juliana. His gray gaze held hers for a minute in the charged silence, then drifted slowly down her body. He smiled and stepped lightly toward her.

Chapter 9

"Good," Tarquin said, taking her hands. "I'm glad to see you're not using paint or rouge. I forgot to tell Mistress Dennison that I don't care for it . . . or at least," he added, "not on you." He stepped away from her, still holding her hands, and scrutinized her appearance again.

"You're very specific about your preferences, my lord duke." Juliana's voice was low and flat as she tried to hide the rush of heat that suffused her skin at his narrow-eyed inspection.

"No more than most men," he said carelessly. "My preferences change from time to time, as I'm sure you'll discover."

"I trust I'll learn my duties quickly enough to please you, my lord duke." She dropped her eyes, knowing that they were blazing with impotent fury.

Tarquin caught her chin between finger and thumb and obliged her to lift her face. He chuckled. "You look ready to consign me to the fires of hell, *mignonne*."

"Unfortunately, I have no pitchfork," she snapped, unable to resist.

"Did I offend you? I beg your pardon," he said with such an abrupt change of tone and manner that Juliana was completely thrown off balance. And before she could recover herself, he had kissed her. A delicate, featherlike brush of his lips on hers that brought goose bumps pricking on her skin.

"I can be a little imperious on occasion," Tarquin said gravely, caressing her cheek with a fingertip. "It's a consequence of my upbringing, I'm afraid. But I give you leave to take me to task at the right moment."

"And when would that be?"

"Times such as this. When we're private and engaged in . . ." He raised a quizzical eyebrow. "In intimate conversation." He continued to stroke her cheek, and insensibly she began to relax, the lines of her face softening, her mouth parting, her eyes losing their fierceness.

When he felt the change in her, Tarquin released her chin with a smile. He left her in the middle of the room and went to pour himself a glass of wine. "Do you care for claret, Juliana?"

"Yes, please." Maybe the members of the Dennisons' seraglio *were* supposed to eschew alcohol during their working hours, but Juliana felt the need of Dutch courage. She took the glass he handed her and gulped down the contents.

With a slight frown, Tarquin took the empty glass from her and placed it on the table. "Are you frightened, *mignonne?*"

"No." But her hands were twisting themselves into impossible knots against the skirt of the robe.

He leaned back against the table, sipping his claret, his eyes seeing right through the brave denial. "Tell me what happened on your wedding night."

Juliana blinked. "You mean apart from nearly suffocating and then hitting my husband with a hot warming pan and killing him?"

"Yes, apart from that."

"Why do you wish to know?"

"I would like to understand certain things," he said.

"Did your husband touch you in the ways of love? Did he arouse you in any way?"

Juliana just shook her head. Sir John had simply fallen upon her on the bed.

"Were you naked?"

She nodded.

"So you know what a man's body feels like? You know what it looks like?" He was asking the questions with an almost clinical detachment.

"I know what it feels like to be almost suffocated," she declared. In truth she could remember little else of that dreadful half hour. John's body had been a great mass of sweating flesh pressing her into the bed, striving and struggling to do something that she knew he hadn't succeeded in doing.

Tarquin nodded. "Then let's assume that you know nothing at all." He set his glass down and hooked the ottoman toward him with one foot. Sitting down, he beckoned her.

Juliana approached tentatively.

The duke drew her between his knees and, with a leisurely movement, untied the girdle at her waist. The robe fell open, and he drew the sides farther apart so he could look upon her body. Juliana shivered. He put his hands on her. They were warm and hard and assured. She stood, his knees pressing against her thighs, her skin alternately hot and icy cold as his hands moved over her hips; his thumbs traced the sharp outline of her hipbones; his breath was warm on her belly. His hands spanned her waist, slipped up over her rib cage, gently cupped her breasts.

When he bent his head and took her nipple into his mouth, Juliana's body became a battleground of sensation, the urge to yield to the glorious liquid warmth seeping through her veins striving against a panicked instinct not to submit, because in doing so she would lose some part of her self.

Her eyes caught her reflection in the mirror. She gazed at her white body, the curve of her breasts and belly, framed in the delicate froth of her robe. The candlelight caught auburn glints in the bent head against the whiteness of her breast. And then his hands moved on her, slipped slowly over her belly. She watched, in a trance, as her eyes grew heavy and glowing, her skin flushed; her lips, moist and pink, parted on a swift breath as he touched her, opened her. It was as if she were watching some other woman, some other man; watching the woman dissolve with the exquisite pleasure that built deep in the pit of her stomach. She was watching, and yet it was she who was dissolving. From her own lips came the little sobbing cries of wonder. It was her own eyes that grew huge as they stared back at her, the irises black and glowing in the jade depths; then her mirror image was engulfed in the rushing climactic wave that filled every pore of her body, so that her eyes closed and her knees turned to honey.

Tarquin drew her down onto his lap as she fell against him. He held her lightly, stroking her hair. His loins were heavy with his own desire as she shifted on his knee and he inhaled the delicate fragrance of the perfume she wore mingled with the rich scents of her fulfillment.

"Come." He lifted her into his arms, reflecting a little wryly that one wouldn't want to carry this luscious body any great distance. He laid her on the bed and stood looking down at her. Her eyes were still dazed, her skin still flushed.

Juliana closed her eyes abruptly. How had it happened? How had she lost herself so completely?

"Open your eyes, Juliana."

She obeyed the soft command almost involuntarily. Tarquin removed his coat and began unbuttoning his waistcoat.

Juliana sat up. She gazed now with candid curiosity as he removed his clothes, every movement orderly and efficient. As he doffed each rich garment, he laid it over the chair. Her eyes widened as he took off the fine cambric shirt. But she had little time to become accustomed to his naked torso before he had pushed off his britches and drawers.

Juliana's breath caught in her throat as she stared at him, realizing helplessly that she was examining him as carefully as he'd scrutinized her when he had opened her robe.

Naked, the Duke of Redmayne was lean and sinewy, muscles rippling beneath taut, smooth skin. He was slim-hipped and broad-shouldered, a line of dark hair creeping over his belly to join the wiry tangle at the apex of his long thighs. Her gaze fixed upon his shaft of flesh, and she remembered feeling it pulsing against her belly when he'd kissed her in the morning room of his house on Albermarle Street.

"Well, ma'am?" He was smiling at the frank curiosity and excitement in her eyes. "Do I please you?"

She wanted him to turn around so she could see his back view, but she couldn't quite manage to ask. She nodded in silence.

As if he had read her mind, he slowly turned his back. Impulsively, Juliana leaned forward and touched his buttocks. The hard muscles tightened at her caress, and she rose to her knees, running a finger up from the cleft, flickering in the path of fine dark hair trailing up his spine. "You feel very different from me."

"Thank the merciful Lord," he said, turning back to her. Leaning over, he slipped his hands to her shoulders beneath the opened robe and pushed the garment from her. "Now, we meet on equal terms, *mignonne*." He twitched the robe from beneath her and tossed it to the floor before coming down onto the bed.

His hand passed over her in a leisurely caress that nevertheless insisted that she lie back. Juliana was both curious and excited. She felt no apprehension, and she'd lost all thought of what had brought them there. Instinctively, she reached to touch his erection, clasping the flesh in her hand as he leaned over her. The corded veins pulsed strongly against her palm, and her finger found the dampening tip. Tarquin murmured something, but Juliana knew that what she was doing was right. Her own excitement grew as she caressed him, feeling him flicker and harden against her hand. She looked up into his face and saw that he, too, was transported, as she had been. That he was lost in his own pleasure, as she'd seen herself in the mirror. Again instinctively, she increased the pressure of her caresses until abruptly Tarquin grasped her wrist and jerked it away from him.

"Enough," he said hoarsely.

"But why? I know you were enjoying it."

"You still have a few things to learn, *mignonne*." He laughed softly as his knee pressed her legs apart.

Juliana parted her thighs. Her hips lifted of their own accord as he slid into her moist, open body. For a moment the stretching fullness in her loins was almost unbearable. She stared wide-eyed into the steady gray eyes holding her gaze.

"Try to relax, Juliana. It'll ease in a minute." He drew back a fraction, then thrust deeply. Her body seemed to split apart, and she heard her own cry of pain. Then everything was smooth and even, and her body was responding to the strong, rhythmic thrusts of his flesh, and the tension that built now was of the most blissful kind. And when it exploded, Juliana dissolved yet again into a scatter of shooting stars.

His body rested heavily on hers, their sweat mingling. Juliana stroked his back as she floated down to earth and took possession of her self again. She could feel him still within her, growing smaller, and a wave of pleasure washed gently through her with the sense that he remained a part of her. Instinctively, she tightened her inner muscles around him and felt the flicker as his flesh responded.

Tarquin kissed the hollow of her throat. "Have patience," he said with a lazy chuckle. He disengaged slowly and rolled away from her. Juliana made a soft murmur of protest at the loss and followed him with her body, curling against him in blissful languor.

Tarquin pushed an arm beneath so her head rested on his shoulder. He caressed her breast, feeling her slide into a light sleep. He lay listening to her breathing, his own eyelids drooping in the candle glow. He hadn't expected such a passionate and trusting response. He'd expected to arouse her; he'd intended to make the loss of her maidenhead as painless as possible. He'd expected to enjoy her as much as he enjoyed most women. He had not expected to be moved by her. But her fresh innocence combined with that lusty, uninhibited passion stirred him. She had every reason to mistrust him, to hold herself back from him, and yet she'd ridden the wave of pleasure with a wonderful candor, giving herself to him and to sexual joy without reservation.

As he held her in his arms, he had the sense that he had found something to cherish. It was a strange, fanciful idea, and he wasn't sure where it had come from. Except that he'd given himself once with such joyful trust and he'd been betrayed. Juliana would not experience such betrayal at his hands.

Juliana stirred and awoke. She burrowed against him with a little murmur of pleasure. "How long was I asleep?"

"About five minutes." He stroked down her back and patted her bottom before extricating himself and sliding off the bed. "Wine, *mignonne*?"

"Yes, please." Juliana stretched and sat up. Blood smudged the long, creamy length of her thigh. She hopped off the bed with a little exclamation. "We should have pulled back the coverlet."

Tarquin turned from the table with a glass of wine. He smiled at her worried domestic frown as she examined the heavy damask for stains. He put down the glass and filled the basin on the washstand with warm water from the ewer. "Come, let me make you more comfortable," he invited, wringing out a washcloth.

Suddenly shy, Juliana approached him hesitantly. She reached to take the cloth from him, but he said, "Let me do it for you."

He gently nudged her thighs apart and Juliana submitted to his deft, intimate attentions, her awkwardness fading when she realized that he was enjoying what he was doing to her. That he was making of the simple cleansing a delicately arousing ritual.

Her eyes were heavy when he straightened and tossed the washcloth back into the basin. "That wasn't so bad, was it, now?" he teased, kissing her mouth.

"I feel most peculiar," Juliana confided matter-of-factly. "As if I've lost touch with the ground."

"Perhaps a little supper will bring you back to reality." Tarquin opened the armoire and drew out a man's velvet chamber robe. He shrugged into it and picked up Juliana's wrapper from the floor. "Put this on again for a little while."

Juliana took it. "A little while" seemed promising. Vaguely, she wondered how long his own robe had been hanging in her armoire. Equally vaguely, she wondered how he'd known it would be there. She took the glass of wine he handed her.

She shook her head when he offered lobster and asparagus but nibbled on a candied fruit, sipping her wine, watching him eat.

"I suppose we should make haste with the marriage ceremony," she said after a minute or two. "If I've conceived, it might be awkward to explain a premature infant."

Tarquin looked up from his supper with a quick frown. "There's no need to discuss that tonight, Juliana."

"But since it's the object of the exercise . . ." She didn't know why she was bringing it up now. It had immediately cast a pall over her rosy glow. But she couldn't seem to stop herself. "I beg your pardon, my lord duke." She sketched a curtsy. "It was very clumsy of me to bring it up. I daresay it's because I'm inexperienced in the art of pleasing men. When I've become more accustomed to life in a bawdy house, I'm certain I won't offend again."

The duke stared at her for a moment; then he chuckled. "What a provoking child you are," he said. "Have another sweetmeat." He passed her the basket.

Juliana hesitated; then, with a tiny shrug, she took a sugared almond and sat down on the chaise longue.

Tarquin's brief nod indicated approval, and he returned to his lobster. "As it happens, I believe we should proceed with the marriage ceremony with all speed," he observed, dabbing his mouth with his napkin. "In my waistcoat pocket you'll find something that might interest you."

Juliana went to the chair where his clothes still lay. She felt in the pocket of his waistcoat and drew out a piece of folded parchment. "What is it?"

"Take a look." He leaned back in his chair, sipping his wine, regarding her closely as she unfolded the paper.

"Oh? It's me!"

"That was the conclusion I came to."

Juliana stared at the poster. There was an artist's likeness of her . . . somewhat crude but accurate enough. The physical description, however, was minute and unmistakable, right down to the freckles on her nose. She glanced up at the mirror, comparing herself with the likeness and the description. Her hair and eyes were the giveaway.

"Where did you find this?"

"They're posted all over town." He selected an asparagus spear with his fingers and lifted it to his mouth.

Juliana read the description of her crime. *Wanted for the murder of her husband: Juliana Ridge of the village of Ashford in Hampshire. Substantial reward offered for any information, however small. Contact Sir George Ridge at the Gardener's Arms in Cheapside.*

"I wonder how much he's offering," she mused, initially more intrigued than alarmed by this evidence of George's pursuit.

The duke shook his head. "Whatever it is, you're not safe outside this house until you're beyond the reach of that country bumpkin. So once the contracts have been drawn up with Copplethwaite, I'll procure a special license. It should all be over by the end of the week."

"I see. And what will I think of your cousin?" Juliana still stood by the chair, still holding the poster.

"You'll undoubtedly dislike him heartily." He refilled his wineglass. "But you need have nothing to do with him in private. You will both lodge in my house in separate quarters. Lucien will leave you strictly alone."

"And once I've conceived, I imagine that will apply to you too, my lord duke?"

"That will depend on you," he snapped. He tossed his napkin to the table and stood up, not sure why her question disturbed him; it was, after all, a perfectly fair question. "It seems not impossible that I might set you up as my mistress after Lucien's death. It would be easy enough to arrange discreetly. My cousin's widow with a child in my wardship would have a natural claim upon my attention and protection."

"I see. A duke's established mistress. I'll be the envy of every courtesan in town, my lord."

"I'll bandy words with you no longer." He strode to his clothes on the chair.

"But can't you understand!" Juliana cried passionately. "Can't you try to understand what I feel?"

Tarquin paused in his dressing and turned to look at her flushed face framed in the flaming halo of her hair, the jade eyes expressing an almost desperate frustration. "I suppose I can," he said eventually. "If you can try to trust in me. I mean you no harm. Quite the opposite."

He dressed swiftly in the silence his words produced, then came over to her and kissed her. He kissed the corners of her mouth, the tip of her nose, and her brow. "There were a few moments this evening when you *didn't* wish to consign me to Lucifer's fires, weren't there?"

Juliana nodded. "Don't go," she said, suddenly sure of one thing she wanted.

"It's best if I do."

Juliana said nothing further, and he left her immediately. She took a sip of her neglected wine. Apparently she was not to have disagreeable arguments or unsettling opinions, or to ask provoking questions. Clearly His Grace of Redmayne didn't like that in a woman. In which case he'd picked the wrong woman for his schemes; she wasn't about to curb her own nature just to fit the duke's image of a suitable mistress.

Lord of hell! She was a mistress. A duke's mistress! The realization hit her for the first time. Abruptly she sat on the bed, aware of every inch of her sensitized skin, the vague soreness between her legs, the utterly pleasurable sense of having been used, filled, fulfilled. Did whores enjoy their work? Did they retire every morning filled with this wonderful, languid bodily joy? Somehow Juliana didn't think so. Did wives feel it? She knew with absolute certainty that the wife of John Ridge wouldn't have. If John hadn't died in the midst of his huffing and puffing, she would be his wedded, bedded wife, condemned never to know the glories that she'd just shared with the Duke of Redmayne.

So what did it all mean? That she should accept with a glad heart the hand fate had dealt her? Count her blessings and embrace the duke with cries of joy?

Oh, no! That was not the way it was going to be. She'd find a way to enjoy the benefits of this liaison while giving the duke a serious run for his money.

Juliana reached for the bellpull to summon Bella, her mind seething with energy, quite at odds with her body's languor.

Chapter 10

Lawyer Copplethwaite was a small, round man whose waistcoat strained over an ample belly. He had a worried air and his wig was askew, revealing a polished bald pate that he scratched nervously.

"Mistress Ridge." He bowed as Juliana entered Mistress Dennison's parlor in response to a summons the following morning. His eyes darted around the room, looking everywhere but directly at her. In fact, he seemed thoroughly ill at ease. He appeared such an unlikely frequenter of a whorehouse that Juliana assumed his discomfort arose from his present surroundings.

She curtsied demurely to the lawyer, then to Elizabeth, who was seated on a sofa beneath the open window, a sheaf of papers in her lap.

"Good morning, *mignonne*." The duke, clad in a suit of dark-red silk edged with silver lace, moved away from the mantel and came over to her. Juliana hadn't been sure how she would greet him after the previous evening. They hadn't parted bad friends, but neither had they parted intimate lovers. Now she covertly examined his expression and saw both a glint of humor in his eyes, and very clear pleasure as he smiled at her.

On a mischievous impulse she curtsied low with an exaggerated air of humility. Tarquin took her hand and kissed it as he raised her. "I may be a duke, my dear, but I don't warrant the depth you would accord a royal prince," he instructed gravely. "Delighted though I am to see such a sweetly submissive salutation." The amusement in his eyes deepened, and she couldn't help a responding grin. She was going to have to get up very early in the morning to best the Duke of Redmayne in these little games.

"I trust you slept well," he said, drawing her farther into the room.

"I never have difficulty sleeping," she said meekly.

He merely raised an eyebrow and drew a chair forward. "Pray sit down. Mr. Copplethwaite is going to read that part of the contracts that concerns you."

The lawyer cleared his throat diffidently. "If I may, madam."

"Yes, of course." Elizabeth handed him the sheaf of papers. There was a moment's silence, disturbed only by the rustling of paper as the lawyer selected the relevant documents. Then he cleared his throat again and began to read.

There were a series of clauses, all very simple, all very much as had been explained to Juliana already. She listened attentively, and most particularly to the clause that concerned her possible failure to conceive within the lifetime of the present Viscount Edgecombe. The lawyer blushed a little as he read this and scratched his head so vigorously, his wig slipped sideways and was in danger of sliding right off its shiny surface.

Juliana tried to keep her own expression impassive as she listened. If she failed to conceive in the viscount's lifetime she would receive a reasonably generous pension on her husband's death. If she did give the duke the child he wanted, then she would receive a large stipend, and she and the child would be housed under the duke's roof until the child's majority. His Grace of Redmayne would be the child's sole guardian and the sole arbiter of his existence. His mother would have all the natural rights of motherhood and would be consulted on decisions concerning the child, but the duke's decision would always be final.

It was perfectly normal, of course. In law children belonged to their fathers, not to their mothers. Nevertheless, Juliana didn't like this cold laying out of her own lack of rights over the life of this putative infant.

"And if the child is female?"

"The same," the duke said. "There is no male entail on the estate. The title will go to Lucien's cousin, Godfrey, but there is nothing to prevent a daughter from inheriting the fortune and the property."

"And, of course, it's the property that concerns you?"

"Precisely."

Juliana nibbled her bottom lip, then turned to the lawyer. "Is that all, sir?"

"All that concerns you, Mistress Ridge."

"You can't tell me how much Mistress Dennison sold me for?" she inquired with an air of wide-eyed innocence. "I should dearly like to know how much I was worth."

The lawyer choked, loosened his collar, choked again. Elizabeth said reprovingly, "There's no need to embarrass Mr. Copplethwaite, Juliana."

"I should think he's accustomed to such questions by now," Juliana replied. "He must have drawn up enough such contracts in his time."

"Three thousand guineas," the duke said casually. "Quite a handsome sum, I think you'll agree." His eyes flickered across her face and then very deliberately over her body.

Juliana curtsied again. "I'm deeply flattered, my lord duke. I trust you won't be disappointed in your investment."

Tarquin smiled. "I think that most unlikely, *mignonne*."

"I don't imagine George is offering such a sum," Juliana mused. "It seems I must be more valuable to you, sir, than to my stepson. And, of course, I go only to the highest bidder."

His eyes flashed a warning. "Put up your sword, Juliana. I'm a more experienced fencer than you."

"If you'd care to sign the papers, Mistress Ridge . . . ?" The lawyer's tactful question broke the awkward moment.

"Whether I care to or not seems irrelevant, sir," Juliana stated acidly, getting to her feet. "Only His Grace's wishes are relevant here."

"Now, now, Juliana, there's no need for impertinence." Elizabeth rose in a swirl of pale silk and billowed across to the secretaire. "Come to the desk. Mr. Copplethwaite, would you bring the documents over here? Thank you. Now, the quill is nice and sharp." She handed Juliana a pen. "There is blue and black ink in the double standish. Whichever you prefer."

Mistress Dennison was clearly anxious to have the business over and done with, signed, sealed, and delivered. She hovered over Juliana, who very deliberately read through every clause before affixing her signature at the bottom of each page. What was she signing away? Her life? Her future? She was committing herself to a destiny laid down for her by these strangers into whose midst she'd dropped like manna from heaven.

A candle stood ready-lit to provide the wax for the seal. Lawyer Copplethwaite punctiliously dripped wax onto the bottom of the page, then impressed his own seal ring to witness her signature. "There, ma'am. I believe that's as right and tight as a document could be." Fussily, he aligned the edges of the sheets, an anxious frown beetling his brow. "If you're satisfied, Your Grace."

"Perfectly, I thank you. However, I have one final task for you, Copplethwaite."

"Yes, Your Grace." The man's worried frown grew more pronounced. "Anything, of course."

"I wish you to witness a marriage," the duke said as casually as if he were proposing a game of whist. "Between Mistress Ridge and Viscount Edgecombe. It's to take place at St. James's, Marylebone, in two hours. I could take you up in my carriage, if you wished."

"But you said the end of the week!" Juliana protested, shocked. "You said you would procure the license after the contracts had been signed,.and it would be done at the end of the week."

"I was able to accelerate matters," he said. "I had thought it in your best interests . . . in the circumstances. Do you object?"

Juliana took a deep breath. "No, I have no objection. It makes little difference when it happens."

"I knew you were a sensible girl," Elizabeth approved briskly. "Let's go to your chamber and make you ready. His Grace has selected a most beautiful bridal gown."

She'd accepted his proposition a mere two days ago! But Juliana was becoming accustomed to the duke's ability to make things happen faster than it would seem possible.

It *was* a beautiful gown. A cream silk dress, opening over a white embroidered petticoat. For half an hour Bella fussed around her, tucking and adjusting at Elizabeth's sharp-eyed direction. She plaited Juliana's hair around her head in a severely restrained coronet before throwing a froth of gauzy lace over her head.

Juliana examined herself in the mirror through the shifting gossamer of the veil and thought of the wedding gown Lady Forsett had had made for her. Juliana had thought it pretty, but compared with this, it had been a dull and dowdy garment, ill fitting at the waist, with a barely existent hoop. The veil had been heavy, clipped to her hair with a hundred painfully tight pins.

She was to be married twice in ten days. The first ceremony had had its farcical elements, but this one was a charade to challenge reason. Juliana adjusted the veil, flicked at the lace ruffles at her elbows, and turned to the door. "Do you accompany me, ma'am? Or do I go alone?"

"Bella is to accompany you as far as the church, my dear. His Grace will be waiting there to give you away."

Juliana felt an almost irrepressible urge to burst into hysterical laughter at the solemnity of Mistress Dennison's voice. It wasn't as if the woman didn't know the truth about the sham marriage and the duke's intended role. And yet she could manage to sound completely convinced and convincing as she put forth this ludicrous version of the truth.

"It's so wonderful, miss," Bella breathed. "To see ye wed, all respectable, like."

"All respectable," Juliana murmured, opening the door. "Yes, of course."

She was unprepared, however, for the excited chorus of girls awaiting her in the hall. They fluttered around her, examining her gown, exclaiming at her good fortune with clearly genuine pleasure. They would take hope and encouragement from the luck of one of their number, Juliana reflected. Where one of them had good fortune, another could soon follow. She responded as warmly as she could, since the truth was not to be told, but was relieved when Mr. Dennison with great ceremony gave her his arm and ushered her outside, into a waiting hackney. Bella climbed in after her and busily straightened Juliana's skirts, making sure they were in no danger of catching in the door.

The church was in a small, quiet lane. Marylebone was almost in the country, and the air was cleaner, the sound of birdsong more easily heard. Bella jumped down from the coach first, and Juliana gathered up her skirts, praying that she would manage this maneuver without disaster. It would be typical of her luck to catch her heel on the footstep and tumble headfirst to the ground.

But the duke appeared in the open doorway. He was looking grave and held out his hand to assist her.

Juliana took the hand and managed to extricate herself and her skirts through the narrow aperture without mishap. "Where's your cousin?"

"Waiting at the altar." He straightened her veil with a deft twitch.

"Do I pass muster, my lord duke?" She couldn't manage to keep the sting from her voice, but he merely nodded.

"You look just as I expected." While she was still trying

to decide whether that was a compliment or not, he had
tucked her hand into his arm. "Ready?"

As I'll ever be. Juliana lifted her head boldly and faced the
open church door. Bella, with an air of great self-importance, bent to straighten the bride's skirts, then solemnly
stood back and watched, dabbing a tear from her eye as the
Duke of Redmayne and Juliana disappeared through the
church doors to meet her bridegroom.

Lucien, standing at the altar with Quentin, looked impatiently toward the door, shuffling his feet on the cold stone.
Lawyer Copplethwaite sat in the front pew, staring intently
into the middle distance. The elderly priest flicked nervously through the pages of the prayer book as if looking
for the right section.

"I can't think why you wouldn't officiate yourself," Lucien muttered. "Keep it in the family."

Quentin's face was carved in granite. "I'd not commit
such sacrilege," he responded in a clipped whisper, wondering why he was there at all. Except that he had never
been able to refuse his brother anything. And he felt a
compulsion to stand by the girl. She was in need of a
friend, however much Tarquin might swear that she would
not be hurt . . . would indeed only be better off by lend-
ing herself to his scheme.

He turned toward the door as the couple entered the
dim nave, Juliana a shimmer of white against the duke's
dark red.

"Tall, isn't she? Quite the Long Meg," Lucien observed
in an undertone. "Hope she's not some hatchet-face into
the bargain. Don't want to be the laughingstock of town."

Quentin's mouth tightened, and his fingers closed over
the simple band of gold in his pocket. The bride and her
escort reached the altar, and Quentin nudged Lucien to
step forward. Juliana, still on the duke's arm, stepped up
beside him. Quentin could detect no hesitation in her
manner, but he could see nothing of her face beneath the
veil.

Juliana peered through her veil at her bridegroom. Her

first impression was of a curiously shrunken figure, hunched and hollow-chested. She felt very tall and robust beside him. It gave her a comforting sense of advantage. She couldn't see his face too clearly, but his pallor struck her powerfully—the dead whiteness of a fish's underbelly. And his eyes were just sockets, deep-set, burning holes as he glanced incuriously at her when the priest began the service. A little prickle of apprehension lifted her scalp, and without volition she turned toward the duke on her other side. He placed his hand on hers as it rested on his arm and smiled reassuringly.

Juliana licked suddenly dry lips. How would she feel at this moment if she were marrying the Duke of Redmayne? Not apprehensive, certainly. It could surely be said that she knew all there was to know about him already.

She wasn't marrying him, but she was inextricably twining her life with his. He intended to be the father of her child. How much closer could two people get? Much closer than any counterfeit marriage could afford. The idea gave her courage, and she heard herself make her responses in a clear, firm voice.

Lord Quentin handed his cousin the ring. Only then did the duke remove the support of his arm from Juliana. She extended her hand. It was not quite steady, but not as shaky as it might have been. The viscount's fingers, however, trembled almost uncontrollably as he tried to slide the ring on her finger. He cursed savagely, muttering that it was deuced early in the day and he needed a drink to steady him. The undertone reached the priest, nervously nodding and smiling as he oversaw the ritual. He looked shocked and uttered a faint protest as the fumbling continued.

The duke moved swiftly. In the blink of an eye he had taken the ring from Lucien and slipped it onto the bride's finger. The priest, still clearly shocked, pronounced them man and wife in a quavering voice.

"Thank God that's over," Lucien declared as soon as the priest's voice had faded into the shadows. "Am I to be vouchsafed a look at this wife of mine?"

"Sir . . . I beg you . . . must you . . ." But Lucien ignored the stammering, violated priest and reached for Juliana's veil with his violently shaking hands. He threw it back and then surveyed her critically in the gloom.

"Better than I expected," he commented. "I need a drink. I bid you join me, madam wife, in a toast to this auspicious event." With a mocking bow he proffered his arm.

He was dressed impeccably and lavishly in emerald-and-gold brocade, but Juliana shuddered at the thought of touching him. Some infection seemed to emanate from him, from his caved-in chest and his thin shoulders, his burning eyes and ghastly green-white complexion. Like some graveyard maggot, she thought, feeling queasy. Some loathsome, crawling inhabitant of the tombs. He was supposed to be sick. But what could he have that would waste him so, would produce this waft of corruption, as if he were rotting from within?

Juliana's eyes darted in almost frantic appeal to Quentin, then up at the duke, as she hesitated. "I imagine we would all like some refreshment," Quentin said before Tarquin could move. "Come, my dear." He took her hand, tucked it under his arm, and Viscountess Edgecombe walked back down the aisle after her wedding on the arm of her husband's cousin. Her husband lounged after them, taking snuff, and Tarquin moved into the sacristy with the priest and Lawyer Copplethwaite, to settle the business side of the ceremony.

Outside Juliana breathed deeply of the sultry air and forced herself to look again at her husband. In the bright sunshine his color looked even worse. The greenish skin was stretched taut on his skull, showing every bone and hollow. He looked as old as Methuselah and as young as Juliana herself. Suddenly he doubled over with a violent coughing fit, his thin chest heaving, perspiration gathering on his brow. She gazed in sympathetic horror while he coughed as if he would vomit up his lungs.

"Can't we do something?" she said to Quentin, who was standing beside her, his face tight and furious.

"No," he said shortly. "He needs cognac."

"What is the matter with him?" she whispered. "The duke said he was ill . . . but what is it?"

"He didn't tell you?" Quentin's eyes flashed with anger, and he looked remarkably like his half brother.

"Didn't tell her what?" Tarquin's voice came from the church steps behind. He glanced at the still-convulsed Lucien, then came down the last step.

"The child does not know what ails her husband," Quentin said harshly. "For shame, Tarquin!"

"Juliana will have nothing to do with Lucien, so what does it matter to her what ails him?" Tarquin said, drawing out his snuffbox. "Your husband is riddled with the pox, *mignonne*. But I promise he will not lay so much as a finger upon you."

Juliana stared at the duke, speechless, as he took a leisurely pinch of snuff, dropped the box into his pocket again, and slapped Lucien hard on the back. "Come, Edgecombe. We'll put a glass of cognac down your gullet, and you'll be right as a trivet."

Lucien straightened, burying his streaming face in his handkerchief. "Odd's blood!" he rasped when he could catch his breath. "Thought I was never goin' to breathe again." He wiped his nose and mouth and thrust the handkerchief back into his pocket. Then he surveyed his wife with a distinct leer. "Sorry about that, m'dear. Not a particularly good first impression for a man to make on his bride, what?"

"No," Juliana said faintly. "Must we continue to stand on the street in this fashion?" She flicked at her bridal white with an expression of deep disgust. Of all the travesties, to be dressed up like this for such a diabolical mockery.

"My carriage is here." Tarquin took her arm, directing her across the street to where stood a light town chaise with the Redmayne arms emblazoned on the panels. "Quentin, do you accompany us back to Albermarle Street?"

His brother hesitated, still angry. But when Juliana looked at him in silent appeal, he gave a curt nod and crossed the street.

"You won't mind if I don't join you?" Lucien popped his head through the open carriage window. "Think I need to quench m'thirst without delay. Can't risk another fit. There's a tavern on the corner." He gestured with his hat.

"By all means," Tarquin said amiably.

"But I'll be there for the bridal feast . . . count on me for that." Laughing, Lucien went off, heading purposefully for the Lamb and Flag on the corner.

"Bridal feast?" Juliana glared at the two men sitting opposite her. "When will this mockery end, my lord duke?"

"Lucien's idea of a jest," Tarquin said. "I had planned no such thing. What I had planned was a visit to the play, followed by supper in the rotunda at Ranelagh. If that would please you, Juliana. D'you care to accompany us, Quentin?"

"If Juliana would permit me to join you," his brother said still coldly. "But maybe she would prefer to retire to her own quarters and weep."

"Oh, I don't believe Juliana is given to such melodrama," Tarquin responded. He was hoping his bracing words would keep her from losing courage. He knew instinctively that if she broke down now, it would be much more difficult for her later.

"And how would you know, sir?" Juliana was hunched into the corner, her baleful eyes never leaving the duke's face.

"An educated guess," he said. "Now, don't fall into a fit of the sullens, child. I'm suggesting an evening of pleasure. You'll not see Lucien—indeed, it's possible you won't see him until you have to make your society debut. Oh, I sent notices of the marriage to the *Morning Post* and the *Times,* so you can expect to receive bride visits within the week, I imagine."

"Without my husband's support, I suppose?"

"Oh, it's hardly Lucien's kind of thing. But Quentin and I will be there to lend our own support. Won't we, dear brother?"

"Of course." Quentin realized that whether he wished it or not, he was now deeply entangled in his brother's scheme. Juliana had embroiled him much more effectively than Tarquin. Juliana, who could be no match for Tarquin . . . no match for Lucien . . . would need all the friendship and protection he could provide. Her eyes were shadowed as they gazed out of the window, her mouth taut, her hands tightly knotted in her lap.

She was so young. So vulnerable. So innocent. Poor child. She could never have dreamed she'd find herself caught up in this twisted scheme of the Duke of Redmayne's. Tarquin had always preferred a devious route to his goals, and this was as cunning and artful as any route he'd ever taken. But how inexcusable that he should involve someone as unprotected and as inexperienced as Juliana.

He glanced sideways at the still figure of his brother beside him. Tarquin was leaning back against the squabs, arms folded, eyes half-closed. But Quentin knew they were resting intently on Juliana. Tarquin's mouth was slightly curved as if he found something amusing or pleasing. Startled, Quentin felt a curious softness emanating from his brother. He had always been able to read Tarquin's mood; it was a skill that arose from the years of closeness, from the years when he'd worshiped his half brother and tried to emulate him.

He no longer tried to emulate him . . . no longer chose to. Quentin had found his own path, and it was not his brother's. But the bond between them was as strong as ever. And now Quentin, to his astonishment, sensed a tenderness in Tarquin—a warmth, as he looked at Juliana, that belied the dispassionate cynicism of his manner.

Quentin returned his gaze to Juliana, so tense and still in her bridal white, the veil thrown back so that her hair blazed in the dimness of the carriage. If Tarquin was stirred by her in some way, then perhaps this would not turn out as badly as Quentin feared.

The chaise slowed and drew up. Juliana came out of her bitter, angry reverie. She looked out of the window and recognized the house on Albermarle Street. The house that was to be her home for the foreseeable future. And if she managed to give the duke the child he desired, then it would be her home for many, many years.

The footman opened the door. Tarquin jumped lightly to the ground, disdaining the footstep, and held out his hand to Juliana. "Welcome to your new home, Lady Edgecombe."

Juliana averted her face as she took his hand and stepped to the ground, Quentin following. Her anger burned hot and deep as the earth's core. How could he have wedded her to that defiled wreck of a man without telling her the truth? To his mind she was no more than an expensive acquisition with no rights to knowledge or opinion. He'd asked for her trust, but how could she ever trust in his word when he would keep such a thing from her?

But she would be revenged. Dear God, she would be revenged a hundredfold. The resolution carried her into the house with head held high, and her dignity didn't desert her even when she caught her heel on the doorstep and had to grab the bowing footman to stop herself from falling to her knees.

Quentin jumped forward to steady her with a hand under her elbow.

"Thank you," she said stiffly, moving away from both Quentin and the footman.

"Juliana has a tendency to topple and spill," Tarquin observed. "In certain circumstances she can produce the effect of a typhoon."

"How gallant of you, my lord duke," she snapped, roughly pulling the veil from her head and tossing it toward a rosewood pier table. It missed, falling to the marble floor in a shimmering cloud.

"Well, let's not brawl in front of the servants," Tarquin

said without heat. "Come with me and I'll show you your apartments." Cupping her elbow, he urged her toward the stairs.

Left behind, Quentin picked up the discarded veil, placed it carefully on the table, then made his way to the library and the sherry decanter.

Juliana and the duke reached the head of the horseshoe stairs.

"As I've already mentioned, I thought you might like to use the morning room as your own private parlor," the duke said with a determined cheerfulness, gesturing down the corridor to the door Juliana remembered on the first landing. "You'll be able to receive your own friends there in perfect privacy."

What friends? Juliana closed her lips firmly on the sardonic question. "Your bedchamber and boudoir are at the front of the house, on the second floor." He ushered her up the second flight of stairs to the right of the landing. "You'll need an abigail, and I've engaged a woman from my estate. A widow—her husband was one of my tenant farmers and died a few months ago. She's a good soul. Very respectable. I'm sure you'll deal well together."

He didn't say that he'd decided that Juliana needed a motherly soul to look after her, rather than one of the haughty females usually engaged as abigails to ladies of the fashionable world.

Juliana was still silent. He flung open a pair of double doors.

"Your bedchamber. The boudoir is through the door on the left." He gestured for her to precede him into a large, light chamber furnished in white and gold. The enormous tester bed was hung with gold damask, the coverlet of white embroidered cambric. The furniture was delicate, carved spindle legs and graceful curving arms and backs, the chaise longue and chairs upholstered in gold-and-white brocade. Bowls of yellow and white roses perfumed the air. Juliana's feet sank into the deep pile of the cream carpet patterned with gold flowers as she stepped into the room.

"Oh, what an elegant room!" Her bitter anger faded as she gazed around in delight. The involuntary comparison of this epitome of wealth and good taste with the ugly, heavy, scratched, dented, and faded furnishings in Sir John Ridge's house would not be quashed.

Tarquin smiled with pleasure, then wondered faintly why this chit of a girl's approval meant so much to him. Juliana had bounced over to the door of the boudoir, and he could hear her delighted exclamations as she explored the small, intimate room. "How pretty it is." She came back to the bedchamber, her eyes shining. "I never expected to find myself inhabiting such elegant surroundings," she confided.

"You will grace them, my dear," Tarquin said, an involuntary smile still on his lips at the sight of her ingenuous pleasure.

"Oh, I dareswear within ten minutes the entire chamber will look as if a typhoon hit it," she retorted.

Tarquin held out his hands to her. "Come, cry peace. I meant no offense. Actually, I find your . . . your haphazard locomotion very appealing."

Juliana regarded him incredulously. "I fail to see how anyone could find clumsiness appealing."

"There's something utterly alluring about you, Juliana. Whether you're on your head or your heels." His voice was suddenly a caress, his smile now richly sensual, issuing an irresistible invitation.

Juliana stepped toward him as the clear gray eyes drew her forward like the pull of gravity. He held her by the shoulders and looked down into her upturned face. "There are so many more enjoyable things for us to do, my sweet, than quarrel."

She wanted to tell him that he was a deceitful whoreson. She wanted to curse him, to bring down a plague on his house. But she simply stood, gazing up at him, losing herself in his eyes while she waited for his beautiful mouth to take hers. And when it did, she yielded with a tiny moan of sweet satisfaction, opening her lips for him, greedily pushing her own tongue deep into his mouth, inhaling the scent of his skin, running her hands through his hair, urgently pulling his face to hers as if she couldn't get enough of him.

He bore her backward to the bed, and she fell in a tumble of virginal white. His face hovered over hers, no longer smiling, expressive now of a deep, primitive hunger that set answering pangs deep in her belly. He was pushing up her skirts and petticoats, ignoring the awkward impediment of the hoop. His free hand loosened his britches, then slid beneath her bottom, lifting her on the shelf of his palm as he drove within her.

Juliana gasped at the suddenness of his penetration, but her body welcomed him with joy, her hips moving of their own accord, her buttock muscles tight against the warmth of his flat palm. He supported himself on one hand as he moved within her in short, hard thrusts. And her belly contracted with each thrust, the spiral tightening until a cry burst from her lips and waves of pleasure broke over her. His head was thrown back, his neck corded with effort, his eyes closed. Then he spoke her name in a curious wonder, and his seed gushed into her with each pulsing throb of his flesh, and when she thought she could bear no more, a surge of the most exquisite joy flooded every cell and pore of her body.

"Such enchantment," Tarquin murmured as he bent and kissed the damp swell of her breast rising above her décolletage.

Juliana lay sprawled beneath him, unable to move or speak until her racing heart slowed a little. With an effort she raised a hand and touched his face, then let it flop back again onto the coverlet. "I got lost somewhere," she murmured.

Tarquin slipped gently from her body. "It's a wonderful landscape to roam."

"Oh, yes," Juliana agreed, pushing feebly at her disordered skirts. "And one doesn't even need to get undressed for the journey," she added with an impish chuckle, suddenly invigorated. She sat up. "Where are my husband's apartments?"

"On the other side of the house, at the back." The duke stood up, refastening his britches, regarding her with a quizzical frown.

She slid off the bed, shaking down her skirts. "And where are *your* apartments, sir?"

"Next door to yours."

"How convenient," Juliana observed, beginning to unpin her loosening hair.

"Let me show you just how convenient." He turned to the armoire on the far side of the room. "Come, see."

Juliana, still pulling pins from her hair, followed curiously. He opened the door, and she gasped at the rich mass of silk, satin, and taffeta hanging there. "What's that?"

"I told you I've been busy with your wardrobe," he said. "But that's not what I wish to show you right now." He pushed the garments aside and stepped back so Juliana could see into the interior.

She saw a door at the back of the armoire.

"Open it," he said, enjoying her puzzlement.

Juliana did so. The narrow door swung open onto another bedchamber quite unlike her own. No dainty, feminine chamber, this one was all dark wood and tapestries, with solid oak furniture and highly polished floors.

"Oh," she said.

"Convenient, wouldn't you agree?" His eyes were alight with amusement.

"Very." Juliana stepped back, shaking her hair free of its plaited coronet. "Did you install it specially?"

He shook his head. "No, it was put in by the third duke, who, it was said, like to play little tricks on his duchess. He was not a pleasant man, by all accounts. But I imagine we can put it to better use."

"Yes." Juliana was beginning to feel dazed again. "Does everyone know of its existence . . . the viscount, for instance?"

"No. It's known to very few people. And I'll vouch for

it that Lucien is not one of them. He doesn't know this house well."

"Lord Quentin?"

"Yes, he knows, of course."

"Just as he knows everything about this scheme?" She ran her fingers through her hair, tugging at the tangles.

"Yes."

"And what does he think of it?"

"He completely disapproves," Tarquin stated flatly. "But he'll come round. He always does." He turned back to the armoire. "Shall we choose a gown suitable for Lady Edgecombe to wear to the play and a visit to Ranelagh?"

Why not? The man was an avalanche, rolling over all obstacles, unstoppable. And, although it confused her to realize it, for the moment she did not want him to stop.

Chapter 11

George Ridge emerged from the Cross Keys Bagnio in midafternoon feeling very much the man-about-town. He turned on his heel, enjoying the swish of his new full-skirted coat of puce brocade. His hand rested importantly on his sword hilt as he looked along Little Russell Street, debating whether to go into the Black Lion Chop-House for his dinner or return to the Gardeners' Arms to see if his posters had born fruit.

The ordinary table at the Gardener's Arms offered a reasonable meal, and the fellow diners tended to be hard drinkers with a taste for crude conversation and lewd jests. In general it suited George very well, but last night, when the ordinary table had been cleared of dinner and set up for gambling, he'd discovered that his fellow diners were deep gamesters. As the bottles of port circulated and the room grew hotter, George had grown louder and merrier and very incautious, peering with bleary bonhomie at the dice and throwing guineas across the table with an insouciance that later shocked him. He hadn't had the courage as yet to calculate his losses.

His father would have gone berserk if he'd known. But, then, Sir John had been an old prude, except in his taste for young women, and he'd been very careful with his wealth.

George had never been to London before his present visit. His father considered it a place for wastrels and idlers, inhabited by loose women and men ready to cut your throat for a groat.

George had enjoyed the loose women this afternoon in the bagnio. Three of them. Three very expensive women. His pockets were a deal lighter now than they had been when he'd left the Gardener's Arms that morning. But it had been worth every guinea. He supposed it was usual for London whores to drink champagne. Cider was all very well for a red-cheeked, wide-hipped country doxy in the barn or behind a haystack, but painted women in lawn shifts, with fresh linen on their beds, obviously had higher expectations.

But as a consequence he found himself guiltily aware that in twenty-four hours he'd probably spent enough to cover the farrier's bill for a twelvemonth. And if he returned to the Gardener's Arms, he would inevitably get drawn into the dicing later. A modest dinner at the Black Lion and a visit to the playhouse would definitely be the prudent course this evening. And since the Theatre Royal was but a couple of steps from the chophouse, he could be sure of arriving before the doors opened at five o'clock so he could get a decent seat in the pit.

He examined the silver lace on his new cocked hat with pride before carefully placing it on his head, ensuring that the pigeon's wings on his pigtail wig were not disarranged. He tapped the hilt of his sword with the heel of his hand and gazed around imperiously, as if about to issue a challenge. A shabby gentleman in a skewed bag wig hastily crossed to the other side of the street as he approached George with his belligerant stance. London was full of aggressive young men-about-town who thought it famous sport to torment vulnerable pedestrians.

George gave him a haughty stare, flicking a speck of snuff from his deep coat cuff. He didn't wear a sword in the country, but he'd realized immediately that in town it was the mark of a gentleman. He had purchased his present weapon from an armorer in Ebury Street, having been assured by that craftsman that it was not a mere decoration—that in the hands of a skilled swordsman, such as His Honor must be, it would be a most deadly weapon, and a powerful protection.

With a little nod of satisfaction George strolled toward the Black Lion. Having experienced the pleasures of London, he was determined that he would spend some weeks of every year in town—in the winter, of course, when the land needed less attention.

Juliana would make him a more than satisfactory consort. She'd grown up in a gentleman's establishment, educated in all the areas necessary for a lady. She knew how to behave in the best society . . . better than he, himself, George was obliged to admit. George was his father's son. The son of a blunt, poorly educated landowner, who was more interested in his crops and his woods, his sport, his dinner and the bottle, than in books or music, or polite conversation. But Juliana was a lady.

But where in the name of Lucifer was she? George's self-satisfaction and pleasure in the day suddenly evaporated. It was all very well making these happy plans, but they were castles in the air without the flesh-and-blood girl to make them real. He *had* to have her as his wife. He wanted her in his bed. He wanted to see the superiority and contempt chased from her eyes as she acknowledged him as her husband and master.

Juliana, with her eyes that could be as cold and green as the deepest ocean; Juliana, with her full mouth that could curl into a derisive smile that shriveled a man; Juliana, with that swirling forest fire of hair and the long limbs, and the full, proudly upstanding breasts.

He would have that Juliana, obedient and docile in his house and in his bed. Or he would see her burn at the stake.

George turned into the Black Lion and ordered a bottle of burgundy. He *would* find her, if he had to pay a hundred guineas to do so.

Juliana was in a very different frame of mind, Quentin thought as the three of them sat at dinner. On the two previous occasions he'd been in her company, she'd been clearly distressed, and this morning, bitterly angry into the bargain. But now her eyes were luminescent jewels, her pale skin had a glow that seemed to come from within. She was bright and bubbly, with ready laughter and a quick wit that showed an informed mind. She threw impish challenges at Tarquin, and occasionally a darting glance that always made the duke smile.

Quentin was neither a prude nor a stranger to women, despite his calling. It didn't take a genius to deduce that Lady Edgecombe had been enjoying some bedsport that afternoon. His brother's indulgent amusement and the unmistakable caress of his eyes when they rested on Juliana clearly indicated that however much at odds they might be in some things, the Duke of Redmayne and his cousin's bride were clearly well matched in the bedchamber.

Quentin supposed he should be disapproving. But he was not a hypocrite. He'd lent his countenance to Tarquin's abominable scheme—reluctantly, it was true, but he was still a part of it. If Juliana took pleasure in the duke's lovemaking, then it could be said that she was not really being coerced in this aspect, at least, of the arrangement.

Juliana wasn't sure whether her feeling of heady enjoyment in this dinner was a residue of the afternoon or had to do with the novel position in which she found herself. The only woman at the table, she was the focus of attention. At Forsett Towers, she'd been relegated to a cramped corner of the table, enjoined to be silent unless spoken to, and had thus endured interminable dinners, passing some of the most tedious hours of her life. At this table, whenever she opened her mouth to speak, both the duke and his brother paid her close and flattering attention.

"What is the play we're to see?" She reached for her

wineglass. A footman moved swiftly to catch the cascade of cutlery set in motion by her floating sleeve.

"Garrick as Macbeth," Tarquin replied with a twitch of amusement as she glared in mortification at the errant ruffles.

"There'll be a farce, too, no doubt," Quentin said. "And since Garrick appointed Thomas Arne as the musical director, one can be sure of lively entertainment during the musical interludes."

"I've never been to the play." Juliana held her sleeve clear of the table as she reached for a basket of pastries. "At home the mummers would come at Christmas, and occasionally during the fair, but there was never a real play."

"I trust you'll enjoy the experience." Tarquin was surprised at how enchanting he found her enthusiastic chatter and ready laughter. This was a Juliana he'd only fleetingly glimpsed hitherto. She also had a healthy appetite. Either no one had told her it was considered ladylike to modify one's enthusiasm for the table in public, or she had simply ignored the stricture. Probably the latter, he thought with an inner smile. Her conversation was both amusing and intelligent. Her guardians had clearly not neglected her education, however much they might have endeavored to stifle her personality.

"Have I a smut on my nose, my lord duke?" Juliana inquired, brushing her nose with a fingertip.

"I don't see one."

"You seemed to be looking at me with particular intensity," she said. "I made sure something was amiss with my appearance."

"Not that I can see." He pushed back his chair. "If you've finished, my dear, I suggest we adjourn to the drawing room for tea."

"Oh, yes." Juliana flushed and jumped to her feet, sending her chair skidding across the polished floor. "I should have thought, I beg your pardon. I'll leave you to your port."

"No need," Tarquin said, steadying the chair so she

could move easily around it. "Quentin and I are not overly fond of sitting long at the table. Isn't that so, brother?"

"Absolutely," Quentin agreed. "I see no reason why Juliana should sit in solitary state in the drawing room while we sozzle ourselves on port."

"Lucien, of course, would have a different view," Tarquin observed.

Juliana glanced quickly over her shoulder at him, but his expression was as dispassionate as his tone. What difference to the atmosphere would her husband's presence make? A significant one, she reckoned.

But she didn't allow such thoughts to interfere with her pleasure in the evening. She had fallen into this situation, and she might as well enjoy its benefits.

They drove to Covent Garden in the duke's town chaise, Juliana gazing out of the window, intrigued as London moved onto its nightly revels. It was the first time she'd been out in the evening since she had stepped off the coach at the Bell, and when they turned into Covent Garden, she saw it had a very different aspect from the daytime scene. The costermongers and barrow boys had gone, the produce stalls packed up for the day. The center of the Garden was now thronged with ladies accompanied by footmen, soliciting custom, and boys darting through the crowd crying the delights to be enjoyed in the specialized brothels masquerading as coffeehouses and chocolate shops.

Beneath the columns of the Piazza strolled fashionable people, quizzing the scene as they made their way to the Theatre Royal, whose doors stood open. It was now just before six o'clock, and the crowd at the doors was a seething mass of humanity, fighting and squabbling as they pushed their way inside to find a last-minute seat.

Juliana looked askance at the melee and wondered how she was to get through there with her wide hoop. She was bound to tear something in the process. "Doesn't the play begin at six?"

"It does." Tarquin handed her down to the cobbles before the theater.

"But if we have no seats—"

"We do, my dear," Quentin reassured with a smile. "Tarquin's footman arrived at the doors at four o'clock in plenty of time to secure us a box."

So that was how the privileged managed such things. Juliana raised an eyebrow and decided she liked being one of their number. She had the duke and Lord Quentin on either side of her as they approached the massed doorway. How it happened she couldn't tell, but a path materialized through the crowd and she was suddenly inside the theater, her gown in one piece, not even a ruffle torn, both shoes still on her feet, and her hoop behaving itself impeccably. She had a vague impression that her two escorts had touched a shoulder here and there, uttered a few words in low voices, edged an impeding body to one side. However it had been done, they were inside.

The orchestra was playing but could barely be heard above the buzz and chatter as people strolled between the seats, pausing to chat to friends or calling across heads to attract attention in other parts of the pit. Above the racket the cries of the orange sellers were pitched shrill and imperative.

"This way." Juliana was deftly ushered to a box overlooking the stage, where a footman in Redmayne livery stood bowing as they entered. Tarquin didn't release Juliana's elbow until she was seated at the front of the box. "Now, if you don't try to explore, you'll be safe and sound," he said, sitting beside her.

"I shan't go short of entertainment." Juliana leaned over the edge of the box. "If the play is half as absorbing as the crowd, I shall be very well satisfied. Why do they have those iron spikes along the stage?"

"To stop the audience jumping onto the stage." Tarquin smiled at her rapt expression. "You see the rather burly men behind? They're an added deterrent."

Juliana laughed. "I am so glad I came to London." Then she flushed, a shadow dimming the vibrancy of her expression. "Or I would be in different circumstances."

Quentin touched her shoulder in brief sympathy. Tarquin chose to ignore the comment. There was a moment of awkward silence; then the orchestra produced an imperative drumroll. The curtain went up, and David Garrick strode onto the stage to deliver the prologue to the evening's entertainment.

Juliana listened, entranced, as the play began. The audience continued to buzz and hum, carrying on their own gossipy conversations throughout, but Juliana was unaware of anything but the stage. It didn't occur to her as in the least strange that Macbeth should be played in contemporary costume, with Garrick in the title role dressed in the full regalia of a Hanoverian officer.

At the first interval she sat back with a little sigh of contentment. "How magical. It's quite different hearing the words from reading them, even aloud."

"I'm glad it pleases you, *mignonne*." Tarquin stood up. "If you'll excuse me for a minute, there's someone I must visit." He strolled off, and Juliana returned her attention to the crowd. An argument seemed to be turning nasty in the front row, and a man was threatening to draw his sword. Someone bellowed in jocular fashion and threw a handful of orange peel over the two opponents. There was laughter, and the moment of tension seemed to have dissipated.

Juliana glanced across the pit to the boxes opposite. She saw the duke directly opposite, standing behind the chair of a woman dressed in dark gray, almost black, with a white fichu at the neck and her hair tucked severely under a white cap. She was looking up at Tarquin as he spoke to her.

"Who's the duke talking to?"

Quentin didn't look up from his own perusal of the crowd. "Lady Lydia Melton, I imagine. His betrothed." There was something false in his studied, casual tone, but Juliana was too astonished by this intelligence to give it any thought.

"His betrothed?" She couldn't have kept the dismay from her voice even if she'd tried. "He's to be married?"

"Did he not tell you?" Still, Quentin neither looked at her nor at the object of the discussion.

"No . . . it seems there's a great deal he didn't tell me." All her pleasure in the evening vanished, and the bitter resentment of the morning returned.

"I daresay he thought his betrothal was irrelevant to you . . . to everyone," he added softly.

"Yes, irrelevant," she said acidly. "Why should it matter to me?"

"Well, it won't be happening for quite a while," Quentin told her, his voice flat. "The marriage was to have taken place two months ago, but Lydia's grandfather died and the entire family have put on black gloves. They'll be in mourning for the full two years."

"Then why's she at the play?" Juliana demanded tartly. "It seems hardly consistent with deep mourning."

"It *is* Macbeth," Quentin pointed out. "They'll leave before the farce."

"Seems very hypocritical to me." Juliana squinted across the playhouse, trying to get a better look at Lady Lydia Melton. It was difficult to form an impression in the flickering light of the flambeaux that lit the stage and the pit. "How old is she?"

"Twenty-eight."

"She's on the shelf," Juliana stated.

"I should refrain from passing judgment when you don't know the facts," Quentin said sharply. "Lydia and Tarquin have been betrothed from the cradle, but the death of Tarquin's mother three years ago postponed the marriage. And now Lydia's grandfather's demise has created another put-off."

"Oh. I didn't mean to sound catty." Juliana gave him a chastened smile. "I'm just taken aback."

Quentin's expression softened. "Yes, I can imagine you might be."

Juliana stared hard across the separating space and suddenly noticed that the lady was looking directly at her. It was clear that Juliana herself was under discussion when

Tarquin raised a hand in a gesture of acknowledgment and Lady Lydia bowed from the waist. Juliana responded in like manner. "I wonder what they're saying about me."

"I imagine Tarquin is explaining that you're Lucien's bride," Quentin observed. "The Meltons were bound to wonder what he and I were doing in a box at the theater with a strange lady."

"But won't they think it strange that the viscount isn't with us so soon after the wedding?"

"No," Quentin said without elaboration.

The orchestra began another alerting drumroll, and Tarquin disappeared from the Meltons' box. A few minutes later he appeared beside Juliana.

"You didn't tell me you were betrothed," she whispered accusingly as the second act began.

"It's hardly important," he returned. "Hush, now, and listen."

Juliana found it hard to concentrate on the rest of the play. She was wondering when Tarquin would have chosen to tell her about his fiancée. She was wondering what would happen to their arrangements when the new duchess took up residence. Presumably, the mistress and her child would be established in one wing of the house and the duchess and her children in another, and the duke would move between his two families as and when it pleased him.

Perhaps her present charming apartments rightfully belonged to the duke's wife. Surely with that proximity, not to mention the concealed connecting door, they must. So presumably she would have to move out of them when the new duchess took up residence.

Juliana opened and closed her fan with such violence that one of the dainty painted sticks snapped. Startled, both her escorts looked sideways.

The duke placed a restraining hand on hers, still roughly flicking the fan in her lap. She turned and glared at him with such fury, he could almost imagine being scorched by the flames in her eyes. There was one thing about Juliana,

he reflected ruefully: One always knew where one stood
with her. She was so full of passions of every kind that she
was incapable of masking her emotions.

"If you wish to quarrel, let's do so later," he whispered.
"Not in the middle of a crowded playhouse. Please, Juliana."

Juliana pointedly turned her eyes back to the stage, her
mouth taut, her jaw set, her back as rigid as if a steel poker
ran down her spine. Tarquin exchanged a glance with his
brother, whose response was far from sympathetic.

The Melton party, as Quentin had predicted, left before
the farce. They left so discreetly, Juliana didn't see them go.
When she looked toward the box as the torches were lit
again to illuminate the pit, she saw it was empty.

Tarquin leaned over the box and hailed an orange seller.
She came up with a pert smile and tossed two oranges up
to him. He caught them deftly, throwing down a sixpence.
She grinned and curtsied, tucking the coin between her
ripe breasts bubbling over the neck of her gown, which was
kilted to show both calves and ankles. "Want to come and
get it back, sir?" she called with a lascivious wink. "No
'ands allowed. An' if ye double it, there's no knowin'
where it'll end up."

Tarquin laughingly refused the invitation. He took a
small knife out of his waistcoat pocket and began to peel an
orange. He broke off a segment and held it to Juliana's lips.
"Open wide, my dear."

"I am not in the mood for teasing." She closed her lips
firmly. But she took the orange segment in her fingers,
rather than open her mouth for him to feed her, and offered a formally polite thank-you.

Tarquin gave her the remainder of the orange without
further remark, peeled the other one, and shared it with
Quentin, who was coming to the conclusion that Juliana
was perhaps not quite the victim he'd believed her to be.

Her delight in the farce was so infectious that all previous
tension dissipated. Tarquin and Quentin wouldn't normally
have stayed for this low comedy that had the pits in hyster-

ics, but Juliana was so entranced, found the bawdiest comments so hilarious, that they sat back and simply enjoyed her enjoyment.

As the curtain came down, she wiped tears of laughter from her eyes with a fingertip. "I haven't laughed so much since I saw Punch and Judy at the fair in Winchester."

George Ridge had also greatly enjoyed his evening, much preferring the farce to the long-winded, ponderous speeches of the tragedy, although he'd been quite impressed with the sword fights, which had seemed very realistic. And Lady Macbeth had dripped chicken blood, and the ghost of Banquo had been horridly gouged and smothered.

He made his way out of the pit, allowing the tide of humanity to carry him. At the door a crowd of gallants was gathered around a painted bawd and her collection of whores. They were bargaining for the women, with the sharp-eyed madam missing nothing as she auctioned off her girls. George hesitated, fancying a particular bold-eyed wench in a canary-yellow gown. Then the bawd shouted, "Ten guineas to the gentleman in the striped weskit," and shoved the girl forward into the arms of the man so described, who eagerly handed over ten guineas, which the bawd dropped into a leather satchel at her waist.

George decided he'd spent enough money on women for one day. He'd return to the Gardener's Arms and take his supper there, then maybe throw the dice a few times. He would set himself a strict limit so that he'd be in no danger of outrunning the carpenter.

He pushed his way out of the stuffy heat of the theater and drew a deep breath of the fresher air outside. He seemed to be getting accustomed to the stench of London, since it troubled him much less now. He was debating whether to take a sedan chair back to Cheapside, or save the fare and walk on such a fine night, when he saw her.

He stared, unable to believe his eyes, his heart jumping erratically. Juliana was on the other side of the street, facing him. She was talking animatedly to her two escorts, men

whose dress made George immediately feel shabby and
countrified. It didn't matter that he'd ordered his suit from
a tailor on Bond Street. Compared to the two men with
Juliana, he could have been wearing a laborer's smock and
carrying a pitchfork.

And Juliana. He'd never seen her like this. In fact, if it
weren't for her hair and the expression on her face and the
voluptuous figure he'd lusted after for weeks, he would
have thought his obsession had bested his senses. She was
dressed as finely as any of the ladies he'd gawped at going
into St. James's Palace or strolling in Hyde Park. Again,
there was that indefinable air of fashion and quality about
her clothes and the way she wore them that relegated
George Ridge to the farmyard. He recognized that Lady
Forsett would eat her heart out if she could see her erstwhile charge tricked out in such style. Such a wide hoop,
and the most shockingly low neckline to her lavender silk
gown.

He moved backward into the shadows so she wouldn't
see him if she chanced to look across the street. Then he
stood and continued to stare at the three of them. Who was
she with? Had she turned whore? It was the only explanation he could think of—that somehow in the days since
she'd arrived in London, alone and friendless, she'd managed to snag a rich and well-connected protector. Or
maybe two. She was laughing and talking to her companions with an ease and informality that seemed to imply
either long acquaintance or a degree of intimacy.

It was an explanation that made perfect sense to George.
He licked his lips involuntarily, imagining how the life of a
whore would change the haughty and inexperienced country girl he had known. But how would she respond to the
prospect of returning to Hampshire as the wife of Sir
George Ridge, when she'd dabbled in the playgrounds of
fashionable London?

A chaise drew up on the other side of the street, obscur-
ing them from his view. He darted out of the shadows in
time to see one of the men hand Juliana into the carriage.

Both men followed her, and the door was closed. George stared at the ducal coronet emblazoned on the panels. He couldn't read the Latin motto or identify the arms, but he knew the carriage belonged to a duke. Juliana, it seemed, was flying high. Perhaps too high for a simple country landowner, however wealthy.

He pushed his way to a hackney that had come to a halt by a group of inebriated men, who were arguing about where they should continue their evening. George shoved roughly through them and into the hackney before they realized what was happening. "Follow the carriage ahead. The black-and-yellow one," George shouted at the jarvey, banging on the roof with his sword hilt.

The hackney started forward with a jolt, and its intended passengers turned and bellowed in startled fury. They made a halfhearted attempt to follow, one of them hanging on to the window straps for a few yards, cursing George for a sneak thief before falling off into the gutter.

George leaned anxiously out of the window, trying to keep the black-and-yellow carriage in sight as they bowled around a corner. The jarvey seemed to be enjoying the chase, took the corner on two wheels, and George was flung back against the cracked, stained leather squabs. He righted himself with a curse and leaned out of the window again.

" 'Ere y'are, guv. Ranelagh Gardens," the jarvey yelled down, coming to a halt before the wrought-iron gates. "Ye want me to go on in after 'em?"

"No, I'll go on foot." George jumped down, paid the jarvey, and hurried into the gardens, paying his half-a-crown entrance fee before making his way to the rotunda, where he guessed he would find them.

For the rest of the evening he dogged Juliana's footsteps, always careful to keep himself out of her line of sight. He watched her eat supper in one of the boxes in the rotunda, listening to the orchestra in the center. She was animated, but he could see no sign of a physical relationship with her two escorts. If she was there as their whore, he would have expected to see wandering fingers, a kiss or two, definitely flirtation; and yet, despite her elegant gown, the trio reminded him of a young girl being taken for a treat by two indulgent uncles.

Greatly puzzled, he followed them back out of the garden just as dawn was breaking. He set another hackney in pursuit of the yellow-and-black chaise, and when the ducal carriage stopped outside a house on Albermarle Street and its three passengers alighted, he instructed the jarvey to drive on past. He fixed the house in his memory as the three disappeared into its lighted hallway. Then he sat back and contemplated the evening's puzzles.

Juliana had entered the house with two men. It could only mean that she had joined the oldest profession in the world. And joined it high up the ladder. But she was still his father's murderess. A whore couldn't expect to duck such a charge, however powerful her protector.

He would find out what he could about the two men; then he would wait his moment. Then he would surprise her.

Chapter 12

"Good morning, my lady."

Juliana disentangled herself from the strands of a warm and fuzzy dream as bright sunlight poured over the bed. She blinked and hitched herself onto an elbow.

A small woman, round as a currant bun, with faded blue eyes and gray hair beneath a neat white cap, stood by the bed where she'd just pulled back the curtains to let in the daylight. She bobbed a curtsy.

"Good morning," said Juliana. "You must be . . ."

"Mistress Henley, m'lady. But the family call me Henny, so if ye'd care to do the same, we'll do very well together."

"Very well, Henny." Juliana sat up and gazed around the handsome bedchamber, memory of the evening returning. She blushed as her eye fell on the heap of carelessly discarded clothes by the window. The duke had insisted on playing lady's maid when they'd come back from Ranelagh and had shown little regard for the fine silks and delicate lawn of her undergarments. "I beg your pardon for leaving my clothes in such a mess," she said.

"Good heavens, my lady, what am I here for?" Henny responded cheerfully. "I'll have them picked up in no time while you take your morning chocolate." She turned to pick up a tray and placed it on Juliana's knees. Steam curled fragrantly from the spout of a silver chocolate pot.

Juliana's eyes widened at this unheard-of luxury. The routine at Forsett Towers had had her dressed and breakfasting by seven o'clock every morning. Lady Forsett had been a firm believer in the evils of the soft life on the young, and on winter mornings Juliana had had to crack the ice in the ewer before she could wash.

Carefully she poured the chocolate into the wide, shallow cup. The china was gold-rimmed and paper thin, alarmingly fragile. She leaned back against the pillows and took a cautious sip, then, emboldened, took a biscuit from the matching plate and dunked it into the chocolate. A soggy morsel splashed back into the cup when she carried the biscuit to her lips, and drops of chocolate splattered the coverlet.

"Is something the matter, my lady?" Henny, shaking out the folds of the lavender silk dress, turned at Juliana's mortified exclamation.

"I've spilled chocolate all over the bed," she said, biting her lip as she rubbed at the splashes. "I'm certain it'll stain."

"The laundress won't be defeated by a little chocolate." Henny bustled over to examine the damage. "Dearie me, it's hardly anything."

"It looks like a lot to me," Juliana said disgustedly. "Perhaps I'd better drink it sitting in a chair." She handed the tray to Henny and jumped out of bed.

"I give you good day, madam wife."

Juliana whirled to the door that had opened without warning. Lucien came into the room. He was fully dressed but looking very disheveled, as if he'd slept in his clothes. He carried a glass of cognac and regarded his wife with a satirical gleam in his bloodshot, hollowed eyes.

"My lord." She took a hasty step backward, catching the hem of her nightgown under her heel.

"Lud, but you seem surprised to see me, my lady. I made sure it was customary for a husband to visit his bride on the morning after their wedding night." He sipped brandy, his eyes mocking her over the rim of his glass. But there was more than mockery in his gaze. There was a touch of repulsion as he examined the shape of her body beneath the fine lawn of her nightgown.

Juliana decided abruptly to return to bed. "You startled me, my lord," she said with as much dignity as she could muster. She climbed back into bed, pulling the covers up to her neck. "Henny, I'll take my chocolate again."

The woman gave her the tray back and curtsied to the viscount. "Should I leave, my lord?"

"No," Juliana said swiftly. "No, there's no need for you to go."

Lucien merely smiled and shrugged. He lounged over to the bed and perched on the end. "So you passed a pleasant evening, I trust." He took a gulp of cognac.

It seemed best to play this straight . . . behave as if it were a perfectly ordinary conversation with a man who had every right to be where he was. "Yes, thank you, sir. We went to the play and after to Ranelagh." She dunked another biscuit into her cup with what she hoped was an air of insouciance and successfully conveyed it, intact, to her mouth.

"Insipid entertainment!" Lucien's lip curled. "If you really wished to see the town, madam, you should put yourself in my hands."

"I doubt His Grace would approve of such a scheme," she responded, leaning back against the pillows, her eyes suddenly narrowed.

Lucien gave a shout of laughter that disintegrated into another of his violent coughing spasms. He doubled over on the bed, the emaciated body racked as his chest convulsed and he grabbed for air.

"There, there, my lord. Take it easy, now." Henny took the cognac from his hands and stood waiting until the spasms diminished. "Drink it down, sir." She handed it back with the air of one who knew the remedy. Presumably, as an old family retainer, she knew their skeletons.

Lucien drained the glass in one gulp and sighed with relief. "Forgive me, m'dear. An unpleasant habit for a bridegroom." He grinned, and Juliana noticed for the first time that he was missing four of his front teeth. It was hard to pinpoint his age, but even at her most generous estimate, he was too young to be losing teeth to decay.

"Now, what was it you said that made me laugh . . . ? Oh, yes . . . Tarquin most certainly wouldn't look kindly on my acting as your guide to London life." He chuckled, but carefully this time.

Juliana nodded thoughtfully. It was not difficult to imagine the Duke of Redmayne gnashing his teeth in such a case. Not difficult . . . indeed, positively delicious . . . an utterly delectable prospect . . .

"Good morning, Lady Edgecombe. . . . Ah, Lucien. I see you're paying your bride a morning visit." The Duke of Redmayne materialized from her thoughts. Juliana, startled, turned to the doorway. Tarquin, in a brocade chamber robe, lounged against the doorjamb, but his indolent air was belied by the harsh light in his eyes.

For some reason no one in this household thought it appropriate to knock upon her door, Juliana reflected. "I give you good day, Your Grace." She took another sip of chocolate, trying to appear as if she were perfectly accustomed to entertaining gentlemen in bed in her nightgown. Of course, it was a perfectly appropriate venue for both husbands and lovers, and she had one of each. A bubble of laughter threatened. Hastily she put down her cup and pushed the tray to safety on the far edge of the bed.

"You seem mighty free with my lady's bedchamber, Tarquin," Lucien sneered. "Should I play the outraged husband, I wonder?"

"Don't be a fool." Tarquin looked merely bored by his cousin's barb as he strolled into the room. "I suppose you haven't been to bed as yet?"

"You suppose right, dear boy." Lucien held his empty glass to the light. "Dear me, empty again. I swear the glass must have a leak. D'you still keep a decanter in your room, Redmayne?"

"Go to your own chamber, Lucien," Tarquin instructed in the same bored tone. "Your man is waiting for you, and I'm certain you'll find everything necessary for your comfort."

Lucien yawned profoundly and stood up. "Well, perhaps you're right. Desolated to bring this enchanting little chat to a close, my dear bride."

"I consider it merely postponed, sir."

Tarquin's air of indolent boredom vanished. "I beg your pardon, Juliana?"

Juliana's smile was all innocence. "I merely said I look forward to continuing the discussion with my husband, sir. Is something wrong?"

Tarquin looked so dumbfounded, she was hard-pressed to keep a straight face.

"Can't keep a wife from her lawful husband, y'know, Tarquin," Lucien stated, fumbling with his snuffbox. He had no idea why Juliana should be intent on needling the duke, but he was more than willing to join in the mischief.

Tarquin walked to the door and opened it. "Good day, Lucien."

Lucien looked hurt. "Throwing me out of my own wife's bedchamber, cousin? Seems I have the right to throw *you* out, not the other way round."

"Get out." The duke's voice was very soft, but the pulse in his temple was throbbing and his nostrils were pinched and white.

Lucien glanced toward Juliana, who, having decided prudently to withdraw from the confrontation, avoided eye contact. She didn't care for the look of the Duke of Redmayne at the moment and was not prepared to provoke him further by obviously aligning herself with the viscount. At least not until she'd formulated a coherent plan.

Lucien shrugged and made for the door, knowing that without an ally he couldn't hold his ground. He wasn't too sure what the issue was anyway, but, surprisingly, it seemed

that young Juliana was not a completely compliant participant in the duke's schemes. He offered his cousin a mocking bow as he went past him into the corridor.

"Lady Edgecombe will ring when she needs you,
Henny," the duke said curtly, still holding the door.

The abigail bobbed a curtsy, picked up Juliana's neglected chocolate tray, and bustled out.

"Now, just what was all that about?" The duke came
over to the bed.

"All what?" Juliana's smile was as innocent as ever. "My
husband came to visit me. We were talking."

"I see." Tarquin's eyes searched hers. "Are you throwing
down the glove, Juliana?"

"Why ever should I do such a thing?"

"I don't know. But if you are, I should warn you that I
will pick it up."

"There would be little point in throwing it, my lord, if
you did not. . . . Not," she added sweetly, "that I am, of
course."

Tarquin stood frowning at her. She was radiating mischief, vibrating with a current of energy that seemed to
make her hair crackle. But he couldn't begin to think what
pleasure or point there might be for her in cultivating Lucien, unless it was to annoy Tarquin himself. Deciding not
to encourage her by pursuing the subject further, he
changed the topic with an amiable smile. "I forgot to tell
you last night that you'll probably receive a bridal visit this
morning from Lady Lydia Melton and her mother."

"Oh? Your betrothed is very kind," she said distantly.

"It's hardly kindess to pay a duty visit to her fiancé's
newly acquired relative, who also happens to be living under his roof."

"No, I suppose not," Juliana mused. "Is she aware, I
wonder, that this newly acquired relative is also installed in
the duchess's apartments?"

"Don't be absurd."

Juliana plaited the coverlet with busy fingers. "I presume
I'll be moved elsewhere once your marriage is celebrated

. . . or will this arrangement be terminated when I conceive your child?"

"You seem determined to quarrel with me this morning," Tarquin observed. "I woke up half an hour ago feeling as if I'd been touched by magic." His voice deepened, his eyes glowed, and his mouth curved in a smile of rich sensual pleasure. "The memory of you was on my skin, running in my blood."

Leaning over her, he planted his hands on the pillow on either side of her head. Juliana couldn't tear her eyes from his, so close to her now, compelling her response. His breath was warm on her cheek, his mouth poised above hers . . . poised for an eternity until, with a little moan of defeat, she grasped his face with her hands and pulled his mouth to hers. She kissed him hungrily, pushing her tongue into his mouth, tasting him, drawing his own special scent into her lungs. He kept himself still for her exploration, leaving her with the initiative, until, breathless, she released his face and moved her mouth from his.

"A much more pleasing greeting," Tarquin said, smiling. "Are you always bad-tempered in the morning? Or did you not get enough sleep last night?"

"My questions were perfectly reasonable," Juliana replied, but her voice was low and sweet, her mouth soft, her eyes aglow.

He sat down on the bed beside her. "Maybe I should have mentioned before that I was to be married, but I really didn't think it important. No matter what our arrangements are my dear, I must be married at some point. And no matter what I might prefer," he added a trifle ruefully, "I have a family duty."

"Would you rather not marry Lady Lydia?" Juliana forgot her own concerns in this much more intriguing question.

"It's a marriage of convenience," he explained evenly. "In my position one does not wed for anything else. For amusement, passion—love, even—one keeps a mistress. Surely that doesn't come as a surprise?"

"No, I suppose not. Do you have other mistresses? Someone . . . someone you love, perhaps?" Her fingers were busier than ever with the counterpane, and she couldn't look up at him.

All expression died out of Tarquin's eyes; his face became blank, featureless. "Love, my dear, is a luxury a man in my position must learn to do without."

She looked up now, startled at the bitterness she sensed beneath his flat tone. "Why must you learn to do without it?"

"What an inquisitive child you are." He looked at her for a moment in silence as she gazed back at him with frank curiosity. "If a man has power and wealth, he can never really trust the sincerity of those around him. Perhaps it takes a certain amount of trust to be able to love," he said simply.

"How wretched!" Juliana reached a hand to touch his as it rested on the bed. "Have people pretended to love you, then, but all they wanted was what you could give them?"

He looked down at her hand curled over his. Such an instinctive and generous gesture of comfort, he thought, gently sliding his hand out from under hers. "When I was young and foolish," he said lightly. "But I learned my lesson."

"At least people pretended to like you," Juliana said thoughtfully. "No one even *pretended* to like me. I don't know which would be worse."

"Of course people liked you," he protested, shocked despite his own cynicism at this matter-of-fact statement from one so young and appealing.

Juliana shook her head. "No," she stated. "I wasn't what anyone wanted, except Sir John, of course. I do think he genuinely liked me . . . or perhaps it was only lust. George said he was a perverted old man who lusted after schoolgirls."

Tarquin leaned over and caught her chin on the tip of his finger, lifting it to meet his steady gaze. "*I* like you, Juliana."

Her eyes gazed into his, searching for evidence of the kindly lie beneath the surface. She couldn't see it; in fact, his eyes were suddenly unreadable, glittering with a strange intensity that made her uncomfortable. She blundered onto a new tack, shattering the mesmerizing focus like a sheet of crystal under a fork of lightning.

"So when Lady Lydia becomes your duchess, where had you intended to put me?"

Tarquin dropped her chin, the strange mood broken. "I hadn't intended to *put* you anywhere. Of course, if you produce an heir to Edgecombe, you will move to your own suite of apartments, both in this house and at Redmayne Abbey. Where you choose to be will be entirely up to you. If you wish to leave this house and set up your own establishment, then you may do so; the child, however, will remain here."

"And if I do not have a child?"

"I thought we had discussed this with Copplethwaite," he said, impatiently now.

"The question of your marriage was not raised."

With an air of forbearance, he began to enumerate points on his fingers. "After my marriage . . . after your husband's death . . . whether or not you have a child, you will be free to take up residence at Edgecombe Court as the viscount's widow. However, the child, if there is one, will remain under my roof. If there is no child, the arrangement is perfectly simple. If there is, and you choose to live elsewhere, you will have generous access to the child. I thought that had all been made clear."

"I daresay I'm a trifle slow-witted, Your Grace."

"And the moon is made of cheese."

Juliana fought a silent battle to keep her bitter resentment hidden. All her instincts rebelled against this cold, rational disposition of maternal rights. Supposing she and the duke fell out irrevocably, had some dreadful quarrel that couldn't be papered over? How was she to continue under his roof in such circumstances? And how could she possibly move out and leave her own child behind?

But of course, for the Duke of Redmayne, both she and the child were possessions. Women were bought and sold at all levels of society. Starving men sold their wives in the marketplace for bread. Royal princesses were shipped to foreign courts like so much cattle, to breed and thus cement alliances, to join lands and armies and treasure chests. She'd known all this since she'd been aware of a world outside the nursery. But how hard it was to see herself that way.

Tarquin was regarding her with a quizzical frown. When she remained quiet, he gently changed the subject: "Do you have plans for today?"

The question startled her. She'd been ruled by others all her life—ruled and confined in the house on Russell Street. It hadn't occurred to her that freedom to do what she pleased and go wherever she fancied would be one of the rewards for this oblique slavery.

"I hadn't thought."

"Do you ride?"

"Why, yes. In winter in Hampshire it was the only way to travel when the roads were mired."

"Would you like a riding horse?"

"But where is there to ride?"

"Hyde Park for the sedate variety. But Richmond provides more excitement." Her delighted surprise at this turn of the conversation sent a dart of pleasure through him. How easy she was to please. And also to hurt, he reminded himself, but he quickly suppressed that thought. "If you wish, I'll procure you a horse from Tattersalls this morning."

"Oh, may I come too?" She threw aside the covers and leaped energetically to her feet, her nightgown flowing around her.

"I'm afraid not. Ladies do not frequent Tattersalls." His eyes fixed on the swell of her breasts, their dark crowns pressing against the thin bodice. "But you may trust me with the commission," he said slowly. "Take off your nightgown."

Juliana touched her tongue to her lips. "Someone might come in."

"Take it off." His voice was almost curt, but she didn't mistake the rasp of passion.

She unfastened the laces at her throat and drew the gown slowly up her body, sensing that he would enjoy a gradual unveiling. When she threw it aside and stood naked, his eyes devoured her, roaming hungrily over her body, but he made no attempt to reach for her.

"Turn around."

She did so slowly, facing the bed, feeling her skin warm and flushed with his scrutiny as if it were his hands, not his eyes, that were caressing her.

Tarquin unfastened his robe with one swift pull at the girdle and came up behind her. His hands slid around her waist, cupping the fullness of her breasts, and she could feel his turgid flesh pressing against her buttocks. Then his hands moved over her belly, traced the curve of her hips, stroked the cheeks of her buttocks.

Juliana caught her breath at the insinuating touch of his fingers sliding down the cleft of her bottom and between her thighs, opening the moist, heated furrow of her body. Lust flooded her loins, tightened her belly, sent the blood rushing through her veins. She moved against his fingers, her own hands sliding behind to caress his erect shaft until she could feel his breath swift and hot against the nape of her neck.

"Put your palms flat on the bed."

Juliana obeyed the soft, urgent command, aware of nothing now but his body against hers and her own aching core begging for the touch that would bring the cataclysm. His hands ran hard down her bent back, tracing the curve of her spine, then gripped her buttocks as he drove into her. It felt different—wildly, wonderfully different—his hard belly slapping against her buttocks with each powerful, rhythmic thrust that drove his flesh deeper and deeper inside her. She could hear her own little sobbing cries; her head dropped onto the rumpled sheets, her spine dipped. Her mouth was dry, the swirling void grew ever closer . . . the moment when her body would slip loose from its moorings. His fingers bit deep into the flesh of her hips and his name was on her lips, each syllable an assertion and a declaration of his pleasure.

Juliana fell slowly, as slowly as a feather drifting downward on a spring breeze. The void came up to meet her, and she was lost in its swirling sensate wonder. She toppled forward onto the bed and Tarquin came with her, his body pressed to her back, his hands now around her waist, holding her tightly as his own climax tore him asunder. His face was buried in the tangled flame-red hair on her neck, and his breath was hot and damp on her skin. The void receded and the tension left her limbs inch by inch, and her body took his weight as his strength washed from him with the receding wave of his own joy.

It was a long while before Tarquin eased himself upright onto his feet. He drew his robe together again and reached down to stroke Juliana's back. "*Mignonne,* come back."

"I can't. I'm lost," she mumbled into the coverlet. "That felt so different."

He bent over her and rolled her onto her back. He stroked her face with a fingertip, and his eyes were dark with the residue of passion and something that looked remarkably like puzzlement. "I don't know what you are," he said simply. He kissed her and then, quietly, he left her.

Juliana sat up slowly. Her body thrummed. At the moment she didn't know what she was either. A bride, a mistress . . . a whore? A woman, a girl? A person or a possession?

And if she no longer knew herself, she knew the duke even less.

Chapter 13

It was noon when Juliana left her apartments, dressed for the day in a wide-hooped yellow silk gown opened over a green-sprigged white petticoat. She felt very much the fashionable lady appearing at such a disgracefully late hour and dressed in such style. Lady Forsett, a firm believer in domestic industry, would have disapproved mightily. Ladies of the house didn't put off their aprons and dress for the day's leisure until just before dinner.

The thought made her chuckle and she gave a little skip, recollecting her position when she caught the eye of a curtsying maidservant who was clearly trying to stifle her grin. "Good day to you," Juliana said with a lofty nod.

"My lady," the girl murmured, respectfully holding her curtsy until Lady Edgecombe had passed her.

Juliana paused at the head of the stairs, wondering where to go. She had seen the mansion's public rooms yesterday and was a little daunted at the prospect of sailing down the horseshoe stairs and into the library or the drawing room. Strictly speaking, she was only a guest in the house, although her position was somewhat ambivalent, whichever way one looked at it. Then she remembered that she had her own private parlor.

She opened the door onto the little morning room, half-afraid she would find it changed, or occupied, but it was empty and just as she remembered. She closed the door behind her and thought about her next move. A cup of coffee would be nice. Presumably she had the right to order what she pleased while she was there. She pulled the bell rope by the hearth and sat down on the chaise longue beneath the window, arranging her skirts tastefully.

The knock at the door came so quickly, it was hard to imagine the footman who entered at her call could have come from the kitchen regions so speedily. But he appeared immaculate and unhurried in his powdered wig and dark livery as he bowed. "You rang, my lady."

"Yes, I'd like some coffee, please." She smiled, but his impassive expression didn't crack.

"Immediately, madam. Will that be all?"

"Oh, perhaps some bread and butter," she said. Dinner wouldn't be until three, and the morning's activities had given her an appetite.

The footman bowed himself out, and she sat in state on the chaise, wondering what she was to do with herself until dinnertime. There were some periodicals and broadsheets on a pier table beneath a gilt mirror on the far wall, and she had just risen to go and examine them when there was another light tap on her door. "Pray enter."

"Good morning, Juliana." Lord Quentin bowed in the doorway, then came in, smiling, to take her hand and raise it to his lips. "I came to inquire after you. Is there anything I can do for you . . . anything you would like?"

"Employment," Juliana said with a rueful chuckle. "I'm all dressed and ready to see and be seen, but I have nowhere to go and nothing to do."

Quentin laughed. "In a day or two you'll have calls to return, and I understand Tarquin is procuring you a riding horse. But until then you may walk in the park, if you'll accept my escort. Or you could visit a circulating library and the shops. There's a sedan chair at your disposal, as well as the chaise. But if you prefer to walk, then a footman will accompany you."

"Oh," Juliana said faintly, somewhat taken aback by such a variety of options. "And I suppose I may make use of the duke's library also?"

"Of course," Quentin responded. "Anything in this house is at your disposal."

"Did His Grace say so?"

Quentin smiled. "No, but my brother is openhanded to a fault. We all live on his bounty to some extent, and I've never known him to withhold anything, even from Lucien."

Juliana could believe in the duke's generosity. It was one thing about him that she felt was not prompted by self-interest. She had a flash of empathy for him, thinking how painful it must be for him to sense when his generosity was abused.

"Do you live here, my lord?"

"Only when I'm visiting London. My house is in the cathedral close in Melchester, in Hertfordshire, where I'm a canon."

Juliana absorbed this with a thoughtful nod. Canons were very important in the church hierarchy. She changed the course of the subject. "Why does my husband live here? Doesn't he have a house of his own?"

The footman appeared with the coffee, and Quentin waited to answer her. Juliana saw that there were two cups on the tray. Obviously, the servants made it their business to know where their masters were in the house.

"It was part of the arrangement Tarquin insisted upon," Quentin told her after the footman had left. He took a cup from her with a nod of thanks. "For your benefit. Obviously, you would be expected to reside under the same roof as your husband. Lucien's own establishment is uncomfortable, to put it mildly. He's besieged by creditors. And, besides, Tarquin can keep an eye on him if he stays here."

"Ensure he doesn't molest me?" Juliana raised an eyebrow.

Quentin flushed darkly. "If I believed that Tarquin

would not protect you, ma'am, I would not be a party to this business."

"Would you have a choice?" she inquired softly. "Your brother is very . . . very persuasive."

Quentin's flush deepened. "Yes, he is. But I like to believe that he could not *persuade* me to do something against my conscience."

"And this manipulative scheme is *not*?" Juliana sounded frankly incredulous as she took a piece of bread and butter from the plate. She regretted the question when she saw how distressed Quentin was. She bore him no grudge— indeed, sensed that he would stand her friend and champion without hesitation if she asked it of him.

"How can I say it isn't?" he said wretchedly. "It's an abominable design . . . and yet it will solve so many embarrassments and difficulties for the family."

"And the family interest, of course, is supreme?"

"For the most part," he said simply. "I'm a Courtney before I'm anything else. It's the same for Tarquin. But I *do* believe he will ensure that you don't suffer from this . . . and . . ." He paused uncomfortably. "Forgive me, but it does seem to me that you could benefit from this scheme if you don't find Tarquin himself distasteful."

Juliana was too honest to lie. She set down her cup, aware that her cheeks were warm. "No," she said. "It's all very confusing. I hate him sometimes and yet at others . . ." She shrugged helplessly.

Quentin nodded gravely and put down his own cup. Taking her hands in a tight clasp, he said earnestly, "You must understand that you may count on me, Juliana, in any instance. I have some influence over my brother, although it may seem as if no one could have."

His gray eyes were steady and sincere resting on her face, and she smiled gratefully, feeling immeasurably comforted. It was the first real statement of friendship she'd ever been given.

Another knock at the door interrupted the moment of tense silence, and the butler appeared. "Lady Melton and

Lady Lydia, madam," he announced. "I took the liberty of showing them into the drawing room."

"Thank you, Catlett," Quentin replied swiftly. "Lady Edgecombe will be down directly. . . . Don't worry," he said to Juliana with a quick smile as the butler departed. "I'll lend you my company for the ordeal."

"Will it be one?" Juliana examined her reflection in the mirror and patted her hair with a nervous hand.

"Not at all. Lydia has the sweetest nature in the world, and Lady Melton is not too much of a gorgon."

"The duke seems not inclined to marry Lady Lydia," Juliana said, licking her fingertip and smoothing her eyebrow. "He said it was a marriage of convenience." She caught sight of Quentin's expression in the mirror behind her, and her heart jumped at the bleak frustration, stark in his eyes. Then he'd turned aside and opened the door, holding it for her. Vividly now, she remembered his studied indifference at the theater, an indifference that she'd been convinced had masked a deep tension.

But this was not the moment for examining the puzzle. Juliana tucked it away for future reflection and prepared for her first social encounter as Lady Edgecombe. It was only as she was crossing the hall to the drawing room that she realized she had no story to explain her marriage to the viscount. Who was she? Where had she come from? Had the duke said anything to the Meltons at the play? If so, what?

Panicked, she stopped dead in the middle of the hall, seizing Quentin's black silk sleeve. "Who am I?" she whispered.

He frowned, puzzled; then his brow cleared. "A distant cousin of the Courtneys from York. Didn't Tarquin tell you . . . but, no, of course he didn't." He shook his head.

"I could cut his tongue out!" Juliana whispered furiously. "He is the most inconsiderate, insufferable, dastardly—"

"My dear Juliana." The duke's soft voice came from the

stairs behind her. "Could you be referring to me?" His eyes twinkled.

She whirled on him and caught her heel in the hem of her gown. There was a nasty ripping sound. "Oh, hell and the devil!" she exclaimed. "Look what you've made me do!"

"Go and ask Henny to pin it up for you," Tarquin said calmly. "Quentin and I will entertain your guests until you're ready."

Juliana gathered up her skirts and cast him what she hoped was a look of utter disdain. But he pinched her nose lightly as she swept past him to the stairs, and she stuck out her tongue with lamentable lack of dignity. Their chuckles followed her upstairs.

When she entered the drawing room twenty minutes later, Tarquin came forward immediately. "Lady Edgecombe, pray allow me to make you known to Lady Melton and Lady Lydia Melton." He took her hand, drawing her into the room.

The two ladies, seated side by side on a sofa, bowed from the waist as Juliana curtsied. They were both dressed in black, Lady Melton also wearing a black dormeuse cap that completely covered her coiffure. Her daughter wore a more modest head covering of dark gray. But the overall impression was distinctly melancholy.

"I am honored, ma'am," Juliana murmured. "Pray accept my condolences on your loss."

Lady Melton smiled fleetingly. "Lady Edgecombe, I understand you only recently arrived from York."

Juliana nodded and took the fragile gilt chair Tarquin pushed forward. Lady Lydia smiled but said little throughout the interview, leaving the talking to her mother. Juliana was far more interested in the daughter than the mother, noting a sweet but not particularly expressive face, a pair of soft blue eyes, a somewhat retiring disposition. The duke was formally polite with both ladies—distant, it seemed to Juliana, unlike his brother, who was warm and attentive. She noticed that most of Lady Lydia's shy smiles were directed at Lord Quentin.

The visit lasted fifteen minutes, and Juliana was gratefully aware that she was being steered through it by the Duke of Redmayne. He answered most questions for her, but in such a way that it appeared she was answering for herself. He delicately introduced neutral, superficial topics of conversation that took them down obstacle-free avenues of purely social discourse and touched on subjects that he knew would be familiar to Juliana. When the ladies took their leave, Juliana was confident enough to think she might be able to manage the next one on her own.

Quentin and the duke escorted the ladies to their carriage. Juliana watched from the drawing-room window. It was Quentin who handed Lady Lydia into the carriage, while Tarquin did the honors for her mother—which was odd, Juliana thought. Lydia smiled at Quentin as she settled back on the seat, and he solicitously adjusted the folds of her train at her feet.

And then, with blinding impact, it struck Juliana that if she was asked who was affianced to whom, she would guess Quentin and Lady Lydia were to make a match of it. It would explain Quentin's strangeness at the theater, and it would certainly account for that fierce, bleak look she'd surprised on his face when she'd carelessly repeated what Tarquin had said about his impending marriage. It seemed she had put her foot in it with her usual clumsiness.

As she watched, Quentin walked off down the street after the carriage, and the duke turned back to the house. She heard his voice in the hall and waited for him to come back to her, but he didn't. She'd expected a word of approval . . . a moment's conversation about the visit . . . something, at least. Crossly, she went into the hall.

"Where's His Grace, Catlett?"

"In the library, I believe, my lady."

She turned down the corridor to the library at the back of the house. She knocked and marched in.

Tarquin looked up from his newspaper with an air of surprise.

"Did I conduct myself appropriately, my lord duke?" she said with an ironic curtsy.

Tarquin laid down his newspaper and leaned back in his chair. "I have offended you again, I fear. Tell me what I've done wrong so that I can correct my faults."

This assumption of chastened humility was so absurd, Juliana burst into a peal of laughter. "I fear you're a lost cause, my lord duke."

Before the conversation could go further, the butler appeared in the open door behind her.

"Visitors for Lady Edgecombe. I've shown them to your private parlor, madam."

Juliana turned, startled. "Visitors. Who?"

"Three young ladies, madam. Miss Emma, Miss Lilly, and Miss Rosamund. I thought they would be more comfortable in your parlor." Not a flicker of an expression crossed his face.

Had Catlett guessed the ladies from Russell Street were of a different order from Lady Melton and her daughter? Or had he assumed she would entertain her own friends in her own parlor?

"Excuse me, Your Grace." With a smile and curtsy she left him and hurried upstairs to her own private room.

Tarquin raised an eyebrow to the empty room and shrugged. The only woman he'd ever lived with until now had been his mother. Apparently he had something to learn in his dealings with the gentler sex—and it seemed that Juliana Courtney, Viscountess Edgecombe, was going to provide the education. Absently, he wondered why the prospect wasn't more irritating.

Juliana hurried up to her parlor, vaguely surprised at how eager she was to see her friends from Russell Street. She hadn't had much time to get to know them, but living under one roof with them even briefly had fostered the kind of easy camaraderie that came out of shared laughter as well as shared anxieties.

"Juliana, this is the most elegant parlor," Rosamund declared as Juliana came in.

"Lud, but the whole mansion is in the first style of elegance." Lilly floated across the room to embrace Juliana. "You are the luckiest creature. And just look at your gown! So pretty. And real silver buckles on your shoes, I'll be bound." The eye of the expert took in every detail of Juliana's costume.

"I swear I'll die of envy," Emma lamented, fanning herself. "Unless, of course, there is some unpleasantness here." Her eyes sharpened as she looked at Juliana over her fan. "You must have to pay for all this in some way."

"Yes, tell us all about it." Rosamund linked arms with Juliana and pulled her down onto the sofa beside her. "You can say anything you wish to us."

Juliana was tempted to confide the whole as they sat around her radiating both complicit sympathy and alert curiosity. But an instant's reflection canceled the dangerous impulse. She must learn to keep her own secrets better than she had done so far. If she hadn't yielded to weakness in the first instance and told Mistress Dennison her story, she wouldn't be in this tangle now.

"There's nothing to tell," she said. "It is exactly as you see it. I was wed to Viscount Edgecombe yesterday, and he and I both reside under the Duke of Redmayne's roof."

"So the duke didn't buy you for himself?" Emma pressed, leaning forward to get a closer view of Juliana's face.

"In a manner of speaking he did," Juliana said cautiously.

"So both he and the viscount are your lovers." Lilly smoothed her silk gloves over her fingers, her hazel eyes sharply assessing.

"Not exactly."

"La, Juliana, don't be so mysterious!" Emma cried. "Everyone wants to know how you managed such a piece of amazing good fortune. There's nothing strange about being shared . . . particularly when you're provided for with settlements. You are, of course?"

"Yes." Juliana decided that it would be simpler to let them believe that she was shared by the duke and his young cousin. It wasn't a total fabrication, anyway. "I'm well provided for, and I suppose you could say that I belong to both the duke and the viscount." She rose and pulled the bell rope. "Will you take ratafia, or sherry . . . or champagne?" she added with wicked inspiration. "Do you care for champagne?"

"La, how wonderful," Lilly declared. "You can order such things for yourself in this house?"

"Anything I please," Juliana said with a hint of bravado as the butler arrived in answer to the summons. "Catlett, bring us champagne, if you please."

"My lady." Catlett bowed and left without so much as a flicker of an eyelid.

"See," Juliana said with a grin. "I have the right to command anything I wish."

"How enviable," Rosamund sighed. "When I think of poor Lucy Tibbet . . ." A cloud of gloom settled over Juliana's three visitors, imparting a cynical, world-weary air to the previously bright and youthful countenances.

"Lucy Tibbet?" she prompted.

"She worked in one of Haddock's millinery shops," Emma said, her usually sweet voice sharp as vinegar. "Keep away from Mother Haddock if you value your life, Juliana."

"She's every bit as bad as Richard Haddock," Rosamund said. "We all thought when he died, his wife would be easier to work for. But Elizabeth is as mean and cruel as Richard ever was."

Catlett's arrival with the champagne produced a melancholy silence broken only by the pop of the cork and the fizz of the straw-colored liquid in the glasses. Catlett passed them around and bowed himself out.

"What's wrong with a millinery shop?" Juliana sipped champagne, wrinkling her nose as the bubbles tickled her palate.

"It's a whorehouse, dear," Lilly said with a somewhat pitying air. "They all are in Covent Garden . . . so are the chocolate houses and coffeehouses. It's just a different name to satisfy the local constables. We can't call them whorehouses, although everyone knows that's what they are."

The others chuckled at Juliana's quaint ignorance. "The Haddocks rent out shops and shacks in the Piazza . . . usually for three guineas a week. They pay the rates and expect a share of the profits."

"Not that there ever are any profits," Lilly said. "Lucy spent ten pounds last week on rent and linen and glasses that she had to buy from Mother Haddock, and she had only sixpence for herself at the end of the week."

"She'd given Richard a promissory note before he died for forty pounds," Rosamund continued with the explanation. "He'd bailed her out of debtors' prison once, and she was supposed to pay him back every week. But she can't do that out of sixpence, so Mother Haddock called in the debt and had her thrown into the Marshalsea."

"We're having a collection for her," Lilly said. "We all try to help out if we can."

"You never know when it might be you," Rosamund added glumly.

"Some of the bawds will make an interest-free loan if they like one of the girls who's in trouble," Lilly said. "But Lucy made a lot of enemies when she was doing well for herself, and now she's down on her luck, none of the bawds will lift a finger."

"And the jailers at the Marshalsea are really cruel." Emma shuddered. "They torment the prisoners and won't give them food or coal or candles if they can't pay the most outrageous sums. And Lucy doesn't have a penny to her name."

"But how much does she need?" Juliana's mind raced. She'd seen enough in her few days in London to find Lucy's plight appalling but believable. After all, the duke had gone to great pains to show her how easy it was for an unprotected girl to slip into the sewer. And once in, there was no way out.

"She needs the forty pounds to free herself from Mother Haddock," Rosamund replied. "The girls at Russell Street have put together ten pounds, and we hope the other houses will contribute too."

"Wait here." Juliana sprang to her feet, spilling champagne down her bodice. She brushed at the drops impatiently. "I'll be back in a moment." She put down her glass and whisked herself from the parlor.

Tarquin was crossing the hall on his way to the front door when she came racing down the stairs, holding her skirts well clear of her feet.

"My lord duke, I need to speak with you, it's most urgent."

He regarded her impetuous progress with a faint smile. Her eyes glowed with a zealot's fire, and her tone was vehement. "I'm at your service, my dear," he said. "Will it take long? Should I instruct the groom to return my horse to the mews?"

Juliana paused on the bottom step. "I don't believe it should take long . . . but then again it might," she said with a judicious frown. "It rather depends on your attitude, sir."

"Ahh." He nodded. "Well, let's assume that my attitude will be accommodating." He turned back to the library. "Catlett, tell Toby to walk my horse. I'll be out shortly."

Juliana followed him into the library, closing the door behind her. It seemed simpler to come straight to the point. "Am I to have an allowance, sir?"

Tarquin perched on the arm of a sofa. "I hadn't given it any thought, but, of course, you must have pin money."

"How much?" she asked bluntly.

"Well, let's see . . ." He pulled on his right earlobe with a considering frown. "You already have an adequate wardrobe, I believe?" He raised an inquiring eyebrow.

"Yes, of course," Juliana said, trying to restrain her impatience. "But there are—"

"Other things," he interrupted. "I do quite understand that. If you were to take your place at court, of course, two hundred pounds a year would be barely sufficient for personal necessities, but since that's not going to happen, I would have thought—"

"Who said it wasn't going to happen?" demanded Juliana, momentarily deflected from her original purpose.

Tarquin looked perplexed. "I thought it was understood. Surely you don't wish to enter society?"

"I might," she said. "I don't see why I shouldn't have the option."

Tarquin's perplexity deepened. He'd had a very clear idea in his head of how Juliana would conduct herself under his roof, and joining the exclusive court circles had not been part of it. He remembered how she'd seemed to encourage Lucien's company that morning—another contingency he hadn't considered. Was it just mischief on her part? Or was she going to be more trouble than he'd bargained for?

"Let's leave that issue for the moment," he said. "I suggest we settle on fifty pounds a quarter at this stage. I'll instruct my bankers accordingly." He stood up and moved toward the door.

"Well, could I have forty pounds now, please?" Juliana stood between him and the door, unconsciously squaring her shoulders. She had never been given money of her own and had never dared ask for it before. But she reasoned that since she was now a viscountess, she was entitled to make some demands.

"Whatever do you want such a sum for?"

"Do I have to tell you how I spend my pin money?"

He shook his head. "No, I suppose not. Are you in some difficulties?"

"No." She shook her head vehemently. "But I have need of forty pounds . . . well, thirty I suppose would do . . . but I need it immediately."

"Very well." Still clearly puzzled, Tarquin went to the desk and opened the top drawer. He drew out a strongbox, unlocked it, and selected three twenty-pound notes. "Here you are, *mignonne*."

"That's sixty pounds," she said, taking the notes.

"You may have need of a little extra," he pointed out. "Will you give me your word you're in no difficulties?"

"Yes, of course, how should I be?" she said, tucking the notes into her bosom. "Thank you very much. I'm very much obliged to you, my lord duke." Spinning on her heel, she half ran from the library, again holding her skirts clear of her feet.

Tarquin stood frowning for a minute. Did that urgent request have anything to do with her visitors from Russell Street? It seemed likely. Highly likely, and he wasn't at all sure that he approved of Juliana's subsidizing Elizabeth Dennison's harlots. But she did have the right to some money of her own, and he didn't have the right to dictate how she should spend it. He found he'd lost interest in his ride and stood in fiercely frowning silence in the middle of the room.

"There, that's forty pounds." Juliana placed two of the bills on the table in her parlor before the astounded eyes of her friends. "So you won't need to spend your own money for Lucy's bail. Shall we go at once?"

"But . . . but is this your own money, Juliana?" Even the down-to-earth Lilly was astonished.

"In a manner of speaking," she said airily. "The duke gave it to me as part of my allowance. I wasn't sure whether I was to have one or not, but Lord Quentin said His Grace was generous to a fault, so I thought I'd put it to the test. And there you are." She indicated the riches on the table with a grandiose flourish, rather spoiling the effect by adding, "It isn't as if he can't afford it, after all."

"Well, I for one won't question such good fortune," Lilly said, tucking the notes into her beaded silk muff. "And I know Lucy won't."

"Then let's go at once." Juliana energetically strode to the door. "Do you know how to get there? Can we walk?

Or should I order the carriage?" she added with another grand gesture.

"We can't go ourselves," Rosamund protested, shocked.

"But you have a footman downstairs."

"It's still no place for ladies," Emma explained. "The jailers are horrid and rude, and they'll ask for all sorts of extras before they'll release Lucy. Mr. Garston will go for us. They won't intimidate him."

"They won't intimidate *me,*" Juliana declared. "Come, let's go. We'll hail a hackney, as there's not a moment to lose. Heaven only knows what miseries Lucy's enduring."

This consideration overrode further objections, although her companions were still rather dubious as they followed her down the stairs, where they collected the Dennisons' footman, Juliana told Catlett that she expected to be back for dinner, and they stepped out into the warm afternoon.

Chapter 14

W here are you off to, Lady Edgecombe?" Quentin was coming up the front steps as they emerged from the house. He bowed courteously to her companions.

"To the Marshalsea," Juliana said cheerfully. "To bail someone out."

"To the Marshalsea?" Quentin stared at her. "Don't be absurd, child."

"The footman will accompany us," she said, gesturing to the flunky behind her.

"The footman may accompany your friends, but Lady Edgecombe does not go to a debtors' prison," Quentin stated.

"Truly it would be best to ask Mr. Garston to go for us, Juliana," Emma put in, laying a tentative hand on Juliana's arm.

"Tarquin would flay me alive if I permitted it," Quentin declared.

Juliana regarded him steadily. "I understood I was free to go where I please."

"Not to the Marshalsea."

"Not even if you accompanied me?"

"Juliana, I have not the slightest desire to visit a debtors' prison."

"But you're a man of the cloth. Surely you have a duty to help your fellow man in need? And this *is* an errand of mercy." Her voice was all sweet reason, her smile cajoling, but Quentin was aware of a powerful determination behind the ingenuous facade.

"Why not follow your friend's suggestion and ask this Mr. Garston to go for you?"

"But that will take time. And that poor girl shouldn't languish in that place a minute more than necessary. I heard that the jailers torture the inmates for money, when of course they can't have any funds, because if they did, they wouldn't be there in the first place." Her eyes sparked with indignation and her cheeks were pale with anger, all pretense of ingenuous cajoling vanished. "You have a duty, Lord Quentin, to help those in trouble. Don't you?"

"Yes, I like to think so," Quentin said dryly. He was uncomfortably reminded that as a canon of Melchester Cathedral, he hadn't spent much time tending a flock. He was beginning to wonder why he'd ever felt Juliana needed protection and guidance. At this moment she hardly seemed like anyone's victim.

"We have the money," Juliana continued. "All forty pounds of Lucy's debt. And if the jailers demand more, I shall tell them to go hang," she added with a flashing eye. "If we allow them to get away with extortion, they'll do it to everyone."

"I'm sure you will keep them in line," Quentin murmured. "I pity the man who tries to stand in your path."

"Oh, you sound just like the duke," Juliana said. "So toplofty. But I tell you straight, my lord, you won't persuade me out of this."

"You are right that I am obliged to help those in trouble." His mouth took a sardonic quirk that made him look even more like his half brother. "I am also obliged to keep people *out* of trouble. And I assure you, my dear Juliana, you will be up to your neck in hot water if Tarquin discovers you've been roaming around a debtors' prison."

Juliana was standing on the top step, half facing the open front door. Out of the corner of her eye she caught sight of Lucien crossing the hall toward the drawing room. "If my husband doesn't object, I fail to see why the duke should," she said with a flash of inspiration. "I do beg your pardon for teasing you, Lord Quentin. Of course you mustn't trouble yourself over this for another minute."

She gave him a radiant smile and turned to the three young women. "I'll be back in an instant. Wait here for me." She hurried into the house, leaving Quentin staring uneasily after her, unsure whether he'd heard her aright.

"Oh, dear," Emma said. "Do you think Juliana is perhaps a little impetuous?"

"I fear that 'a little' is something of an understatement, ma'am," Quentin said. "Surely she's not intending to enlist Edgecombe's support?"

"I believe so, my lord," Rosamund said, her brown eyes wide and solemn in her round face.

"Excuse me." Quentin bowed briefly and strode into the house in search of Tarquin, leaving the women still on the steps.

Juliana had followed Lucien into the drawing room and closed the door behind her. "My lord, I need your leave to go on an errand," she stated straightaway.

"Good God! What's this?" Lucien exclaimed. "*You* are asking *me* for permission?"

"Indeed, my lord." Juliana curtsied. "You are my husband, are you not?"

Lucien gave a crack of laughter. "That's a fine fabrication, my dear. But I daresay it has its uses."

"Precisely," she said. "And since you are my husband, yours is the only leave I need to run my errand."

Lucien's harsh laugh rasped again. "Well, I'll be damned, m'dear. You're setting yourself up in opposition to Tarquin, are you? Brave girl!" He flipped open an enameled snuffbox and took a liberal pinch, his eyes like dead coals in his grayish pallor.

"I'm not precisely in opposition to His Grace," Juliana said judiciously, "since I haven't consulted him on the matter—indeed, I don't consider it his business. But I *am* consulting *you*, sir, and I would like your leave."

"To do what?" he inquired curiously.

Juliana sighed. "To go to the Marshalsea with bail for a friend of my friends."

"What friends?"

"Girls from the house where I was living before I came here," she said a touch impatiently, hoping that the duke wouldn't suddenly appear, summoned by Lord Quentin.

Lucien sneezed violently, burying his face in a handkerchief. It was a few minutes before he emerged, a hectic flush on his cheeks, his eyes streaming. "Gad, girl! Don't tell me Tarquin took you out of a whorehouse!" He chuckled, thumping his chest with the heel of one hand as his breath wheezed painfully. "That's rich. My holier-than-thou cousin finding me a wife from a whorehouse to save a family scandal. What price family honor, eh!"

Juliana regarded him with ill-concealed distaste. "You may believe what you please, my lord. But I am not and never have been a whore."

Lucien raised a mock-placatory hand. "Don't eat me, m'dear. It doesn't matter to me what you were . . . or, indeed, what you *are*. You could have serviced an entire regiment before dinner, for all that I care."

Juliana felt her temper rise. Her lip curled and her eyes threw poisoned daggers at him. Firmly she told herself that Viscount Edgecombe was not worth her anger. "Will you give me leave to go to the Marshalsea, my lord?" she demanded impatiently.

"Oh, you may have leave to do anything you wish if it'll irritate Tarquin, my lady." He chuckled and wheezed. "By all means visit the debtors' prison. By all means choose your friends from the whorehouses of Covent Garden. By all means do a little business of that sort on the side, if it appeals to you. You have my unconditional leave to indulge in any form of debauchery, to wallow in the stews every night. Just don't ask me for money. I don't have two brass farthings to rub together."

Juliana paled and her freckles stood out on the bridge of her nose. "Rest assured, I will ask you for nothing further, my lord." She dropped an icy curtsy. "If you'll excuse me, my friends await me."

"Just a minute." He raised an arresting hand, impervious to her anger. "Perhaps I'll accompany you on this errand. Lend a touch of respectability . . ." He grinned, the skin stretched tight on his skull. "If your husband bears you company, Tarquin will have to gnash his teeth in silence."

Juliana wasn't happy at the prospect of enduring her husband's company. On the other hand, the idea of thwarting the duke had an irresistible appeal. He did, after all, have it coming.

"Very well," Juliana murmured.

"Well, let's be about this business." He sounded relatively robust at the prospect of sowing mischief and moved to the door with almost a spring in his step. Juliana followed, her eyes agleam now with her own mischief.

Just as they reached the front door, Quentin and the duke emerged from the library.

"Juliana!" Tarquin's voice was sharp. "Where do you think you're going?"

She turned and curtsied. "For a drive with my husband, my lord duke. I trust you have no objections."

The duke's mouth tightened and an ominous muscle twitched in his cheek. "Lucien, you're not encouraging this outrageous scheme."

"My wife has asked for my permission to help a friend, and I've offered her my company in support, dear boy." Lucien couldn't hide his glee. "Wouldn't do for Lady Edgecombe to go alone to the Marshalsea . . . but in my company there can be no objection."

"Don't be absurd," the duke snapped. "Juliana, go upstairs to your parlor. I'll come to you directly."

Juliana frowned at this curt order. "Forgive me, my lord duke, but my husband has commanded my presence. I do believe that his commands must take precedence over yours." She curtsied again and whisked herself out of the house before Tarquin could gather his wits to react.

Lucien grinned, offered his cousin a mock bow, and followed his wife.

"Insolent baggage!" Tarquin exclaimed. "Who the hell does she think she is?"

"Viscountess Edgecombe, apparently," his brother said, unable to hide a wry smile. It wasn't often that Tarquin was routed.

The duke stared at him in fulminating silence; then he spun on his heel and strode back to the library. He left the door ajar, so after a moment's hesitation Quentin followed him.

"If that child thinks she can use Lucien to provoke me, she'd better think again," the duke said, his mouth a thin, straight line, his eyes cold and hard as agate. "What could she possibly hope to gain by such a thing?"

"Revenge," Quentin suggested, perching on the wide windowsill. "She's a lady of some spirit."

"She's a minx!" The duke paced the room with long, angry strides.

"They won't come to any harm," Quentin soothed. "Lucien will—"

"That drunken degenerate is only interested in putting one over on me," Tarquin interrupted. "He's not concerned about Juliana in the least."

"Well, no one need know about it," Quentin said.

"No one need know that Viscountess Edgecombe in the company of three whores went to the rescue of a pauper harlot in the Marshalsea!" Tarquin exclaimed. "Goddammit, Quentin! They may not recognize Juliana, but they will certainly recognize Lucien."

"Not if they take a closed carriage," Quentin suggested lamely.

A dismissive wave showed what Tarquin thought of this

possibility. He resumed his pacing, an angry frown knotting his brow. Lucien would cause whatever evil he could. Juliana was only a country innocent, and she had no idea what she was dealing with. Somehow he would have to put a stop to her foolish alliance with Lucien.

George Ridge climbed up from the basement steps of the house opposite the duke's mansion on Albermarle Street and stood watching the group of four women and a man followed by a footman stroll down the street. He stood with his feet apart, adjusting his waistcoat with a complacent tug, his right hand resting on his sword hilt. He'd been watching the house on Albermarle Street since midmorning, and nothing he'd seen made any sense. Last night he'd assumed that Juliana had been bought for the night by the two men who'd taken her into the house. But now it seemed as if she lived there. His first thought was that it was a whorehouse and the men were visiting her there. But two ladies, evidently irreproachable in their somber clothes, had arrived in a carriage with an earl's arms on the panels. Then the two men he'd seen the previous night had escorted them back to the carriage with all due ceremony and courtesy. Then the three young women, accompanied by a footman, had arrived. Some altercation had occurred, he was convinced, between Juliana and one of the two men who seemed to live in the house, and now there she was in the company of yet another man, prancing down the street with the other women.

None of it made any sense. Juliana's dress was fine as fivepence and didn't look in the least whorish, but there was an air about her present companions that he would swear labeled them as Impures. High Impures, certainly, but definitely not fit companions for a young lady of Juliana's birth and breeding. And what of the man whose arm she held? Unsavory-looking creature, George thought, although the view from his hiding place was partially obscured by the iron railings. Something very rum was going on, and the sooner he got to the bottom of it, the sooner he'd be able to decide on his next move.

He stood for a few more minutes until the party reached the end of the street; then he strolled off toward the mews at the back of the house. Someone there would tell him to whom the house belonged. It would be a start.

"Don't you think we should get a hackney, sir?" Juliana inquired as they emerged onto the crowded thoroughfare of Piccadilly.

"Oh, all in good time . . . all in good time," Lucien responded easily. "I've a mind to show myself to the world in such charming company. It's a rare sight for me to be surrounded by a bevy of the doves of Venus. We're bound to meet up with some of my friends . . . an acquaintance or two. Introduce you, m'dear wife . . . and of course your friends . . . your previous fellow laborers." He chuckled.

Juliana's lips thinned. She wasn't prepared to sacrifice her reputation just to annoy the duke. Lucien was taking matters too far.

A hackney carriage trundled along Piccadilly toward them, and with swift resolution she hailed it. "Forgive me, my lord, but I don't believe we have the time for social dalliance." She tugged on the handle of the carriage door as it came to a stop beside them. "I think we can all fit in, if you don't mind sitting on the box, sir." She offered him a placating smile and was taken aback by the flash of sullen anger in the ashy coals of his eyes.

"I say we walk along Piccadilly, madam."

Juliana's smile remained unwavering as her three friends were handed into the coach by the footman. "Indeed, my lord, but we cannot spare the time. Poor Lucy could even now be dying of starvation in that place. We don't have a minute to lose." She turned to follow her companions into the hackney. Seating herself, she leaned out of the still-open door.

"If you don't wish to sit on the box, my lord, perhaps you could follow us in a separate hackney."

Lucien glowered at her. Juliana coaxed, "Please come, my lord. If I go alone, His Grace will feel he has cause to be vexed with me. But as you so rightly said, if you come, he'll have to bite his tongue."

It worked. The viscount, still glowering, climbed onto the box beside the jarvey. "The Marshalsea," he growled. The jarvey cracked his whip and the hackney moved off, the footman leaping onto the step behind, hanging on to the leather strap.

"Why are you so set on this, Juliana?" Lilly fanned herself in the warm interior, her languid air belied by the sharpness of her gaze. "I warrant it has to do with more than Lucy's plight."

"Perhaps it has," Juliana said with a serene smile. "But Lucy's situation is the first consideration."

Rosamund was sitting in silence in a corner, the muslin collar of her short cloak drawn up around her ears as if she were hiding from something. When she spoke, her voice was husky and awkward. "Forgive me, Juliana, I don't wish to pry. But . . . but that is your husband who's accompanying us?"

"Yes, for my sins," Juliana replied with a shudder. Once out of the viscount's presence she couldn't hide her repulsion.

"He's a sick man," Rosamund said hesitantly. "I don't know if—"

"He's poxed," Lilly stated flatly. "There's no need to beat about the bush, Rosamund, we all know the signs. Have you been in his bed, Juliana?"

Juliana shook her head. "No, and I shall not. It's not part of the arrangement."

"Well, that's a relief!" Emma sighed and relaxed. "I didn't know what to say . . . how to warn you."

"There's no need. I've had fair warning," Juliana responded, looking out of the window to conceal her expression from her companions. "And I'm in no danger . . . at least not of that sort," she couldn't help adding in a low voice.

"It's to be hoped we don't catch something in the Marshalsea," Rosamund muttered. "There's jail fever and all sorts of things in that place. Just breathing the air can infect you."

"Then you may stay in the hackney," Juliana said. "The viscount and I will go inside and procure Lucy's release."

"I'm certainly coming in," Lilly said stoutly. "You don't know Lucy. She won't know to trust you."

"No, she's had so much ill luck," Emma agreed with a sigh. "She won't know whom to trust."

The carriage came to a rattling halt on the uneven cobbles in front of a fearsome high-walled building. Great iron gates stood open to the street, and ragged creatures shuffled through them, exuding a desperate kind of defeat.

"Who are they?" Juliana gazed out of the door as the footman opened it.

"Debtors," Lilly said, stepping down to the road ahead of her.

"But they aren't incarcerated."

"No, they're paroled from dawn to dusk so they can beg—or work, if they can find something," Emma explained, following Juliana to the cobbles. "And they have visitors, who bring them food, if they're lucky. There are whole families in there. Babies, small children, old men and women."

Lucien clambered off the box, the maneuver clearly costing him some effort. He stood for a minute wheezing, leaning against the carriage, sweat standing out on his pallid brow. "I must be mad to agree to such a ridiculous scheme," he muttered, mopping his forehead with his handkerchief. "You go about your business, madam wife. I'm going to settle my chest in that tavern over yonder." He gestured to a ramshackle building with a crooked door frame and loose shutters. Its identifying sign was unreadable and hung by a single nail over the door. "Come to me in the taproom when you're finished with your errand of mercy."

Juliana silently resolved to send the footman through that unsavory-looking door, but she curtsied meekly to her husband, eyes lowered to the mud-encrusted cobbles.

Lucien ignored the salutation and hurried off, the smell of cognac drawing him like a dog to a bone.

"Oh, dear, I thought the viscount was going to negotiate for us," Rosamund said, dismayed.

"We have no need of Edgecombe for the moment." Juliana gathered up her skirts and set off toward the gate, watching her feet warily as she picked her way through the festering kennel in the middle of the street, praying she wouldn't catch her high heel on an uneven cobble.

The gatekeeper stared blearily at them as they stopped at his hut. His little eyes were red-rimmed and unfocused, and he smelled most powerfully of gin. He took a swig from the stone jar on his lap before deigning to answer Juliana's question.

"Lucy Tibbet?" He wiped his mouth with the back of his hand. "Tibbet, eh? Now, who'd 'ave put 'er in 'ere?"

"Mistress Haddock," Lilly said.

"Oh, that bawd!" The gatekeeper threw back his head and guffawed, sending a foul miasma into the steamy summer air. "Lucifer, but she's an 'ard one, she is. Worse than that 'ubby of 'ers. That Richard. Lor' bless me, but 'e was worth a bob or two, weren't 'e?"

"If by that you mean he took every penny his girls earned, I'd agree with you," Lilly said acerbically. She was clearly made of sterner stuff than Rosamund and Emma, who were hanging back, holding their skirts well clear of the matted straw and rotting vegetables littering the cobbles.

"You one of 'em, missie?" The gatekeeper leered. "Mebbe we could come to some arrangement, like."

"And maybe you could tell us where to find Mistress Tibbet," Juliana said, stepping forward. The gatekeeper drew back involuntarily from the tongues of jade fire in her eyes, the taut line of her mouth, the tall, erect figure. This lady looked as if she were unaccustomed to meeting with opposition, and she held herself with an assurance that whores generally lacked.

"Well, now, mebbe I could, my lady . . . fer a consideration," he said, pulling his whiskery chin.

"I have forty pounds here to pay her debt," Juliana said crisply. "In addition I will give you a guinea, my good man, if you make things easy for us. Otherwise, we shall manage without you."

"Oho . . . hoity-toity, aren't we!" The gatekeeper lumbered to his feet. "Now you listen 'ere, my fine lady. The name's Mr. Cogg to you, an' I'll thankee to show a little respect."

"And I'll thank you to mind your manners," Juliana said. "Are you interested in earning a guinea or not?"

"Ten guineas it'll be to secure 'er release." His eyes narrowed slyly.

"Forty guineas to pay off her debt, and one guinea for your good self," Juliana said. "Otherwise, I shall visit the nearest magistrate and arrange for Mistress Tibbet's release with him. And you, Cogg, will get nothing."

The gatekeeper looked astounded. He was unaccustomed to such authoritative young women at his gates. In general, those who came to liberate friends and relatives were almost as indigent as the prisoner. They addressed Mr. Cogg as *sir*, with averted eyes, and crept around, keeping to the shadows. They were not comfortable with magistrates, and in general, a threatening word or two was sufficient to ensure a substantial handout for the gatekeeper.

Lilly had stepped up to Juliana's shoulder, and she, too, glared at the gatekeeper. Emma and Rosamund, emboldened by their friends' stand, also gazed fixedly at Mr. Cogg.

After a minute the gatekeeper snorted and held out his hand. "Give it 'ere, then."

Juliana shook her head. "Not until you've taken us to Mistress Tibbet."

"I'll see the color of yer money, first, my lady." He drew

himself upright, but even standing tall, his eyes were only on a level with Juliana's. She regarded him as contemptuously as an amazon facing a pygmy.

"I'm going to find a magistrate." She turned on her heel, praying the bluff would work. It could take hours to find a magistrate and hours to secure Lucy's release by that route. And Juliana always hated to alter her plans. Having once set her heart and mind on walking out of this place with Lucy, she was loath to give up.

" 'Old on, 'old on," the gatekeeper grumbled. He knew that if a magistrate ordered the prisoner's release, he'd see not a penny for himself. A golden guinea was better than nothing. He took another swig from his stone bottle and came out of his little hut, blowing his nose on a red spotted handkerchief. "This a-way."

They followed him across a yard, thronged with people. Two small boys darted between the legs of the crowd and cannoned into the gatekeeper, whose hands moved seamlessly, clouting them both around the ears even as he continued to walk. The boys fell to the ground, wailing and rubbing their ears. A woman screamed at them and came running over, waving a rolling pin. The children scrambled to their feet and disappeared so quickly, it was almost as if they'd never been there.

The gatekeeper went through another gate into an internal courtyard, as busy as the other. There were cooking fires there, and women scrubbing clothes at rain butts. The stick-thin bodies were clad in rags, the children half-naked, for the most part. The scene reminded Juliana of the gypsy encampments in the New Forest during her childhood.

But inside the building things were very different. Here there was sickness and despair. Rail-thin, hunched figures sat on the filthy stone stairs, their eyes blank, as the gatekeeper, followed by Juliana and her companions, puffed his way upward. Juliana glimpsed rooms off the landings—rooms without furniture, with unglazed windows and straw on the floor. And in the straw lay huddled bodies, crumpled like pieces of discarded paper. The air reeked of death and desolation. These people were dying there. These were the folk for whom there was no salvation. Who had no one in the world with money either to procure their release or to ensure them at least sufficient bread to keep body and soul together.

Her three companions were silent, looking neither to right nor left, avoiding the sight of the horrors that hovered on the edges of their own lives. The horrors that inevitably came to the old and infirm of Covent Garden if they weren't clever or lucky enough to provide for the uncertain future.

"She's in 'ere." Mr. Cogg stopped at an open doorway at the top of the last staircase. He was breathing heavily, sweat running down his face. "Lucy Tibbet!" he bellowed into the dimly lit attic room. "Lucy Tibbet . . . show a leg there."

A faint groan came from the far wall, and Lilly pushed past him and almost ran into the room, her pink skirts swinging gracefully. The others followed, blue and palest green, bending together over a shape on the straw. They looked like summer butterflies in a dungeon, Juliana thought as she crossed the room to join them, her nose wrinkling at the powerful stench emanating from a tin bucket in the corner.

Lucy lay in the straw, her eyes half-closed. She was filthy, her hair matted, shoeless and clad only in a torn chemise. The hectic flush of fever was on her thin cheeks, and a clawlike hand fluttered in Lilly's palm.

"Sweet heaven, what have they done to you?" Emma cried, dropping to her knees on the dirty straw. "Where are your clothes?"

"Jailer took them," Lucy croaked. "To pay for bread and water. Until there was nothing left . . ." She turned her head on the straw, two tears trickling from behind her closed eyelids. "They took my good shift and gave me this one in its place. I suppose I should be thankful they didn't leave me naked."

"Oh, how wicked!" Rosamund's tears fell onto the straw.

"We've come to take you out of here," Juliana said, seeking in brisk action to mask her own appalled distress. "Rosamund, if you lend Lucy your cloak, it will protect her a little until we can get her into the hackney."

Rosamund eagerly unclasped her cloak. Lilly lifted Lucy from the straw and draped the soft silk garment around her shoulders. The contrast between the shimmering silk and the girl's filthy, matted hair, thin cheeks, and torn shift was shocking.

"Can you walk?" Juliana half lifted Lucy to her feet and held her as she swayed dizzily.

"My head's spinning." Lucy's voice was weak and shaky. "I haven't stood up for days."

"You'll feel stronger in a minute," Emma said, stroking Lucy's emaciated arm. "I could drive a knife into Mother Haddock!" she added ferociously. "We didn't know you were in here until a few days ago. The bawd told her girls to keep quiet about it if they didn't want to find themselves joining you."

"There has to be a way to get even," Lilly muttered, staring around the attic as if taking it in for the first time. "She intended you should die in this hole."

"We'll think about getting even later." Juliana slipped a supporting arm around Lucy's waist. "Lilly, you take her other arm."

The gatekeeper was still in the doorway, watching the scene with scant interest. His little eyes focused sharply, however, when he saw Lucy on her feet. "Eh, you don't leave 'ere until I gets me money."

Lilly, at a nod from Juliana, withdrew the two crisp notes from her muff. "This is the sum of her debt." Mr. Cogg stretched out a hand for them, but she held on to the notes.

"However did you—"

"Hush, dear, don't talk until we're safely outside," Rosamund said, patting Lucy's hand. "We'll explain everything then."

"Give it 'ere, then." Mr. Cogg snapped his fingers.

"It has to be paid to Mistress Haddock," Juliana said. "I'm not giving it to you until you give me a receipt for it."

Mr. Cogg shot her a look of intense dislike. "Fer such a young thing, you knows yer way around," he grumbled, turning back to the stairs. "Where was you brung up, then? In a moneylender's?"

It was intended to be a deep insult, but Juliana merely laughed, thinking that Sir Brian Forsett's example when it came to money dealings could as well have been set in a moneylender's.

She wrote out the receipt herself and stood over Mr. Cogg as he put his mark to it. Then she laid the forty pounds on the rickety table in his hut. "I have only a twenty-pound note. Does anyone have a guinea to give to this kind gentleman?"

Rosamund produced the required coin and they left the Marshalsea, Lucy hobbling on her bare feet between Juliana and Lilly. The footman and the hackney carriage were waiting where they'd left them; of Lucien there was no sign.

"Fetch Viscount Edgecombe from the tavern, if you please," Juliana instructed the servant, who was staring with unabashed curiosity at the pathetic scarecrow they were lifting into the hackney.

Lucy sank onto the cracked leather squabs with a groan. "Are you hungry, dear?" Emma inquired tenderly, sitting beside her and chafing her hands.

"I don't feel it anymore," Lucy told her, her voice still low and weak. "It was painful for the first week, but now I feel nothing."

"Where are we to take her?" Lilly sat opposite, a frown drawing her plucked eyebrows together. "We can't take her back to Mother Haddock."

"What about Mistress Dennison?" Juliana was looking out of the window, watching for her husband.

"No," Rosamund said. "She's already said she won't help Lucy."

"Lucy refused a wealthy patron that Mistress Dennison presented to her," Emma explained.

"He was a filthy pervert," Lucy said with more strength than she'd shown hitherto. "And I didn't need him or his money then."

"She was in the keeping of Lord Amhurst," Lilly said. "Mistress Dennison had arranged the contract and thought Lucy owed her a favor. It was only for one night, apparently."

"One night with that piece of gutter filth!" Lucy fell back, exhausted, and closed her eyes.

"Anyway, that's why Mistress Dennison won't help her," Rosamund stated.

"She can come back with me," Juliana declared with rather more confidence than she felt. The duke was not going to be best pleased with her as it was. Asking him to house the indigent Lucy in her present condition was a favor no one would blame him for refusing even in his most charitable frame of mind.

"Well, that's settled." Lilly sounded relieved as she set the seal on Juliana's offer. "And while you're getting better, Lucy, we'll try to persuade Mistress Dennison to take you in when you're ready to work again."

"She's quite good-hearted, really," Emma put in. "In fact they both are if you keep on the right side of them."

A discussion began on the likelihood of the Dennisons' relenting, but Juliana continued to peer out of the window toward the tavern. The footman finally reemerged and trotted back to the hackney. He was alone.

"Beggin' your pardon, m'lady, but his lordship says as how he's not ready to leave just yet and you should go on without him."

"Damn," Juliana muttered. The viscount was not a reliable partner in crime. Without him at her side things would go harder for her when they got back to Albermarle Street, and she wouldn't be able to refer Tarquin's complaints to her husband, as she'd intended doing. She debated going in after Lucien herself, then decided against it. If he was far gone in cognac, she'd achieve only her own discomfort.

"Very well. Tell the jarvey to return to Albermarle Street," she instructed, withdrawing her head from the window. Lucy was huddled between Lilly and Rosamund, a tiny, frail figure in her thin shift against the butterfly richness of the other women. She didn't look more than twenty. What kind of life had she led so far that she could have been condemned so young to such a hideous death?

Chapter 15

The carriage drew up on Albermarle Street and Juliana alighted, reaching up to help Lucy as her friends half lifted her down.

"Should we come in with you?"

Juliana, after a moment's reflection, shook her head. "No, I think I'd better do this alone, Emma. It could be a little awkward. I can manage to get Lucy up the steps without help."

"If you're sure," Rosamund said, trying to conceal her relief but not quite succeeding.

"You would be better employed persuading the Dennisons to shelter Lucy when she's recovered her strength," Juliana said, supporting Lucy with a strong arm at her waist. "I'll come to Russell Street tomorrow and tell you how she is. Also," she added with an intent frown, "I have an idea that I want to talk over with you all. And the other girls, too, if they'd be interested."

"Interested in what?" Lilly leaned forward, her eyes sharp.

"I can't explain here. I have to think it through myself first, anyway." She smiled and raised a hand in farewell. "Until tomorrow."

There was a chorus of good-byes as she supported Lucy

up the steps to the front door. Catlett opened it before she could knock, and for once his impassive expression cracked when he saw her companion. Juliana couldn't blame him. Lucy was a dreadful sight. Rosamund's incongruous, delicate, muslin-frilled cloak only accentuated her half-naked condition. However, Juliana merely nodded to Catlett as she helped the girl into a chair in the hall.

Lucy fell back, her face whiter than milk, her eyes closed, her heart racing with the effort of getting from the carriage to the chair. Juliana stood looking at her, for the moment nonplussed. What orders should she give? There must be spare bedchambers in the house, but did she have the right to dispose of one without the duke's leave? Probably not, she decided, but there didn't really seem to be much option.

"Catlett, would you ask the housekeeper to show me to—"

"What in the devil's name is going on here?"

Juliana spun round at the duke's voice. So he hadn't recovered his good humor in her absence—not that she'd expected that he would have. She glimpsed Quentin behind him, overshadowed by his brother, not so much by height as by Tarquin's sheer presence.

She cleared her throat and began, "My lord duke, this is the woman we brought from the Marshalsea, and—"

"Catlett, you may leave." The duke interrupted her with this curt order to the servant, who was staring at the pale, crumpled figure of Lucy, as fascinated as if she were a two-headed woman at the fair.

"Now you may continue," Tarquin said as Catlett melted away into the shadows behind the stairs.

Juliana took a deep breath. "If you please, sir—"

Lucy moaned faintly, and Quentin, with a muttered exclamation, pushed past his brother and bent over her.

Juliana tried again. "She's been starved," she said, her voice stronger as she thought of Lucy's plight. "Tortured with starvation and left to die in that filthy place. She needs to be looked after, and I said she could come here."

"Indeed, Tarquin, the girl has been shockingly mistreated." Quentin straightened, his expression stricken. "We should send for the physician as soon as she's put to bed."

The duke looked over at Lucy and his expression softened for a minute, but when he turned his eyes back to Juliana, they cooled again. "For the time being you may take her upstairs and hand her over to Henny. She will know what to do for her. But then I would like to speak with you in my book room."

Juliana stepped back from him and dropped a curtsy. "Thank you, my lord duke. I am yours to command." She lowered her eyes in feigned submission and thus missed the spark of reluctant amusement that flared in his eyes. When she looked up, it was extinguished. He gave her a curt nod and stalked off to his book room.

"Come, Juliana, I'll help you get the poor girl upstairs. She's barely conscious." Quentin lifted Lucy into his arms, seeming unaware of her filthy clothes and hair pressed to his immaculate white shirt and gray silk coat. He carried her to the stairs, Juliana following.

"I'll put her in the yellow bedchamber," Quentin said almost to himself, turning right at the head of the stairs. "Then we'll ring for Henny."

He laid Lucy on the bed and drew the coverlet over her with all the tenderness of a skilled nurse. Juliana rang for Henny and then sat on the edge of the bed beside Lucy. "How *dare* they?" she said with soft ferocity. "Look at her! And that place was full of skeletons . . . little children. . . . Oh, it's disgusting!"

"I wish it were possible to change such things," Quentin said uncomfortably.

"But *you* could!" Juliana sprang to her feet, her eyes flashing with a zealot's enthusiasm. "You and people like you. You're powerful and rich. You could make things happen. You *know* you could."

Quentin was saved from a reply by the arrival of Henny,

who took charge with smooth efficiency, showing no apparent surprise at the condition of her patient.

"Come, let's leave Henny to tend her." Quentin drew Juliana toward the door. "And you must go to Tarquin."

Juliana grimaced. "He seems very vexed."

"You could say that." A smile touched his mouth. "But if you play your cards right, he won't remain so. Believe it or not, he's really a very fair man. He was easygoing as a boy . . . except in the face of injustice or deliberate provocation." Quentin's smile broadened as he recollected certain incidents of their shared boyhood. "At those times we all learned to keep out of his way."

"I don't seem to be able to stay out of his way," she said with a helpless shrug. "If I'd been able to do that, I wouldn't be living here now."

Tarquin had been trying to recapture a sense of control over events. He couldn't understand how a chit of a girl could have such a profoundly disturbing effect on the smooth running of his life. But ever since he'd seen her through the peephole, naked in the candlelight, she'd exerted some power over him . . . a power that had intensified as he'd introduced her to the ways of passion. He was moved by her. He no longer knew what to expect—from her, from himself. It was not a pleasant sensation; indeed, he found it almost frightening.

When Juliana tapped at the door, he flung himself into the chair behind the massive mahogany desk and picked up a sheaf of papers. "Enter." He didn't look up from the documents as the door opened.

Juliana stood in the doorway, waiting for him to acknowledge her. Instead he said, still without looking up, "Close the door."

Juliana did so and stepped into the room. Her chin went up. If he was intending to humiliate her by this insulting treatment, he would find it didn't work. Without invitation she sat down casually on a chair, her wide skirts flowing gracefully around her, and picked up a copy of the *Morning Post* from a side table.

Tarquin glanced up, and that same glimmer of reluctant laughter sprang to his eyes as he surveyed the red head bent over the newspaper, the graceful curve of her neck, the absolute resistance radiating from the still figure. Viscountess Edgecombe wasn't yielding an inch.

He put the papers aside and said, "Let's not beat around the bush, *mignonne*. As I understand it, you intend to form an alliance with Lucien. Is that correct?"

Juliana's eyebrows lifted. "I don't know what you mean, sir. The viscount is my husband. I am absolutely allied with him in the eyes of the Church and the law."

Tarquin's lips thinned. "I tell you straight, Juliana, that I will not tolerate it. Also, as of now, you will have nothing further to do with Mistress Dennison's girls. They will not visit you here, and you will not visit them. You mustn't be tainted with the whorehouse."

"But am I not already tainted? What am I but your whore, bought under contract to a bawd?"

"You are my mistress, Juliana. That doesn't make you a whore."

"Oh, come now, my lord duke," she said scornfully. "You bought me for three thousand pounds, as I recall. Or was it guineas? I'm flattered that I should be worth so much to you, but I suppose the breeding aspect to this arrangement makes me more valuable. I may be naive, but I *do* know that men don't buy their mistresses. They buy whores."

"I think you've said all there is to say on that subject," the duke said coldly. "Repeatedly, I might add. I will now repeat myself. You will have no further contact with the girls on Russell Street. Henny will take care of that unfortunate creature upstairs until she's well enough to leave, at which point I'll give her a sum of money that will enable her to establish herself without a protector."

Quentin had said the duke was generous to a fault. It seemed he hadn't exaggerated, and this liberal benevolence toward a girl he didn't know from Eve rather took the edge off Juliana's hostility. However, since it didn't suit her plans to be cut off from Russell Street, the battle must continue.

"You're very kind, sir," she said formally. "I'm certain Lucy will be suitably grateful."

"For God's sake, girl, I'm not asking for gratitude," he snapped. "Only for your obedience."

"As I'm aware, I owe obedience only to my husband, sir."

"You owe obedience to the man who provides for you," he declared, standing up in one fluid movement. Juliana had to force herself to stand her ground as she found herself looking up at him.

He leaned forward, his flat palms resting on the desk. "You have already played into Lucien's hands by encouraging him to embarrass me. God only knows who saw you this morning. Who knew where you were going. Whom he will tell. He paraded you through the streets of fashionable London with a trio of High Impures, and he played you for a fool, you silly child. These naive schemes of retaliation will hurt you a damn sight more than they'll hurt me."

Juliana paled. It hurt her that he believed Lucien had made a fool of her. Surely, she deserved more credit than that. "Your cousin's conduct doesn't appear to have affected your standing in society so far, sir," she said with icy calm. "I fail to see why his wife should alter the situation." She curtsied again. "I beg leave to leave you, sir."

Tarquin came out from behind the desk. He took her chin and brought her upright. "Don't do this, Juliana," he said quietly. "Please."

She looked up at him, read the sincerity in his eyes and the harsh planes of his face. She recognized that he was offering her an opening to back down without loss of face, but her anger and resentment ran too deep and too hot to be swept away so easily.

"My lord, you reap what you sow."

For a long moment their eyes held, and she read a confusion of emotion in his. There was anger, puzzlement, resignation, regret. And beneath it all a torch of desire.

"So be it," he said slowly. "But bear in mind that *you* also reap what you sow." He bent his head to take her mouth with his. It was a kiss of war, and her blood rose to meet the power and the passion, the bewildering knowledge that she could fight tooth and nail yet respond with desperate hunger to the touch and the feel, the scent, the taste, the glorious rhythms, of his body.

When he released her, his gaze still held hers, taking in the full red richness of her lips, the delicate flush of desire against the creamy pallor of her cheeks, the deep jade depths of her eyes, the flame of her hair. He could feel her arousal pulsing like an aura, and he knew she was as aroused by the declaration of war as she was by passion.

"You have leave to leave me," he said.

Juliana curtsied and left, closing the door gently behind her. She passed an unfamiliar footman as she walked down the corridor toward the hall. "Do you know if Viscount Edgecombe has returned to the house?"

"I don't believe so, my lady."

He kept his eyes fixed on the middle distance beyond her head, and it occurred to Juliana that, with the exception of Henny, the servants in this house had been trained to avoid eye contact with their employers.

"Would you inform me when he does return?" she asked pleasantly. "I shall be in my parlor."

The footman bowed and she went on her way, her mind whirling as she tried to organize her thoughts. She couldn't free her mind from the bubbling volcano of her body. The duke had started something with that kiss that wouldn't be soon extinguished. She wondered if he'd known it . . . if it was the same for him. She guessed grimly that he knew what he'd done to her, and that unlike her, he was able to control his own responses.

Upstairs in the yellow bedchamber she found Lucy propped up on pillows, with Henny feeding her gruel. "Oh, you look so much better," she said, approaching the

bed. Lucy's hair was clean, although dull and straggly, and
her thin face was no longer grime encrusted. She wore a
white nightgown that clearly swamped her, but her dark
eyes had regained some life.

She turned her head toward Juliana and smiled weakly.
"I don't know who you are. Or where I am. But I owe you
my life."

Juliana shook her head briskly. She'd done no more than
any compassionate human being would have done, and
gratitude struck her as both unnecessary and embarrassing.
"My name's Juliana," she said, sitting on the edge of the
bed. "And you're in the house of the Duke of Redmayne.
I'm married to his cousin, Viscount Edgecombe."

Lucy looked even more bewildered. She shook her head
as Henny offered her another spoonful of gruel. "I don't
think I could eat any more."

"Aye, I daresay your belly's not used to being full,"
Henny said cheerfully, removing the bowl. "I'll leave you
with her Ladyship. Just ring the bell if you want me." She
indicated the rope hanging beside the bed and bustled out.

"How do you know Lilly and the others?" Lucy asked,
lying back against the pillows.

"Ah, there hangs a tale," Juliana said with a grin. "But
you look as if you need to sleep, so I'll tell you later, when
you're stronger."

Lucy's eyes were closing and she did not protest. Juliana
drew the curtains around the bed and tiptoed from the
room. She went to her own parlor and stood at the window, looking out over the garden, her brow knitted in
thought. Tarquin could prevent Lucy's friends from visiting
her in his house, but she couldn't see how he could prevent
her from visiting Russell Street if she had her husband's
permission to do so. It sounded as if he thought he could,
but how would he do so?

By compelling Lucien to withhold his permission, of
course. He could do that by withdrawing his financial support. So she had to get to Lucien before the duke did. She
had to find a way to persuade him to stand against Tarquin,

whatever pressure was brought to bear. It ought to be possible. Lucien didn't strike her as particularly clever. Vindictive, spiteful, degenerate, but not needle-witted. She should be able to run rings around him if she came up with the right motivation.

Quentin walked into the garden below her and strolled down a flagstone path. He carried a pair of secateurs and stopped beside a bush of yellow roses. He cut half a dozen and then added another six white ones from the neighboring bush. Juliana watched him arrange them artistically into a bouquet, a little smile on his face. It was astonishing how different he was from his half brother. In fact, it was astounding how vastly different the three Courtney men were from each other. Lucien was utterly vile. She believed that Tarquin, beneath the domineering surface, was essentially decent. She was not afraid she would come to harm under his protection. But he lacked his brother's sensitivity and gentleness.

Quentin came back into the house with his bouquet of roses, and she wondered who they were for. Lady Lydia, perhaps?

The thought popped into her head. Something had given her the impression that that would be a match made in heaven. And from what she'd seen, she guessed it was a match they both yearned for. Or at least *would* yearn for if they thought it could ever be a possibility. But the Duke of Redmayne stood between them. And the duke had little interest in taking Lady Lydia to wife—he was merely satisfying an obligation. Maybe she could change that. People often didn't know how to get out of their own tangles. Witness herself, she thought wryly.

There was a tap at her door, and Lord Quentin came in at her response. He carried the roses, and for a minute she thought they were for her. But he said with a quick smile, "I thought your friend might take comfort from some flowers. They have such a lovely scent and they're so fresh and alive. I don't wish to burst in upon her unannounced, so I wondered if you would accompany me to her chamber."

"Yes, of course." Juliana sprang to her feet. Her hoop swung in a wide arc as she hastened eagerly to the door. A small round table rocked under the impact of the hoop. She paused to steady the table automatically before resuming her swift progress. "She was feeling sleepy when I left her, but it would be lovely to open one's eyes on a bowl of roses. Aren't they beautiful?"

Quentin smiled as she buried her nose in their fragrance. "You have only to give order for the servants to cut some for your own apartments."

Juliana looked up quickly, afraid that he might have read her mind earlier. "Oh, I would pick them myself," she said. "But someone has already put roses in my bedchamber and boudoir." She accompanied him down the corridor to Lucy's chamber, wishing she had the art of small talk to cover her moment of awkwardness.

She opened Lucy's door quietly and tiptoed in, peeping behind the bed curtains. Lucy opened her eyes and offered a tired smile.

"Lord Quentin has brought you some roses." Juliana stood aside so that Quentin could approach the sickbed. "I'll ring for a maid to put them in water." She reached for the bellpull, then stepped back in case Quentin wished to talk to Lucy alone. He might intend to have a pastoral conversation. But Quentin's voice was cheerful, and more avuncular than clerical, as he asked Lucy how she did and laid the roses on the bedside table.

"The maid will look after these. I don't wish to disturb your rest."

"Thank you, sir." Lucy's smile brightened considerably. "I don't know what I've done to deserve such kindness."

"You don't have to deserve it," Juliana stated with a touch of indignation. "When someone's been so ill treated, they're entitled to all the compassion and care that decent people can offer. Isn't that so, Lord Quentin?"

"Indeed," he agreed, even as he wondered why he

found her passionate declaration such a novel concept. As a man of the cloth, he should have been expounding the principle himself, but somehow it hadn't crossed his mind until now. The poor were a fact of life. Cruelty and indifference were everywhere in their lives. If he'd thought of their plight at all, he'd simply considered it to be one of the inevitable evils of their world. The rich man in his castle, the poor man at his gate. Juliana was opening his eyes on a new landscape.

Lucy looked incredulous, and he was glad he hadn't shown his own surprise at Juliana's revolutionary doctrine. "I'll leave you to your rest," he said. "But should you ever wish to talk to me, please send for me." He bowed and eased out of the room.

"What would I talk to him about?" Lucy inquired, struggling up on the pillows. "I wouldn't dare to send for him."

"He's a clergyman," Juliana informed her, sitting on the edge of the bed. "So if you wanted to talk on churchy matters, then, of course, he'd be available."

"Oh, I see." Lucy looked less bewildered. "Tell me your story, Juliana. I feel much stronger now."

Juliana told her as much as the other girls knew, breaking off when a maid entered to put the roses in water. Henny came in a few minutes later with a hot posset for the invalid. Juliana left to dress for dinner.

In her bedchamber she examined herself in the cheval mirror, frowning at her untidy appearance. Her morning's activities in the Marshalsea had wreaked havoc with her earlier elegance. It was disconcerting to think that she'd had her confrontation with the duke looking like a grubby schoolgirl. That hadn't prevented him from kissing her, however. She knew she hadn't mistaken the desire in his eyes, and surely he couldn't have feigned the passion of that kiss. Perhaps he found scruffy gypsies arousing. Bella at Russell Street had described in her worldly way some of the strange fancies of the men who visited there. Nuns and schoolgirls . . . who was to say the duke was any different?

Henny bustled in at that point, and she put the interesting question aside, submitting to the deft, quick hands of the abigail, who plaited her hair and arranged the unruly curls that wouldn't submit to the pins into artful ringlets framing her face. She didn't ask Juliana's opinion about her gown but chose a sacque gown of violet tabby opened over a dark-green petticoat. She arranged a muslin fichu at the neck, adjusted the lace ruffles at her elbows, twitched the skirt straight over the hoops, handed her a fan and her long silk gloves, and shooed her downstairs like a farmer's wife with her chickens. But Juliana found this treatment wonderfully comforting. She had not the slightest inclination to argue with the woman or play the mistress to her servant.

"Ah, well met, my lady. Shall we go down together?" Lucien emerged from his bedchamber as she passed. His voice was slightly slurred, his eyes unfocused, his gait a trifle unsteady. The reek of cognac hung around him. "Don't in general dine at m'cousin's table. Dull work, except that the wine's good and his chef is a marvel. But thought I'd honor my bride, eh?" He chuckled in a restrained fashion so that it brought forth no more than a wheeze. "Take my arm, m'dear."

Juliana took the scarlet-taffeta arm. It was utterly unimpeachable for her to go into dinner on her husband's arm. But how it would plague the Duke of Redmayne! She smiled up at Lucien. "After dinner, my lord, perhaps I could speak with you in private."

"Only if you promise not to bore me."

"Oh, I can assure you, sir, I shall not bore you." Her eyes, almost on a level with his, met and held his suddenly sharp gaze as he looked across at her. Then he smiled, a spiteful smile.

"In that case, my lady, I shall be honored to give you a moment of my time." He stood aside with a bow to allow her to precede him into the drawing room.

Chapter 16

George Ridge sat staring into his turtle soup with the air of a man who has undergone a deep shock. Around him the noise and revelry in the Shakespeare's Head tavern rose to a raucous level as the customers washed down the tavern's famous turtle soup with bumpers of claret. A group of Posture Molls was performing in the middle of the room, but George barely noticed their lewdly provocative positions as they exposed the most intimate parts of their bodies to the patrons. Posture Molls operated on a look-but-don't-touch principle, arousing the spectators to wild heights but refusing to make good the promises of their performance.

It was a lucrative business and ran less risk of the pox than more conventional whoredom. But George was unmoved. He believed in getting his money's worth and considered this form of entertainment to be a snare and a delusion. When the girls crawled around to pick up the coins showered upon them by the overexcited audience, he turned his back in a pointed gesture of dismissal. One of the women approached him, her petticoat lifted to her waist. She pushed her pelvis in his face and reached to stroke his hair. He slapped her hand away and cursed her, half rising from his chair in a threatening movement.

"Stinking whoreson," the woman said, her lip curling. "You look but you don't pay. A plague on you." She spat contemptuously into the sawdust at his feet and stalked off, still holding her shift to her waist as she went in search of a more appreciative member of the audience.

George took up his tankard of punch and drained it, reaching forward to the bowl in the middle of the table and ladling the fragrant contents into the pewter tankard. He gulped down half of it and returned to his turtle soup.

Juliana was married to a viscount! He dropped his spoon into the pewter bowl with a clatter as for the first time this fact really penetrated his brain. He hadn't been able to credit it at first, when the groom in the stables had told him nonchalantly that he was in the employ of the Duke of Redmayne. George had offered a description of the two men he'd seen with Juliana, and the groom had identified them as the duke and his brother, Lord Quentin. A description of the sickly-looking gentleman who'd gone off with the women that morning brought forth a contemptuous curl of the lip and the information that it must have been Viscount Edgecombe, His Grace's cousin. And then the startling words: "Just married yesterday. Brought 'is wife back 'ere . . . poor creature!"

Wife! It wasn't possible, but the groom had absolutely identified Lady Edgecombe as a lady with unmistakably striking hair and a taller than usual figure. There could be no possible doubt.

George picked up his spoon again. No sense wasting an expensive delicacy. He scraped the bowl with his spoon, then wiped it out with a hunk of bread. Then he sat back and glared at the grimy wall. Behind him there were bursts of laughter and applause. He sneaked a look over his shoulder and then hastily turned his eyes away. Two women were apparently coupling on a table. George found it deeply offensive. Such depravity didn't go on in Winchester, or even in the stews of Portsmouth, where you could find a sailor and his whore making the beast with two backs on every park bench.

He would have left the Shakespeare's Head at this point, except that he'd ordered a goose to follow the soup, thinking that a good dinner might quell the roiling turmoil in his belly. If Juliana was truly married to a viscount, then she couldn't marry George Ridge. Unless it had been a Fleet marriage. The thought gave him some hope, so he was able to face the platter of roast goose swimming in its own grease with more enthusiasm than he might otherwise have shown.

He chewed with solemn gusto, tearing the bird apart with his fingers, spearing potatoes on the point of his knife, heedless of the grease running down his chin, as he drank liberally of the bottle of claret that the landlord had thumped down at his elbow. He was now oblivious of the riotous goings-on behind him. A Fleet marriage seemed more and more likely. How could Juliana in such a few days be truly married to a duke's cousin? George didn't know much about the highest echelons of the aristocracy, but he was pretty certain they didn't marry on a whim. And they didn't marry women with no name, even if they were gently bred, as Juliana certainly was. So it must be some whoredom arrangement. Presumably she'd been tricked by an illegal ceremony. It made perfect sense, since George had had difficulty imagining Juliana's seeking her bread by selling her body.

Feeling immeasurably more cheerful, he wiped his chin with his sleeve and called for a bottle of port and a dish of lampreys. Juliana would have to be grateful for the prospect of rescue once she understood the falsity of her present position. He, of course, would have to be very magnanimous. Not many men would wed a harlot. He would be sure to point this out to Juliana. That and the promise to remove all suspicions of her involvement in his father's death should produce abject submission to his every fancy.

He grinned wolfishly and stuck his fork into the dish of eellike fish, scooping them into his mouth without pause until the dish was empty; then he launched an attack on a steamed pudding studded with currants.

Two hours later, overcome by sleepiness, but having first ensured that he was sitting firmly upon his money pouch, he allowed his head to fall upon the table and was soon snoring loudly amid the debris of his dinner. No one took the slightest notice of him.

Viscount Edgecombe took a gulp of cognac and gave a crack of amusement as he stared at his wife in her parlor after dinner. "By all means, I'll show you the town, m'dear." He hiccuped once and chortled again. "I can show you some sights. Gad, yes." He drained his glass and laughed again.

Juliana said steadily, "His Grace will not care for it."

"Oh, no, that's for sure." Lucien blearily tried to focus his eyes, producing only a squint. "He'll forbid it, of course." He frowned. "Could make himself a nuisance, you know."

"But you're not under his control, are you, sir?" She opened her eyes wide. "I can't imagine your submitting to the orders of anyone."

"Oh, ordinarily, I wouldn't," he agreed, refilling his glass from the decanter. "But I'll tell you straight: Tarquin holds the purse strings. Very generous, he is, but I'd not care to risk his closing the purse on me. I can't tell you how expensive it is to live these days."

"Why does he finance you?" She waited for a coughing fit to subside as he choked on the cognac.

"Why, m'dear, in exchange for agreeing to this sham marriage," he told her with a final wheeze.

"Then surely you could say that if he doesn't continue, you'll repudiate me as your wife," suggested Juliana, idly smoothing the damask on the sofa where she sat.

Lucien stared at her. "Gad, but you're a devious creature. Why's it so important to have at Tarquin?"

Juliana shrugged. Lucien presumably didn't know the full details of her contract with the duke. "I object to being manipulated in this way."

A sly look crept into Lucien's hollowed eyes. "Ah," he said. "Tarquin said you would do his bidding. Have something on you, does he?"

"Merely that I am friendless and without protection," she said calmly. "And therefore dependent upon him."

"So why would you want to put his back up?" The sly look hadn't left his eyes. "Not in your interests, I would have said."

"I have a legal contract that he can't renege upon," Juliana replied with a cool smile. "It was drawn up by a lawyer and witnessed by Mistress Dennison. He is obliged to provide for me whatever happens."

Lucien produced his skeletal grin at this. "Out of the goodness of my heart, m'dear, I'll tell you you'll have to get up very early in the morning to put one over on Tarquin."

"That may be so," Juliana said with a touch of impatience. "But I wish to go to Covent Garden. I wish to see what it's like there, how the people live, particularly the women. Your cousin wouldn't take me to the places I wish to visit, but you can. Since you spend your time there, anyway, as I understand it, taking me along shouldn't inconvenience you in any way."

"Well, I daresay it won't. But it'll inconvenience Tarquin." He took more cognac and surveyed her costume critically. "Of course, society women do frequent the bagnios. Poor Fred always has some courtier's lady in tow."

"Poor Fred?"

"Prince of Wales. Everyone calls him Poor Fred—poor devil can never get anything right, leads a dog's life. His father loathes him. Humiliates him in public at every opportunity. Wouldn't change places with him for all the crowns in Europe."

"So there wouldn't be anything really objectionable about my coming with you?"

He choked again on his cognac. "Nothing objectionable! Little simpleton!" he exclaimed. "It ain't respectable, m'dear girl. But not everyone in society is as high starched as my estimable cousins." He set his glass down with a snap. "It'll be worth it, just to see Tarquin's face. We'll do it, and if he threatens to cut me off, I'll threaten him back."

"I knew you had spirit," Juliana declared warmly, hiding her revulsion under a surge of triumph. "Shall we go at once?"

"If you like." Lucien surveyed her again with a critical frown. "Don't suppose you've a pair of britches, have you?"

"Britches?" Juliana looked astonished. "I *did* have, but—"

"No matter," he said, brusquely interrupting her. "You've too many curves to be appealing. No way you could look like a lad, however hard you tried."

For a moment Juliana could think of nothing to say. She remembered the look of repulsion in his eyes when he'd seen her in her nightgown. Finally she asked slowly, "You like your women to dress up as lads, sir?"

He grimaced. "I prefer the lads themselves, my dear. But if it must be a woman, then I've a fancy for the skinny kind, who can put on a pair of britches and play the part."

Dear God, what else was she going to learn about her husband? She'd heard of men who liked men, but it was a capital crime, and in the bucolic peace of Hampshire such preferences carried the touch of the devil.

"What a little innocent you are," Lucien mocked, guessing her thoughts. "It'll be a pleasure to rid you of some of that ignorance. I'll introduce you to the more unusual amusements to be had in the Garden. And who knows, maybe you'll take to them yourself. Fetch a cloak."

Juliana had a moment of misgiving. What was she getting herself into? She was putting herself in the hands of this vile, pox-ridden degenerate . . . but, no, she wasn't. She had money of her own and could return home at any time without his escort. And she *did* want to see for herself what happened to the women who earned their living in the streets of Covent Garden.

"I'll only be a moment." She went to the door. "Will you await me here?"

"My pleasure," he said with a bow. "So long as the decanter's full." He strolled to the table to refill his glass.

Juliana took a dark hooded cloak from her wardrobe and clasped it at her throat. She wore no jewelry because she had none, except for the slim gold band on her wedding finger, and the richness of her gown was concealed by the cloak. It made her feel a little easier about this expedition, almost as if she were going incognito.

She hastened back to her parlor, where Lucien was slumped on the sofa, sunk in reverie, twirling the amber contents of his glass. He looked up as she came in, and it seemed to take a minute for recognition to enter his dull eyes. "Oh, there you are." He stood somewhat unsteadily, and Juliana noticed that his speech had become more slurred in the few minutes she'd been absent.

"Are you sure you're well enough to go out?"

"Don't be a fool!" He threw back his head and in one movement poured the remaining liquid in his glass down his throat. "I'm fit as a flea. And I've no intention of spending the evening in this mausoleum." He weaved his way toward her where she stood in the doorway and rudely pushed past her.

Frowning, she followed him out of the house and into a passing hackney.

Five minutes later Tarquin emerged from the drawing room. He had decided to go to White's Chocolate House on St. James's Street for an evening's political discussion and a game of faro. Taking his cloak and gloves from the footman, he told him to leave the front door in the charge of the night watchman since he expected to be back late. He then went forth into the balmy evening. It didn't occur to him to ask where Juliana might be. He assumed she was in her parlor, or sitting with the invalid in the yellow bed-chamber.

Juliana, swathed in her cloak, sat back in a corner of the hackney, watching the scene through the window as the vehicle stopped and started through streets as thronged as if it were midmorning. The main thoroughfares were lit with oil lamps, but when they turned onto a side street, the only light came from a link boy's lantern as he escorted a pair of gentlemen, who walked with their hands on their sword hilts.

Covent Garden was as lively as it had been the previous evening. The theater doors were already closed, the play having begun, but the hackney took them to the steps of St. Paul's Church and halted. Juliana alighted, drawing her cloak tightly around her. Lucien followed somewhat unsteadily and tossed a coin up to the jarvey, who, judging by his scowl, considered it less than adequate payment.

A noisy crowd was gathered before the steps of the church; a man played a fife barely heard above the ribald yells and drunken curses as the throng swayed and surged.

"What's going on over there?"

Lucien shrugged. "How should I know? Go and look."

Juliana made her way to the outskirts of the crowd, standing on tiptoe to see over the heads.

"Push your way to the front," Lucien said at her shoulder. "Politeness won't get you anywhere in this place." He began to shove his way through the throng, and Juliana followed, trying to keep at his heels before the path closed behind him. She remembered how Tarquin and Quentin had cleared a way through the crowd at the theater; but they'd done it almost by magic, never raising their voices or appearing to push at all. Lucien cursed vilely, using his thin body like a battering ram, and he received as many curses as he threw out. Somehow they reached the front of the crowd.

A man in rough laborer's clothes stood on the steps, beside him a woman in a coarse linen smock and apron, her hair hidden beneath a kerchief. Her hands were bound and she had a rope halter around her neck. She kept her eyes on the ground, her shoulders hunched as if she could make herself invisible. The crowd roared with approval when the man caught her chin and forced her to look up.

"So what am I bid?" he called loudly above the noise. "She's good about the 'ouse. Sound in wind and limb . . . good, strong legs and wide 'ips." He touched the parts in question and the woman shivered and tried to draw back. But the man grabbed the loose end of the halter and jerked her forward again.

Lucien laughed with the crowd. Juliana, horror-struck, glanced up at him and saw such naked, malevolent enjoyment on his face that she felt nauseated. "What's going on?"

"A wife-selling. Isn't it obvious?" Lucien didn't take his eyes off the scene on the steps as the husband enumerated the wretched woman's various good points.

Suddenly a voice bellowed above the crowd. "Ye've 'ad yer fun, Dick Begg. Now, let's be done with this." A brawny man pushed his way to the steps and jumped up beside the couple. The woman flushed deepest crimson and tried to turn aside, but her husband jerked again on the halter he still held, and she was able only to avert her head.

"Ten pound," the newcomer declared. "An' ye leave 'er alone from now on."

"Done," the husband announced. Both men spat on their palms and clapped them together to seal the bargain. The second man counted ten coins into the other's hand while the crowd roared its approval again; then he took the end of the halter and led the now weeping woman away from the crowd, toward the rear of the church.

Dick Begg pocketed his coins. "Good riddance to bad rubbish," he stated, grinning. "Niver did get on wi' the bitch anyways."

"How disgusting!" Juliana muttered. She'd heard of such auctions but had never seen one before. The crowd was dispersing now that the entertainment was over, until a fight started up between two burly costermongers. They were going at each other with bare fists, and swiftly a cheering, catcalling circle formed around them.

It was Lucien's turn to look disgusted. "Animals," he

said with a curling lip. He strode away toward the Green
Man tavern, not troubling to wait for Juliana.

She followed him into the low-ceilinged taproom, her
eyes immediately beginning to water with the tobacco
smoke that hung in a thick blue haze in the air.

"Blue ruin!" Lucien bellowed at a passing potboy as he
pulled out a bench at a long table and sat down. The bench
was as filthy as the stained encrusted planking of the table.
Juliana brushed ineffectually at the grime and then sat
down with an internal shrug. Her cloak was dark and
would keep most of it off her gown.

"Not too nice in your tastes, I trust," Lucien said with a
sneer.

"Not overly," Juliana responded evenly. "But this place
is a pig sty."

"Don't let mine host hear you saying that." Lucien
chuckled. "Very proud of his establishment is Tom King."
He slapped a sixpence on the table when the potboy appeared with a stone jar and two tankards. "Fill 'em up."

The lad did so, wiping the drips from the table with his
finger, which he then licked. His hands were as filthy as his
apron, and his hair hung in lank, greasy locks to his shoulders. He took the sixpence and vanished into the crowd as
someone else yelled for him. He didn't arrive quickly
enough, apparently, because he was greeted with a mighty
clout that sent him reeling against the wall.

Juliana gazed at the scene in horrified fascination, blinking her watering eyes. When Lucien pushed a tankard
toward her with the brisk injunction "Drink," she carried
it to her lips and absently took a large gulp.

Her throat was on fire, her belly burning as if with hot
coals. She doubled over the table, choking, her eyes streaming.

"Gad, what a milksop you are!" Lucien thumped her
back with his flat palm, using considerable force. "Can't
stomach a drop of gin!" But she could hear his malicious
amusement as he continued to pound her back. Presumably, she was reacting exactly as he'd intended.

"Leave me alone!" she said furiously, straightening and shaking off his hand. "Why didn't you warn me?"

"And spoil my fun?" He clicked his tongue reprovingly.

Juliana set her lips and pushed the tankard as far from her as she could. She wanted a glass of milk to take away the taste, but the thought of asking for such a thing in this place was clearly absurd.

"Gad, it's Edgecombe!" A voice called from the mists of smoke. "Hey, dear fellow, what brings you here? Heard you'd become leg-shackled."

Three men weaved their way through the room toward them, each carrying a tankard. Their wigs were askew, their faces flushed with drink, their gait distinctly unsteady. They were young, in their early twenties, but the dissipation behind the raddled complexions and bloodshot, hollowed eyes had vanquished all the bloom of youth.

Lucien raised a hand in greeting. "Come and meet my lady wife, gentlemen." He rose from the bench and bowed with mock formality as he indicated Juliana. "Lady Edgecombe, m'dear fellows. Madam wife, pray make your curtsy to Captain Frank Carson, the Honorable Bertrand Peters, and the dearest fellow of them all, Freddie Binkton." He flung his arm around the last named and hugged him before kissing him soundly.

Juliana stood up and curtsied, feeling ridiculous in these surroundings, but not knowing how else to behave. The three men laughed heartily and bowed, but she sensed a hostile curiosity in all their expressions as they scrutinized her in the dim light.

"So why the devil did ye take a wife, Lucien?" Captain Frank demanded, having completed his examination of Juliana. "Thought you was sworn to bachelorhood."

"Oh, family pressure, m'dear." Lucien winked and took another swig of his tankard. "My cousin thought it would avoid scandal."

They all went into renewed laughter at this, and Juliana sat down again. There was something indefinably horrible about the group. They made her skin crawl, and she could

feel their covert glances even though they appeared now to
ignore her, all of them absorbed in some scandalous tale of
the captain's. She glanced toward the door, where an elegant lady stood, a footman at her back, deep in conversation with a rotund gentleman in an old-fashioned curly
wig.

As Juliana watched, the elderly gentleman counted out
five coins into the lady's hands. She passed them to the
footman, who pocketed them; then she tucked her arm
into the gentleman's, and they entered the tavern and went
up a rickety pair of stairs at the rear of the taproom. The
footman leaned against the doorjamb, idly picking his
teeth, watching the passersby.

The woman had looked too prosperous to be soliciting
on the streets, Juliana reflected. And certainly too well
dressed to be taking her clients to a back room in this
noisome place. She must remember to ask Lilly to explain
it.

"Lud, madam, you're not drinking?" the Honorable
Bertrand declared in mock horror. "Lucien, Lucien, you
neglect the dear lady shamefully."

Lucien grinned. "Tried her on blue ruin, but it didn't
seem to suit her. What else can I offer you, my dear? Ale,
perhaps? Port?"

"Milk punch, if you please, sir," Juliana said, her nerves
prickling as she realized they wanted to make sport of her
in some way. She glanced around, but there would be no
help available in this riotous assembly. A couple were rolling around on the floor, the woman's legs in the air, her
skirts tumbled about her head, exposing her body to the
waist. Juliana felt sick. She pushed back the bench and
stood up.

"If you'll excuse me, my lord, I find I have the headache.
I'll take a hackney outside."

"Oh, but I don't excuse you," Lucien slurred, grabbing
her hand and pulling her back beside him. "You owe obedience to your husband, madam, and your husband bids
you keep him company and drink your milk punch."

Juliana thought she could probably break Lucien's hold without too much difficulty, but the eyes of the others were fixed upon her with a sinister intensity, waiting to see what she would do. She couldn't break free from them all if they tried to hold her. No one in this place would come to her aid. And she would be utterly humiliated. And Lucien would relish every minute of it. It was what he'd enjoyed about the wife-selling. The woman's total degradation had made him lick his lips like a hyena salivating over a rotting carcass.

She sat down again with a calm smile. "As you please, my lord."

Lucien looked a trifle disappointed; then he clapped his hands and bellowed for the potboy to bring milk punch. Juliana sat still, trying to maintain her calm smile and an air of nonchalant interest in her surroundings. The woman on the floor was on her hands and knees now, the man behind her, striking her flanks with his open palms as he mimicked the act of copulation to the roaring acclamation of his audience, who raised their tankards in a series of cheering toasts. The woman was laughing as much as anyone, throwing her head back and thrusting backward as if to meet him with orgasmic enjoyment.

Juliana kept the disgust from her face. She noticed that Lucien seemed to have no interest in the scene, although his friends were participating in the general uproar, thumping their tankards on the table and yelling encouragement.

"Does she get paid for that?" she inquired casually.

Lucien looked startled at the question. His blurry eyes searched her face suspiciously. She gave him a bland smile as if nothing about this place could possibly disturb her.

"I daresay," he said, shrugging. "It's not my idea of entertainment." He pushed back the bench and stood up. "Come."

"Where are we going?"

"To show you a few of the other entertainments available in this salubrious neighborhood. You did ask me to introduce you to London society . . . and your wish is ever my command, my dear ma'am.'' He bowed ironically.

Juliana curtsied in the same vein and took his arm, determined not to give him the satisfaction of seeing her dismay.

"Oh, must we go?" lamented the captain, getting unsteadily to his feet.

"Oh, yes. Wherever Lucien and his wife go, we go, too,'' Bertrand said, draining his tankard. "Wouldn't wish 'em to want for company on this bridal evening." He took Juliana's other arm, and she found herself ushered to the door and out into the Piazza.

"Where to now?" Freddie asked, looking around with an assumption of alert interest.

"Hummums," answered Lucien. "Show m'lady wife here what goes on in the steam rooms.''

"I don't think a steam room would be a good idea," Juliana demurred. "Won't it ruin my gown?"

"Gad, no, ma'am!" laughed the captain. "They'll take all your clothes from you and give you a towel. Very friendly place, the hummums."

Juliana was not going to the hummums, however friendly. She walked in the midst of her escort, awaiting her moment to break free. They had reached the corner of the Little Piazza, and she paused at the kiosk selling the obscene prints that she'd seen with the duke. "What do you think of these, gentlemen?" she asked with a smile.

Distracted, they peered into the kiosk. Juliana slipped her arms free and turned swiftly. Too swiftly. Her foot slipped on a patch of nameless slime on the cobbles, and she grabbed at the nearest object to save herself. Captain Frank proved a reliable support, although he laughed heartily at her predicament. When she was stable again, her heart was beating violently against her ribs, the captain was holding her too tightly for comfort, and she could see no escape from the hummums.

"I've a mind for a cockfight," announced Bertrand, slipping an arm through Lucien's. "What d'ye think, Lucien? It's been a while since we had a wager on the birds."

"By the devil's grace, so it has." Lucien was immediately diverted. "Madam wife, here, will enjoy it, I'll be bound." He gave Juliana his skeletal grin, and his eyes were filled with spiteful glee. "What d'ye say? The Royal Cockpit or the hummums, m'dear?"

At least in the cockpit she could keep her clothes on. And surely she could endure the cruelty if she kept her eyes closed. "The cockpit, if you please, sir." She managed another insouciant smile and achieved a certain satisfaction in seeing that her carefree response had disconcerted her husband.

"Let's to it, then!" Bertrand hailed a hackney. "After you, Lady Edgecombe."

She found herself hustled into the dark interior, the others piling in after her with much laughter. But there was an edge to their merriment that filled her with trepidation.

"The Royal Cockpit, jarvey." Lucien leaned out of the window to shout their direction. The jarvey cracked his whip, and the horses clopped off toward St. James's Park.

Chapter 17

❧❧❧

It was three o'clock in the morning when Tarquin returned home. He nodded at the night porter, who let him in, and headed for the stairs. The man shot the bolts again and returned to his cubbyhole beneath the stairs.

The duke strode into his own apartments, shrugging off his gold brocade coat. His sleepy valet jumped up from his chair by the empty fireplace and tried to stifle a yawn.

"Good evening, Your Grace." He hastened to take the coat from his employer, shaking it out before hanging it in the armoire. "I trust you had a pleasant evening."

"Pleasant enough, thank you." Tarquin glanced toward the armoire with its concealed door, wondering if Juliana was awake. Presumably she'd retired hours ago. His valet tenderly helped him out of his clothes and handed him a chamber robe. The duke sat at his dresser, filing his nails, while the man moved around the room, putting away the clothes, drawing back the bed curtains, turning down the bed.

"Will that be all, Your Grace?"

The duke nodded and dismissed him to his bed. Then he stepped through the door in the wardrobe and softly entered the next-door chamber. The bed was unslept in.

Henny snored softly on the chaise longue. Of Juliana there was no sign.

"Where the devil—"

"Oh, lordy me, sir!" Henny jumped to her feet at the sound of his voice. Her faded blue eyes were filmed with sleep. "You did give me a start." She patted her chest with a rapid fluttering hand.

"Where's Juliana?" His voice was sharp, abrupt.

"Why, I don't know, Your Grace. I understand she went out with Lord Edgecombe. They haven't returned as yet. But His Lordship is never one to seek his bed before dawn," she added, smoothing down her apron and tucking an escaping strand of gray hair back under her cap.

Tarquin's initial reaction was fury, mingled immediately with apprehension. Juliana could have no idea where and how Lucien took his pleasures. She was far too innocent of the urban world even to imagine such things. It was that very innocence that he'd believed would make her a compliant tool in his scheme. And now it was the same innocence combined with that defiant spirit that was leading her into the horrors of Lucien's world. Perhaps he'd erred in his choice. Perhaps he should have involved a woman who knew her way around the world, who would have entered a business contract with her eyes open. But such a woman would not have been virgin. And a whore could not be the mother of the heir to Edgecombe.

But he'd made his choice and was stuck with the consequences. He'd assumed he'd be able to put a stop to her mischief with Lucien, but he hadn't expected her to move so fast. He would learn the lesson well.

"Is everything all right, Your Grace?" Henny sounded troubled, a deep frown drawing her sparse eyebrows together, as she examined the duke's livid countenance. "If I did wrong—"

"My good woman, of course you didn't," he interrupted brusquely. "Lady Edgecombe is not in your charge. Take yourself to bed now. She won't need you tonight."

Henny looked a little doubtful, but she curtsied and left

the chamber. Tarquin stood for a minute, tapping his fingernails on a tabletop, his mouth grim.

He turned on his heel and went back to his own chamber, where he threw off the chamber robe and dressed swiftly in plain buckskin britches, boots, and a dark coat. The sword at his waist was no toy, and his cane was a swordstick. He strode downstairs again, and the puzzled night porter hurried to open the front door.

"Do you know what time Lord and Lady Edgecombe left?"

"No, Your Grace. I understood from Catlett that they left quite early, before Your Grace."

The duke cursed his own stupidity. Why hadn't he thought to check on her before he went out? He'd completely underestimated her, assuming her defiance to be no more than that of a thwarted schoolroom miss.

He left the house and called to a link boy, standing in a doorway opposite, his oil lamp extinguished at his feet. The lad shook himself awake and came running across the street. "Where ye goin', m'lord?"

"Covent Garden." It would be Lucien's first and probably last stop of the evening.

The lad busily trimmed the wick of his lantern before striking flint on tinder. The yellow glow threw a welcoming patch of illumination as the lad hurried along beside the duke, trotting to keep up with Tarquin's swift, impatient stride.

Juliana gulped the fresh air of St. James's Park, trying to get the stench of blood out of her nostrils. She couldn't rid her mind of the images, however. Even though she'd kept her eyes shut much of the time, the torn and mangled birds lying inert in the sawdust ring, surrounded by blood-soaked feathers like so many bloody rags, tormented her inner vision. She could still hear the deafening uproar as the wild betting had grown increasingly frenzied with each new pair of cocks, armed with silver spurs, being set down in the pit. Open mouths screaming encouragement and curses, drink-suffused eyes filled with greedy cruelty, the astonishing determination of the birds, fighting to the death even when clearly mortally wounded, were indelibly printed on her mind, and for the first time in her life she'd been afraid she would swoon.

Somehow she'd held on, aware of Lucien's quick glances at her deathly pallor, her closed eyes. She would not give him the satisfaction of breaking down at this hideous sight. His eyes, sunk in their dark sockets, grew more spiteful as the ghastly business progressed. Vaguely, she was aware that he was losing money hand over fist. Bertrand had cheerfully handed over a fistful of coins when Lucien turned out his empty pockets with a vile oath. But it wasn't until the fourth pair of birds had been tearing each other apart for forty-five minutes, blood and feathers spattering the audience on the lower ring of seats, that Lucien stood up from the matted bench and announced that he'd had enough of this insipidity.

Juliana had staggered out of the circular room, into the warm night. She wanted to crawl behind a bush and vomit her heart out. But she would not give her loathsome husband the pleasure.

"Well, my dear, I trust you're enjoying your introduction to London entertainments." Lucien took snuff, regarding her with a sardonic smile.

"It's certainly an education, my lord," she responded, both surprised and thankful that her voice was clear and steady.

Lucien frowned, glowering at her in the flickering light of the flambeaux illuminating the path from the cockpit to the gate. The woman was proving a disappointment. He'd expected her to break before now.

"Gad, man, but I've a thirst on me to equal a parched camel's," Frank Carson declared, loosening his already crumpled cravat. "Let's to the Shakespeare's Head. I've a mind for some dicing."

"Aye, good thought," Freddie approved, wiping his perspiring forehead with a lace-edged handkerchief. "You comin', Edgecombe?"

"Indeed," the viscount said. "The night's but barely begun. Come, madam wife." He grabbed Juliana's elbow and dragged her beside him down the path and onto the street. "Hackney! Hey, fellow. You there, idle bastard!" He waved belligerently at the driver of a cab, smoking peacefully in the stand of hackneys touting for customers emerging from the Royal Cockpit.

The jarvey cracked his whip and directed his weary horse across the street. "Where to, guv?"

"Shakespeare's Head." Lucien clambered up, leaving Juliana to follow. Her petticoat was grimy from the filthy matting in the cockpit, her dainty slippers soiled with something unidentifiable but disgusting. She drew her cloak tighter around her, despite the warmth of the night, and huddled into the shadowy corner as the others rowdily entered the vehicle.

She was extremely weary, and growing increasingly frightened. There was a frenzy to her husband's behavior, an alarming glitter in his burning eyes. His color was, if anything, worse than usual, and his breath rasped in his chest. She knew instinctively that he intended to make game of her in some way. Foolishly, she had attempted to ally herself with him in opposition to the duke. Foolishly she had thought she'd found the perfect motive for Edgecombe's cooperation. Foolishly she'd thought she could use him for her own ends. But Lucien was not cooperating with her. He was using her for his own amusement. And he wasn't finished yet.

There was nothing she could do, outnumbered as she was, but watch and wait and try to escape. Maybe they would become so involved in the gambling, so besotted with drink, that she could slip away without their noticing. Maybe a visit to the outhouse at the tavern would give her an opportunity.

Covent Garden was still thronged, but the crowd's inebriation had reached a new peak. Voices were loud and slurred, raised in anger and curses as often as in laughter. Men and women swayed over the cobbles, clutching stone jugs of gin, and Juliana watched a woman tumble in a drunken heap into the kennel, spilling the drink all over her. The man she was with fell on her with a roar, throwing her skirts up over her head to chanting encouragement from passersby.

Juliana averted her eyes. She had no idea whether the woman was a willing participant in what was going on, or merely insensible. She didn't seem to be struggling. Someone screamed from one of the shacks under the Piazza, a loud squeal like a stuck pig. Juliana shuddered, her scalp crawling. A woman came flying out of the building, wearing only a thin shift. A man raced after her, wielding a stick. His face was suffused with fury, the woman's pale with terror. Juliana waited for someone to intervene, but no one took any notice as the woman weaved and ducked through the crowd, trying to escape the ever-swinging stick.

"Filthy whore—up to her tricks again," Bertrand said, grinning. "The trollops think they can get away with murder."

"So what's she done?" Juliana demanded, her eyes snapping in the flickering orange light from flambeaux and oil lamps.

Bertrand shrugged. "How should I know?"

"Cheated, most like," Frank said. "It's what they all do. Cheat their customers, cheat their whoremasters, cheat their bawds. They all need a spell in Bridewell now and again. Shakes 'em up."

Juliana swallowed her rage. It would only amuse them. There had to be a way to improve the conditions under which these women sold themselves. She understood that it was the only living available to them . . . understood it now from bitter experience. But surely they need not be so vulnerable to the merciless greed of those who exploited them.

She found herself being ushered with a determined arm

toward a tavern, where the door stood open to the square and raucous, drunken voices poured forth with the lamplight on a thick haze of pipe smoke.

A bare-breasted woman swayed over to them with a tray laden with brimming tankards of ale. "What can I do fer ye, m'lords?" She winked and touched her tongue to her lips in a darting, suggestive fashion.

"Ale, wench!" Bertrand announced, slapping her backside with unnecessary vigor so that the tray shook in her hand and the ale spilled over. "Clumsy slut," he said with an offhand shrug, pulling out a bench from under one of the long tables.

Juliana sat down with the rest. She was parched, and ale was a welcome prospect. On the other side of the room, through the harsh babble of clamoring voices, she could hear the bets being called amid oaths and exclamations as the dice were rolled. There was a sharp edge of acrimony to the hubbub, a warring note that made the hairs on her nape prickle in anticipation of the violence that bubbled just beneath the surface of the apparent excitable jocularity.

A tankard of ale was thumped in front of her. The resulting spill dripped into her lap, but she'd long given up worrying about her clothes on this horrendous evening. If a soiled petticoat and a beer stain on her gown were the worst that would happen, she'd count herself fortunate. She drank deeply and gratefully.

After a few minutes, when it seemed that her companions were absorbed in wagering on the possible dimensions of a spreading ale spill, she rose to her feet, trying to slide unobtrusively away.

Lucien's hand shot out and grasped her wrist. She looked down at the thin white fingers and was distantly surprised at how strong they were. The blood fled from her skin beneath the grip. "Where are you off to, madam wife?" he demanded, his tone acerbic, his words slurred.

"The outhouse," she responded calmly. "You're hurting me."

He laughed and released her wrist. "It's out the back, past the kitchen. Don't be long now."

Juliana made her way through the room. She was accosted at almost every step by drunken revelers and dice players, but she avoided eye contact and shook the grasping hands from her arm with a disdainful air.

The privy was in an enclosed backyard, and Juliana could see no escape route. She wrestled with her skirts in the foul darkness, her head aching with the noise and the smoke, and her bone-deep weariness. How was she to get away? Lucien would delight in thwarting any attempt, and his friends would cheerfully lend their physical support. It wasn't worth risking the humiliation of defeat and Lucien's malevolent amusement.

She paused for a moment in the inn doorway before reentering the taproom. Lucien was watching the door, waiting for her reappearance. He beckoned imperatively and rose unsteadily to his feet as she approached. "We're going to play," he announced, taking her elbow. "You shall stand at my shoulder, madam wife, and smile on the dice."

Juliana could see no option, so she forced a smile of cheerful compliance and accompanied them to the dice table. They were greeted with rather morose stares, and room was somewhat unwillingly made for them at the table. Juliana yawned, swaying with exhaustion as the excitement grew with each throw of the dice. Lucien's voice grew increasingly slurred. A hectic flush stood out against his greenish pallor, and his eyes burned with a febrile glitter as the level in the brandy bottle he now held went steadily down.

He won initially and, thus encouraged, began to bet ever more immoderately. And as he grew more excited, so his losses mounted. He'd lost all his own money at the cockpit and now ran through Bertrand's loan, threw down his watch, a ring, and his snuffbox before resorting to IOUs, tossing them onto the table with reckless abandon. It was clear to Juliana through her sleepiness that his fellow players were not happy with these scrawled scraps of paper, and finally one of them declared disgustedly, "If you can't play with goods or money, man, I'll not throw again. I've no use for promises."

"Aye, what good's a piece of paper when a man wants to buy ale?" The chorus swelled and the faces pressed closer to the table, glaring at Lucien.

"Devil take you all," he swore. "My IOUs are as good as gold, I'll have you know. Underwritten by His Grace, the Duke of Redmayne. Present them at his house on Albermarle Street in the morning, and he'll pay you with interest."

"Who wants to wait till mornin'?" There was a rumble around the table, and one man half rose from his seat. He had massive fists, like sledgehammers, and a wandering eye that lent added menace to his drunken squint. "Pay up, *my lord*," he said with sneering emphasis, "or I'll 'ave the coat off yer back."

Lucien fumbled for his sword but not before Captain Frank Carson had hurled back his chair and leaped to his feet, his sword in his hand. "You dare to insult the honor of a gentleman!" he bellowed, his eyes rolling back in his head as he struggled to focus them. "Have at you, sir!" He lunged across the table. The burly man sidestepped with surprising agility, and the candlelight flickered on the blade of a cutlass. A woman screamed and the crowd in the taproom drew closer, some standing on their chairs to get a better view.

Juliana was now wide-awake. Her eyes flew to the door, tantalizingly open. But eager spectators pressed close behind them, and she was pinned to the table's edge. The mood in the room was ugly. Lucien and his friends, with drawn swords, faced a veritable army of knife-wielding rogues. The dice lay abandoned in the middle of the table, and the rowdy clamor died as a moment of expectant silence fell.

It was Freddie Binkton who broke the menacing tension. They were hopelessly outnumbered, their retreat cut

off by the spectators. "Let's not be hasty, now," he said
with a nervous titter. "Lucien, dear fellow, you must have
something about you to raise a bit of blunt. We can all
contribute something." He patted his pockets as if he could
conjure coins from their depths.

"I'd put in my watch," Bertrand said, adding dolefully,
"but I wagered it on that damn red cock . . . had no
more spirit than a mewling lamb. Gave up without a fight
. . . lost my watch . . . worth all of fifty guinea . . .
lost it for a paltry ten-pound wager." His voice trailed off
with his wandering attention, the sword in his hand drooping.

As if acceding to the truce, the ruffianly group lowered
their knives, relaxed their aggressive stance, and glared at
Lucien, waiting for his response.

Lucien looked around, his mouth tight, a pulse throbbing in his temples, the same febrile flush on his face, as
garish as a clown's paint. Juliana, standing so close to him,
could feel the savage fury emanating from his skin,
mingling with the sour smell of fear and sweat. His gaze fell
on her, and she shrank back, instinctively trying to merge
with the people around her. Something flared suddenly in
the pale-brown eyes, and he smiled slowly with a ghastly
menace.

"Oh, I believe I've something to sell," he said, barely
moving his lips.

"No!" Juliana whispered, her hand at her throat as she
understood what he intended. "No, you cannot!"

"Oh, but I believe I can, madam wife," he said airily.
"Wives are their husbands' chattel. You are mine, and I
may dispose of you how I please. You should be glad to be
of service, my dear." His hand shot out and gripped her
wrist again in that painful vise. "Someone bring me a
length of rope. We should do this properly."

"Come now, Lucien, it isn't right," Frank mumbled,
half-apologetically. He looked uneasily at Juliana, who simply stared back at him, unseeing in her horror.

"Don't be such a ninny," Lucien said with a petulant

scowl. "It's not for you to say what's right or not when it comes to my wife. Ah, rope." He took the rope handed him by a grinning ostler and looped it into a halter. "Here, madam. Bend your head."

"No!" Juliana pulled back from him, terrified as much by the evil embodied in the grinning death's-head countenance as by his intention. Someone grabbed her arms and pulled them behind her so she was forced to stand still. Lucien, still with that venomous grin, roughly pulled the halter over her head. Hands tugged and pulled at her, shoving her up onto the table. She fought them, her rage now superseding her terror. She kicked and scratched, barking her shins on the edge of the table as she was pushed and pulled and dragged upward. But despite her struggles, they got her onto the table, and Lucien seized the end of the halter.

Juliana, blinded by her wild rage, kicked at him, catching him beneath the chin with the sole of her shoe. He went reeling backward, dropping the rope. She made to jump from the table, but two men grabbed her ankles, holding her still as Lucien came up again, his eyes narrowed, one hand to his chin.

"Bitch," he said softly. "You'll pay for that."

She would have kicked him again if they hadn't been holding her ankles so tightly. She swayed dizzily on her perch, nausea rising in her throat, a cold sweat breaking out on her back. How had she walked into this nightmare? She'd known Lucien was vile, but not even in her darkest imaginings could she have suspected him capable of such viciousness. But the duke had known. He had always known what his cousin was capable of. He'd known but it hadn't stopped him from using her . . . from exposing her to this evil.

Lucien was calling in a drunken singsong, "So what am I bid for this fine piece, gentlemen? Shall we start at twenty guineas?"

A chorus of responses filled the air. Juliana looked down and saw little red eyes peering greedily up at her, stripping her naked, violating her with their lascivious grins. She couldn't move, her ankles were circled so tightly, and Lucien was pulling on the rope so that it cut into the back of her neck.

George Ridge awoke from his postprandial sleep as the shouts around him grew even more raucous. He raised his head, blinking, for a moment disoriented. He remembered where he was when he saw that he'd been sleeping in the midst of the detritus of his dinner. He belched loudly and lifted the bottle of port to his lips. There was a swallow left, and he smacked his lips, set the bottle down, and turned to call for another.

His eyes fell on the scene at the far side of the room. At first he couldn't make out what was going on, the noise was so loud, the crowd so thick. They were wagering on something, and there was a frenzied edge to the bidding that struck him forcefully. He blinked, shaking his head to rid his brain of muzziness. Then he blinked again and sat up.

Juliana was standing on the table. It couldn't be anyone else. Not with that tumbling forest fire of hair, those jade-green eyes flashing with such desperate fury, that tall, voluptuous figure.

But what in the devil's name was going on here? He pushed back his chair and stood up slowly, trying to isolate the words from the general hubbub. He heard someone call, "A hundred guineas. Come, gentlemen. My wife is worth at least that."

Wife! He approached the outskirts of the crowd. The bidding was getting livelier. A hundred and fifty, two hundred. Juliana stood like a stone. The man holding the rope, the man calling himself her husband, worked the crowd to renewed frenzy as he began to point out Juliana's attractions.

George's mouth was dry. He swallowed, trying to produce some saliva. The situation was unbelievable, and yet it was real. He pushed through the crowd, cleared his throat. "Five hundred guineas!" His voice sounded cracked and feeble, and at first no one seemed to hear him. He tried again, shouting. "I bid five hundred guineas for her."

Juliana heard George's voice, penetrating the trance into which she'd retreated from the unbearable humiliation, the waves of terror sucking at her. *Don't look at him. Don't react.* The instruction screamed in her brain even through her daze. She mustn't acknowledge him. If she refused to know him, then he couldn't prove her identity. She was still Viscountess Edgecombe. She was still under the protection of the Duke of Redmayne. Dear God, was she?

"Five hundred guineas," Lucien said, turning to George with another of his savage grins. "Why, sir, that's a jump bid if ever I heard one. But she's a prime article, and you've a fine eye."

George didn't seem to hear him. He was staring at Juliana, willing her to look at him. But she was a graven image, her eyes fixed straight ahead. He reached to touch her ankle, and she didn't move.

"Any advance on five hundred for my dear wife, or shall this gentleman have her?" Lucien called out merrily. "He's got a bargain, I'm telling you."

"There are times, Edgecombe, when you surprise even me with the depths of your depravity." The cool voice cut through the raucous merriment as the Duke of Redmayne crossed the room from the door, where he'd been standing unnoticed for the last few minutes.

The nightmare had such a grip upon her that for a moment Juliana didn't react. Then the clear tones of salvation pierced her trance. Slowly she turned on her perch, George forgotten in the flood of incredulous relief. He'd come for her.

"Tarquin . . ." It was more plea than statement, as if she still didn't dare to believe that he was there.

"I'm here," he affirmed. His voice was a caress, the soft reassurance balm to her agonized soul. His gray gaze encompassed her, all-seeing; then he turned on Lucien.

Lucien shrank back against the table as his cousin's livid eyes blazed at him. A muscle twitched in the duke's cheek, but he said nothing, merely tapped one clenched fist into the palm of his other hand. Then, very slowly, he brought up the fist and—almost gently, it seemed—touched Lucien on the edge of his chin. The viscount fell back into the crowd without a sound.

A murmur passed through the throng as the duke's eyes ran slowly around them. Suddenly a wicked blade flickered in his hand at the end of the swordstick. He still said nothing, but the crowd fell back, and the two men holding Juliana's ankles stepped away from the table.

George Ridge cleared his throat. He didn't know what was going on here, but he could see his prize slipping away from him. The newcomer spun round at the sound, and George flinched from the piercing stare, as cold and lethal as an arrowhead. He dropped his gaze in involuntary submission to this unknown but infinitely more powerful force.

Tarquin turned back to Juliana. He reached up and lifted her to the ground. He removed the halter and threw it into the crowd.

His eyes were still those he'd turned upon Lucien, cold and deadly, but he touched her hair, brushing a strand from her forehead. His long fingers moved fleetingly over the curve of her cheek. "Are you hurt?"

She shook her head. Her voice was barely a whisper, but she managed to say frankly, "Only my pride."

Surprise glimmered in his eyes, softening the implacable steadiness of his gaze. Any other woman would have broken down in tears and hysteria. But Juliana was unique. "Can you walk?"

Her knees were quivering uncontrollably, but there was something in his appraising scrutiny that gave her strength to say "Of course," even as she clutched his arm for support. Somehow she put one foot in front of the other as the crowd fell back. Then they were outside. Dawn was breaking, and a curious quiet had fallen over the Piazza and the square. A few bodies lay sleeping under the colonnades, a pair of slatternly women leaned in a doorway, drinking ale between yawns. A shout and a crash came from Tom King's coffeehouse as a man flew through the door to land in the gutter, where he lay in a heap, clutching a stone jar of gin.

The duke raised a finger and a hackney appeared as if by magic. Tarquin gave Juliana a boost into the interior with an unceremonious hand under her backside and followed almost in the same movement, pulling the door shut with a slam.

For the first time in hours Juliana was no longer terrified. The gloomy, musty interior of the carriage was a haven, private and utterly protected. Faint gray light came through the window aperture, showing her the duke's countenance as he sat opposite, regarding her in reflective silence.

"What are you thinking?" Her voice sounded shrunken, as if the events of the night had leached all strength from it.

"Many things," he replied, running his fingertips over his lips. "That you are the most perverse, stubborn, willful wench it's ever been my misfortune to have dealings with. . . . No, let me finish answering the question." He held up an arresting hand as Juliana's mouth opened indignantly. "That Lucien's evil tonight surpassed even my expectations; and most of all, that I should never have let you set eyes on him."

"So you're sorry you devised this demonic scheme?"

"No, I didn't say that. But I deeply regret involving you."

"Why?"

Tarquin didn't immediately reply. It was on the tip of his tongue to say simply that she wasn't cut out for the role, not sufficiently compliant. It was how he believed he would have responded just a few short hours ago. But something had happened to him when he'd seen her on that table, exposed to the sweating, lusting, depraved gaze of London's vicious underworld. When he'd seen her freshness, her simplicity, her ingenuous candor mentally fingered by that vile mob, he'd known a rage greater than any he could remember. And to his discomfort and confusion that rage was directed at himself as much as at Lucien.

"Why?" Juliana repeated. "Am I not sufficiently biddable, my lord duke?" As her terror receded, her bitterness grew. On one level Tarquin was as guilty of that hideous violation as Lucien had been. "I'm sorry to have put you to such inconvenience this evening." She tore angrily at a loose cuticle on her thumb, stripping the skin away with her teeth.

Tarquin leaned over and took her hand from her mouth. He clasped the abused thumb in his warm palm and regarded her gravely in the growing light. "I'm willing to accept a hefty share of the blame for this night's doings, Juliana, but you, too, bear some responsibility. You chose to cultivate Edgecombe to be avenged upon me. Will you deny it?"

Honesty forced her to shake her head. "But what else would you expect me to do?"

The exasperated question brought a low, reluctant chuckle to his lips. "Oh, I expected you to be good and obedient and allow me to know what's best for you. Foolish of me, wasn't it?"

"Very." Juliana tried to extricate her hand, but his fingers closed more firmly around hers.

"I will ensure that Lucien doesn't come near you ever again. Do I have your assurance that you won't seek him out?"

"I learn from my mistakes, sir," she said with acid dignity.

"I shall endeavor to learn from mine," he said wryly, releasing her hand as the carriage came to a halt on Albermarle Street. "And maybe we can look forward to a harmonious future."

Maybe, Juliana thought, but without too much optimism. She'd finished with Lucien, but after tonight she was more than ever determined to help the women of Covent Garden.

Her head swam suddenly as she stepped to the pavement.

Her knees buckled under an invincible wash of fatigue, and she reached blindly for support. Tarquin caught her against him, holding her strongly.

"Easy now, *mignonne*." His voice steadied her, and she leaned into the warmth and strength of his hold.

"I'm all wobbly," she mumbled apologetically into his coat. "I don't know why."

He laughed softly. "Well, I do. Come on, let's get you to bed." He lowered his shoulder against her belly and tipped her over. "Forgive the indignity, sweetheart, but it's the easiest way to accomplish the task."

Juliana barely heard him. She was almost asleep already, her body limp and unresisting as he carried her inside.

Chapter 18

Tarquin awoke to filtered sunlight behind the bed curtains. The covers had been thrown back, and his naked body stirred deliciously as he felt the moist, fluttering caresses over his loins. Juliana's skin was warm against his, her hair flowing over his belly, her breath rustling on his inner thighs. Her fingers were as busy as her mouth, and he closed his eyes on a wave of delight, yielding to pleasure. His hand moved over her curved body, caressing the small of her back, smoothing over her bottom, tiptoeing over her thighs. He felt her skin quiver beneath his fingers and smiled.

He'd helped her undress and tumbled her into bed in the clear light of a rosy dawn, and by the time he'd thrown off his own clothes and prepared to join her, she'd been sleeping like an exhausted child, her cheek pillowed on her hand. He'd slipped in beside her, wondering why he chose to share her bed only to sleep when his own waited next door. He made it an invariable practice never to spend an entire night with his mistresses, but there had been something so appealing about Juliana. The deep, even breathing, the dark crescent of her eyelashes against the pale cheeks, the dusting of freckles across the bridge of her nose, the turn of her bare shoulder against the pillow, the vibrant cascade of her hair escaping from her lace-trimmed night-cap. Unable to resist, he'd slid in beside her, and she'd stirred and nuzzled against him like a small animal in search of warmth and comfort.

He'd fallen asleep smiling and awoken with the same smile. Now he smacked her bottom lightly. "*Mignonne,* come up."

Juliana raised her head and turned on her belly to look up at him. "Why?" She pushed her hair away from her face and gave him a quizzical smile.

"Because you are about to unman me," he replied.

Juliana reversed herself neatly and stretched her body over his, her mouth nuzzling the hollow of his throat, her loins moving sinuously over his. "Better?" she mumbled against his pulse.

With a lazy twist of his hips he entered her as she lay above him. He watched the surprise dawn in her eyes, to be followed immediately by a wondering pleasure. "This is different."

He nodded. "If you kneel up, you'll find it's even more so."

Juliana pushed herself onto her knees. She gasped at the changed sensation and slowly circled her body around the hard, impaling shaft. She touched his erect nipples with a feathery fingertip, searching his face for his response, chuckling when he groaned with pleasure.

"Does it feel good when I do this, sir?" She rose on her knees, then slowly sank down again, arching her back as she grasped her ankles with her hands. His flesh pressed against her body's sheath, and she suddenly lost interest in Tarquin's reaction as a wave of glorious sensation broke over her. She cried out, her body arched like a bow, the near unbearable tension building in ever tightening circles.

Tarquin lay still, knowing she needed no help from him to reach this peak. He watched her through half-closed eyes, reveling in the innocent candor of her joy. And when she cried out again, he grasped her hips and held her tightly as she rocked on his thighs with each succeeding wave of her climax.

"But what happened to you?" she gasped when she could finally speak, tears of joy glistening in her eyes. "Did I leave you behind?"

"Not for long," he promised softly. The exquisitely sensitized core of her body lay open for his touch, and he played delicately upon her as Juliana moved herself over and around him, her tongue caught between her teeth as she concentrated on her lover's pleasure, her own ever present but taking secondary importance. But when he drove upward with another almost leisurely twist, she was surprised yet again by the rushing, heated flood of ecstasy that dissolved muscle and sinew like butter in the sun.

He gripped her hips, his fingers biting deep into the rich curves, holding her as if she were his only anchor to reality in the storm-tossed sea of sensual bliss. And when it was over and he became aware of the lines and contours of his body on the mattress, of the dust motes in the ray of sun creeping through the curtains, he drew her down to lie along his length, his hand stroking over her damp back, his flesh diminishing slowly within her.

What was it about this woman that she could so transport him? Make him forget everything but the glories of their joining? What was it that made him want to protect her, to make her happy? He was thirty-two, affianced from childhood to a perfect match—a woman who would be his wife but who would not object to his mistresses. A woman who knew the rules of their society. A woman he *wanted* to marry. So why, then, did the prospect suddenly seem drab? When he thought of the well-ordered years ahead, he felt dull and depressed. But why? He and Lydia were two grown people who knew what each expected of the other. His marriage would follow the rules of all successful relationships. He gave people what they expected from his money, position, and influence, and he made sure he received what he was due in his turn.

It had always worked before, but it wasn't working with

Juliana. He was convinced that another woman in her position would have jumped at the chance of a title and a comfortable settlement for life. But not Juliana. She wasn't interested in what he had to offer; she seemed to want something more. She wanted something from *him*. Something far deeper than mere material offerings. And the thought stirred him, filled him with a restless excitement, was the source of this sudden impatience with his carefully laid-out future.

And holding this long, luscious body, feeling her jade gaze on his face, fiery tendrils of hair tickling his nose, he understood deep at his core that he lacked something fundamental to his happiness. He held it in his arms, but he couldn't grasp it and make it his. He didn't know how to. It was embodied in Juliana's unusual, tempestuous, forthright spirit, and he didn't know how to capture it. He didn't understand Juliana's rules.

He pulled himself up sharply. Juliana was a novelty, he told himself as she slept the brief sleep of satiation on his breast. He was confusing his fascination with her novelty with something deeper and unnameable. She was young and fresh. Her spirit amused him, her passion touched him. Her courage and resolution moved him. With luck she would be the mother of his child. In the best of all possible worlds she would remain his mistress as she mothered his child. There was no place—no need—for deeper, unnameable emotions.

Juliana stirred and opened her eyes. She kissed his neck sleepily. "I forgot to mention that George Ridge was in the tavern last night."

His hand stilled on her back. "Good God! What in heaven's name made you forget such a thing?"

"There was so much else to worry about," she said, sitting up, brushing hair out of her eyes. "And then I got so wobbly, and everything else went out of my head."

"I suppose it's understandable." He reached lazily for one full breast, cupping it in his palm, a fingertip circling the nipple. "Did he see you?"

"He could hardly miss me when I was standing on the table with a rope around my neck." She drew back from his caressing hand with a shiver, saying abruptly, "I don't seem to feel like being touched."

Tarquin dropped his hand immediately, his expression suddenly drawn with anger. "Lucien will pay in full measure for what he did to you," he promised savagely. "When he comes back to the house, he will pay." He stood up abruptly and strode to the window, staring out into the bright morning.

Juliana looked at his rigid, averted back and shivered slightly at the powerful anger she sensed. She wasn't to know how much of it was directed at himself. "I'll get over it," she said. "It was only a passing moment just then." She sat hunched on the bed, her arms crossed protectively over her breasts. "It all came back . . . the cockfight, and the wife-selling before, and the gin—"

"Gin?" he exclaimed, swinging back to the room, diverted from his bitter self-reproach. "Lucien permitted you to drink gin?"

"He forced it on me. I didn't know what it was." Her eyes flashed with her ever-ready temper.

Tarquin silently added it to the score he would settle with his cousin and said calmly, "Let's return to George Ridge. He recognized you?"

Juliana nodded, accepting the change of subject as an apology of some kind. "Enough to bid five hundred pounds for me."

Tarquin frowned. He stood beside the bed, his hands on his hips, his air as self-possessed as if he was fully dressed instead of starkly, and most beautifully, naked. "What did you do?"

"Nothing," she said somewhat absently, now thoroughly distracted by the sight of him, her eyes dwelling on the spare frame, the play of muscle, the lean, sinewy length of thigh. His sex was quiescent, but as her eyes lingered on the soft flesh, it flickered and rose beneath the intent gaze as if responding to an unspoken wish.

Tarquin appeared unaware. "What do you mean, you did nothing? You must have responded in some way."

Juliana reached forward to touch him, her tongue peeping from between her lips, a little frown of concentration on her brow.

Tarquin stepped back, observing with a smile, "I think I'd better don a chamber robe if we're to have a sensible discussion here." He turned to pick up his robe from the chaise longue. Juliana's gaze feasted on his lean back, the cluster of dark hair in the small of his back, and the dark trail that led downward to vanish in the cleft between the taut buttocks. Her fingers itched to slide between his thighs, and in another moment she would have sprung from the bed, but he slung the robe around his shoulders, thrusting his arms into the sleeves, and turned back to the bed, tying the girdle firmly at his waist.

Juliana couldn't hide her disappointment. Tarquin chuckled. "I'm flattered, *mignonne*. You certainly know how to compliment a man."

"It wasn't flattery," she denied with a sigh, wriggling beneath the covers again.

"Now, answer my question. What do you mean by 'nothing'?"

"It seemed sensible to behave as if I didn't know who he was," she explained. "I couldn't think too clearly, but I thought that if I refused to acknowledge him, then he would find it harder to identify me. If I deny that I'm Juliana Ridge, it's only his word against mine."

"Mmmm." Tarquin pulled at his chin. "That was quick thinking. But in the long term your guardians could identify you."

"But I could still deny it. And you could vouch for my identity as a whole other person. Who would challenge the Duke of Redmayne?"

Juliana showed a touching faith in the ability of the aristocracy to circumvent the law. But while Tarquin might be able to use his rank and influence to intimidate George Ridge and possibly the Forsetts, rank and influence would do little good before the bar. "It would be best if Ridge didn't see you again," he stated after a moment of frowning thought. "Keep to the house for the time being, unless you're with me . . . or possibly Quentin."

Juliana's face dropped. She couldn't do that and meet with her friends on Russell Street. "I'm not afraid of George," she protested. "I can't agree to be a prisoner just because that idiot George is hanging around. He's such a blockhead, he couldn't find his way out of a cloak bag. It was different when I was friendless and had no protection, but how could I be at risk when I have the mighty protection of His Grace of Redmayne?" She gave him a sweet smile, pulling the sheet up to her chin. "You are surely a match for a country lout, my lord duke."

"And that's exactly why you're not to go out without me or Quentin as escort." He bent over and kissed her lightly. "Do the sensible thing for once and oblige me in this." His gray gaze was calm, his voice quite without threat, but Juliana knew she'd been given fair warning.

After Tarquin left her, Juliana leaped from bed, rang for Henny, and began to plan for the day. She would take every precaution. She would travel only in a closed carriage, and she wouldn't show her face on the streets, at least not unless it was absolutely necessary.

Lucy was sleeping when she visited her on her way down to breakfast. Even in sleep the girl was beginning to look better already. It was as if her spirit had reentered her body and she was once more taking a grip on the world.

Juliana tiptoed out without waking her and went down to the breakfast parlor, where she found Quentin at breakfast. He looked up and cast a swift, almost involuntary, glance over her that made her immediately pleased with her gown of pale-green muslin over a pink petticoat. Henny had worked her usual magic with her hair, making a virtue of the unruly ringlets, arranging them artfully at her ears.

Quentin rose to his feet, bowing with a smile. "The

house has taken on a quite different air, my dear, since you came to join us. May I carve you some ham?"

"Thank you." Juliana took the chair pulled out for her by an attentive footman. She frowned slightly, wondering what he meant by "a different air." When people said things of that nature to her, they were usually scolding, but Lord Quentin had no such manner about him. "Is it a pleasanter air, sir?" she asked tentatively.

Quentin laughed. "Oh, most definitely. The house feels altogether lighter and merrier."

Juliana smiled broadly. "I hope His Grace agrees with you."

"Agrees with what?" Tarquin entered the room, taking a chair at the head of the table. He cast an eye over the *Gazette* beside his plate.

"Lord Quentin was so kind as to say that I've made the house merrier." Juliana took a piece of bread and butter, confiding cheerfully, "I'm not accustomed to being told such things. Mostly people say I make life uncomfortable for them."

The duke pursed his mouth consideringly. "Perhaps it amounts to the same thing for some people."

"How ungallant, my lord duke!"

"I suppose some people might actually enjoy chasing all over town after you at three o'clock in the morning."

"Oh! How could you speak of that now!" she exclaimed, her eyes flashing with indignation. "That is *most* unchivalrous!"

Tarquin smiled faintly. "My dear, as you said to me so aptly once, you reap what you sow." But to Juliana's relief he turned to Quentin with a change of subject. "No word on when you must leave us?"

"No, the archbishop seems perfectly content to keep me kicking my heels in London while he ponders my bishop's request."

"Well, I shall be loath to see you leave," the duke said civilly. "So I hope the pondering continues for a while longer."

Juliana soon excused herself and left the brothers to their breakfast. It seemed sensible to wait until the duke had gone about his morning's business before making her own move, so she lurked in the upstairs hallway, listening to the comings and goings in the hall below, waiting for the duke's departure.

He left shortly before noon, having first called for his horse. Juliana ran to her bedchamber and watched from the window as he rode up the street on a powerful piebald hunter. That left only Quentin. She hurried down the stairs and asked Catlett to call her a chair.

"My lady, surely you would prefer to take His Grace's conveyance?" Catlett said disapprovingly.

Juliana remembered that Quentin had told her the duke's own chair was at her disposal. If she used it, she would be under the protection of Tarquin's own men. She could always say she assumed that was as good as having his own escort, if he challenged her on her return.

"Yes, thank you, Catlett," she said with a sweet smile. "I wasn't sure whether His Grace was using the chair himself."

Somewhat mollified, Catlett bowed and sent the boot boy round to the mews for the sedan chair. The bearers brought the chair into the hall, where Catlett assisted Juliana inside; then he instructed the bearers to "Look alive, there. And be careful of 'Er Ladyship. No jolting." Leaning into the chair, he inquired, "Where shall I tell them to take you, m'lady?"

"Bond Street," Juliana said off the top of her head. She'd redirect the chairmen when they were outside.

They trotted off with her up Albermarle Street, oblivious of the man standing in a doorway opposite. They didn't notice him as he set off after them, almost at a jog in his haste not to lose them, sweat breaking out profusely on his forehead with his exertion, his waistcoat straining across his belly, his habitually red face turning a mottled dark crimson.

Juliana waited until they'd turned the corner onto Piccadilly. Then she tapped on the roof with her fan. "I've changed my mind. Carry me to Russell Street, if you please," she said haughtily.

The chairman looked a little surprised. Covent Garden addresses were not for the likes of Lady Edgecombe. But he shouted the change to his companion carrying the rear poles, and they set off in the new direction.

George hailed a sedan chair and fitted his ungainly bulk inside. "Follow that chair. The one with the coronet."

The chairmen hoisted the poles onto their muscular shoulders, taking the strain of their passenger's weight with a grimace. Then they set off after the chair emblazoned with the ducal coronet, their pace considerably slower than their quarry's.

Juliana alighted at the door of the Dennisons' house. She smoothed down her skirts and glanced up at the house that had once been her prison. First a refuge, then a prison. She could see her own third-floor window, where she'd lain in bed at night listening to the occupants of the house at work. What would have happened to her if the innkeeper hadn't sent for Elizabeth Dennison? She would never have known Tarquin, Duke of Redmayne, that was for sure. Her hand drifted to her belly. Did she even now carry his seed?

Briskly dismissing the thought, she said to the chairmen, "You had best wait for me here."

The lead chairman tipped his hat and adjusted the pads on his shoulders where the poles had rested. His companion ran up the steps to hammer on the knocker. Juliana followed him with the same haughty air of before, silently challenging them to question what she could be doing in such a place.

Mr. Garston opened the door and looked for a moment completely startled. Then he bowed as he'd never bowed to Juliana Ridge. "Pray step within, m'lady."

Juliana did so. "I've come to see Miss Lilly and the others." She tapped her closed fan in her palm and looked pointedly around the hall, as if finding its furnishings wanting in some way. To her secret delight Mr. Garston seemed a little intimidated, a little unsure of how to treat her. It was small revenge for their first meeting, and the subsequent occasions when he'd barred the door to her.

"Would ye care to wait in the salon, m'lady?" He moved with stately step to the room she remembered so vividly, flinging open the double doors.

The salon had been cleaned and polished, but the smell of wine and tobacco, and the girls' perfume, still lingered from the previous evening, despite the wide-open windows. It was a decadent combination of odors. Juliana wandered to the window and stared out at the scene in the street outside. Sunshine did much to mute the grimness: the one-legged child, hobbling on a crutch, thrusting his upturned cap at passersby with a whining, singsong plea for a penny; the woman asleep or unconscious in the gutter, a bottle clutched to her breast. Two gentlemen emerged from Thomas Davies's bookshop opposite, at Number 8. They had the air of learned men, with their flowing wigs and rusty black frock coats. Both carried leather-bound volumes, and they were talking earnestly. They stepped over the woman without so much as looking down and brushed past the crippled child, ignoring his pathetic pleas as he followed them down the street. Pleas that turned rapidly into curses when it became clear they were not going to put a penny in his cap.

As the child hopped, muttering, back to his position in the shadow of the bookshop doorway, Juliana frowned in puzzlement. There was something not quite right about him. She stared, leaning out of the window into the narrow street. Then she saw it. The child's leg was bent up at the knee and fastened with twine around his thigh. He was not one-legged at all. But he must be in the most awful discomfort, she thought, compassion instantly chasing away the moment of distaste at the fraud. Presumably he had a beggars' master, who had hit upon this cheat. Perhaps he was fortunate he hadn't been mutilated permanently.

Shuddering, she turned from the window as the door opened on a babble of excited voices.

"How is Lucy, Juliana?" Rosamund, her pretty face grave with concern, was the first into the room. The others followed in a gay flutter of filmy wrappers and lace-edged caps. They were still in dishabille, as Juliana remembered from her own days in the house. They wouldn't dress formally until just before dinner.

"She was sleeping when I left. But I think she's recovering quickly. Henny is looking after her." Juliana perched on the arm of a brocade sofa. "His Grace will not permit her to have visitors, because she needs to rest," she explained tactfully. "So I'll have to act as your messenger."

Fortunately no one questioned this polite fabrication, and Lilly launched into a description of the Dennisons' reaction to Lucy's plight and the request that they consider taking her in when she was well enough to work again.

"Mistress Dennison was pleased to say that since Lucy appeared to have His Grace's favor, then they would consider it," Emma said, sitting on the sofa and patting Juliana's arm confidingly.

"What a difference it makes to have an influential patron," sighed Rosamund, shaking her curls vigorously.

"Actually, I don't think it has much to do with the duke," Lilly declared acerbically. "It's just that Mistress Dennison would be delighted to thwart Mother Haddock."

There was a chuckle at this; then Lilly said, "So what was this plan you had, Juliana?"

"Ah." She opened and closed her fan restlessly. "Well, I thought that if we all banded together, we could look after each other. Protect each other so that what happened to Lucy couldn't happen again."

"How?" asked one of the girls with a mop of dark-brown curls and a sharp chin.

"If everyone in the various houses agreed to contribute a small sum every week from their earnings, we could have a rescue fund. We could pay debts like Lucy's . . . bail people out of debtors' prison."

The circle of faces looked at her in dubious silence.

Then someone said, "That might be all right for us . . . and for girls in some of the better houses, but for most of them, they don't earn enough to keep body and soul together after they've paid their whoremasters for the drink and the candles, and coal, and a gown, and linen. Molly Higgins told me she spent over five pounds last week because she had to have wax candles for her clients and new ribbons for her nightcap because she can't look shabby if she's to attract the right kind of customers. And the five pounds didn't include the present she had to give to madam to keep her sweet."

"But if they didn't have to buy all those things from their masters, then they would be better off," Juliana pointed out.

"But those are the terms on which they rent the places where they do business," Emma pointed out with an air of patience, as if explaining self-evident truths to an infant.

"But if they all refused to accept those terms, and if we managed to collect enough money to lend them for those necessary supplies, then they wouldn't be dependent on the whoremasters and bawds."

"It seems to me that you're talking of a vast deal of money," a dark girl said, nibbling a fingernail.

"Money's the key to everything," Rosamund replied gloomily. "I don't see how we can do it, Juliana."

"It's not money so much as solidarity," Juliana persisted. "If everyone agrees to put in what they can, you'd be surprised how it will mount up. But everyone has to take part. Everyone has to agree to stand by each other. If we do that, then we can stand up to the bawds and whoremasters."

There was another doubtful silence, and Juliana realized she had her work cut out. These women were so accustomed to a life of exploitation and powerlessness that they couldn't grasp the idea of taking their lives back. She opened her reticule and drew out her remaining twenty-pound note.

"I'll start the fund with this." She put the note on the table in front of her.

"But, Juliana, why should you contribute?" Lilly asked. "You're not one of us. In fact, you never have been."

"Oh, but I am," she said firmly. "My position is a little different, a little more secure, but I'm still in a situation I didn't choose, because I was alone and friendless and vulnerable. I was as much exploited as any one of you. And I'm as much dependent on the goodwill of a man who wouldn't call himself my whoremaster, but in essence that's exactly what he is."

Juliana glanced involuntarily toward the window as she said this, suddenly afraid that she might see the Duke of Redmayne standing there. If he heard himself described in such terms, his reaction didn't bear thinking about. But, then, he wasn't a man to appreciate the unvarnished truth when applied to his own actions.

"We should discuss it with the girls in the other houses," Lilly said. "If no one else wants to take part, then it won't work. We couldn't do it all ourselves."

"No," Juliana agreed. "It must be a real sisterhood."

"Sisterhood," mused Rosamund. "I like that word. I like what it means. Will you come with us to talk to the others, Juliana? You sound so convincing . . . so certain. And it was your idea."

Juliana nodded. "But not today." She didn't explain that she thought she'd been out of the house long enough. An extended absence would inevitably come to the duke's notice, but a short airing in his own chair would probably draw no more than a sigh and a raised eyebrow in their present state of accord.

"It would be best if we could gather everyone together," Emma said. "We should send round a message with a meeting place and a time."

"Where should we meet?" All eyes turned to Lilly, who seemed to have the role of natural leader.

"The Bedford Head," she said promptly. "We'll ask Mistress Mitchell if she'll lend us the back room one forenoon. She won't be busy then."

Juliana had seen the Bedford Head during her nightmare

with Lucien. It was a tavern in the center of Covent Garden—not a place she was eager to revisit. However, needs must when the devil drives, and the Garden was bound to be less wild in the morning.

A footman entered with tea and cakes and the message that Mistress Dennison requested Lady Edgecombe's company in her parlor when she'd completed her visit with the young ladies.

"A request, not a demand," Juliana mused with a wicked grin. "That's a novelty."

A chorus of laughter greeted this, and the mood lost its solemnity. The conversation became as light and fizzy as champagne, with much laughter and fluttering of fans. Juliana had once wondered if their gaiety was genuine, not merely a performance to hide their real feelings, but she'd soon become convinced that it was perfectly real. They allowed little to upset them. Presumably because if they stopped too often to reflect and look around, they'd never laugh again.

She'd never enjoyed female company before. Her friends in Hampshire had been restricted by Lady Forsett to the vicar's solemn daughters, both of whom had regarded Juliana as if she were some dangerous species of the animal kingdom, shying away from her whenever they were alone in her company. Of course, she had developed the reputation as a hoyden when she'd fallen from the great oak at the entrance to Forsett Towers and broken her arm. It had been a youthful indiscretion, but one that had blackened her among the ladies of the county. The cheerful and undemanding camaraderie of the women on Russell Street was therefore a delightful new experience.

Outside George Ridge was engaged in idle conversation with the duke's chairmen. Initially they'd regarded the large young man, sweating in his lavishly trimmed coat of scarlet velvet, with contempt and suspicion. But it didn't take them long to figure out that he was the classic pig's ear struggling to make a silk purse of himself. Their manner became more open, although none the less slyly derisive.

"So what kind of a house is this?" George gestured to the front door with his cane.

" 'Ore'ouse, like as not." The chairman spat onto the cobbles and resumed picking his teeth. "An 'igh-class one, mind ye."

"The lady didn't look like a whore," George remarked casually, feeling for his snuffbox.

"What? Lady Edgecombe?" The second chairman guffawed. "Proper little lady she is . . . or so that maid of 'er's says. 'Is Grace keeps a wary eye on 'er. Told Mistress 'Enny she needed a bit o' motherin'. 'E didn't want no 'ighfalutin abigail attendin' to 'er."

"That so?" The first chairman looked interested. "A'course, Mistress 'Enny's yer brother's mother-in-law, so I daresay she'd tell ye these things."

"Aye," the other agreed with a complacent nod. "Tells me most everythin'. Except," he added with a frown, "what's goin' on wi' that girl what 'Er Ladyship brought to the 'ouse yesterday. Mr. Catlett said as 'ow 'Is Lordship weren't best pleased about it. But Lord Quentin, 'e told 'im 'e 'ad a duty . . . or summat like that." He spat again, hunching his shoulders against a momentary sharp breeze coming around the street corner. "Blessed if I can get a thing outta 'Enny, though. Mouth's tighter than a trap."

"So what's Lady Edgecombe doing visiting a whorehouse?" George wondered aloud. Both chairmen looked at him suspiciously.

"What's it to you?" There was a belligerence to the question, and George thought that perhaps he'd got as much out of them as he was going to.

He shrugged. "Nothing, really. It's just that I thought I saw her in the Shakespeare's Head last even. With a group of men. Perhaps her husband . . . ?"

Both men spat in unison. "The viscount's no 'usband fer anyone. Can't think what persuaded 'im to take that poor young thing to wife. A dog's life, 'e'll lead 'er."

"But 'Is Grace is keepin' an eye out," his companion reminded him. "Eh, man, the affairs of the quality is no concern of ours. Couldn't understand 'em in a million years."

"Aye, that's a fact."

They both fell into a ruminative silence, and George finally offered a brief farewell and walked away. The mystery was growing ever deeper. Was Juliana really married to the viscount, who'd tried to sell her last night? Or was she embroiled in some whore's masquerade? The latter seemed the most likely, since it was impossible to imagine the real Viscountess Edgecombe taking part in that business in the tavern. A man of the viscount's breeding would never expose his wife to such ghastly humiliation. Whores were paid to participate in such playacting. But if the duke's servants believed she was truly wedded to the viscount, then something very deep was afoot. The woman, Mistress Henny, an old family retainer who'd been assigned to look after Juliana, was a very convincing detail in the narrative. But why would Juliana be part of such a deception?

Money, of course. She had left her husband's home without a penny, hadn't even taken her clothes. Somehow she'd fallen under the duke's influence, and he was requiring her to earn her keep by playing this part. He'd come to her rescue last night, so he must be deeply involved. But did he know that the strumpet he was employing was wanted for murder? Perhaps someone should tell him.

George turned into a tavern under the Piazza and called for ale. Perhaps he should confront Juliana before exposing her to her protector. Maybe she would be so intimidated by seeing him and understanding how much power he now held over her, that she would capitulate without a murmur. So long as she wasn't legally married, then nothing stood in the way of his own possession. She hadn't appeared to recognize him last night, but she'd been in great distress then and probably unaware of anything around her. He would ensure that next time she looked him full in the face and acknowledged his power.

George drained his tankard and called for a bottle of burgundy. He was beginning to feel that he would soon steer a path through this muddle and emerge triumphant. All he had to do now was to waylay Juliana when she was alone and with no easy exit. He would easily convince her to see which side her bread was buttered.

The burgundy arrived, but after a few sips he stood up and walked restlessly to the tavern door. The thought of Juliana drew him like a lodestone. His feet carried him almost without volition back to Russell Street, where he took up a stand on the steps of the bookshop, apparently minding his own business.

Juliana found Mistress Dennison friendly and hospitable. She bade her sit down and pressed a glass of sherry on her, then sat down herself and said with crisp matter-of-factness, "Do you know yet whether you've conceived?"

Juliana nearly choked on her sherry before she reminded herself that in this household there were no taboo intimate subjects when it came to female matters.

"It's too early to tell, ma'am," she responded with creditable aplomb.

Mistress Dennison nodded sagely. "You do, of course, know the signs?"

"I believe so, ma'am. But anything you wish to impart, I should be glad to hear."

Mistress Forster had broken her silence on all such matters only once, to tell Juliana that if she missed her monthly terms, she could assume she had conceived. Juliana suspected that there was more to the business than that bald fact, so she was grateful for Elizabeth's interest.

Elizabeth poured herself another glass of sherry and began to describe the symptoms of conception and the method of calculating the date of an expected birth. Juliana listened, fascinated. Mistress Dennison minced no words, called a spade a spade, and left no possibility for misunderstanding.

"There, child. I trust you understand these things now."

"Oh, yes, completely, ma'am." Juliana rose to take her leave. "I'm very thankful for the enlightenment."

"Well, my dear, you must always remember that even when a girl leaves here for such a splendid establishment as yours, she is still one of my girls. Any questions you may have, you will find the answers here. And when the time comes, I shall gladly assist at the birth. We are a close family, you understand." She smiled warmly at Juliana.

"I trust you'll see your way to opening your family to Lucy Tibbet, ma'am." Juliana dropped a demure curtsy. "His Grace has been kind enough to say that he'll give her a sum of money when she leaves his house so she'll be able to set herself up, but she will need friends. As we all do," she added.

Mistress Dennison looked a trifle vexed at being pressed on this matter, but she said a little stiffly, "His Grace is all condescension as always, Juliana. Lucy is very fortunate. Perhaps more than she deserves. But it's to be hoped she's learned a valuable lesson and will be a little more obedient in future."

Juliana dropped her eyes to hide the tongues of fire. "I'm sure you will do what you think best, ma'am."

"Yes, indeed, child. I always do." Elizabeth inclined her head graciously. "And I daresay, if Lucy is truly penitent, then Mr. Dennison and I will see our way to assisting her."

"Ma'am." Juliana curtsied again and turned to leave the room before her unruly tongue betrayed her. In her haste she tripped over a tiny spindle-legged table and sent the dainty collection of objets d'art it supported flying to the four corners of the room. "Oh, I do beg your pardon." She bent to pick up the nearest object, and her hoop swung wildly and knocked over an alabaster candlestick on a low table.

"Never mind, my dear." Elizabeth rose rather hastily to her feet and reached for the bellpull. "A servant will see to it. Just leave everything as it is."

Juliana backed cautiously from the room, her high color due not to embarrassment but to hidden anger.

She made her way down the stairs. The women had all retired to their chambers to dress for the day's work. A maid bustled across the hall with a vase of fresh flowers for the salon. Juliana glimpsed a footman refilling the decanters on the pier table. In a couple of hours the clients would begin to arrive.

Mr. Garston bowed her ceremoniously out of the door, clicking his fingers imperiously to the idling chairmen. "Look sharp, there. 'Er Ladyship's ready fer ye."

The chairmen snarled at Garston but jumped to attention as Juliana came down the steps. As she turned to step into the chair, she saw George watching her from the steps of the bookshop at Number 8. He offered her a clumsy bow, his lips twisting in a humorless grin. Juliana frowned as if in puzzlement. She spoke in carrying tones.

"Chairman, that man over there is staring at me in the most particular way. I find it offensive."

The first chairman touched his forelock. "Ye want me to wipe the grin off 'is face, m'lady?"

"No," Juliana said hastily. "That won't be necessary. Just carry me back to Albermarle Street."

George cursed her for an arrogant strumpet. How dare she look through him as if he were no more than a slug beneath her feet? What did she think she was playing at? But now that he'd found her, now that he knew that she went out alone, he could plan his campaign. Next time she left Albermarle Street alone, he would take her. He'd bring her to a proper respect for her late husband's heir. He returned to his burgundy with renewed thirst.

Chapter 19

The duke had not returned when Juliana got back to the house. One less confrontation to worry about, she thought cheerfully. The longer she could keep him in ignorance of her excursions to Russell Street, the simpler life would be. George was a damnable nuisance, though. If he was going to dog her footsteps at every turn, she was going to have to tell Tarquin, which would mean admitting her own journeyings. For some reason she had absolute faith in the duke's ability to dispose of George Ridge in some appropriate fashion . . . and she also had a grim foreboding that he'd be able to put a stop to her own activities if he chose. But that was a bridge to be crossed later.

She sat down at the secretaire in her parlor and drew a sheet of paper toward her. Dipping the quill into the standish, she began to set out a list of items the Sisterhood's fund would have to cover if it was to do any good. They could support only their contributing members, she decided, although that would leave out many of the most vulnerable women of the streets. The ones who sold themselves for a pint of gin against the tavern wall, or rolled in the gutter with whoever would have them for a groat. But one had to start great enterprises with small steps.

A footman interrupted her calculations with the message that His Grace was at the front door and wished her to join him. Puzzled, she followed the footman downstairs. The front door stood open, and as she approached, she heard Tarquin talking with Quentin.

"Ah, there you are, *mignonne,*" he called as she appeared on the top step. "Come and tell me if you like her."

Juliana caught up her skirts and half tumbled down the stairs in her eagerness. Tarquin was standing beside a roan mare with an elegant head and aristocratic lines.

"Oh, how pretty she is." She stroked the velvety nose. "May I ride her?"

"She's yours."

"Mine?" Juliana stared, wide-eyed. She had never had her own mount, having to make do with whatever animal no one else wished to ride in Sir Brian's stables—doddery old riding horses for the most part, ready to be put out to pasture. "But why would you give me such a wonderful present?" A glint of suspicion appeared in her gaze, and she stepped almost unconsciously away from the horse.

"I promised to procure you a mount," he said smoothly. "Did you forget?" He could almost see the suspicions galloping through her mind, chasing each other across her mobile countenance. She was wondering what he wanted in exchange.

"No, I haven't forgotten," she said cautiously. "But why such a magnificent animal? I've done nothing to deserve her, have I?"

"Oh, I don't know," he said solemnly. "I can think of certain things, *mignonne,* that have given me limitless pleasure." His eyes were filled with a seductive smile, making clear his meaning, and Juliana felt her cheeks warm. She glanced sideways at Quentin, who appeared to be taking an inordinate interest in a privet hedge.

Juliana nibbled her bottom lip; then she shrugged and stepped up to the mare again. She decided not to spoil her pleasure in the gift by worrying about whether there were strings attached. If there were, she would ignore them. She took the mare's head between her hands and blew gently into her nostrils. "Greetings."

Once again Tarquin was entranced by her ingenuous delight. Her pleasure in his gift filled him with a deep satisfaction that had nothing to do with his intention to keep her so happy and busy that she had neither the time nor the inclination to cause him further trouble.

Quentin smiled with his brother. You couldn't find two women more different from one another than Lydia Melton and Juliana Courtney, he reflected. The one so quiet and composed, with the pale gravity of a cameo. The other a turbulent, wildfire creature, ruled by passion. The comparison struck him to the heart with the familiar shaft of pain that came whenever he thought of Lydia. Of how impossibly unfair it was that Tarquin should have her and not truly want her, and he should be left on the outside, watching, his heart wrung with love and loss. But he must bow his head to God's will. Railing against the Almighty's plans was no proper behavior for a man of the cloth.

"What will you name her?" he asked abruptly.

Juliana patted the silken curve of the animal's neck. "Boadicea."

"Now, why that, in heaven's name?" Tarquin's eyebrows shot into his scalp.

"Because she was a strong, powerful woman who did what she believed in." Juliana's smile was mischievous, but her jade eyes were shadowed. "An example for us all, sir."

Tarquin smiled with resigned amusement and gestured toward the man holding the horses.

"This is Ted, Juliana. He's your groom, and he'll accompany you wherever you go."

Juliana looked startled. The man wore a leather jerkin and britches instead of livery. He had a broken nose, and his face had the misshapen appearance of one that had been in contact with a variety of hard objects over the years. He was very tall and very broad, but Juliana had the impression that his bulk was not fat, but muscle. His hands were huge, with hairy knuckles and splayed fingers.

He offered her a morose nod of the head, not a smile cracking his expression, not a glint of humor or pleasure in his eyes.

"Everywhere?" she queried.

"Everywhere," Tarquin repeated, the smile gone from his eyes.

"But I have no need of a bodyguard," Juliana protested, horrified at the implications of such a restriction.

"Oh, but you do," Tarquin declared. "Since I can't rely upon you to take sensible precautions, someone must take them for you." He reached out a hand and lightly caught her chin in his palm. "No Ted, no horse, Juliana."

It appeared he knew of her expedition. Juliana sighed. "How did you find out? I didn't think you'd come back."

"Not much goes on under my roof without my knowledge." He continued to hold her chin, his expression grave. "Do you accept the condition, Juliana?"

Juliana looked again at the morose Ted. Was he to be spy as well as protector? Presumably so. How was she to manage the projected visit to the Bedford Head in his dour company? Well, she'd get around him somehow. She returned her attention to Boadicea, saying by way of answer, "I should like to ride her immediately."

"It wants but ten minutes to dinner," Quentin said, amused.

"After dinner you may ride her in the park during the promenade, with Ted's escort," Tarquin suggested, hiding his relief at her capitulation. "Everyone will be wondering who you are. You'll create quite a stir."

Juliana laughed at this, not displeased with the idea. "I'd better tidy myself before dinner." She dropped a mischievous curtsy to the brothers and ran back inside.

Quentin chuckled, linking his arm in his brother's as they returned inside. "If she needs protection, Ted's as good a man as any for the task."

Tarquin nodded. "The best." They both smiled, each with his own boyhood memories of the taciturn, uncompromising gamekeeper, who'd taught them to ride, to

tickle trout, to snare rabbits and track deer. Ted Rougley
was utterly devoted to the Courtney family, with the exception of Lucien, and his loyalty was unwavering. Tarquin
would never give him an order, but if he made a request,
Ted would carry it out to the letter. Juliana would find it
hard to take a step unguarded.

"I understand Juliana needs to be kept away from that
stepson of hers, but what of Lucien?" Quentin asked as
they entered the dining room.

Tarquin's nostrils flared, his mouth becoming almost invisible. "He hasn't returned to the house as yet. I'll deal
with him when he does."

Quentin nodded and dropped the subject as Juliana came
into the room.

"So," Juliana said conversationally, helping herself to a
spoonful of mushroom ragout. "I'm to receive no visitors
and go abroad only escorted by that morose-looking bodyguard. Is that the way it's to be?"

"My dear, you may have all the visitors you wish—"

"Except my friends," she interrupted Tarquin.

"Except Mistress Dennison's girls," he finished without
heat.

"I suspect I am going to be bored to tears," she stated,
sounding remarkably cheerful at the prospect.

"Heaven preserve us!" the duke declared, throwing up
his hands in mock horror. "The combination of you and
boredom, my dear Juliana, doesn't bear thinking of. But
you will meet plenty of people. There will be those who
come to pay a bridal visit. You may go to Vauxhall and
Ranelagh, the play, the opera. You will be introduced to
people there, and I daresay you'll be invited to soirees and
card parties and routs."

"Well, that's a relief," Juliana said as cheerfully as before,
popping a roast potato into her mouth.

Tarquin smiled to himself. Quentin sipped his wine, reflecting that there was a rare softness, an indulgence, in
Tarquin's eyes when they rested on the girl, even when
they were sparring.

Juliana left them when the port decanter appeared, saying she wished to get ready for her ride, and the brothers sat over their port in companionable silence, each with his own thoughts.

Twenty minutes later Juliana's head peeked around the door. "May I come in again, or is it inconvenient?" she asked delicately. Chamber pots were kept in the sideboard for the convenience of gentlemen sitting long over their port, and she knew better than to burst in unannounced.

"Come in by all means," Tarquin invited, leaning back in his chair, legs stretched out and ankles crossed. Quentin saw the warm, amused look spring into his eyes again.

"I thought since you must have chosen my riding dress, you'd like to see what it looked like." Juliana stepped into the room. "It's very beautiful." She couldn't disguise her complacence as she presented herself expectantly for their admiration. "Don't you think the velvet on the collar and cuffs is a clever touch?" She craned her neck to examine her reflection in the glass of the fireplace. "It does such nice things for my eyes and skin." With a critical frown she adjusted the angle of her black, gold-edged hat. "I've never had such an elegant hat, either."

Tarquin smiled involuntarily. He'd amused himself giving orders for this wardrobe, but his enjoyment was tripled with Juliana's clear pleasure and the fact that his eye had been accurate. The green cloth coat and skirt with a cream silk waistcoat and dark-green velvet trimmings accentuated the lustrous jade of her eyes and her vivid hair. The nipped waist of the jacket and graceful sweep of the skirt made the most of the rich lines of her body.

She swept them both a curtsy, then rose and twirled exuberantly. The train of her full skirt swirled and wrapped itself around the leg of a table. With a muttered curse she extricated herself before any damage could be done.

"You look enchanting," Quentin declared. "Tarquin has always had a good eye when it comes to women's clothes."

"Do you spend this amount of time and trouble, not to

mention money, on all your mistresses' wardrobes?" Juliana tweaked at her snowy linen cravat, smoothing a fold.

Quentin turned aside to hide his grin as Tarquin stared in disbelief at the insouciant Juliana. "Do I what?"

"Oh, was that indiscreet of me?" She smiled sunnily. "I didn't mean to be. I was only interested. It's unusual, I believe, for men to take such an interest in women's clothes."

"Let's drop the subject, shall we?" The duke sat up straight, his brows coming together in a fierce frown.

"Oh, very well." She shrugged. "But how many do you have?"

"How many what?" he demanded before he could stop himself.

"Mistresses."

Tarquin's face darkened, his indulgent equanimity destroyed. Quentin hastily intervened, pushing back his chair and getting to his feet. "Juliana, my dear, I think you had better go for your ride. I'll escort you to the mews and see you mounted." He had swept her from the room before she could say anything else devastating, and before Tarquin could give voice to his bubbling wrath.

"Not exactly the soul of tact, are you?" Quentin observed in the stable yard.

"Did you think it an indelicate question?" Juliana asked airily, stepping up to the mounting block. "I thought it perfectly reasonable." She settled into the saddle, her skirts decorously arranged, and shot Quentin a mischievous grin that he couldn't help but return.

"You're incorrigible, Juliana."

Ted mounted a sturdy cob and examined Juliana critically. "The roan's fresh, ma'am. Think ye can 'andle her wi'out a curb?"

"Of course." Juliana nudged the mare's flanks, and Boadicea plunged forward toward the street. Juliana, unmoved, pulled back on the reins and brought the animal to a stop.

Ted grunted. "Seat's all right," he commented with a nod at Quentin. "Daresay she'll do."

Quentin raised a hand in farewell as the horses walked sedately out of the yard; then he went back into the house to fetch his hat and cane. It was a beautiful afternoon, and a stroll in Hyde Park was a pleasing prospect.

Juliana threw out a few conversational gambits to her escort but received only monosyllabic responses. Soon she gave up and settled down to enjoy her ride in private. She was so intent on managing Boadicea and displaying herself to advantage that she didn't see George slip out of a doorway as they clopped down Albermarle Street. She didn't notice him following at a steady pace and a safe distance; she was far too busy looking around, assessing the reactions of fellow travelers to her passing. It was gratifying to receive curious and admiring glances when at home she was accustomed to drawing not so much as a second look.

Ted, however, was aware of their follower. He took his charge on a roundabout route to the park, down side streets and through alleys, always at a pace that wouldn't outstrip a determined pursuer. The man dogged them every step of the way.

George was filled with an impotent rage. He'd been waiting for her to emerge for hours, imagining how he would go up to her, how he would scoop her up from the street, bundle her away. But she was still way beyond his reach, accompanied by that ugly-looking customer who gave the unmistakable impression of a man who would know how to handle himself in a fight.

George was in the grip of an obsession. He'd lost all interest in the fleshly pleasures of London; his dreams both waking and sleeping were filled with Juliana and the corrosive fear that even though he was so close to her, yet he might still be too far. He had followed her back to Albermarle Street from Russell Street and taken up his usual stand on the basement steps opposite. He'd watched with greedy, predatory eyes when she'd appeared on the steps with the two men and the roan mare. He couldn't hear what they said, but it was clear they were discussing something pleasing. He watched her go into the house, and his gut twisted at the bitter reflection that the men behaved toward her with a consideration more suited to a respectable wife than to a harlot.

And now she was riding through London, dressed in the very peak of fashion, on a well-bred and very expensive lady's horse, in the company of a groom. He had to get his hands on her. Force her to acknowledge him. His hands curled into fists at the thought of how she'd looked straight through him. It had been with such conviction that he could almost have believed that he was mistaken—that this pampered creature of fashion was not Juliana Ridge, the neglected and unsophisticated country girl, his father's murderess and the legal owner of a substantial portion of George Ridge's inheritance.

But he knew from the way his loins were afire and his blood ran swift whenever he was in her vicinity that he was not mistaken. This was Juliana. *His* Juliana.

His quarry turned into Hyde Park, and he dodged behind a tree as they reined in the horses and seemed to be having a discussion about which direction to take. He could achieve nothing by continuing to follow them. He couldn't haul her from her horse . . . not here . . . not now. They would return to Albermarle Street eventually, and he'd do better to scout around there while he waited, but he couldn't bring himself to turn his back on Juliana. His eyes drew him forward onto the tan strip of sand running beside the pathway, where they put their horses to the trot and then to a canter, too fast now for him to keep them in sight.

He could sit and wait for them to come full circle, or he could go back to his post. His belly squalled, reminding him that he'd been so intent on his vigil, he'd had no dinner. He decided to return to the Gardener's Arms and drown his frustrations. He would return to watch and await his opportunity in the morning. It was the sensible decision, but he still had to force himself to walk away.

Juliana settled comfortably into the roan's rhythm. The mare had an easy gait and seemed to be enjoying the exercise as much as her rider. The dour Ted kept pace on his cob.

They were on their second circuit when she saw Quentin on the path ahead, walking toward them with a lady dressed in black taffeta. Juliana recognized Lady Lydia despite the heavy black veil concealing her face. She drew rein as she came up with them. "I give you good day, Lady Lydia. Lord Quentin."

For a moment she read dismay in Quentin's eyes, and she was convinced her interruption was unwelcome; then his customary serene smile returned. "Dismount and walk with us awhile." He reached up a hand to help her down. "Ted will take Boadicea."

"Boadicea? What an unusual name for such a pretty lady," Lydia said in her soft voice, responding to Juliana's curtsy with her own, but not lifting her veil.

"She's pretty," Juliana agreed, "but I believe she has a mind of her own." She handed the reins to Ted and took Quentin's other arm, turning with them on the path. "How fortuitous that we should all meet like this. I didn't realize you were going to be in the park, too, Lord Quentin."

"It was a sudden impulse," he responded. "Such a beautiful afternoon."

"Yes, quite lovely," Lydia agreed. "I couldn't bear to be inside another minute. We are still in strict mourning, of course, but there can be no objection to my taking a walk when I'm veiled."

"No, of course not," Quentin said warmly.

"Are you enjoying London, Lady Edgecombe?"

"Oh, immensely, Lady Lydia. It's all so very new to me. Hampshire is such a backwater."

Quentin kicked her ankle at the same instant she realized her mistake.

"Hampshire?" Lydia put up her veil to look at her in surprise. "I thought your family came from York, in the north."

"Oh, yes," Juliana said airily. "I was forgetting. I used to visit relatives in Hampshire and liked it much better than York. So I always think of it as home."

"I see." Lydia's veil fell again. "I didn't know there were any Courtneys in Hampshire."

"My cousin's family," Juliana offered. "A very distant cousin."

"How curious that you should be closer to a distant cousin's relatives than to your own," Lydia mused, puzzled.

"Lady Edgecombe has some unusual views on the world," Quentin said flatly. "I'm sure you must wish to continue your ride, Juliana. It must be dull work walking when a new mount awaits you."

Juliana wasn't sure whether he was getting rid of her for his sake or hers, but she took her cue, signaling to Ted, who rode a little way behind them, leading Boadicea.

Lydia put up her veil again to bid her farewell. "I do hope we'll be like sisters," she said, kissing Juliana's cheek. "It will be so pleasant to have another woman in the house."

Juliana murmured something and returned the kiss. She glanced again at Quentin. His face was almost ugly, and she knew he was thinking, as was she, of Tarquin's setting up two families under his roof. Installing the woman Quentin loved as the mother of one of them.

Juliana was no longer in any doubt that Quentin loved Lydia Melton, and she suspected his love was reciprocated. Tarquin had admitted that he did not love Lydia, yet he was her betrothed. There must be a way to sort out this tangle. Quentin was not quite such a magnificent catch as his brother, but he was still the younger son of a duke, wealthy in his own right, and clearly destined for great things in the Church. He would be an excellent match for Lydia—once her engagement to Tarquin could be broken off.

But that would leave Tarquin without a wife. Without a mother for his legitimate heirs.

A problem for another day. She remounted with Ted's assistance, waved a cheerful farewell to Quentin and his lady, and trotted off. "Have you known the Courtney family for long, Ted?"

"Aye."

"Forever?"

"Aye."

"Since His Grace was a boy?"

"Since 'e was nobbut a babby."

That was a long sentence, Juliana thought. Maybe it was a promising sign. "Have you known Lady Lydia and her family for long?"

"Aye."

"Always?"

"Aye."

"So they've known the Courtneys for always?"

"Aye. Melton land marches with Courtney land."

"Ah," Juliana said. That explained a lot, including a marriage of convenience. Ted might well prove a useful source of information if she picked her questions correctly. However, his lips were now firmly closed, and she guessed he'd imparted as much as he was going to for the present.

She dismounted at the front door and Ted took the horses to the mews. Juliana made her way upstairs. As she turned toward her own apartments, she came face-to-face with Lucien. Her heart missed a beat. Tarquin had said she'd never have to face her vile husband again. He'd said he would deal with him. So where was he?

"Well, well, if it isn't my not so little wife." Lucien blocked her passage. The slurring of drink couldn't disguise the malice in his voice, and his eyes in their deep, dark sockets burned with hatred. His chin was blue-bruised. "You left in such a hurry last night, my dear. I gather the entertainment didn't please you."

"Let me pass, please." She kept her voice even, although every millimeter of skin prickled, her muscles tightened with repulsion, and the hot coals of rage glowered in her belly.

"You weren't so anxious to be rid of me yesterday," he declared, gripping her wrist in the way that sent a wave of remembered fear racing through her blood. He twisted her wrist and she gave a cry of pain, her fingers loosening on the riding crop she held. He wrenched it from her slackened grasp.

"What an unbiddable wife you've become, my dear." Catching a clump of her hair that was escaping from her hat brim, he gave it a vicious tug as he pulled her closer to him. "I promised you would pay for that kick last night. It seems you're getting quite above yourself for a Russell Street harlot. I think I must teach you proper respect."

Out of the corner of her eye Juliana caught the flash of movement as he raised the whip. Then she screamed, with shock as much as pain, as it descended across her shoulders in a burning stripe.

Lucien's eyes glittered with a savage pleasure at her cry. He raised his arm again, at the same time pulling brutally on her hair as if he would tear it from her scalp. But he'd underestimated his victim. It was one thing to take Juliana by surprise, quite another to face her when she'd had a chance to gather her forces. She had learned over the years to control the worst of her temper, but she made no effort to quench it now.

Lucien found he had one of the Furies in his hands. He clung on to her hair, but she seemed oblivious of the pain. The whip fell to the ground as her knee came up with lethal accuracy. His eyes watered, he gasped with pain. Before he could protect himself, she kicked his shins and was going for his eyes with her fingers curled into claws. Instinctively, he covered his face with his hands.

"You filthy bastard . . . son of a gutter-born bitch!" she hissed, driving her knee into his belly. He doubled over on an anguished spasm and was racked with a violent coughing fit that seemed to pull his guts up from his belly. Juliana grabbed up the whip, raised her arm to bring it down across his back.

"Jesus, Mary, and Joseph!" Tarquin's voice pierced the scarlet circle of her blind rage. He had hold of her upraised wrist and was forcing her arm down. "What in the name of damnation is going on here?"

Juliana struggled to regain control. Her bosom was heaving, her cheeks deathly pale, her eyes on fire, seeing nothing but the loathsome, squirming shape of the man who had dared to raise his hand to her. "Gutter sweeping," she said, her voice trembling with fury. "Slubberdegullion whoreson. May you rot in your grave, you green, slimy maggot!"

Tarquin removed the whip from her hand. "Take a deep breath, *mignonne*."

"Where were you?" she demanded, her voice shaking. "You said I would never have to see him again. You *promised* you would keep him away from me." She touched her sore scalp and winced as the movement creased the stripe across her back.

"I didn't know until just now that he'd returned," Tarquin said. "I wouldn't have let him near you if I had. Believe me, Juliana." She was shivering violently and he laid a hand on her arm, his expression tight with anger and remorse. "Go to your apartments now and leave this with me. Henny will attend to your hurts. I'll come to you shortly."

"He hit me with that damned whip," Juliana said, catching her breath on an angry sob.

"He'll pay for it," Tarquin said grimly. Fleetingly, he touched her cheek. "Now, do as you're bid."

Juliana cast one last, scornful look at the still convulsed Lucien and trailed away, all the bounce gone from her step.

Tarquin said with soft savagery, "I want you out of my house within the hour, Edgecombe."

Lucien looked up, struggling for breath. His eyes were bloodshot, filled with pain, but his tongue was still pure venom. "Well, well," he drawled. "Reneging on an agreement, my dear cousin! Shame on you. The shining example of honor and duty has feet of clay, after all."

A pulse flicked in Tarquin's temple, but he spoke without emotion. "I was a fool to have thought it possible to have an honorable agreement with you. I consider the contract null and void. Now, get out of my house."

"Giving up on me at last, Tarquin?" Lucien pushed himself up until he was sagging against the wall. His deep-sunk eyes glittered suddenly. "You promised me once you would never give up on me. You said that you would always stand by me even when no one else would. You said blood was thicker than water. Do you remember that?" His voice had a whine to it, but his eyes still glittered with a strange triumph.

Tarquin stared down at him, pity and contempt in his gaze. "Yes, I remember," he said. "You were a twelve-year-old liar and a thief, and in my godforsaken naïveté I thought maybe it wasn't your fault. That you needed to be accepted by the family in order to become one of us—"

"You never accepted me in the family," Lucien interrupted, wiping his mouth with the back of his hand. "You and Quentin despised me from the first moment you laid eyes on me."

"That's not true," Tarquin said steadfastly. "We gave you every benefit of the doubt, knowing the disadvantages of your upbringing."

"Disadvantages!" Lucien sneered, the blue bruises standing out against his greenish pallor. "A demented father and a mother who never left her bed."

"We did what we could," Tarquin said, still steadily. But as always, even as he asserted this, he wondered if it was true. It was certainly true that he and Quentin had despised their scrawny, deceitful, cunning cousin, but they had both tried to hide their contempt when Lucien had come to live among them, and then, when Tarquin had become his guardian, they had both tried to exert a benign influence on the twisted character. Tried and most signally failed.

For a moment he met his cousin's eyes, and the truth of their relationship lay bare and barren for both of them. Then he said with cold deliberation, "Get out of my house, Edgecombe, and stay out of my sight. I wash my hands of you from this moment."

Lucien's mouth twisted in a sly smile. "And how will that look? Husband and wife living apart after a few days of marital bliss?"

"I don't give a damn how it will look. I don't want you breathing the same air as Juliana." Tarquin turned contemptuously.

"I'll repudiate her," Lucien wheezed. "I'll divorce her for a harlot."

Tarquin turned back very slowly. "You aren't good enough to clean her boots," he said with soft emphasis. "And I warn you now, Edgecombe, you say one word against Juliana, in public or in private, and I will send you to your premature grave, even faster than you can do yourself." His eyes scorched this truth into his cousin's ghastly countenance. Then he swung on his heel and stalked away.

"You'll regret this, Redmayne. Believe me, you'll regret it." But the promise was barely whispered and the duke didn't hear. Lucien stared after him with fear and loathing. Then he dragged himself down the passage to his own apartments, soothing his mortified soul with the promise of revenge.

Chapter 20

Lucien emerged at twilight from Mistress Jenkins's Elysium in Covent Garden. He bore the well-satisfied air of a man who has relieved both mind and body. Jenkins's flogging house was a highly satisfactory outlet for anger and frustration. The Posture Molls knew exactly how to accommodate a man, whichever side of the birch he chose to be, and he had given free rein to his need to punish someone for the humiliation of his debacle with his wife and Tarquin's subsequent edict.

His eyes carried a brutal glint, and his mouth had a cruel twist to it as he strolled up Russell Street and into the square. But it didn't take long for the reality of his situation to return. He'd been thrown out of his cousin's house, cut off from that bottomless and ever-open purse. And he had a cursed woman to blame for it.

He entered the Shakespeare's Head, ignored the greetings of acquaintances, and sat down in morose silence at a corner table, isolated from the company. He was well into his second tankard of blue ruin when he became aware of a pair of eyes fixed intently upon him from a table in the window. Lucien glared across the smoke-hazed taproom; then his bleary gaze focused. He recognized the overweight man looking as if he was dressed up to ape his betters, squashed into the clothes of a fashionable man-about-town, his highly colored face already suffused with drink. As Lucien returned the stare, the man wiped a sheen of grease from his chin with his sleeve and pushed back his chair.

He made his ponderous and unsteady way through the crowded tables and arrived in Lucien's corner. "Beggin' your pardon, my lord, but I happened to be here last even when you were selling your wife," George began, as intimidated by the death's-head stare and the man's sickly, greenish pallor as he was by the depthless malice in the sunken eyes.

"I remember," Lucien said grudgingly. "Five hundred pounds you offered for her. Fancied her, did you?"

"Is she truly your wife, sir?" George couldn't disguise the urgency of his question, and Lucien's eyes sharpened.

He buried his nose in his tankard before saying, "What's it to you, may I ask?"

George started to pull back a chair, but the viscount's expression forbade it. He remained standing awkwardly. "I believe I know her," he said.

"Oh, I should think you and half London knew her," Lucien responded with a shrug. "She came from a whorehouse, after all."

"I thought so." George's flush deepened with excitement. "She's not truly your wife, then. A Fleet marriage, perhaps?"

"No such luck." Lucien laughed unpleasantly. "I assure you she's Lady Edgecombe all right and tight. My cursed cousin made sure of that. A plague on him!" He took up his tankard again.

George was nonplussed. His disappointment at hearing that Juliana was legally wed was so great that for a moment he could think of nothing to say. He'd convinced himself that she couldn't possibly be what she seemed, and now all his plans came crashing around his ears like the proverbial house of cards.

"So why are you so interested in the whore?" Lucien demanded.

George licked his dry lips. "She murdered my father."

"Oh, did she now?" Lucien sat up, his eyes suddenly alive. "Well, that doesn't surprise me. She half killed me this afternoon. If I had my way, I'd put a scold's bridle on her, strap her in the ducking chair, and drown her!"

George nodded, his little eyes glittering. "She's a murderess. I won't rest until I see her burn."

"Take a seat, dear fellow." Lucien gestured to the chair and bellowed at a potboy, "A bottle of burgundy here, you idle lout!" He leaned back in his chair and surveyed George thoughtfully. "It seems we have a desire in common. Tell me all about my dear wife's sordid history."

George leaned forward, dropping his voice confidentially. Lucien listened to the tale, his expression unmoving, drinking his way steadily through the bottle, for the most part forgetting to refill the other man's glass. He had no difficulty reading the lust behind Ridge's desire for vengeance, and he knew it could be put to good use. The man was a country-bred oaf, with no subtlety. But when the twin devils of lust and vengeance drove a man, he could be an invincible enemy under proper direction. A most valuable tool.

If Lucien could expose Juliana, could see her quivering in the dock to receive the death sentence, Tarquin's disgrace would be almost as devastating as the girl's. His damnable pride would crumble in the dust. He'd be the jesting stock of London.

George finished the story and drained his glass. "I thought I would tell the duke first," he said, looking mournfully at the empty bottle. "Expose Juliana to him and see what he says."

Lucien shook his head. "Depend upon it, he knows it all."

George pointedly picked up the empty bottle and upended it into his glass. "How can you be sure?"

"Because he as good as told me." Lucien finally beckoned the potboy for another bottle. "Told me the harlot would do his bidding. Thought then he must have something on her. Something to hold over her." His voice was becoming increasingly slurred, but the spite in his eyes grew more pronounced.

"If I laid a charge against her," George said eagerly, "if I did that, she'd have to answer it, even if she denied that she was who she was. But if I could get her guardians to identify her as well as myself, well, surely that should convince the magistrates."

Lucien looked doubtful. "Problem is, Tarquin's up to every trick. A man has to be sharp as a needle and slippery as an eel to put one over on him."

"But even the duke couldn't withstand the testimony of Juliana's guardians. She lived with them from the time she was four years old. If they swear and I swear to her identity, surely that would be enough."

"It might. So long as Tarquin didn't get wind of it first." Lucien stared into his glass, swirling the rich red contents. "It might be easier to work on the whore herself."

"Kidnap her, you mean." George's eyes glittered. "I've been thinkin' along those lines myself. I'd soon get a confession out of her."

George stared into the middle distance. Only when he had Juliana in his hands would he be able to satisfy this all-consuming hunger. Then he would be at peace, able to reclaim his rightful inheritance. He was no longer interested in having her to wife. But he knew he would get no rest until he'd indulged this craving that gnawed at his vitals like Prometheus's vultures.

Lucien's mouth moved in a derisive, flickering smile. He could read the man's thoughts as if they were spelled out. Slobbering, incontinent bumpkin . . . couldn't wait to possess that repellently voluptuous body. "I think we should attempt the legitimate route first," he said solemnly, enjoying the clear disappointment in his companion's fallen face. "Lay a charge against her with the support of her guardians. If that doesn't work, then . . ." He shrugged. "We'll see."

George traced a dark, rusty stain in the table's planking

with a splayed fingertip. Red wine or blood, it could be either in this place. The realization entered his befuddled brain that if Juliana was in prison, guards could be bribed. He could have her to himself for as long as it would take. Either plan would give him the opportunity he craved.

He looked up and nodded. "I'll go back to Hampshire in the morning. Lay the matter before the Forsetts. Where will I find you, my lord?"

Lucien scowled, remembering anew that he was now condemned to lodge under his own besieged and uncomfortable roof. "My house is on Mount Street, but here's as good a place as any other. Leave a message with Gideon." He gestured with his head toward the man filling pitchers of ale at the bar counter before taking up his glass again, partially turning his shoulder to George in a gesture that the other man correctly interpreted as dismissal.

George pushed back his chair and stood up. He hesitated over words of farewell. It seemed too inconclusive simply to walk away, but there was no encouragement from the viscount. "I bid you good night, sir," he said finally, receiving not so much as a grunt of acknowledgment. He walked away, intending to return to his previous bench, but he was filled with a restless energy, a surge of elation at the thought that he was no longer alone in his quest. He went outside instead. A slatternly young woman approached him with a near toothless smile.

"Half a guinea, honorable sir?" She thrust her bosom at him, her black eyes snapping.

"Five shillings," he returned.

She shrugged, took his hand, and led him off to the bulks beneath the market holders' stalls. For five shillings, it wasn't worth taking him to her room on King Street, where she'd have to pay for candles and probably change the linen.

"The Bedford Head on Wednesday forenoon."

The word flew around the houses of Covent Garden,

dropping in the ears of languid women gathered in parlors
in the morning's dishabille, idly comparing notes of their
previous night's labors, sipping coffee, discussing fashions
in the latest periodicals. The word was brought by women
from Mistress Dennison's establishment. It was whispered
to heads bent in an attentive circle and received with
hushed curiosity. The words *sisterhood* and *solidarity* were
spoken on tongues stumbling over the unfamiliar concepts.
And the Russell Street women went on to the next house,
leaving the seed to germinate, with Lucy's former plight as
fertilizer.

Mistress Mitchell of the Bedford Head had listened to
Lilly's explanation that a group of Covent Garden cyprians
wished to have a small party to celebrate a birthday. She
was asked to provide refreshments, and Lilly didn't bat an
eyelid at Mistress Mitchell's exorbitant price for such simple fare as coffee, chocolate, and sweet biscuits. She tripped
out of the Bedford Head with a cheerful smile, leaving
Mistress Mitchell in frowning thought.

Why would the women wish to rent private space for a
party when any one of them could have entertained the
others under her own bawd's roof? There wasn't a High
Impure in the Garden whose abbess would refuse permission for such an event.

Mistress Mitchell went on her own rounds, consulting
her fellow abbesses. None could come up with an explanation. It was decided that Mistress Mitchell would position
herself at the peephole to the back room on Wednesday
forenoon. With the aid of a glass against the wall, she
would be able to hear the women's conversation.

While she was sitting with Lucy, Juliana received a message
from Lilly that the meeting was arranged for Wednesday
forenoon. Lucy was sufficiently strong now to leave her bed
and was ensconced on the chaise longue beneath the window. Juliana read the note, which contained a variety of

messages for Lucy from Russell Street, and then handed it to her companion.

Lucy looked up from the letter. "What is this meeting, Juliana?"

Juliana explained. "It's time we did something," she finished with her usual vehemence. "These people make their living out of us, why should they get away with treating us as badly as they please?"

Lucy looked puzzled. "But not you, Juliana. You're not involved at all. Who's making their living out of you?"

"The duke paid Mistress Dennison three thousand guineas for me," Juliana responded succinctly. "I was bought and sold like a slave, simply because I had no protection, no money of my own, no friends, and nowhere to turn. If the Sisterhood had existed then, I would have had somewhere to go. A few guineas would have made all the difference. And think what it would have done for you."

Lucy leaned back, the letter lying open in her lap. "I don't think you understand the power of the whoremasters and bawds, Juliana."

"I understand it as well as I wish to," Juliana retorted. "And I know that it's that defeatist attitude, Lucy, that gives them the power that they have." She turned at a knock on the door, calling "Come in" before recollecting that it was Lucy's bedchamber not her own.

Tarquin entered the room. Lucy, who'd seen her host only the once when she'd been brought into the house, struggled to stand up.

"Don't disturb yourself," Tarquin said, coming over to the chaise longue. "I wished to find out how you were feeling."

"Oh, much better, Your Grace," Lucy stammered, flushing as she adjusted her wrapper. "I . . . I'm sure I'll be able to leave in the morning if—"

"There's no need for that." He bent to pick up the letter that had fluttered to the floor from Lucy's lap. "You're very welcome under my roof until Henny considers you fit to leave." He handed her back the letter, and Juliana couldn't tell whether he'd seen the contents or not. He hadn't seemed to glance at it, but one could never tell with Tarquin. His eyes were everywhere even when he seemed at his most unconcerned.

He took a pinch of snuff and glanced around the room. "I trust you're quite comfortable, ma'am."

Lucy's flush deepened at both the question and the courtesy title. "Oh, yes, indeed, Your Grace. I can't express my gratitude enough for your kindness. I'm sure I don't deserve such—"

"Of course you do!" Juliana interrupted fiercely. "You are as deserving of kindness and consideration as any other human being. Isn't that so, my lord duke?" Her eyes hurled the challenge at him.

"Oh, Juliana, you mustn't say such things," Lucy protested faintly. "Indeed, I don't wish to be a nuisance."

"You aren't being. Is she, sir?"

Tarquin shook his head with a wry quirk of amusement but refused to be drawn. He pushed himself off the windowsill and tipped her chin, lightly kissing her mouth. "When you've completed your visit with Lucy, come and see me in my book room."

Juliana, thrown off course by the kiss, glanced at Lucy, who was studiously rereading her letter. Lucy, of course, wouldn't think twice about a gentleman's playful dalliance with his mistress.

"I wish you a speedy recovery, ma'am." Tarquin bowed to the flustered Lucy and left them.

"Oh, he's so kind," breathed Lucy.

"It seems so," Juliana said, ruffled. "And yet I don't believe he ever does anything that doesn't suit him. I don't believe he would ever really put himself out for someone. He's kind only when it doesn't inconvenience him. But he would as easily leave someone bleeding by the roadside if his direction took him elsewhere or he didn't have the time to help."

Even as she spoke, she remembered how he'd come to her rescue when Lucien was tormenting her and how overpoweringly grateful she'd been to see him. Lucien was now banned from the house because he'd hurt her. Family quarrels were incredibly inconvenient, and yet the duke had sacrificed his peace to champion Juliana. Of course, he'd exposed her to the dangers of Lucien in the first place, so strictly speaking it was his responsibility to repair the damage.

Lucy was looking reproachful but understanding, and Juliana remembered that she had yet to explain Tarquin's generous offer to set the girl on her feet again. It was certainly kind of him but would hardly inconvenience him. He had so much wealth, he wouldn't notice such a sum. Quentin had said his brother was generous to a fault, but was it true generosity when one could give without the slightest sacrifice to oneself?

However, she was obliged to listen to Lucy's astonished gratitude, singing the duke's praises to the heavens when she heard of her good fortune.

Tarquin was seated at his desk, rewriting a speech his secretary had written for him to give to the House of Lords that evening. His secretary was a worthy soul, but somewhat dull, and the duke was convinced the speech would send its presenter to sleep halfway through it, let alone his audience. Not that his peers would pay much attention to the most exciting debate. They'd be snoring off a large and bibulous dinner, for the most part.

He looked up as Juliana came in on her knock. She curtsied demurely. "You wished to see me, my lord duke?"

He pushed back his chair and beckoned to her. When she came to him, he took her hands in his, turning them palm up. To her astonishment he raised them to his lips and kissed her palms. "How are your bruises, *mignonne*?"

"My shoulders are still sore, despite Henny's arnica," she responded, her voice strangely thick. His breath rustled warmly over her hands, which he now held clasped together against his mouth. He kissed each pointed knuckle in turn, his tongue darting snakelike between her bent fingers, each moist, swift, unexpected stroke lifting the fine hairs on her nape, her skin prickling with excitement.

"Have you forgiven me for not getting to Lucien in time?" The wicked little caresses continued, his lips now nuzzling the backs of her hands, his teeth playfully grazing the skin.

Juliana was losing her grip on reality. She barely heard his words. Her feet shifted on the Persian carpet, and she gazed down at the top of his bent head, distractedly noticing how his hair waved thickly back from his broad forehead. How could she say she hadn't forgiven him for anything when one loving touch could turn her body to molten lava?

He looked up, folding her hands securely in his. His eyes were smiling but his tone was grave. "There is so much to enjoy, *mignonne*. Can we take a pleasanter path from here on?"

Juliana could find no words. Her body said one thing, her mind another. How could she possibly forget that she was still captive to his plan? She was still to bear his child, to give it up to his sole control, to live a life of deceit, emotionally dependent on the duke's continuing favor. She looked down at him, her eyes bewildered but her tongue silent.

After a long minute Tarquin released her hands. There was regret in his eyes, but he said in an equally normal tone, "I think it's time for you to return Lady Melton's visit. One mustn't be backward in the courtesies."

"No," Juliana agreed, eagerly grasping this ordinary topic as a lifeline through the labyrinth of her confusion. "Should I go alone?"

"No, I'll take you up in my phaeton." He examined her appearance with a critical air. "I don't care for the breast knot on that gown. It spoils the line of the bodice."

Juliana looked down at the little posy of silk orchids sown to the low neck of her gown. "I thought them pretty."

"So they are, but not on you. They're too frilly . . . fussy." He waved a hand in an impatient gesture. "Your bosom needs no decoration."

"Oh," said Juliana.

"Change your gown now, and tell Henny to remove the flowers before you wear it again."

"As you command, my lord duke." Juliana swept him a low curtsy. "Do you have any other instructions regarding my costume, sir?"

"Not for the moment," he replied, ignoring her sardonic tone. "Except that I have yet to see you in the blue-sprigged muslin. It opens over a dark-blue petticoat, as I recall. There's a lace fichu that will be sufficiently modest for paying a visit to a house in mourning."

Juliana confined her response to another exaggeratedly submissive curtsy. Tarquin's eyes glowed with amusement. "You may have half an hour." He sat down at his desk again, picking up his quill in pointed dismissal.

Juliana stalked upstairs to change into the required gown. It was such a wonderful relief to be simply annoyed with him again. Her emotions were so much clearer when she was responding to his dictatorial manner than when he confused her with softness and the spellbinding invitation of his caresses.

He was awaiting her in the hall when she came down just within the half hour, carrying her gloves and fan. She paused on the bottom step, tilting her head to one side inquiringly as she invited his inspection.

Tarquin solemnly ran his eyes from the top of her head to the toe of her kid slippers. Then he described a circle with his forefinger. Juliana stepped to the hall and slowly turned around.

"Yes, much better," he pronounced. "Let us go. The phaeton is at the door."

He handed her up and took his seat beside her. "It won't be necessary to spend more than fifteen minutes with Lady Melton. If she's unavailable, you may leave your card."

"But I don't have a card."

"Yes, you do." He reached into his breast pocket and handed her a crisp white card on which, in an elegant hand, was inscribed, "Viscountess, Lady Edgecombe." "My secretary took the task upon himself. He has a good hand, I'm sure you'll agree."

"Better than mine," Juliana responded, turning the card between her fingers. It seemed to give her a sense of permanence, as if she could really begin to see herself as Lady Edgecombe. As if nothing could now dislodge her from this extraordinary peak.

At the Melton residence Tarquin handed the reins to his groom, who leaped from the back ledge to take them, and stepped to the street. Juliana gathered her skirts around her and prepared to alight, holding prudently on to the side of the carriage as she gingerly put her foot on the top step.

"I think it might be safer all round if I lift you down," Tarquin said, observing these wise precautions. Taking her around the waist, he swung her to the ground and remained holding her waist until he was certain she was firmly lodged on her two feet.

His hands at her waist were hard and warm, and he held her for a fraction longer than strictly necessary. Juliana felt the old confusion rushing back, but then he was ushering her up the steps through the door held by a bowing footman, and into the hall. He handed the footman his card and gestured to Juliana that she should do the same. The footman bowed them into the salon.

Once more in possession of her senses, Juliana looked around with interest. The furnishings were old-fashioned and heavy, for the most part draped in dark holland covers. The curtains were pulled halfway over the long windows, plunging the room into gloom.

"Lady Melton observes the most strict mourning," Tarquin answered her unspoken question. He took a pinch of snuff and leaned against the mantel, his eyes, suddenly inscrutable, resting on Juliana.

"Lucy received a letter from her friends this morning?" Juliana jumped, guilt flying flags in her cheeks. Had he read the note in its entirety? He couldn't have had time, surely. But if he had, he would know of the projected meeting on Wednesday forenoon. And he would know she was intending to be there. "Do you object?" She took refuge in challenge, hoping annoyance would explain her sudden flush.

"Not at all. Should I?" He continued to regard her in that unreadable fashion.

"I can't imagine why you would. But since you won't permit her friends to visit her in person, I wasn't sure whether a sullied piece of paper could be allowed through your door."

Tarquin's response died at birth with the return of the footman. Her Ladyship and Lady Lydia would be happy to receive them in the family's parlor.

The family parlor was not much less gloomy than the salon, despite its air of being lived in. The curtains and chair covers were dark and heavy, the pictures all carried a black border, and there were no flowers in the vases.

Lady Melton held out her hand to Juliana with a gracious nod and greeted the duke with a complacent smile. Lydia rose and gave Juliana her hand with a warm smile before offering her reverence to the duke with downcast eyes. He drew her to her feet with a pleasant word of greeting, raising her hand to his lips.

Quentin, who had been seated beside Lydia on the sofa, stood up to greet Juliana with a brotherly kiss on the cheek.

"Quentin, I was unaware you intended to call upon Lady Melton this morning," Tarquin said.

Juliana was immediately aware of a slight stiffening from Lady Lydia beside her, but Quentin said easily that he had been passing the door and thought he would discuss a sermon with Lady Melton, but he was about to take his leave. He bowed to Her Ladyship before kissing Lydia's hand. "I must remember to bring the book of gardens to show you, Lydia, next time I'm passing. The fourteenth-century herb garden is most interesting."

"Thank you, Lord Quentin. I look forward to it." She

left her hand in his for a moment, then very slowly withdrew it, her fingers lightly brushing his as she did so.

Juliana glanced at Tarquin. He appeared to notice nothing, devoting his attention to his hostess. Juliana quirked an eyebrow at this, remembering her old nursemaid's frequent mutter that there's none so blind as those who won't see. But, of course, it wouldn't occur to the Duke of Redmayne that something as frivolous and inconvenient as misplaced love could upset his plans.

"Do sit by me, Juliana," Lydia invited with her soft smile, patting the sofa beside her before picking up her embroidery frame. Juliana took the seat and settled down to observe, maintaining an easy conversation with Lydia with half her mind. The duke remained beside Lady Melton, deep in some discussion. He'd barely exchanged two words with his betrothed, beyond the courtesies, and Lydia showed no sign of feeling neglected. Presumably a marriage of convenience didn't require close attention between the partners.

The arrival of two other somewhat formidable ladies prevented Juliana's making any further observations of the betrothed couple. She was introduced, questioned as to her husband's whereabouts.

"You reside under His Grace's roof at present, I understand," declared the dowager Duchess of Mowbray.

"My husband's house is in need of repair," Juliana replied. "His Grace has kindly offered his hospitality until it's ready to receive us."

"I see. So Edgecombe's residing at Albermarle Street also, Redmayne?"

"My cousin is occupied with the renovations to his house," Tarquin said smoothly. "He finds it more convenient to live there while he supervises the work."

Juliana swallowed a laugh at this astonishing fabrication. Surely no one who knew Lucien would believe it. She glanced covertly around the room, gauging their reactions.

"What's that you say?" demanded the dowager's companion, Lady Briscow, leaning forward and cupping her ear.

The dowager took a speaking trumpet from the lady's hand and bellowed, "Redmayne says Edgecombe is livin' in his own house. The gal's sheltered under Redmayne's roof."

Lady Briscow seemed to take a minute to absorb this, while the boomed words echoed around the room. "Ah," she pronounced finally. "Well, I daresay that's for the best." She turned to examine Juliana. "Very young, isn't she?"

"I am past seventeen, ma'am." Juliana decided it was time to speak up for herself.

"Too young for Edgecombe," declared the lady loudly. "Besides, I thought he didn't care for women."

"Now, Cornelia, that's not a fit subject in front of the young ladies," the duchess protested.

"What's that you say? Thought the man only liked little boys."

"Cornelia!" pleaded the duchess through the ear trumpet. "That's not for the ears of the young ladies."

"Pshaw!" declared Lady Briscow. "Innocence isn't going to do the gal much good with that husband of hers."

"We must take our leave, Lady Melton." Tarquin rose to his feet, his expression as bland as if he'd heard nothing of the preceding exchange. Juliana jumped up hastily, too hastily, and a dish of tea resting on the chair arm crashed to the floor. Dregs of tea splattered on the carpet, and the delicate cup rolled against a chair leg and shattered.

She bent to pick up the pieces with a mortified exclamation. Lydia dropped to her knees beside her. "Oh, pray don't worry, Lady Edgecombe." She gathered up the shards swiftly, her cheeks on fire. The conversation had amused Juliana, but Lydia was deeply shocked. But, then, she was probably as innocent as Juliana had been on her wedding night with John Ridge. Juliana could no longer imagine such naïveté, and yet it was only a few short weeks since she'd been a country virgin with no prospect of ever venturing farther afield than Winchester or Portsmouth.

She stood up, apologizing profusely for her clumsiness, though her diversion had relieved everyone but Lady Briscow, who clearly needed no relief.

Lady Melton said hastily, "It was so easy to do, Lady Edgecombe. Such a stupid place to put the dish. I can't think why the footman would have placed it there."

Juliana attempted to excuse the footman and blame herself, but Tarquin said coolly, "Come, my dear Lady Edgecombe. No harm's done, and you're making a great matter out of a very little one." He swept her with him out of the parlor.

"I wish I weren't so damnably clumsy," Juliana lamented, once more ensconced in the phaeton. "It's so embarrassing."

"Well, on this occasion your clumsiness did everyone a good turn," the duke said wryly. "Cornelia Briscow has the crudest tongue in town."

"But is my husband's . . . uh . . . predilection . . . generally known, then?"

"Of course. He's caused enough scandal in his time to ruin a dozen families. But it's not generally the subject for polite conversation."

"Nor a subject to be mentioned before his bride gets to the altar," she said tartly.

Tarquin glanced sideways at her. "I couldn't imagine what possible good it would do you to know."

He sounded so infuriatingly certain of himself. Did he never question his actions, or their consequences? But he had shown remorse for the whole debacle with Lucien, she reminded herself, so there was nothing to be gained by continuing to pluck that crow.

"Lord Quentin seems to find Lady Lydia's company agreeable," she observed casually after a minute.

"So do most people," the duke said, sounding a trifle surprised at this conversational turn.

"Yes, of course," Juliana agreed. "She's a most charming lady. Very kind, I believe."

"She's certainly that."

"Very pretty, too. I think men find pale fairness most appealing."

"Now, what would you know about it?" Tarquin looked at her again with an amused smile.

"Well, I can't see how they wouldn't. Lord Quentin certainly seems to find Lady Lydia very attractive."

"She's a very old friend," he said with a slight frown. "Quentin has known Lydia from early childhood."

"I wonder when he'll get married," Juliana mused. "Canons do get married, don't they?"

"Certainly. Bishops too." He turned his horses into the mews behind his house. "Quentin will find himself the perfect bishop's wife, one who will grace the bishop's palace and set a fine example to the wives of his clergy, and they'll have a quiverful of children."

He tossed the reins to a groom and jumped to the cobbles. "Come."

Juliana took his proffered hand and jumped down beside him, her hoop swinging around her. She stood frowning at a rain barrel, where a water beetle was scudding across the murky surface.

"Hey, penny for your thoughts?" Tarquin tilted her chin.

She shook her head dismissively. She wasn't about to tell him that she was trying to think of a way to sow a little seed in his stubborn brain. "I was thinking perhaps Lucy might like an airing in the barouche."

"By all means," he said. "But you will take Ted as escort."

Juliana grimaced but made no demur. She dropped him a tiny curtsy and went into the house through the back door.

Tarquin gazed after her. She hadn't been thinking about Lucy at all. Something much more complicated had been going on behind those great green eyes.

He found himself wishing that he could know her thoughts, wishing that he could slide behind her eyes into the private world of Juliana herself. She gave so much of herself, but there was always a little that was kept back. He would like to know her as well as she knew herself . . . maybe even better than she knew herself. And with that urge came another: That she should know and understand him as no one else had ever done.

He shook his head as if to dispel these extraordinary fancies. Romantic nonsense that had no place in his scheme of things. He'd never been troubled by such sentimental notions before. Maybe he had a touch of fever. He passed a hand across his brow, but it felt quite cool. With another irritated head shake he followed Juliana into the house.

Chapter 21

"Here's that horrible man again." Lady Forsett turned from the drawing-room window, her aquiline nose twitching with disdain.

"What horrible man, my dear?" Sir Brian looked up from his newspaper.

"John Ridge's son. Such an uncouth oaf. What can he possibly want now?"

"I would imagine it has something to do with Juliana," her husband observed calmly. Amelia had conveniently forgotten all about their erstwhile ward. He couldn't remember hearing her refer to the girl once since her disappearance.

Lady Amelia's nose twitched again, as if it had located a particularly unpleasant odor. "The child has never been anything but trouble," she declared. "It would be just like her to plague us with that vulgar man."

"I doubt Juliana would be encouraging George Ridge to pester us," Sir Brian pointed out mildly. "Knowing Juliana, I would imagine she would be wishing her stepson to the devil."

"Really, Sir Brian, must you use such language in my company?" Lady Forsett opened and closed her fan with reproving clicks.

"I do beg your pardon, my dear. . . . Ah, Dawkins, show the gentleman in." The footman, who'd arrived to announce the visitor, looked surprised at having his errand anticipated.

"Not in my drawing room," Amelia protested. "He's bound to have manure on his boots. Show him into the morning room."

The footman bowed and removed himself. "I daresay you don't wish to meet Ridge," Sir Brian said, rising reluctantly from his chair. "I'll see him alone."

"Indeed, sir, but I wish to hear what he's come about," his wife declared firmly. "If he has news of Juliana, then I want to hear it." She sailed to the door in a starched rustle of taffeta. "You don't suppose he could have found her, do you, sir?" Her pale eyes reflected only dismay at the prospect.

"I trust not, my dear. The man couldn't find an oak tree if it stood in his path. I daresay he's come to demand Juliana's jointure or some such bluster." Sir Brian followed his lady to the morning room.

George was standing ill at ease in the middle of the small room. He was very conscious of his London finery and tugged at his scarlet-and-green-striped waistcoat as the door opened to admit his hosts. He bowed with what he hoped was a London flourish, determined that these supercilious folk would acknowledge the town bronze he'd acquired in the last week.

"Sir George." Sir Brian sketched a bow in return. Lady Forsett merely inclined her head, disdaining to offer a curtsy. George visibly bristled. She was looking at him as if he'd come to call reeking of the farmyard with straw in his hair.

"Sir Brian . . . madam," he began portentously, "I am come with news that in happier circumstances would bring you comfort, but, alas, in prevailing circumstances I fear it can only bring you the utmost distress." He waited for a response, and waited in vain. His hosts merely regarded him with an air of scant interest. He licked his dry lips and involuntarily loosened his stiffly starched cravat. He was parched, and no mention had been made of refreshment . . . not even a glass of wine.

"Juliana," he tried again. "It concerns Juliana."

"I rather assumed so," Sir Brian said politely. "You seem a little warm, Sir George. I daresay you had a hot ride."

"Devilish hot . . . oh, beggin' your pardon, ma'am." He flushed and fumbled for his handkerchief to wipe his brow.

"Maybe you'd like a glass of lemonade," Amelia said distantly, reaching for the bell rope.

George cast Sir Brian an anguished look, and his host took pity on him. "I daresay the man would prefer a tankard of ale on such a hot afternoon." He gave order to the footman who had appeared in answer to the summons, then turned back to George. "Am I to assume you've found Juliana, Sir George?"

"Oh, yes, yes, indeed, sir." George stepped forward eagerly. Sir Brian stepped back. "But I found her in the most distressing circumstances."

"She is in want?" Lady Forsett asked coldly.

"No . . . no, I don't believe so, ma'am. But the truth is . . . well the truth is . . . not something for the lady's ears, sir." He turned with a significant nod to Sir Brian.

"I can assure you my ears aren't so nice," Amelia said. "Do, I pray you, get to the point."

George took a deep breath and rushed headlong into his tale. His audience gave him all their attention, interrupting him only to press upon him a foaming tankard of ale. Lady Forsett took a seat on a delicate gilt chair and remained motionless, her hands clasped on her fan in her lap. Sir Brian tapped his mouth with a forefinger but other than that showed no emotion.

When George had reached the conclusion of his narrative and was thirstily drinking his ale, Sir Brian said, "Let me just clarify this, Sir George. You're saying that Juliana is now Viscountess Edgecombe, lodged under the roof of the Duke of Redmayne?"

"Yes, sir." George nodded vigorously, wiping a mustache of foam from his upper lip with the back of his hand.

"Legally married?"

"Apparently so."

"Then surely she's to be congratulated."

George looked confused. "She's turned whore, sir. I thought I explained that."

"But she's respectably wed to a member of the peerage?" Sir Brian offered a puzzled frown. "I fail to see how the two states can coexist."

George began to feel the ground slipping from beneath his feet. "She denies who she is," he said. "She ignores me . . . looks straight through me."

"I would never have credited her with so much sense," Amelia murmured.

"Madam, she murdered her husband . . . my father." George slammed his empty tankard onto a table.

"Not so hot, sir . . . not so hot," Sir Brian advised. "There's no need for a show of temper."

"But I will have her brought to justice, I tell you."

"By all means, you must do what seems best to you," Sir Brian said calmly. "I wouldn't stand in your way, my dear sir."

George looked nonplussed. "But if she refuses to acknowledge her identity, and she has the duke's protection, then it will be difficult for me to challenge her masquerade, and I must do that if I'm to lay charges against her. I need you to verify my identification," he explained earnestly, as if his audience might have failed to grasp the obvious point.

Sir Brian's eyebrows disappeared into his scalp. "My good sir, you cannot be suggesting I journey to London. I detest the place."

"But how else are you to see her?" George stumbled.

"I have no intention of seeing her. If, indeed, she is so established, I would be doing her a grave disservice."

"You won't have her brought to justice?" George's eyes popped.

"I find it difficult to believe that Juliana was responsible for your father's death," Sir Brian said consideringly. "It was, of course, a most unfortunate occurrence, but I can't believe Juliana should be punished for it."

"I will see her burned at the stake, sir." George strode to the door. "With or without your assistance."

"That is, of course, your prerogative," Sir Brian said.

George turned at the door, his face crimson with rage and frustration. "And I will have my inheritance back, Sir Brian. Don't think I don't know why it suits you to let her go unchallenged."

Sir Brian raised an eyebrow. "My dear sir, I do protest. You'll be accusing me of ensuring her disappearance next."

George went out, the door crashing shut behind him.

"Dear me, what a dreadful fellow," Sir Brian declared in a bored tone.

Lady Forsett's fan snapped beneath her fingers. "If he has found Juliana and it is as he says, then we cannot acknowledge her. Apart from the scandal over Sir John's death, her present situation is disgraceful. She may be married, but it's certain she took the whore's way to the viscount's bed, and you may be sure there's something most irregular about the connection."

"I doubt Juliana wishes to be acknowledged by us," her husband observed with an arid smile. "I suggest we wish her the best of luck and wash our hands of the whole business."

"But what if that oaf manages to bring her before the magistrates on such a charge?"

"Why, then, my dear, we simply repudiate her. She's been out of our hands since her wedding day. We have no obligation either to help her or to hinder her, as I see it."

"But if she is discovered, then either way you will lose control of her jointure."

Sir Brian shrugged. "So be it. But you may be sure that while I have it, I am making the most of it, my dear. The trust is turning a handsome profit at present. And, besides," he added with another humorless smile, "she may well be carrying a child. In which case her jointure will remain in my hands if she's found guilty of her husband's death. Her first husband's death," he amended. "She really has been remarkably busy. I must commend her industry. But, then, she always did have a surplus of energy."

Amelia dismissed this pleasantry with an irritated wave. "The jointure will remain in your control only if the child can be proved to be Sir John's."

"How would they prove otherwise?"

"It would be a matter of dates," Amelia pointed out. "The child must be born within nine months of Sir John's death."

"Quite so," her husband agreed tranquilly. "Let us see what happens, shall we? If she is found and brought to justice, then we will simply wash our hands of her very publicly. But I trust that won't happen. I really don't wish Juliana injury, do you, my dear?"

Amelia considered this with a frown. "No," she pronounced finally. "I don't believe I do. She was always a dreadful nuisance, but so long as she doesn't cause us any further inconvenience, she may marry a duke if she pleases, or go to the devil with my blessing."

Her husband nodded. "Benign neglect is in everyone's best interests, ma'am. Except, of course, Sir George's."

"Juliana will be a match for that fool," pronounced Lady Forsett.

"And if she's not, then we shall rethink our position." Sir Brian strolled to the door. "I'll be in my book room until dinner."

His wife curtsied and rang the bell rope to tell the servants to air the morning room. The man's pomade had been overpowering, almost worse than the stale sweat it was designed to mask.

Mistress Mitchell crouched closer to the wall, the upturned tumbler pressed to her ear. She could hardly believe what she was hearing. The ungrateful hussies were complaining of their usage, of the terms of their employment, were exchanging stories of mistreatment, and now were proposing to set up against their protectors. They were talking of buying their own supplies of candles, wine, coal. Of having a joint fund to support them in need so they wouldn't have to go into debt to their abbesses or whoremasters. It was unheard of. It was rebellion. And it was all coming from that sweet-tongued serpent that Elizabeth Dennison had placed with the Duke of Redmayne. She'd clearly got above herself since her removal to His Grace's establishment. Didn't she know she owed Mistress Dennison gratitude on her knees? But if she thought she could lead the others astray, then Miss Juliana, or whatever she called herself, was in for a nasty surprise. Indeed, they all were.

Mistress Mitchell forced herself to continue listening, resisting the urge to run immediately to her fellow bawds with the news of this traitorous meeting. She was glad of her restraint when she heard them plan to meet again. There was some discussion as to time and venue, its being agreed that they shouldn't use the same place twice, in case they aroused suspicion. Mistress Mitchell snorted derisively at this. Whatever precautions they took, how could they possibly expect to carry off such a heinous scheme of treachery under the very noses of those who managed them?

She pressed closer to the wall as the murmur of voices grew more indistinct. Then she heard Mother Cocksedge mentioned. She smiled grimly. A most unpleasant surprise could be arranged if they met in Cocksedge's house.

From the scrape of chair on floor, the rustle of skirts, the increased volume of their voices, it sounded as if they were preparing to break up the party, so she took her considerable bulk down the back stairs with creditable speed and was hovering in the taproom as they came tripping down in a chattering group.

"Had a good party, dearies?"

"Yes, thank you, Mistress Mitchell." Deborah dropped a polite curtsy.

"And whose birthday was it?"

There was an infinitesimal silence; then Lilly said firmly, "Mine, ma'am. And I have to thank you kindly for your hospitality."

"Not at all, dearie, not all." The woman smiled and nodded, busily polishing a brass candlestick on her apron. "Anytime, my dears."

Juliana was the last down the stairs. She stood for a moment, listening to this exchange, wondering what it was about the woman that made her uneasy. There was something false about her kindly jollity, something artificial in her smile. Then she realized that the smile came nowhere near the woman's sharp black eyes—that those eyes were shifting and darting around the room, looking everywhere but directly at the group of women.

"Come, Juliana. Will you walk with us to Russell Street?" Lilly turned to her, and Juliana shook herself free of unease. It had been a most heartening meeting. Her proposals had been greeted with more enthusiasm than doubt, although there were some skeptics in the group— those who couldn't believe a whore could exist without the protecting and exploiting arm of a master.

She went outside with the others, nodding farewell to Mistress Mitchell, whose smile revealed blackened stumps in a flaccid mouth. The bawd was of a different order from Mistress Dennison, Juliana reflected. The social hierarchy in this underworld was as rigidly defined as it was in her own world.

She walked arm in arm with Lilly toward Russell Street, glancing over her shoulder, half expecting to see the imperturbable Ted on her heels. She'd managed to evade him with the simple expedient of leaving the house by the back stairs and telling no one. She would face the inevitable fireworks on her return. She didn't have to admit where she'd been. The duke had not mentioned Lucy's letter again, so she assumed he hadn't read the relevant paragraph.

She turned back to Lilly, who was excitedly describing her surprise at how enthusiastic everyone had been at the meeting. Suddenly Juliana jerked her head sideways again. Immediately she cursed herself for the reflex action. George was standing on the corner of Russell Street, gazing at her. He'd seen her turn. He would have seen the startled flash of recognition in her eyes, however rapidly it was suppressed.

She couldn't risk taking a chair now on her own. It would be all too easy for George to follow, to force himself upon her. Now she would have given anything for the sight of the imperturbable Ted. She was aware of George following them down the street. He was making no attempt to hide his pursuit; indeed, his step was almost jaunty. It was almost as if he was mocking her, challenging her to evade him.

When they reached the house, she accompanied the others inside, managing not to look behind her, although the skin on her back prickled. "Is there a back way out of the house?"

"Why?" Lilly looked at her in puzzlement.

Juliana frowned, wondering whether she could take them into her confidence. She settled for half the story. "There's a man following me. I don't wish to speak with him."

"Juliana, who is he?" They all pressed closer, eyes shining with curiosity.

"A man from the past," Juliana said mysteriously. "An odious creature who's been pestering me for days."

"Like that dreadful Captain Waters," Rosamund said. "He followed Lilly around for months. Even after Mr. Garston had warned him off."

"Lud, he was a vile nuisance." Lilly fanned herself vigorously as if she would waft away the memory. "He never paid his bill or brought presents, or even left me a little something for myself. It's no wonder Mr. Dennison barred him from the house."

"But he still came around making sheep's eyes at you." Emma chuckled. "Offered to wed you, didn't he?"

"La! I'd not throw myself away on a wet-handed pauper," Lilly declared with disgust. "I know my worth, let me tell you."

All interest in Juliana's pursuer had been forgotten in this reminiscence, and when she asked again for a way out of the back, Rosamund without further question directed her to a door through the kitchens that opened onto a narrow alley piled with kitchen refuse.

George couldn't believe his luck. Juliana was in the whorehouse again. This time she hadn't been conveyed in the duke's chair and there were no stalwart ducal employees to protect her. There was no sign, either, of the ugly-looking customer who had been accompanying her hitherto. The field was clear. He'd tried the legitimate path with his appeal to the Forsetts. Now he would do what he really wanted to do. He would take her off the street. And he would keep her until he'd had enough of her. Then he would give her up to the magistrates. He didn't need the help of that drunkard Edgecombe. This he could do alone.

But she'd seen him. He'd seen the flash of recognition in her eyes. She wouldn't walk into his arms. Pleased with his cunning, George retraced his steps, looking for the back of the house. Juliana was an artful bitch. She would attempt to give him the slip, and there was only one way she could do that.

Juliana stepped into the narrow alley and looked around, conscious of the door to safety at her back. A mangy dog sniffed at the refuse in the kennel, but there was no other movement in the alley. She slipped into the open and hastened toward Charles Street, a square of light at the end of the gloomy, noisome cobbled corridor. She emerged into the busy street and looked around for a chair or a passing hackney.

Then it happened. One minute she was standing in the sunshine, the next enveloped in a dense, suffocating black-

ness. She had heard nothing, seen nothing. Now her limbs
were caught up in thick folds of material. A hand was
pressed hard against her face stifling her cries. She was
lifted, twisted, bundled, thrust through a narrow aperture,
banging her covered head on the edge of something. Arms
like iron bands clutched her, holding her still and steady. A
whip cracked, and she realized she was in a coach of some
kind. The vehicle lurched forward and the arms around her
tightened. She struggled and kicked, but the hand pressed
the wadded material against her mouth and nose until black
spots danced in front of her eyes and her lungs screamed for
air. She fell still and immediately the suffocating pressure
was eased. She was accustomed to thinking of herself as
big-boned and ungainly, strong enough to break most
holds, but she couldn't fight against suffocation.

She forced herself to keep still. The blanket swaddling
her smelled strongly of horse. As her mind cleared, she
realized that she was in George's hands. Her captor was a
big man, like George, and she could feel his flabbiness, feel
the excess flesh rolling over his frame as he held her against
him. A shudder of revulsion ripped through her. What was
he going to do with her? But she knew the answer to that
perfectly well. In her mind's eye she saw George in his
cups, his little eyes lusting, his loose lips wet and hungry.
She could almost feel his great hands on her body, pulling
the clothes from her, falling onto her as she lay pinned
beneath him, his fetid breath suffocating. . . .

Panic flooded her and she began to struggle again, her
legs flailing desperately against the confining folds of her
skirts and the enfolding blanket. Again the wadded material
pressed against her nose. Again she fought for breath . . .
and then suddenly the vehicle lurched to a halt. There were
confused shouts, bumps. A violent thud that set the coach
rocking as if someone had jumped into the vehicle. The
pressure was abruptly lifted. Her lungs gulped at the hot,
stale air trapped in the musty folds of the blanket.

George was bellowing, still clutching at her but not as
securely as before. She renewed her struggles to free herself

from the blanket. She had no idea what was going on around her, but whatever it was, it gave her a slim chance to escape.

George's arms suddenly went slack, and she tumbled off his knee and onto the floor of the carriage. She rolled over onto her hands and knees and heaved herself upright, throwing off the blanket, emerging pink, breathless, and sweaty . . . to find George slumped unconscious against the squabs of the hackney and Ted, his hand still in a fist, regarding her with undisguised irritation.

"I've better things to do than chasin' all over town looking for you," he stated before throwing open the door and calling up to the box. "Hey . . . jarvey. 'Elp me get rid of this bloke."

The jarvey appeared in the open door. He gazed dispassionately at the unconscious George. "Who'll be payin' me fare, then?"

Ted didn't answer. He grabbed George by the shoulders and hauled him off the bench. " 'Ere, take his legs."

The jarvey obliged. A small crowd had gathered around them, but no one seemed concerned as the two men swung George out of the carriage and propped him up against the wall of a tavern.

"Right," Ted said, brushing off his hands. "Albermarle Street, now, jarvey."

"So ye'll be payin' the bloke's fare as well as your'n?" the jarvey asked suspiciously.

"Ye'll be paid," Ted said impatiently, swinging himself into the vehicle with surprising agility for such a big man. It occurred to Juliana that the thump she'd heard must have been Ted's surprise entrance into the hackney.

"Right y'are." The driver, whistling cheerfully, mounted his box. "Go anywhere, do anything, that's Joe Hogg fer ye. Jest as long as I gets me fare. All in a day's work to me."

Juliana kicked the smelly horse blanket under the seat. Presumably the obliging jarvey had lent it to George. After what she'd seen in the streets of London since her arrival in the city, she was not surprised that George had been able to abduct her without interference.

Ted slumped in a corner, regarding her in morose silence.

"How did you know where to look for me?" Juliana asked tentatively.

" 'Is Grace 'ad an inklin'."

So he had read the letter. But why hadn't he said anything . . . done anything to prevent her giving Ted the slip? But perhaps she hadn't given Ted the slip. "Have you been following me all morning?"

Ted grunted an affirmative.

"So I was never really in any danger from George," Juliana mused, relief giving way to anger. Ted had deliberately let her walk into George's ambush.

Ted made no response. The carriage drew up at Albermarle Street, and Juliana jumped to the ground after Ted. Leaving him haggling with the jarvey, she stalked up the steps and into the house.

"Where's His Grace, Catlett?"

"Here." The duke spoke from the library door before Catlett could answer. His gray eyes were cold as a winter sky, his mouth tight. "Let us go to your bedchamber, Lady Edgecombe." He gestured that she should precede him up the stairs.

Juliana hesitated, then acquiesced, reasoning that she couldn't give full rein to her own outrage in front of the butler. The duke might consider he had a grievance, but she had one as well.

She marched up the stairs and threw open the door of her bedchamber, swinging round to face him as he entered behind her. He slammed the door and, before she could open her mouth, took her by the shoulders and shook her. "Just look at you, Juliana. You look as if you've been dragged through a hedge backward. You're a disgraceful sight." He propelled her toward the cheval glass. "Take a look at yourself! Anyone would think you'd been rolling in a ditch with a farmhand!"

Juliana was so taken aback by this seemingly irrelevant attack that she couldn't speak for a minute. She stared at her image in the glass. Her hair was tumbling loose around her shoulders, bits of fluff and what looked like straw clinging to the curls. Her gown was covered in dust and woolen fibers and what were clearly horse hairs. Her face was smudged with dirt.

She found her voice. "What do you expect me to look like after I've been manhandled by that oaf, rolled in a stinking horse blanket, and half suffocated? And whose fault is it, I should like to know? *You* let me walk into his trap." Her voice shook with renewed anger. "You're an unmitigated whoreson!" She rubbed the side of her hand over her mouth, trying to rid her tongue and lips of still-clinging threads of blanket hair.

"So George is responsible for your state! Dear God, you are an incorrigible chit!" Tarquin exclaimed. "He does what he's been threatening to do for weeks because you almost invite him to, and then you dare blame me for your reckless stupidity."

"Yes, I do," she cried. "Ted was following me all morning. You read Lucy's letter and you knew where I was going, and you told Ted to let George abduct me."

"Oh, now wait a minute!" His hands closed hard over her shoulders again. "Hold your tongue and listen to me. You deliberately exposed yourself to a danger that you knew was out there. You deliberately chose to evade the protection I had provided for you. You did the same with Lucien, and though I'm willing to accept some share of the blame there, I will not shoulder any responsibility for this morning! Do you hear me?" He shook her in vigorous emphasis.

"Maybe I did underestimate George, but you aided and abetted him," Juliana stated, aware, to her fury, that tears were starting in her eyes. "You're a treacherous cur!" She sniffed and dashed a hand across her eyes. "Of all the heartless, vile, despicable things to do. You let me walk into George's trap. You let me be frightened and manhandled. You let me think I was in danger when I wasn't."

"I don't know what you're talking about," he said impatiently. "I had no idea George was on the scene this morning. I knew only that you were planning some expedition with Dennison's girls. I didn't tell you I knew because I rather hoped that your better judgment would prevail. When it didn't, I sent Ted after you. I never tell Ted how to do his job. His instructions were to see that no harm came to you and to bring you back, when I intended to make my feelings known to you in no uncertain terms. How he accomplished his task was his business."

Juliana swallowed, her anger doused as effectively as a fire with a bucket of water. "You didn't tell him to let me be kidnapped?"

"No, of course I didn't. But he obviously thought you needed a lesson. Ted doesn't take kindly to people attempting to get the better of him."

"Oh." Rather forlornly, Juliana wiped her nose with the back of her hand.

Tarquin released his grip on her shoulders, pulled a handkerchief out of his pocket, and briskly wiped her nose and her eyes. "Weeping won't improve your appearance."

"I'm only crying because I'm angry," she said. "Or at least I was. But I still don't see how you can say my actions have nothing to do with you. If you hadn't forbidden me to see my friends, then I wouldn't have had to try to go alone. You have the right to forbid them under your roof, but you don't have the right to prevent me from visiting them under theirs."

"We have a contract," he stated flatly. "And one of its clauses is that you behave in a manner befitting Viscountess Edgecombe. Consorting with whores is not appropriate behavior. Wandering the streets looking like a haystack is not appropriate behavior. Therefore, you will not do it."

Juliana turned away from her image in the glass. It lent too much weight to the duke's argument. She would not back down on her right to choose her friends. But nothing would be served by saying so at this point. "You speak of a contract, my lord duke. Can it be a true contract when one side was blackmailed into signing it?"

"You signed it in exchange for my protection, for the security and comfort of my home, for the assurance that you would never be in want. That's a strange kind of blackmail to my mind." His voice was icy.

"And if I hadn't signed it, you would have betrayed me," she threw at him bitterly.

"Did I ever say that?"

Her mouth opened in astonishment. "No, but . . . but you implied it."

He shrugged. "How you choose to interpret my words is not my responsibility."

"How could you say that?" She stared at him in disbelief. "Of all the treacherous, slippery *snakes*! Oh, go away and leave me alone!" She turned away again with an angry gesture, trying to control her tears.

Tarquin regarded her averted back in frowning silence, running his fingertips reflectively over his lips. He would never have betrayed her to the law, but there was no way Juliana could have known that. He *had*, however, rescued her from a miserable life on the streets and probably a premature, wretched death. The fact that he'd done so for his own ends didn't change that truth. Why wouldn't she just accept the situation? He couldn't understand what she had to object to in her present life. She enjoyed the passion they shared. She was safe from Lucien. She was provided for for the rest of her life. So why did she take such pleasure in defying him? She was the most perverse creature he'd ever had dealings with. If he'd known she would cause him so much trouble when he'd watched her through Mistress Dennison's peephole, he would have looked elsewhere for the tool to control Lucien.

"Go away!" Juliana repeated crossly. "You've made your point. There's no need to gloat."

Gloat! He almost laughed aloud. If anyone should be gloating, it was Juliana. Turning on his heel, he left her to her angry tears.

Chapter 22

"I daresay you've known Lady Lydia all your life," Juliana remarked to Lord Quentin several mornings later, when he returned to her parlor after escorting her visitors to their carriages.

"What makes you say that?" He walked to the window overlooking the garden and stood looking out so she could see nothing of his face.

"Oh, just that you seem very easy together. Like very old friends." She refilled their coffee cups with an air of nonchalance.

In the last few days Lady Lydia had been a frequent visitor to Lady Edgecombe. Somehow her visits coincided with Lord Quentin's seemingly casual presence in Juliana's parlor. Lady Lydia never came alone; she always had some friend or acquaintance of her mother's in tow, a lady anxious to pay a courtesy visit to the new bride. But it was clear to Juliana, at least, that these chaperons were merely a blind. Behind their presence, Lady Lydia and Lord Quentin could talk and smile, brush hands in a fleeting gesture, sit side by side on a sofa, their heads bent together over a book of illustrations.

"We are old friends." Quentin turned from the window

to take his refilled cup, that same bleak look haunting his eyes.

"But you feel more for each other than friendship." Juliana found herself taking the bull by the horns without conscious thought. Her impulses were always getting the better of her, but maybe in this case it might prove helpful.

Quentin said nothing for a minute. He drank his coffee, then said, "Is it that obvious?"

"To me."

"I am trying so hard to control it, Juliana." Quentin's voice was low and anguished, reflecting the misery in his eyes. "But I can't bear the idea of her marrying Tarquin. Of her marrying anyone but me." He began to pace the room from window to door, the words bubbling forth as if Juliana had unplugged a well. "I should go back to Melchester at once. Put myself beyond temptation. But I can't do it."

"Have you finished your business with the archbishop?"

Quentin shook his head. "If only I had, I wouldn't have an excuse to stay . . . to betray Tarquin every minute I'm in Lydia's company."

"You're too harsh with yourself," Juliana said practically. "You're not betraying the duke by sitting with Lydia—"

"I lust after her!" he interrupted in anguish. "God help me, Juliana, but I lust after another man's wife."

"She's not his wife yet," Juliana pointed out.

"Don't split hairs." He sat down, dropping his head in his hands. "It's mortal sin. I know it and yet I can't stop myself."

"But she feels the same way about you."

Quentin raised his head. His face was haggard. "She has said so. God forgive me, but I asked her. I forced her to acknowledge her own sin." He dropped his head in his hands again with a soft groan.

Juliana tucked an errant ringlet behind her ear. All this talk of sin, she supposed, was only to be expected from a man of the cloth, but since it was impossible to believe that Quentin had carried his devotion to Lydia as far as consummation, he did seem to be going overboard with the self-flagellation.

"Why don't you ask the duke to release her?" It seemed a simple enough solution.

Quentin gave a short, bitter laugh. "Sometimes I forget how unworldly you are. Lydia's family would never countenance a match with me. Not when their daughter is destined to be a duchess. Our world doesn't work that way, my dear."

Juliana refused to be satisfied with this. "But Lydia surely is not so mercenary?"

"Lydia! Sweet heaven, no! Lydia is an angel!"

"Yes, of course she is. But if she doesn't care about becoming a duchess, surely she can persuade her parents that she loves someone else."

Quentin shook his head, almost amused by this naive pragmaticism. "Lord and Lady Melton would never give up such an advantageous match for their daughter."

"But supposing the duke offered to release Lydia?" she suggested. "Perhaps he would do it for your sake. If he understood how you feel—and how Lydia feels."

"My dear girl, it would be the same as jilting her. Tarquin would never do that to her . . . or her family. Besides," he added with a rueful sigh, "I could never ask Tarquin to make such a sacrifice. He wants this match. He's done so much for me over the years, I couldn't bring myself to ruin his life."

"Oh, pshaw!" Juliana exclaimed in disgust. "You wouldn't be ruining his life. He'd soon get over it. It isn't as if he's in love with her. And as far as jilting Lydia is concerned, a private rearrangement is no concern of anyone's. It'll be a nine days' wonder at worst."

Quentin wondered if she was right, and for a moment hope flickered. Then it died as swiftly as it had arisen.

"Lydia has been educated to be Tarquin's wife. She will bring him Melton land to augment his own. She knows her duty and she knows what to expect. She will be a good wife and mother to his children, and she'll expect no more than courtesy and consideration in return. She won't think about other women in his life, because she knows that all women of her social status do not marry for love. She knows that she must expect her husband to seek his pleasure outside the marriage bed." The bitterness was back in his voice now. "Tarquin has no truck with sentimentality, Juliana. And love comes into that category."

"I suppose so." Her fingers plucked restlessly at an overblown rose in a bowl beside her chair. The petals showered down. She and Tarquin had had no private talk since their last confrontation. He had been polite and distant, but he hadn't come to her bed. She wondered if he was waiting for an invitation. She had told him to leave her alone, after all.

"Don't you think he could change, Quentin?" She pinched a rose petal between her fingers, not raising her eyes as she asked the question.

"He already has a little," Quentin said thoughtfully. "I think you've had a softening effect on him."

Juliana looked up with a quick flush. "Do you think so?"

"Mmmm. But then you, my dear, are a most unusual young woman." He rose to his feet and took her hand, raising it to his lips. "Unusual, and most perceptive. I didn't mean to burden you with my troubles."

Juliana's flush deepened with pleasure. "You didn't burden me with anything, sir. I'm honored with your confidence."

He smiled again and bent to kiss her cheek. "You have, at least, enabled me to see clearly again. If it's so obvious to you what Lydia and I feel, then it may become obvious to Tarquin also. I don't want that to happen."

"So what will you do?"

"Write to my bishop and ask to return before my mission is completed."

It was a sad—indeed, rather pathetic—solution, Juliana thought, but she merely nodded as if in agreement, and he left her.

She leaned back against the chair and closed her eyes for

a moment. Her hand drifted over her belly. Had she conceived? It was five weeks since her last monthly terms. She
felt no different, none of the signs so painstakingly pointed
out by Mistress Dennison. And yet she had this strange,
deep knowledge inside her body that something different
was going on. She couldn't put words to it, but it was a
definite conviction known in her blood if not in her brain.

She would wait until she was sure, of course, before
telling the duke. In their present state of estrangement he'd
probably be delighted that there was no further need for
their lovemaking. She ought to be pleased herself, but Juliana was too honest to pretend that the thought brought her
anything but a hollow pain. She hated the present coldness,
but some stubborn streak kept her from making the first
move. It was up to the duke to heal the breach if he wanted
to.

" 'E's lodgin' at the Gardener's Arms, in Cheapside, Yer
Grace." Ted took a thirsty gulp of ale. Tracking George
Ridge across London had been hot and thirsty work.

The duke was perched on the edge of the desk in his
book room, a glass of claret in hand, his canary silk coat
and britches a startling contrast to his companion's rough
leathern britches and homespun jerkin. Yet it would be
clear to anyone walking into the room that there was a
definite equality in the relationship between the Duke of
Redmayne and the stalwart Ted Rougley.

"Has he recovered from your little intervention?"

Ted grinned. "Aye, 'e's large as life an' twice as ugly."
He drained his tankard and smacked his lips.

Tarquin nodded, gesturing to the pitcher that stood on
the silver tray at the far end of the desk. Ted helped himself
with a grunt of thanks.

"An' there's summat else ye should know, Yer Grace."
Ted's tone was faintly musing, yet carried a note of some
import. Seeing he had the duke's full attention, he contin-

ued. " 'Cordin' to the missis at the Gardener's, 'e's bin 'avin' a visitor. Regular like."

"Oh?" Tarquin's eyebrows crawled into his scalp.

"Right sickly-lookin' gent, the missis said. Gave 'er the creeps 'e did. All green an' white, with eyes like the dead."

"She has a colorful turn of phrase," Tarquin observed, sipping his claret. "Are we to assume that Lucien and George have set up an unholy alliance?"

He took out his snuffbox and stood for a minute tapping a manicured fingernail against the enamel. He was remembering that George had been in the Shakespeare's Head the night Lucien had put Juliana on the block. Juliana said he'd made a bid on her. It was possible that these two, both bearing grudges against Juliana, and in Lucien's case overwhelmingly against his cousin, should have formed the devil's partnership.

Ted didn't answer what he knew had been a rhetorical question, merely regarded his employer stolidly over his tankard.

"Let's deal with George first," Tarquin said. "We'll pay a little visit to the Gardener's Arms later tonight . . . when the oaf should have returned from his amusements in the Garden. Bring a horsewhip. We must be sure to emphasize my point."

"Right y'are, Yer Grace." Ted deposited his empty tankard on the tray, bowed with a jerk of his head, and left.

The duke frowned into space, twirling the delicate stem of his glass between finger and thumb. He'd been intending to put a stop to George's antics as soon as Ted had tracked him down after the attempted abduction, but if Ridge had joined forces with Lucien, then the situation was much more menacing. Lucien was unpredictable and could be quite subtle in his malevolence. Ridge, as he'd already demonstrated, would rely on brute force. They made a formidable combination.

He stood up suddenly, impelled by a force he'd been fighting for the last couple of days. He wanted Juliana. This estrangement tore at his vitals. It was becoming almost im-

possible to keep up the cool, distant facade. Every day he
looked at her across the dinner table, at the fierce vibrancy
of her hair, the luster of her eyes, the rich curves of her
body. And he held himself away from her. It was torture, a
wrenching on the rack. And Juliana, damn her, was giving
as good as she got. Her stare was as cool as his, her voice as
flat, her conversation never transcending the banality of
small talk between strangers. He wanted to throttle her as
much as he wanted to assuage his aching longing on her
willing, eagerly responsive body.

Never had he felt like this before. As if every carefully
woven strand of his personality was tangled, his life a jum-
bled jigsaw. And all because a seventeen-year-old chit
didn't know what was good for her. What else did she
want of him, for God's sake?

With a muttered oath he flung himself out of the book
room and took the stairs two at a time. He entered Juliana's
parlor without knocking, shut the door behind him, then
stood leaning against it, regarding her in brooding silence.

Juliana had been writing a note to Lilly. At midnight
they were all due to meet at Mother Cocksedge's establishment. Juliana had planned the evening very carefully. She
was going to the opera in a party assembled by one of Lady
Melton's acquaintances. It would be easy enough to slip
away before supper. She could plead a headache, insist on
returning alone in a hackney, and instead have herself
driven to Covent Garden. In the unlikely event that the
duke returned from his own entertainment before her, he
would assume the party was sitting late over supper.

She was explaining in her letter to Lilly that she would
arrive at Cocksedge's just after midnight when Tarquin
burst in. She felt herself flush. Instinctively she thrust the
sheet of vellum to the back of the secretaire.

"My . . . my lord. This is a surprise," she managed to
say, trying for the cold tone she'd perfected recently.

"I miss you, dammit!" he stated, pushing himself away
from the door. "Goddamn you, Juliana. I can't go on like
this. I don't know what you've done to me." He pulled her

up from her chair. He held her face between both hands and kissed her with a deep urgency. His hands moved upward, pulling the pins from her hair, his fingers roughly running through it as he loosened it; all the while his tongue hungrily probed her mouth.

Juliana was so taken aback that for a minute she didn't respond; then a wild, almost primitive, triumph flashed through her veins. She had this power over him. A woman's power. A power she was positive he had never acknowledged before. Now she clung to him, at last after days of deprivation able to give expression to the unquenchable well of passion that bubbled at her core. Her tongue fenced with his, her body reached against him, rubbing, pressing, moving with sinuous temptation, and she felt him hard and urgent against her belly.

Tarquin bore her backward to the sofa, and she fell in a tangle of skirts to sink onto the shiny taffeta. He didn't release her mouth, merely pushed up her skirts to her waist, released his own aching stem, and drove deep into her body. Her legs curled around his back, and her body moved with all the urgency of a passion that had many causes but only one outlet. Anger, hurt, mistrust, desire, all consumed in the flames.

He drew her legs onto his shoulders, his palms running up the firm calves, over the smooth flesh of her thighs above her garters, cupping her buttocks. His eyes were closed as he held her in his hands, and his flesh was plunging deep into the dark, velvet depths of her body. As the little ripples of her approaching climax tantalized his flesh, he opened his eyes and looked down at her. Her own eyes were wide-open, glowing with joy, not a sign of misgiving or withholding beneath the jade surface. She was giving herself to him as if there had never been a word of doubt between them, and he knew, in that moment, that the giving was a true expression of her soul.

And in the same instant he understood what she wanted from him. A gift that came without reservations. The gift of himself. He had beneath him, her body encompassing his as he possessed hers, the possibility of a love for all time. A partner of his heart and soul.

Juliana reached up and touched his face, a look of wonder now in her eyes. He looked transformed. Her breath caught in her throat as she read the message in the intensity of his gaze. This was no longer a man who couldn't believe in the reality of love.

Chapter 23

George Ridge threw the dice. They rolled across the square of table cleared of debris and came to a halt in a puddle of ale. A six and a one. He spat disgustedly on the sawdust at his feet and tipped the bottle of port against his mouth, taking a deep draft. His guineas were scooped up with a gleeful grin by his fellow player, who spat twice in his hand, tossed the dice from palm to palm, murmured a blasphemous prayer, and rolled them. A groan went up from the crowd around the table as they saw the numbers. The one-eyed sea captain had had the luck of the devil all evening.

George pushed back his chair. He'd continued playing long past his limit and had the sinking feeling that his losses were probably greater than he realized. His brain was too addled by ale and port to function well enough for accurate calculation, but in the cold, aching light of day he'd be forced to face reality.

As he struggled unsteadily to his feet, a hand descended on his shoulder and a voice spoke quietly into his ear. It was a voice as cold as a winter sea, and it sent shivers down his spine as if he were about to plunge into such waters.

"Going somewhere, Ridge?"

George turned under the hand on his shoulder and

found himself looking up into a pair of expressionless gray eyes in a lean and elegant countenance. The thin mouth was curved in the faintest smile, but it was a smile as cold and pitiless as the voice. He recognized the man immediately. His eyes darted around the room, looking for support, but no one was paying attention. Their bleary gazes were focused on the play.

"I think we'll find it more convenient to have our little discussion in the stable yard," said the Duke of Redmayne. He removed his hand from George's shoulder. Suddenly George found himself in the grip of a pair of fists that fastened on his elbows from behind as tenaciously as the tentacles of an octopus.

"This a-way, boyo," an encouraging voice said in his ear. George's feet skimmed the ground as he was propelled through the crowded taproom and out into the yard behind the inn.

The night was hot. Two ostlers, sitting on upturned water butts smoking pipes and chatting in desultory fashion, glanced up, at first with scant interest, at the three men who'd entered the yard. Their eyes widened as they took in the curious group. A gentleman in black, gold-embroidered silk looking as if he'd just walked out of the Palace of St. James's; a second gentleman, bulky and red-faced, in a suit of crimson taffeta and a yellow-striped waistcoat; a third man in the rough leather britches and jerkin of a laborer. The second gentleman was beginning to protest, trying to free himself from the grip of the laborer. The elegant gentleman leaned casually against a low stone wall. He carried a long horsewhip that snaked around his silver-buckled shoes of red leather.

"Take your hands off me!" George blustered thickly, finally managing to get a look at the man holding him. He had but a confused recollection of the disruption in the hackney before he'd lost consciousness, but there was something horribly familiar about his captor. He struggled with renewed violence.

"I just want a word or two," the duke said carelessly, snapping the whip along the ground.

George's eyes darted wildly downward. There was something menacingly purposeful about the thin leather lash flickering and dancing across the cobbles. Ted adjusted his grip almost casually, but his victim immediately recognized that he was held even more firmly than before.

"Listen to 'Is Grace, I should," Ted advised. "Listen well, boyo."

Tarquin subjected George Ridge to a dispassionate scrutiny before saying, "Perhaps you would care to explain why you issued such a pressing invitation to Lady Edgecombe. I understand from her that she was not at all inclined to enter your hackney."

Ted shifted his booted feet on the cobbles and gazed about him incuriously, but his grip tightened yet again, pulling George's arms behind his back.

George licked suddenly dry lips. "You have a murderess under your roof, Your Grace. The murderer of my father, Juliana Ridge's late husband." He tried to sound commanding with this denunciation, full of self-confidence and righteous indignation, but his voice emerged stifled and uncoordinated.

"And just, pray, who is this Juliana Ridge?" the duke inquired in a bored tone, withdrawing his snuffbox from the deep-cuffed pocket of his coat. He flipped the lid and took a leisurely pinch while George struggled to make sense of this. Viscount Edgecombe had been convinced the duke knew all Juliana's skeletons.

He took a deep breath. "The woman living in your house. The woman who calls herself Viscountess Edgecombe. She was married to my father, Sir John Ridge of the village of Ashford, in the county of Hampshire." He paused, regarding the duke anxiously. His Grace's expression hadn't changed; he looked merely politely bored.

George continued somewhat desperately, "I daresay, Your Grace, when you found her in the whorehouse you knew nothing of her history . . . but . . ." His voice faded under the duke's now blazing gaze.

"You appear to have lost your wits, sir," the duke said softly, coiling the whip into his hand. "You would not otherwise insult the name of a woman wedded to my cousin, living under my roof and my protection. Would you?"

The last question was rapped out, and the duke took a step toward George, who couldn't move with the man at his back holding his arms in a vise.

"My lord duke," he said, clear desperation now in voice and eyes. "I do assure you I know her for what she is. She has hoodwinked you and she must be brought to justice. Her husband intends to repudiate her as soon as she's brought before the magistrate and—"

"I think I've heard enough," the duke interrupted. He didn't appear to raise his voice, but the two ostlers sat up attentively.

The duke pushed the shiny wooden handle of the whip beneath George's chin, almost gently, except that its recipient could feel the bruising pressure. "The lady living under my roof is a distant cousin of mine from York. You would do well to check your facts before you slander your betters."

The gray eyes pierced George's blurred gaze like an icicle through snow. But George knew the duke was deliberately lying. The man knew the truth about Juliana. But in the face of that bold statement, the derisive glare that challenged him to dispute it, George was dumbstruck.

The duke waited for a long moment, holding George's befuddled gaze, before saying almost carelessly, "Do not let me ever see your face within half a mile of Lady Edgecombe again." He removed the whip, tossed it to Ted, who caught it neatly with one hand.

The duke gazed silently at George for what seemed to the disbelieving Ridge to be an eternity of cold intent; then he nodded briefly to Ted, turned on his heel, and walked out of the yard.

"Well, now, boyo," Ted said genially. "Let's us come to an understanding, shall us?" He raised his whip arm. George stared, horror-struck, as the lash circled through the air. Then he bellowed like a maddened bull as he finally understood what was to happen to him.

Juliana found it impossible to concentrate on the opera, as much because her mind was on the meeting in Covent Garden as because everyone around her was chattering as if the singers on stage were not giving their hearts and souls to the first performance of Pergolesi's new work.

The Italian Opera House in the Haymarket was brilliantly lit throughout the performance with chandeliers and flaming torches along the stage. King George II was in the royal box with Queen Caroline, and Juliana found them more interesting than the incomprehensible Italian coming from the stage. It was probably as close as she would ever get to Their Majesties.

George II was an unimpressive-looking man, florid of face, an untidy white wig standing up around his bullet-shaped head. He had a most disagreeable expression, glaring around at his companions, bellowing critical comments to his aides throughout the performance in his heavily accented broken English that rose easily above the general hubbub.

After the first interval Juliana judged it time to wilt a little. She began to ply her fan with increasing fervor, every now and again sighing a little, passing her hand over her brow.

"Is something the matter, Juliana?" The eldest Bowen daughter, Lady Sarah Fordham, leaned forward anxiously. "Are you unwell?"

"The headache," Juliana said with a wan smile. "I get them on occasion. They come on very suddenly."

"Poor dear." Sarah was instantly sympathetic. She turned to her mother beside her. "Lady Edgecombe is unwell, Mama. She has a severe headache."

"Try this, my dear." Lady Bowen handed over her smelling salts. Juliana received them with another wan smile. She sniffed delicately; her eyes promptly streamed, and she gasped at the powerful burning in her nostrils. Leaning back, she closed her eyes with a sigh of misery and plied her fan with no more strength than an invalid. She'd had to revise her original plan to leave the opera and go to Covent Garden in a hired hackney. Tarquin had insisted she take his own coachman for the evening so she wouldn't be dependent upon Lady Bowen for transport. He'd meant it considerately, but it was a damnable nuisance. Now she would have to get rid of John Coachman.

"I do fear I shall swoon, ma'am," she murmured. "If I could but take the air for a few minutes . . ."

"Cedric shall escort you." Lady Bowen snapped her fingers at Lord Cedric, a willowy, effete young gentleman who happened to enjoy the opera—not that he had much opportunity to do so in the noisy clamor of his mother's box. "Take Lady Edgecombe for some air, Cedric."

Reluctantly, the young man abandoned the soprano-and-tenor duet that he'd been straining to hear. Bowing, he offered his arm to Juliana, who staggered to her feet with another little moan, pressing her hand to her forehead.

Outside, on the steps of the opera house, she breathed the sultry air and sighed pathetically. "I really think I must go home, sir," she said in a weak voice. "If you could make my excuses to your mama and summon my coachman, I need not keep you from the music another minute."

"No trouble, ma'am . . . no trouble at all," he stammered, but without the true ring of conviction. Leaving Juliana on the top step, he ran down to the street and sent an urchin to summon the Duke of Redmayne's carriage. It appeared within five minutes. Juliana was installed within, the coachman instructed to return with all speed to Albermarle Street, and Cedric Bowen hastened back to his music.

Juliana banged on the roof of the carriage as it was about

to turn right onto Pall Mall. The coachman drew rein and leaned down from his box.

"Take me instead to Covent Garden," Lady Edgecombe instructed in her most imperious tones. "I left my fan in a coffeehouse there this morning. I would see if it's still there."

The coachman had no reason to disobey Her Ladyship's orders. He withdrew to the box, turned his horses, and drove to Covent Garden. Juliana tried to control her apprehension, which was mixed with a curious excitement, as if she were embarking on a great adventure. She was hoping that some of the street women would come to the meeting as well as the more highly placed courtesans. It would be convenient for them to take an hour off work and slip into Cocksedge's tavern, where Juliana hoped to convince them that a simple investment of trust and solidarity could make an enormous difference to their working conditions. A few of the High Impures would be unable to leave their establishments to attend, but there were plenty who could find an excuse for visiting clients outside the house, and Lilly had decided to plead sickness early in the evening in order to make her escape from Russell Street.

But Juliana knew that with or without her friends' support, the success of this embryonic plan depended upon her powers of persuasion and her own energy and commitment. She had to make them see her own vision, and see how to make it reality.

She banged on the roof again when they reached St. Paul's Church. "Wait here for me," she instructed, swinging open the carriage door and stepping to the cobbles, managing to avoid a pile of rotting, slimy cabbage leaves just waiting to catch the foot of the unwary. Gathering her skirts in her hands, she picked her way through the market refuse toward Mother Cocksedge's establishment. The church clock struck midnight.

Noise spilled through the open door of the chocolate house run by Mother Cocksedge. Drunken voices, raucous laughter, the shrill skirl of a pipe.

Juliana stepped through the door and blinked, her eyes slowly adapting to the gloom. The sights were becoming familiar. The whores swayed drunkenly in various stages of undress, either touting for custom or satisfying the demands of a customer. Two dogs fought over a scrap of offal in the center of the room amid a loudly wagering circle of young gentlemen, dressed in the finery of courtiers; their cravats were loose, their wigs in disarray, their stockings twisted. Women crowded around them, touching, stroking, petting, receiving kisses and occasional rowdy slaps in exchange, as the young bloods drank from tankards of blue ruin and shouted obscenities to the rafters.

Juliana felt immediately exposed. This was not like slipping upstairs to Mistress Mitchell's back room. But she knew that the women they were hoping to gather tonight would be more comfortable in this place than in a more exclusive and expensive establishment. She pushed her way through to the back of the taproom, her tall figure and flaming hair attracting immediate attention.

"Hey, where're you off to, my beauty?" A young man grabbed her arm and grinned vapidly at her. "Haven't seen you in these parts before."

"Let me go," Juliana said coldly, shaking her arm free.

"Oho! Hoity-toity madam," another young man bellowed, his eyes small and red in a round, almost childlike, face. "Give us a kiss, m'dear, and we'll let you pass." He lurched toward her, leering.

Juliana gave him a push, and he tumbled backward against the table amid shrieks of laughter. Before he could recoup, Juliana had pushed through to the rear of the room.

"Juliana!" Lilly's fierce whisper reached her as she paused, wondering where to go and whom to ask. The young woman beckoned from a doorway. "Quickly. They don't know we're in here, but if they find out, they'll start such a ruckus." She pulled Juliana into the room, slamming the door behind her. " 'Tis the very devil, but there's no key to the door. And the young bloods are always the worst. They'll start a melee at the drop of a hat, and before we know it, we'll be in the middle of a riot."

"I can believe it," Juliana said grimly, shaking out the folds of her gown, which had become crushed as she'd fought her way through the room. "Nasty little beasts."

"Our bread and butter," a woman said from the table, raising a tankard of ale to her lips. "But not for the likes of you, my lady." She smiled sardonically. "It's all very well to be full of grand plans when it's not yer livelihood at stake."

"Now, Tina, don't be so sharp. Let the girl say what she 'as in mind." An older woman in a tawdry yellow dress gave Juliana a much nicer smile. "Come on in, dearie. Take no notice of Tina, she's sour because 'er gentleman jest passed out on 'er an' she couldn't get a penny outta him."

Juliana looked around the room, recognizing amid the substantial group some faces from the earlier meeting. Women sat at the table, lounged on the broad windowsill, perched on the settles on either side of the hearth. They were all drinking, even the Russell Street women, and for the most part those unknown to Juliana looked skeptically at her when she introduced herself.

"Well, let's 'ear what ye've to say," Tina said, still belligerently. "We ain't got all night. Some of us 'ave a livin' to earn."

Juliana decided that attempting to justify her own position would be pointless. Let them believe what they would of her. She had more important matters to concentrate on. The street women were harried and thin-faced, their clothes shabby finery that she guessed had been on other backs before. Beside them, the girls from Russell Street and similar houses looked pampered and affluent, but they all shared something: A wariness, a darting mistrust in their eyes, an air of resignation to the vagaries of fate, as if what security they had today could be gone tomorrow and there was nothing they could do about it. Beside them, the safety and permanence of her own situation must look like heaven. And these were not the poorest of the women out there. There were women and young girls, little more than children, lying against the bulks, winter and summer, with whoever could give them a crust of bread or a sip of gin.

She began to explain her idea, slowly and simply, but soon the images of what she'd seen, the knowledge of what lives these women led, the deep knowledge that she had escaped it by a hairbreadth, took over, and her voice grew passionate, her eyes flashing with conviction.

"It's not inevitable that we should be obliged to live as the bawds and whoremasters dictate. It's not inevitable that we should see our earnings disappear into the pockets of greedy masters. It's not inevitable that we should live in fear of prison for the slightest offense, for the smallest word out of turn. None of this is inevitable if we support each other." She had instinctively used "we" throughout. If she didn't identify with the women, she would seem like a preacher, distant on a pulpit. And, besides, she *did* identify with them, even if her situation was vastly different.

She paused for breath and Lilly jumped in, her eyes misty with tears. "We have to have a fund, as Juliana says. We each put into it whatever we can afford—"

"Afford!" exclaimed Tina, coughing into a handkerchief. "That's rich, that is. It's all right fer you what've got a decent 'ouse an' all found. But fer us . . . there's nowt twixt us an' the devil but a sixpence now an' agin if we're lucky."

"But that's my point," Juliana said eagerly. "Listen, if you didn't have to pay all those expenses, you would be able to contribute to the Sisterhood's fund. Those of us who have the most will put in the most—that's only fair. And the rest contribute what they can. But we'll find our own suppliers for coal and light and food and wine. If we can guarantee a certain amount of business, I'm sure we'll find some merchants willing to do business with us. Willing to give us credit to get started."

"Lord luv us, darlin', but who's goin' to give us credit?" wheezed a woman on the settle, laughing at the absurdity of such a prospect.

"They'll give Viscountess Edgecombe credit," Juliana said stubbornly.

A thoughtful silence fell at this. Juliana waited, her blood on fire with her passionate need to persuade them that they *could* take control of their lives. It had to be possible.

"Ye'd be willin' to put yer name out, then?" Tina looked at her with a sudden degree of respect.

"Yes." She nodded in vigorous emphasis. "I will put my own money in every week, just like everyone else, and I will undertake to find the merchants willing to do business with us."

"But, Juliana, they aren't going to be doing business with *you*," Deborah pointed out. "You have no need to buy supplies to conduct your own business."

Juliana shrugged. "I don't see that that makes any difference."

"Well, if ye don't, then us'll thankee kindly fer yer assistance," Tina stated. "That so, ladies?"

"Aye." There was a chorus of hesitant agreement, and Juliana was about to expand on her plan when the piercing squeal of a whistle drowned her words. There was a crash, a bellow, shrieks, more whistles from the room beyond. The young bloods were calling in their high-pitched excitement, furniture crashed to the floor, the sound of blows.

"Oh, dear God, it's a riot," Emma said, her face as white as a sheet. "It's the beadles."

The women were surging to the back of the room, looking for another door. Someone flung up the casement sash and they hurled themselves at the opening. Juliana just stood there in astonishment, wondering what the panic was all about. The disturbance was all in the room next door. If they stayed quiet, no one would come in. They'd done nothing. They were doing nothing to disturb the peace.

Suddenly a voice bellowed from the open window, "No ye don't, woman. Y'are not gettin' away from me. All right, my pretties, settle down now. Mr. Justice Fielding is awaitin' on ye."

Deborah gave a low moan of despair. Juliana stared at the

glowering face of the beadle in the window, his rod of office raised threateningly. Behind him, two others were wrestling with one of the women who'd managed to get through the window. Then the door flew open. She had a glimpse of the room behind, the scene of chaos, the mass of grinning or scowling faces lost in a frenzied orgy of destruction. Then she saw Mistress Mitchell standing with another woman in a print gown and mob cap. They were both talking to a constable as his fellows surged into the room where the women were now huddling, swinging their batons to left and right, grabbing the women, herding them toward the door.

Juliana was caught up with the rest. She lashed out with a fist and a foot and had the satisfaction of feeling them meet their mark, but it did her little good. She was hustled out, pushed and shoved by the officious and none too gentle constables. And as she looked over her shoulder, Mistress Mitchell smiled with cold triumph.

They had been betrayed, and it was clear by whom. The whoremasters of Covent Garden wouldn't see their nymphs escape the yoke without a fight.

Chapter 24

⟨⟨⟩⟩

The duke's coachman was sitting on an ale bench outside a tavern under the colonnades of the Piazza, pleasantly awaiting the return of his passenger. He could see the carriage and the urchin who held the horses, but he could see little else beyond the sea of bodies eddying around the square. He heard the ruckus from Cocksedge's as just another exploding bubble in the general cacophonous stew and called for another tankard of ale.

"Beadles is raidin' some 'ouse," a shabby bawd observed from the bench beside him. "Daresay some of them varmints from up town are causin' trouble. Breakin' 'eads no doubt, drunk as lords . . . a'course, most of 'em is lords." She cackled and drained her tankard. "Not that that Sir John'll do much more 'an turn a blind eye to *their* goings-on. It's the women who'll suffer, as usual."

She stared into her empty tankard for a minute, then gathered herself to her feet with a sigh. "That ale does go through a body summat chronic." She staggered into the road, raising an imperative hand to a flyter, who stood with his pail and telltale voluminous cloak a few yards away. He trotted over to her, and she gave him a penny. The flyter set his bucket on the cobbles and then spread his cloak as a screen for the woman, who disappeared into its folds to relieve herself in relative privacy.

John Coachman paid scant interest to a sight that could be seen on every street corner in the city. He eyed his carriage in case the disturbance should show signs of coming this way. There were the sounds of running feet, more yelling and cursing, mostly female. With a grunt he hauled himself to his feet and clambered onto the box of the coach to see over the heads to the turmoil across the square.

He could make out little, except a group of constables herding a crowd of women toward Bow Street, presumably to bring them before Sir John Fielding, the local magistrate. Around the beadles and their prisoners surged a crowd of raging women, throwing rotten fruit at the constables, cursing them with fluent vigor. The constables ducked the missiles, ignored the curses, and moved their prisoners along with the encouragement of their rods. The young men from Cocksedge's roared and swayed in a drunken circle before suddenly affected by a common impulse; like lemmings, they turned in a body and reentered Cocksedge's. The sound of breaking glass and smashing furniture was added to the general tumult, Mother Cocksedge's vituperations and desperate pleas rising above it all.

John Coachman began to feel a little uneasy. Where in all this chaos was Lady Edgecombe? Presumably he should have accompanied her on her errand, but she hadn't really given him the opportunity to offer. A little shiver of apprehension ran down his spine at the thought of the duke's possible reaction to this dereliction of duty.

He stood on his box and gazed intently over the throng. The party of women and beadles was reaching the corner of Russell Street. He caught a glimpse of a flaming red head in the midst, and his heart jumped. Then he sat down again with a thump. Lady Edgecombe couldn't possibly be in the company of a group of arrested whores. Presumably she was waiting for the tumult to die down before she came back to the carriage. He couldn't leave the horses to go and look for her, even if he knew where in this inferno she had gone. If she came back to find him not there, they would be worse off than they already were. He yawned, sleepy from the ale he'd been imbibing freely, and settled down on the box, arms folded, to await Lady Edgecombe's return.

Juliana was continuing to struggle and protest as she was borne out of Covent Garden toward Bow Street. She could see only Lilly and Rosamund of the Russell Street girls and hoped that the others had escaped. The beadles couldn't possibly arrest the entire roomful of women, and it seemed to her that they were somewhat selective in the ones they harried along the street. She noticed that several women at the outskirts of the group were permitted to duck away from their captors and disappear into the dark mouths of alleys as they passed. But there was no possibility of such a move for herself. She had a beadle all to herself, gripping her elbow as he half pulled her along.

Rosamund was weeping; Lilly, on the other hand, cursed at her captors with all the vigor of a Billingsgate fishwife. Her face was tight and set, but Juliana didn't think she was going to break down. "Where are they taking us?" she asked.

"Fielding's," Lilly said shortly through compressed lips. "And then Bridewell, I expect."

Juliana gulped. "Bridewell? But what for?"

"It's a house of correction for debauched females," Lilly told her with the same curtness. "Surely you're not so naive you don't know that."

"Yes, of course I know it. But we weren't doing anything." Juliana tried to keep her temper, knowing that Lilly's impatience was fueled by apprehension.

"We were in the middle of a riot. That's all it takes."

Juliana chewed her lip. "Mistress Mitchell was there, together with some grimy-looking creature I assume was Mother Cocksedge."

"I saw her."

"D'you think she put the beadles on to us?"

"Of course." Lilly turned to look at Juliana and her fear

was now clear in her eyes. "We tried to tell you that it's impossible to escape the rule of the bawds," she said bleakly. "I was a fool to be carried away by your eloquence, Juliana. There was a moment this evening when I thought it might happen. We would buy our own necessities, look after each other in illness or ill luck, thumb our noses at the bastards." She shook her head in angry impatience. "Fools . . . we were all fools."

Juliana said no more. Nothing she could say at this moment would improve the situation, and she needed to concentrate on her own plight. She couldn't admit her identity to the magistrates—neither of her identities. She had to keep the Courtney name out of her own disgrace. The duke, for all his deviousness, didn't deserve to have his cousin's wife publicly hauled off to Bridewell.

Hauled off? Or carted? Her blood ran cold, and a clammy sweat broke out on her hands and forehead. Would they drive them to Bridewell at the cart's tail? Was she about to be whipped through the streets of London?

A wave of nausea rose in her throat. She knew it was part of the customary punishment for bawds. But they weren't bawds. They were the slaves of bawds. Surely that would be a lesser offense in the stern eyes of Sir John Fielding.

They reached a tall house on Bow Street, and one of the constables banged on the door with his staff. A sleepy footman answered it. "We've harlots to be brought before Sir John," the constable announced with solemnity. "Creating a fracas . . . debauching . . . soliciting . . . inciting to riot."

The footman looked over his head to the surrounded women. He grinned lasciviously as he noted their disordered dress. Even the well-dressed women had suffered in the arrest and now tried to hold together torn bodices and ripped sleeves. "I'll waken Sir John," he said, stepping back to open the door fully. "If ye takes 'em into the front parlor where Sir John does 'is business, I'll fetch 'im fer ye."

The constables herded their little flock into the house and into a large paneled room on the left of the hall. It was sparsely furnished, with a massive table and a large chair behind it, rather giving the impression of a throne. The women were pushed into a semicircle around the table while another yawning footman lit the candles and oil lamps, throwing a gloomy light over the bare room.

Then silence fell, as deep as a crypt—not so much as the rustle of a skirt, the scrape of a foot on the bare floor. It was as if the women were afraid to speak or to move, afraid that it might worsen their condition. The beadles kept quiet, as if awed by their surroundings. Only Juliana looked around, taking in details of the molding on the ceiling, the embossed paneling, the waxed oak floorboards. She was as scared as the rest of them, but it didn't show on her countenance as she tried to think of a way out of this dismal situation.

After an eternal fifteen minutes the double doors opened and a voice intoned, "Pray stand for 'Is Honor, Sir John Fielding."

As if they had any choice, Juliana thought with a brave attempt at humor, unable to ignore the shiver that ran through her companions.

Sir John Fielding, in a loose brocade chamber robe over his britches and shirt, his hastily donned wig slightly askew, took his seat behind the table. He surveyed the women with a steady, reproving stare.

"Charges?"

"Disorderly be'avior, Sir John," the head beadle spoke ponderously. "Inciting to riot . . . debauchery . . . damage to property."

"Who brings the charges?"

"Mother Cocksedge and Mistress Mitchell, Yer 'Onor."

"Are they here?"

"Awaitin' yer summons, sir." The beadle tapped his staff on the floor and twitched his nose with an air of great self-importance.

"Then summon them."

Juliana turned her head toward the door. The two women bustled in. Mistress Mitchell looked like a respectable housewife in her print dress and mob cap; Mother Cocksedge had thrown her apron over her head and appeared much affected by something, her shoulders heaving, great sobs emerging from beneath the apron.

"Cease yer blubbin', woman, an' tell 'Is Lordship yer complaint," instructed one of the constables.

"Oh, I'm ruint, Yer 'Onor, quite ruint," came from beneath the apron. "It's all thanks to those evil girls . . . them what encouraged the young gennelmen to break up my 'ouse. Flaunted theirselves at 'em, got 'em all excited like, then wouldn't deliver. An' them three . . ." With a dramatic gesture Mother Cocksedge flung aside her apron and pointed at Juliana, Lilly, and Rosamund. "Them three, what ought to know better, they was encouragin' the others, poor souls what don't 'ave 'alf the advantages, to use my establishment fer *h*immoral purposes."

Juliana gasped. "Why, you old—"

"Silence!" The justice glared at Juliana. "Open your mouth once more, woman, and you'll be carted from St. Paul's Church to Drury Lane and back again."

Juliana shut her mouth, seething as she was forced to listen to the two women spin their tales. Mistress Mitchell was all hurt feelings and good nature taken advantage of as she explained that she'd allowed some girls to use her best parlor for a birthday party, but instead they'd been preparing to create a riot at Mother Cocksedge's oh-so-respectable chocolate house. They had a grievance against Mother Cocksedge and intended to be avenged upon her by causing her house to be wrecked by a group of angry young bloods.

They were evil, fallen women with no morals, set on their wicked ways, put in Mother Cocksedge, once more retreating beneath her apron. "But me an' Mistress Mitchell, 'ere, Yer 'Onor, we don't think as 'ow they should all be punished as much as them what lead 'em into evil. Them three from Russell Street."

Mistress Mitchell bristled and agreed with a dignified nod.

Sir John Fielding regarded the two complainants with an expression of distaste. He was as aware as anyone of the true nature of their trade. But they were not on this occasion brought before him, and their complaint was legitimate enough. His head swung slowly around the semicircle of defendants, and his gaze rested on the three chief malefactors.

Lilly and Rosamund immediately dropped their eyes, but the bold-eyed redhead met his accusatory glare head-on, her green eyes throwing a challenge at him.

"Name?" he demanded.

"Juliana Beresford." She spoke clearly and offered neither curtsy nor salutation.

Lilly and Rosamund, on the other hand, both curtsied low and murmured their names when asked, with an "If it please Your Honor."

"Do you have anything to say to these charges?" He gestured to Juliana.

"Only that they're barefaced lies," she replied calmly.

"You were not gathered in this woman's chocolate house?" The justice's eyebrows rose in a bushy white arc.

"Yes, we were, but—"

"You weren't gathered behind a closed door?" he interrupted.

"Yes, but—"

He thumped his fist on the table, silencing her again. "That's all I wish to know. It is against the law for people to gather together for the purposes of incitement to violence and riot. I sentence you and your two companions to three months in the Tothill Bridewell. Those whom you have corrupted are free on payment of a five-shilling fine."

With that he pushed back his chair and rose to his feet, yawning prodigiously. "I sat overlate last even, and then to be dragged from my bed in the small hours to deal with a trio of hotheaded troublemaking harlots is more than a man can abide," he remarked loudly to a somber-suited man who had stood behind him throughout the trial and who now accompanied him from the room.

"Ye'll be showin' a little more respect to yer betters after three months beatin' 'emp," Mother Cocksedge declared, coming up to the three young women with a leer in her little pink eyes. "I doubt Mistress Dennison and 'er man 'll be ready to take ye back afterward. We don't like trouble-makers in the Garden, and don't ye ferget it, missie." She jabbed a finger at Juliana's chest. Juliana would have retaliated if she hadn't been held so tightly by a constable. The urge to spit in the woman's face was almost overpowering, but somehow she resisted it and looked away from the hateful, triumphant grin.

"Rosamund cannot survive Bridewell," Lilly whispered to Juliana. "I can, and you can. But Rosamund is fragile. She'll not last on her feet for more than a week."

"She won't have to," Juliana declared with a confidence she didn't feel. They were binding her hands in front of her with coarse rope, and with each twist and knot she was secured in the chains of powerlessness.

Lilly gave her a scornful look as if to say "Face reality" and endured her own bonds with tight lips. Rosamund continued to weep softly as she was similarly bound. The other women had been hustled from the room and could be heard across the hall, declaring penitence and gratitude as the two bawds paid their fines. They'd just been given a lesson on which side their bread was buttered, and it would be a rainy day in hell before they would contemplate standing up for themselves again.

"Come along, then, me pretties." A beadle grinned at them and chucked Rosamund beneath the chin. "Ye'll spoil them lovely eyes with yer tears, missie. Save 'em for the Bridewell, I should." A hearty laugh greeted this sally, and Juliana, Lilly, and Rosamund were half pushed, half dragged out of the house to an open cart waiting outside.

Juliana waited in sick dread for them to fasten her bound hands to a rope behind the cart and pull her bodice to her waist. But they were shoved upward into the cart, and her relief was so great that for the first time since this ordeal had begun, she thought she might faint. She put an arm around Rosamund and took Lilly's hand in a fierce grip as they stood in the benchless vehicle, swaying and lurching over the cobbles.

Dawn was breaking, and the city streets were filling with costermongers, night-soil collectors, barrow boys, servants of all kinds hurrying to the market. The nighttime din had died down in Covent Garden, replaced with the coarse cries of the market people, the rattle of wheels and the clop of horses. As the cart bearing the three bound women was drawn through the streets, people jeered and threw clods of mud and pieces of rotten fruit; small boys ran along beside the cart, chanting obscene songs.

Juliana thought of being burned at the stake. She imagined being tied to the stake in front of a jeering crowd. She thought of the noose around her neck, mercifully squeezing consciousness from her body before they lit the faggots. She lived that nightmare and thus defeated the ghastly reality of the humiliating journey.

John Coachman had fallen asleep on the driver's box. He'd intended to nod off for a minute or two, but when he awoke, it was almost full light. He leaped from the carriage with an oath, still thick with sleep but his heart pounding with fear. Abandoning his horses, he plunged across the Garden, dodging the market folk as they put up their stalls. He'd seen Lady Edgecombe disappear in this direction, but where had she gone then? He stood wildly looking around as if he would see her sitting at her ease under the Piazza. But he knew that something was very wrong. And he'd slept through it. The duke would have his hide and throw him without a character into the street to starve.

"Lost summat, mate?" a friendly carter inquired, pausing with his laden basket of cabbages delicately balanced on his head.

John Coachman looked bewildered. "My lady," he stammered. "I've lost my lady."

The carter chuckled. "Covent Garden's the place fer

losin' a lady friend, mate. But there's plenty 'ere where that one came from."

The coachman didn't attempt to explain something that he didn't understand himself. His great fear was that Lady Edgecombe had been abducted, a fine lady in this den of iniquity. It wouldn't be the first time. And it must have happened at least an hour ago. She could be anywhere in the city's maze of mean, narrow streets and dark, dank courts.

"D'ye 'ear of the business last night at Cocksedge's?" the carter asked, reaching in his pocket for his clay pipe, his basket immobile on his head despite his movements. He struck flint on tinder and lit the pungent tobacco.

The coachman hardly heard him. He was still gazing frantically around, trying to think of his next course of action.

"A group of them 'igh-class nymphs was taken up by the beadles at Cocksedge's," the informative carter rattled on between leisurely puffs. "Incitin' a riot, or so the old bawd says. Got summat agin 'em, I'll bet. She's got the evil eye, that one, make no mistake."

Slowly the words sank in. John remembered the scene he'd witnessed earlier. The flame-red hair stuck in his memory. "What's that you say?"

The carter repeated himself cheerfully. "Took 'em to Fielding's, so I 'eard, but . . ." He stared after the coachman, who was now racing back to his carriage and the stamping, restless horses.

John Coachman clambered onto the box, cracked his whip with a loud bellow of encouragement, and the horses broke almost immediately into a canter, the coach swaying and lumbering behind. They sideswiped a stall and the owner raced after them, yelling curses. A child was snatched just in time from beneath the pounding hooves by an irate woman. A mangy dog dived between the wheels of the carriage and miraculously emerged unscathed on the other side.

Outside the magistrate's house on Bow Street, the

coachman pulled up his sweating horses and with trembling hands descended to the street and ran up the steps to bang the knocker. The footman who answered was lofty and unhelpful until he saw the ducal coronet on the panels of the carriage. Then he was all affability. Yes, there had been a group of whores brought before Sir John an hour or so ago. Three of them sentenced to Tothill Bridewell, the others let off with a fine that their bawds had paid. And, yes, one of the women sent to Tothill had been a tall green-eyed redhead. He vaguely remembered that she'd been wearing a dark-green gown.

John Coachman thanked the man and retreated to his carriage. His world seemed to have run amuck. Lady Edge-combe taken up for a whore; hauled off to Tothill Bride-well. It made no sense. And yet there was no other explanation for Her Ladyship's inexplicable disappearance.

He turned his horses toward Albermarle Street, his mind reeling. It was backstairs gossip that there was something smoky about the way Lady Edgecombe had come to the house. The whole marriage with the viscount reeked to the heavens. And she was installed in the chamber next to the duke, her bridegroom now gone from the house.

He knew well, however, that the conclusions he drew would avail him nothing when facing the duke's wrath. It was with sinking heart that he drove into the mews, handed the horses over to a groom, and entered the house by the back door.

The house was in its customary quiet but efficient early-morning bustle, waxing, polishing, brushing, dusting. The kitchen was filled with the rich aromas of bacon and black pudding, the boot boy and scullery maid carrying steaming salvers into the servants' hall. The coachman knew he would have to confide in Catlett if he was to speak with the duke. And he knew that he must speak with His Grace before many minutes had passed.

He approached the august figure of Catlett, seated at the head of the long table sampling his ale and examining with a critical eye the offerings laid before him by the boot boy.

The lad's mouth watered as he watched the dishes move down the table. He and the scullery maid would have to wait until everyone had eaten before they'd be allowed to rummage for scraps to break their own fasts.

"Eh, John Coachman, and 'ow be you this fine mornin'?" Catlett asked genially, spearing a chunk of black pudding with the end of his knife.

"I'd like a word in private, if ye please, Mr. Catlett." The coachman turned his hat between his hands, his eyes filled with anxiety.

"What? In the middle of me breakfast?"

"It's very urgent, Mr. Catlett. Concerns 'Er Ladyship and 'Is Grace."

Catlett irritably pushed back his chair. "Best come into me pantry, then. You, lad. Put me plate on the 'ob to keep 'ot. I'll dust yer jacket fer ye if 'tis a mite less 'ot than 'tis now."

Wiping his mouth with a napkin, he led the way to his pantry. "So what is it?"

He listened, his eyes widening, as the coachman told him of the night's happening and the total absence of Lady Edgecombe.

"Taken up fer a whore?" Catlett shook his head in incredulity. " 'Ow could that be?"

"Dunno. Accident, I daresay. She went to fetch a fan, got caught up in the riot." John snapped his fingers.

"Sir John wouldn't send Lady Edgecombe to Tothill Bridewell," Catlett declared. "So she must not 'ave told 'im 'oo she is."

"Aye. But why?"

"Not fer us to ask," Catlett pronounced. "But 'Is Grace must be told at once. Ye'd best come wi' me to 'is chamber. 'E's only been back fer a couple of hours."

The coachman followed Catlett into the front of the house and up the stairs. A parlor maid, waxing the banister, gave him a curious look, then dropped her eyes immediately as Catlett clipped her around the ear. "You got nuthin' better to do, my girl, than gawp at yer betters?"

"Yes, sir . . . Mr. Catlett . . . no, sir," she mumbled.

Outside the duke's bedchamber Catlett said, "Wait 'ere." He pushed open the door and entered the darkened chamber. The bed curtains were drawn around the bed. He twitched them aside and coughed portentously.

The duke seemed to be deeply asleep, an arm flung above his head, his face in repose curiously youthful, his mouth relaxed, almost smiling.

Catlett coughed again and, when that produced no response, went to draw back the window curtains, flooding the room with light.

"What the devil . . . ?" Tarquin opened his eyes.

"I beg your pardon, Your Grace, but it's a matter of some urgency." Catlett moved smoothly back to the bed, his practiced working accents crisp and well modulated.

Tarquin struggled up onto an elbow and blinked at the man. "Why are you waking me, Catlett, and not my valet?"

Catlett coughed. "I thought, Your Grace, that you'd prefer as few people as possible to be a party to the situation."

Tarquin sat up, instantly awake. His eyes flew to the armoire and its concealed door. *Juliana.* She hadn't returned when he'd come in earlier, but he hadn't thought twice about it. She was with his own coachman, escorted by the formidable and ultrarespectable Lady Bowen.

"Tell me."

"John Coachman's waiting outside, Your Grace. It's probably best if he tells it in his own words." Catlett bowed.

"Fetch him."

Visibly trembling, the coachman approached the duke's bed. He was still twisting his hat between his hands, his cheeks flushed as he stammered through his recital. The duke listened without a crack in his impassivity, his eyes flat, his mouth thin.

When the coachman had finished his tale and stood miserably pulling at his hat brim, eyes lowered, the duke flung aside the bedclothes and stood up. "I'll deal with you later," he said grimly. "Get out of my sight."

The coachman scuttled off. Catlett moved to pull the bell rope. "You'll be wanting your valet, Your Grace."

"No." Tarquin waved him away. "I'm perfectly capable of dressing myself. Have my phaeton brought round immediately." He threw off his nightshirt and pulled a pair of buckskin britches from the armoire.

Catlett left with a bow, and Tarquin flung on his clothes, his mind racing. He could think of no rational explanation for Juliana's predicament. But, then, Juliana didn't need logical reasons for getting herself into trouble, he thought grimly. He knew that George Ridge couldn't have been involved, since he'd been occupied elsewhere. It was the kind of vengeance that would appeal to Lucien, certainly, but he hadn't the patience to orchestrate such a sophisticated plan. He was a man who acted on vicious impulse. But what in the name of all that was good had taken Juliana, against his express orders and her own past experiences, to Covent Garden at the height of the night's debauchery?

Simple mischief? Pure deviltry? Another demonstration of her refusal to yield to his authority? Somehow he didn't think it was that simple. Juliana wasn't childish . . . hotheaded, certainly; but she was also surprisingly mature for her years—a product presumably of her loveless childhood. She was probably involved in another misguided mission like the one that had taken her to the Marshalsea. For some reason the women of Russell Street held a dangerous fascination for her.

He ought to leave her in Bridwell for a few days, he thought wrathfully, thrusting a thick billfold into the pocket of his britches. She'd soon learn just how dangerous a fascination it was.

But he knew it was fear more than anger that spoke. The purity of his anger was muddled with a piercing dread. He couldn't endure the idea of Juliana's being hurt or frightened. It was as if some part of himself was suffering and he couldn't detach himself from the pain.

It was inexplicable, and a damnable nuisance. He strode out of his chamber, slamming the door behind him, and headed at a run for the stairs.

"Good morning, Tarquin. Where are you off to at the peep of day?" Quentin's voice hailed him from the library as he crossed the hall. Quentin, always an early riser, looked fresh and serene.

"Juliana has contrived to get herself sent to Bridewell," he told Quentin tersely. "Against my better judgment I'm about to spring her loose before she endures too much punishment in that hellhole."

Quentin stared in disbelief. "But how for mercy's sake did—"

"I've no idea," Tarquin interrupted. "The temperamental chit is a loose cannon. And, by God, I'm going to keep her on a leash in future!"

"I'll accompany you." Quentin dropped the prayer book he'd been carrying onto a side table.

"There's no need. I can handle Juliana without assistance."

"I'm sure you can." Quentin followed him out into the bright morning. "Nevertheless, you might need a supporting cast. You don't know what you're going to find."

Tarquin shot him a bleak look, and their eyes held for a minute. They both knew that Quentin's remark was not lightly made. Then the duke climbed with an agile spring into the waiting phaeton, followed by his brother.

Quentin felt Tarquin deliberately relax as he took up the reins. He glanced up at his profile and saw that all emotion was wiped clear from his countenance. He was not fooled by this apparently calm exterior. He'd been convinced for some time now that the careless affection Tarquin showed for his *mignonne* masked a much deeper feeling.

Tarquin whipped up his horses. It was the only indication of his urgency as he fought to subdue the images

of what Juliana could be going through at this moment.
She was so intractable, so bold and challenging, that it
wouldn't be long before she would provoke the jailers to
break her spirit. They had crude but sure methods of doing
so.

Chapter 25

Juliana stumbled forward under a vigorous shove from her escort, through a doorway and into a long, narrow, filthy room. An iron-barred door clanged behind her. A minute or two earlier the cart had drawn up in a stinking courtyard, surrounded by a high wall. The three women had been hauled down to the cobbles by two men wielding rods, and driven like cattle into the low building. Rosamund had tripped over an uneven flagstone and, unable to help herself with her bound hands, had fallen to her knees. One of the jailers had promptly brought his rod down on her shoulders, cursing her vilely. Sobbing piteously, she'd managed to stand up again and totter forward.

Now the three women stood with their bound hands facing a sea of hostile, predatory eyes as the women in the dimly lit room stared at them, hungrily taking in the quality of their clothes. The walls were of bare brick, glistening and slimy with oozing damp; the air was dank and foul; the only light came from a minute window high up in the far wall under the roof timbers. Far too high to reach from the ground, and far too small to admit even a climbing boy.

The women, for the most part clad only in ragged underpetticoats, coarse stockings, and clogs, stood in front of rows of massive tree stumps beating hanks of hemp with heavy wooden mallets. Juliana saw with dread that several of them wore leg irons, shackling them to the stumps. The dull, rhythmic pounding bounced off the stone walls. A woman with a slit nose cackled as Rosamund gave a low moan and swayed.

"First time 'ere, is it, dearies?" She dropped her mallet and came over to them. Her hands were flayed and bleeding from the hemp. Juliana wondered what crime had merited the slit nose, even as she drew back from the unequivocal malice in the woman's eyes. The woman reached for Rosamund's muslin fichu. "Fancy gewgaws ye've got. Fetch quite a pretty penny, they will."

"Leave her alone," Juliana snapped.

The woman's eyes narrowed dangerously, and she tore the fichu from Rosamund's quivering neck. "I'll 'ave 'er clothes, and your'n, too, missie. Soon as the day's work's done. An' if ye don't watch yer tongue, we'll strip ye nekkid. We knows 'ow to tame a proud spirit in 'ere. Innit so, girls?"

There was a chorus of agreement, and the eyes seemed to move closer, although the women remained at their posts. Juliana involuntarily turned to the jailer as if seeking protection.

The man merely laughed. "Don't go upsettin' Maggie. She'll scratch yer eyes out soon as look at ye. An' 'er word goes in 'ere. What 'appens in 'ere, when y'are locked up fer the night, is none of me business." He moved in front of them and sliced their bonds with his knife. "Get to work now. Them three stumps over there." He gestured to three unoccupied work sites, the massive mallets resting atop.

Maggie followed them over and stood, hands on hips, as the jailer pulled three thick hanks of hemp from a basket on the wall and threw them onto the stumps. The woman reached over and took Rosamund's shrinking hand. "This'll not last long," she observed, turning the small white hand over in her grime-encrusted, blood-streaked palm. "I give ye an hour, an' yer 'ands'll be bleedin' so 'ard ye won't be able to bear it to touch the mallet." She cackled, and a ripple of mirth ran around the room from the others, who had taken a rest from their labors to watch the induction.

The jailer grinned. "Them what won't work goes in the pillory."

Rosamund was dazed with fright and was weeping so hard now, she couldn't take anything in, but Juliana and Lilly both looked to where the man's finger was pointing. A wall pillory, the holes high enough to keep the victim on her toes and to put an intolerable strain on her shoulders. Above it inscribed the legend: *Better to work than stand thus.*

Juliana picked up the mallet and brought it down on the hemp with an almighty swing. The weight of the mallet astounded her, and any effect of the blow on the hemp was invisible. The stuff had to be pounded until the core fibers split and could be separated from the thick fibrous covering. After three blows her wrists ached, the skin of her palms was beginning to rub, and the hemp showed no more than a slight flattening. She glanced at Rosamund, who was tapping feebly through her tears and making no impression at all on her hank. Lilly, tight-lipped, white-faced, was swinging her mallet above her shoulder and bringing it down with resolute violence. In a short while she'd be exhausted, Juliana thought apprehensively. If she was exhausted, she wouldn't be able to continue.

She glanced again at Rosamund's hemp, then swiftly picked up her own partially split hank and swapped it with Rosamund's barely touched one. Lilly gave her a quick approving nod, whispering, "Between us we should be able to keep her going."

"Eh, stop yer jabberin' over there." The jailer came toward them swinging his rod. "There's no time fer talkin'. Ye'll 'ave six of 'em ready by noontime, or ye'll find yerself at the whippin' post."

A chilling desperation took a hold on Juliana. She could see no way out. There was no one to appeal to. They were imprisoned in this fetid hole so far from civilization that they could have dropped off the face of the earth for all the contact they would have with the outside world. But surely someone would be wondering where she was. The coachman would be looking for her. Someone would discover what had happened.

But why would they do anything to help her? What right had she to expect help? The duke would be thinking that it served her right. To obtain her release, he'd have to acknowledge his connection with a convicted whore in a house of correction. She couldn't imagine why anyone, let alone the Duke of Redmayne, would wish to do that.

Except, of course, to protect his investment. Furiously, she swung the mallet, ignoring the pain in her hands, ignoring the drops of blood that began to fall on the stump and made the handle of the mallet slippery. She welcomed the anger because it defeated the dreadful, numbing desperation that she knew instinctively was her greatest enemy.

She and Lilly must do their own six hanks and share Lilly's if they were to keep her from the pillory—or worse, the whipping post. In this hellhole, inhabited by the dregs of humanity, the weak would go to the wall. Juliana knew that she would be able to stand up to the jailer, and to the vile Maggie, as long as she kept her strength and diverted the deadening sense of helplessness. Lilly, too, would be difficult to break. But Rosamund stood not a chance. Her spirit was already broken, and to watch her complete disintegration would provide merry sport for the degraded wretches who surrounded them.

Sir John Fielding regarded his visitors in polite astonishment. "Lady Edgecombe among the whores I sent to Tothill Bridewell? My dear sir, surely you must be mistaken."

"I don't believe so," Tarquin said, his mouth so thin and tight it was barely visible. "Red hair, green eyes. Tall."

"Aye, I marked her well. A bold-eyed wench," the magistrate opined, stroking his chin. "Now you mention it, she did seem rather out of the common way for strumpets. But why wouldn't she identify herself? How could she get caught up—"

"Forgive me for interrupting." Quentin stepped forward. "I believe it must have had something to do with Juliana's interest in the lives of the street women." He coughed discreetly. "She was much exercised over young Lucy's plight, if you recall, Tarquin. Insisted upon bringing her out of the Marshalsea. I believe it would be in character for her to . . . to extend her field of operations, if you will."

Tarquin nodded tersely. "It would certainly be in character."

"What's that you mean to say, your lordship?" Sir John looked puzzled. "Don't quite catch your meaning. What interest could a lady have in a whore's life?"

"The inequities of their position, I believe, troubles Lady Edgecombe most powerfully," Quentin explained gravely.

"Well, I'll be damned. Out to reform them, is she?" Sir John took up a dish of coffee and guzzled it with relish.

"Probably not reformation, Sir John," Quentin said, sipping his own coffee. "Juliana is of a practical turn of mind."

"Not when it comes to self-preservation," Tarquin stated grimly.

"Well, if she's been meddling in the profits of the likes of Mitchell and Cocksedge, it's no wonder she aroused the wrath of the demons," Sir John observed. "Devil take it, sir, but His Lordship should keep a tighter rein on his wife."

"Oh, believe me, Sir John, from now on the tightest rein and the heaviest curb," Tarquin promised, setting aside his coffee dish and standing up with an abrupt movement. "If you'll provide me with an order for her release, sir, we'll be about our business."

"Aye, Your Grace. Aye, indeed." The magistrate summoned his somber-suited secretary, who'd been listening with wagging ears to the conference. "Write it up, Hanson. Immediate release of Lady Edgecombe."

"I believe Her Ladyship called herself Juliana Beresford, sir," the secretary reminded. "It's down as that in the register of committal."

"I daresay she thought her real identity might prove an embarrassment for you," Quentin murmured to his brother.

"Juliana is always such a paragon of consideration," Tarquin retorted.

They waited, the duke in visible impatience, for the secretary's laborious penning of the order. Tarquin almost snatched it from the man, thrusting it into his coat pocket, throwing a curt thank-you over his shoulder to Sir John as he strode from the room, Quentin on his heels.

"How long has she been in there, d'ye reckon, Quentin?" Tarquin's voice was taut, his face a mask as he whipped up his horses, setting them at a racing pace through the rapidly crowding streets.

Quentin glanced at his fob watch. It was nine o'clock. "They were at Fielding's just before dawn. Reached Bridewell maybe two hours later."

"Seven o'clock, then. Two hours." A note of relief crept into his voice. It would take a lot longer than that to break Juliana. "Has she talked to you about this obsession she has with the whores?" He kept out of his voice his annoyance that she had not confided in him—an annoyance that was directed more at himself than at Juliana. He hadn't questioned exactly what she'd been doing in Covent Garden on her last excursion, which had led to George's attempted abduction. He'd assumed she'd been simply meeting her friends for her own entertainment. Now it seemed there may have been more to it.

"A little. Usually when we've been sitting with Lucy. Juliana's own experiences, I believe, have made her particularly sensitive to the women's plight. Exploitation, as she calls it."

"Death and damnation!" Tarquin overtook a lumbering dray on the narrow street, so close he shaved the varnish on the phaeton. "Exploitation! Who the hell has exploited *her*?"

"You have."

Tarquin's expression blackened, and his eyes took on the flat glitter of anger. But he said nothing, and Quentin prudently held his own peace.

The forbidding building of the Tothill Bridewell loomed before them. Tarquin drew his horses to a halt before the massive iron gate. The postern gate swung open and an ill-kempt guard stepped through. He took in the equipage and the haughty impatience of the driver. He tugged his forelock in a halfhearted gesture. "Sure ye 'aven't come to the wrong place, good sirs?"

Tarquin jumped from the phaeton. "Take the reins," he instructed, thrusting them into the astonished guard's hands. "Where will I find the keeper of this place?"

"Eh, Yer 'Onor, at 'is breakfast, I don't doubt." The guard looked in alarm at the two pawing horses that had become his charge. "In 'is 'ouse," he added helpfully.

"And where might that be?" Quentin asked swiftly, sensing Tarquin was within an inch of throttling the guard.

"'Cross the yard, on the left. 'Ouse that stands alone."

"Thank you." Quentin fished out a sovereign. "For your trouble. There'll be another when we return." Then he set off after Tarquin, who had already disappeared through the postern gate.

The yard was surrounded by high walls. A whipping post stood prominently in the middle, stocks and a pillory beside it. To one side a massive treadmill turned, groaning with each revolution. A team of women, petticoats kilted to their knees, feet bare, wearily trod its circumference, a jailer with a long-lashed whip exhorting them to greater effort as he paced around them.

One quick glance told both men that Juliana had not been harnessed to that barbarous toil. Tarquin banged on the door of a squat cottage standing apart from the long, narrow, low-pitched building that housed the Bridewell.

"All right . . . all right . . . I'm a-comin'." The

door opened and a woman poked her head out. She would once have been pretty, smooth-cheeked, with merry blue eyes and golden hair. But her face now was pitted with smallpox, her eyes shadowed with spite and the barren acceptance of a barren existence, her gray-streaked hair hanging in lank ringlets to her scrawny shoulders. Her eyes widened as she took in the visitors.

"I wish to have speech with the keeper of this place," Tarquin stated brusquely. "Fetch him, my good woman."

" 'E's at 'is breakfast, my lord." She bobbed a curtsy. "But if'n ye'd care to step this way." She gestured behind her into a dingy, smelly passageway.

Tarquin took the invitation, Quentin on his heels. The passage gave onto a square room, reeking of stale fried onions and boiling cods' heads. A man in a filthy waistcoat, collar unbuttoned, sleeves rolled up, was scooping boiled tripe into his mouth with the blade of his knife.

He looked up as the door opened. "Agnes, I told you I weren't to be disturbed. . . ." Then his voice faded as he saw his visitors. A sly look came into his eyes. He wiped his dripping chin with the back of his hand and said in a fawning tone, "Well, what can Jeremiah Bloggs do fer ye, good sirs?"

Tarquin could see he was already calculating how much of a bribe he could squeeze out of whatever this situation was. Keepers of the prisons earned no salary, but they were free to extort and "fee" both prisoners and their visitors for anything they could come up with.

"I have an order for the release of a woman brought in here by mistake this morning," he said, laying the document on a corner of the dirt-encrusted table. "If you'd be so good as to have her fetched."

The sly look intensified. Bloggs stroked a loose-flapping lower lip with a thumb tip. "Well, it ain't quite that easy, 'onored sir."

"Of course it is," snapped the duke. "This document states that the prisoner Juliana Beresford is to be released immediately. Without let or hindrance. If you have difficulty performing your duties, my good man, I shall ensure that you are replaced by someone who does not."

The sly look became a malevolent glare. "I don't know where she might be 'eld, Yer 'Onor," he whined. "There's a dozen or so wards, includin' the lunatic ones. Per'aps ye'd like to look fer 'er yerselves. Might be quicker, like."

"Certainly. But you are accompanying us."

Muttering under his breath, the keeper abandoned his tripe, drained his mug of blue ruin, picked up a massive ring of keys, and stomped ahead of them out to the court.

The stench of excreta overwhelmed them the minute the door was opened onto the building. Quentin choked. Tarquin pulled out his handkerchief and held it to his nose, his expression even grimmer than before. The keeper was unaffected by the reek. He maneuvered his large bulk down the passage, stopping at each barred ward, unlocking the door and gesturing sullenly that they should look in.

Thin, dull-eyed women looked back at them without pausing in the rhythmic pounding of their mallets. Rats rustled through the filthy straw at their feet; their jailers sat taking their ease on stools against the walls, occasionally swinging their rods when they judged someone was slacking.

Quentin couldn't keep the horror from his face. He had always known these places existed and, indeed, had assumed that houses of correction were necessary for the smooth running of society. But in the face of this unutterable reeking misery, he began to question his assumptions. He glanced at his brother. Tarquin's countenance was utterly impassive—a sure sign of turmoil within.

At the sixth ward they stopped outside an iron-bound door. Mr. Bloggs inserted the key. "If she ain't in 'ere, sirs, I can't think where she'd be. Less'n she be lunatic already; or they've put 'er on the treadmill. Which it's to be 'oped they 'aven't. Seein' as 'ow it's all a mistake, like." He grunted with what could almost have been a chuckle at the thought of an innocent suffering from such an error.

"Can't think what Sir John could be a-doin', makin' such a mistake." He swung the door open and stood aside.

Juliana was lost in the rhythm of the mallet. She allowed her eyes to see only the hemp in front of her. As the fibers began to separate, a grim satisfaction filled her. She thought of nothing more than the disintegration of the hemp. The pounding was in her ears, in her blood, the condition of her hands a distant agony that she knew instinctively she mustn't focus upon. Beside her Lilly pounded away. Without exchanging a glance they flipped Rosamund's pathetic work from one stump to another. But despite their efforts Rosamund's hands were bleeding and mangled within the first hour, as Maggie had gleefully foreseen, and her tears mingled with the blood dripping onto the hemp.

There had to be a way out of this nightmare. But Juliana's brain was deadened by the numbing, repetitive noise and the creeping dullness of fatigue. She'd had no sleep for twenty-four hours, and this work would presumably continue until nightfall. It wasn't possible to think, to do anything, but force her body through the motions and watch the hemp.

At the moment the door opened, Rosamund cried out. The mallet dropped, bouncing on the tree stump. She stared with fixed intensity at her hands, her eyes widening in horror. She raised her eyes to gaze wildly around the room, as if coming to a realization of her surroundings for the first time; then, with another cry of despair, she crumpled to the filthy straw.

Juliana dropped to her knees, Lilly beside her. They ignored the commotion at the door. Lilly lifted Rosamund's head, laying it in her lap. Juliana wanted to chafe her hands but didn't dare to touch them. Her own stung unmercifully now that her concentration had been broken, but she stroked Rosamund's deathly white cheek.

"Fetch some hartshorn and water, man!" She threw the instruction over her shoulder in the direction of where she'd last seen the jailer.

Maggie cackled. "'Arts'orn and water. And would m'lady like 'er smellin' salts, then? Or a burned feather, per'aps?"

Juliana was on her feet in one bound. She turned on the grinning woman, her eyes spitting rage, her bloody hands raised. Maggie took a step backward as the flaming-haired Fury advanced on her.

"Juliana! Don't make matters worse than they are."

She whirled toward the door as the quiet voice crashed through her crimson rage. His voice was quiet but his eyes were hot as lava, and there was a white shade around his taut mouth, a muscle twitching in his cheek. Juliana saw only anger—no indication of his agonies of the last hour, not a hint of the glorious rush of relief as he saw her unbroken and not seriously harmed.

"What are *you* doing here?" She couldn't believe the petulant words even as they emerged from her lips. She wanted to rush to his arms, to be folded in the power of his body, secure in the knowledge of his protection. She wanted to be soothed and cuddled, to hear the soft words of love on his lips. She'd chosen to believe that if he came for her, it would be because it suited his purposes, not because he wished to. But as he stood there, such fearsome rage in every taut muscle, she felt a deeper disappointment than she'd ever known.

Her eyes flew to Quentin standing behind the duke, his expression a rictus of horror. Quentin would understand what had brought her to this. He would see, where his brother didn't, her weakness and her unimaginable relief that the ordeal was over.

"I might ask the same of you," the duke replied, coming toward her.

He took her hands, his own warm and strong, and turned them over. His rage knew no bounds at what he saw, and it was all he could do to keep himself from cradling the torn, bruised flesh, soothing the hurts with the balm of his kisses. But this was not the time. She was safe, and he had to get her out of this filthy place of terror before he did anything else.

"Come," he said, his voice curt with anxiety. He turned to the door.

Juliana snatched her hands from his grasp, their pain as nothing compared to the surge of angry disbelief. Did he really expect her to walk out with him, abandoning her friends?

"I'll not leave here without Lilly and Rosamund." She picked up her mallet again. "They're here because of me. They have no more business being here than I do. Those spawn of a gutter bitch betrayed us, and I'll not leave my friends in this hell. I neither need nor want your intervention." She raised the mallet with both bloody hands and brought it down again, fighting with every muscle the screaming agony of her torn flesh.

Tarquin swung back to her with an incredulous *"What?"* Quentin suppressed a smile at the sight of his unflappable brother so completely confounded.

Juliana ignored the question, and Tarquin, frowning fiercely, looked at the pathetic, crumpled body of the girl on the floor, the white-faced desperation of the other girl, and he suddenly felt ashamed.

It was not an emotion to which he was accustomed. Impatiently, he snatched the mallet from Juliana, throwing it to the floor. "Quentin, take her out of here while I arrange about the others." He seized her in his arms and spun her across to his brother, who caught her against him.

"I'm not leaving without them!" Juliana's protest was muffled against Quentin's black waistcoat.

"Juliana, for once in your short life do as you're bid," Tarquin declared dangerously.

"Come," Quentin murmured. "Tarquin will negotiate their release."

Juliana looked from one brother to the other and saw only truth and confidence in their eyes. "Rosamund will need to be carried," she said matter-of-factly. "We must find a litter for her."

"You may leave that with me. Now, get out of this foul air. There's no knowing what infection lurks in it. . . . Bloggs, a word with you." He jerked his head at the keeper, whose eyes now glittered. Unless he'd misunderstood, he was about to receive a substantial bribe. He oiled his way over to the duke, who'd withdrawn to the far corner of the ward.

Juliana allowed Quentin to draw her away. When they reached the sunshine of the courtyard, she took the air in great gulps. "Did you know such places existed, Quentin?"

"Yes," he said shortly. "But I'd never been inside one before." The horror of what he'd seen still lingered in his eyes. He drew her toward the postern gate, anxious to leave the last vestiges of this hell behind.

"I won't be defeated," she said with low-voiced determination, stepping out into the street beside him. "I won't let those evil women get the better of me."

"In God's name, Juliana! You can't possibly take on the world of vice all on your own." He took the horses from the relieved guard, handing him another coin.

"I won't do it alone," she said fiercely. "People like you will help me. People like you with the power to challenge the exploitation and the misery. Then things would change."

Touched by her fervency, Quentin was unwilling to spoil her dreams with his own cynicism.

"Here's Tarquin," he said with relief. The duke, carrying Rosamund in his arms, Lilly a pace or two behind, appeared at the gate, Jeremiah Bloggs at his side, a beatific smile on his face as he counted again the wad of notes that had bought the women's release. The duke hadn't even haggled over the terms, just peeled off the bills with an expression of disgust and contempt that ran off the keeper like water on a greased hide.

Juliana hurried over to them. "We must get Rosamund to the physician . . . but no, Henny will be able to look after her as well as any physician. They can't go back to the

Dennisons' until we discover whether Mistress Dennison had anything to do with the plot."

Once again Juliana was turning his house into a rescue mission and convalescent home for ill-used strumpets. Tarquin surprised himself with a wry grin. He lifted Rosamund into the phaeton and refrained from comment. He had one interest, and only one. He intended to have Juliana stripped, scrubbed, and in bed without a moment's delay.

Quentin climbed up and took Rosamund on his lap, cradling her tightly. Lilly, silent, white-faced, and shivering violently in the aftermath of this sudden escape from hell, took her seat beside him.

"There's not enough room for me," Juliana said. "I'll take a hackney. . . . Oh, but I don't have any money. My lord duke, could you . . . ?"

"No, I could not!" he snapped. "If you think I'm going to let you out of my sight again, you are vastly mistaken, my child." He half lifted her onto the step, put a hand under her backside with his customary familiarity, and shoved her upward. "You'll have to squash up."

"I would, but the hoop's in the way." Juliana struggled to sit down on the inch of bench available between Lilly and the driver's seat.

"Then take it off."

"Here?" She looked askance at the open street.

"Yes, here," he affirmed flatly. "Get down again." He reached up and pulled her to the ground. "Turn around and lift up your skirts."

After an instant's hesitation Juliana obeyed with a shrug. After everything else that had happened, being divested of her hoop before the gaze of curious passersby seemed little more than a minor inconvenience. She noticed, however, that Quentin discreetly averted his eyes when she raised her skirts, revealing the frothy if now grimy folds of her underpetticoat.

Tarquin deftly untied the tapes at her waist and freed the

whalebone panniers. He tossed them from him into the side of the street and once again boosted Juliana into the phaeton, climbing up beside her.

She gathered the soft folds of her gown and petticoats about her and made herself as small as possible. Tarquin's thigh pressed hard against hers as he occupied the remaining space on the bench and gave his horses the office to start. Juliana touched Lilly's hand, as much for her own comfort as to offer it. Lilly gave her a wan smile, and they both looked at Rosamund, held tightly in Lord Quentin's arms. Her eyes were open, staring sightlessly up at the sky from her deathly pale countenance. She appeared to be in a state of shock, immobile and unaware of her surroundings.

Rosamund was not cut out for the hand life had dealt her, Juliana thought. Lilly could manage to live it without loss of self. Indeed, she often enjoyed it. Most of the girls on Russell Street could take pleasure in their lot. They found plenty to laugh about; they shared a close camaraderie. They were not in want, and there was always the possibility of a grand and secure future if luck looked in their direction. But there was also the possibility of a Bridewell. Of a Marshalsea. Of spreading their legs beneath the bulks at Covent Garden for half a loaf of bread. But they chose not to brood about the consequences of ill luck, and who could blame them?

Grimly, Juliana acknowledged that alone she couldn't work miracles. She glanced sideways at the duke's unyielding countenance. He would make a powerful advocate if he could be persuaded to wield his influence. But that was a forlorn hope.

Unless . . . Her bruised hand touched her belly. Soon she must tell Tarquin of the child she carried. Presumably he'd be delighted. Maybe he'd be so delighted that he'd be open to suggestion. Willing to exert himself in someone else's interests for once. But then again, maybe he'd simply become even more protective of her, even more anxious that she should not be sullied by contact with Covent Garden life. Maybe he'd just keep her even more closely confined, to protect his unborn child. She and that child were his investment, after all. And he was a man who looked after his investments.

Chapter 26

George Ridge stepped out of the sedan chair, wincing as the skin on his back creased with the movement. He glowered up at the cracked stone facade of Viscount Edgecombe's town house on Mount Street. The building had a seedy, run-down air, the brass on the door unpolished, the windows dingy, the paintwork scuffed. Despite the early hour a small group of men, whom George immediately recognized from both dress and manner as bailiffs, were gathered lounging against the iron railings at the bottom of the steps leading to the front door. As George approached the steps, their air of weary waiting dissipated, and they straightened, eyes suddenly alert.

"Ye 'ave business with 'Is Lordship, sir?" one of them inquired, picking his teeth with a dirty fingernail.

"What's it to you?" George pushed past him, scowling.

"Jest that if Yer 'Onor's goin' to get that door open, y'are a sight cleverer than we are," the man said scornfully. " 'Oled up in there, tighter than a chicken's arse."

George ignored him and hammered on the knocker. There was no response. He stepped back, looking up at the unyielding facade, and glimpsed a face in an upstairs window, peering through the grime. He hammered again and this time, after a few minutes, heard the scraping of bolts.

His companions heard it too and surged up the steps. The door opened a crack. A disembodied hand grabbed George's sleeve and dragged him through the aperture. The door crashed shut on a bailiff's foot. There was a roar of outrage from outside, then violent banging on the knocker, setting a dusty porcelain figurine on a table shivering on its pedestal.

"Viscount's upstairs." The body belonging to the hand was skinny, the narrow face weasellike, with a pair of very long incisors that jutted beyond the thin lips. The man jerked his head toward the stairs. "First door on the left." Then he slithered away into the shadows beyond the staircase.

George, his scowl deepening, stomped up the stairs, which were thick with dust. His eyes were red with drink and burned with a rage so fearsome it was almost inhuman. George Ridge was a goaded bull, only one thought and one aim in view. Vengeance on the man who had ordered him thrashed like a serf. A vengeance he would obtain through Juliana. The Duke of Redmayne had made it painfully clear that Juliana's health, reputation, and general well-being were vitally important to him. Juliana would burn at the stake in Winchester marketplace. And before she did, her stepson would possess her . . . would bring her arrogant contempt to the dust. He would see her humbled, he would see her protector powerless to protect. And with her conviction he would regain his own inheritance.

He pushed open the door at the left of the staircase. It creaked on unoiled hinges, revealing a sparsely furnished apartment, its air of neglect failing to mask its handsome proportions and the elaborate moldings on the ceiling.

Lucien was slumped in a sagging elbow chair by a grate filled with last winter's ashes. A cognac bottle was at his feet, another, empty, lying on the threadbare carpet. A glass dangled from his fingers.

He jerked upright as George entered. "Dick, you bastard, I told you I . . . oh." He surveyed his visitor with

an air of sardonic inquiry. "To what do I owe this pleasure?"

"You're going to help me," George stated. He bent to
pick up the cognac bottle, raised it to his lips, and drank
deeply.

Lucien's eyes sharpened. Something very interesting had
occurred. Sir George had lost his air of bumbling, overawed
ineptitude.

"Help yourself, dear boy," Lucien invited, his languid
tone belied by the arrested look in his eyes. "There's more
where that came from. At least I trust there is."

"Thankee." George drank again, his throat working as
the fiery liquid burned down his gullet to add fuel to the
fire that raged in his belly.

"So how can I be of assistance?" Lucien took back the
bottle and tilted it to his own mouth. "Damnation, it's
empty! Ring the bell for Dick, dear fellow." He gestured
to the frayed bell rope beside the door.

George pulled on it, half expecting it to come away in
his hand, but faintly, from the bowels of the silent house,
came the jangle of the bell.

"I am going to take Juliana," he said, pacing the room,
each movement generating a painful stab, reminding him
with hideous clarity of his humiliation at the hands of the
duke's groom. "And this time I'll not be stopped."

"Oh?" Lucien sat up, the gleam of malevolent curiosity
in his eye intensifying.

"I intend to abduct her tomorrow," George said, almost
in a monotone, as if he were reciting a well-learned lesson.
"I will have a closed carriage ready, and we'll take her
immediately to Winchester. The Forsetts will be compelled
to identify her if the magistrates demand it. And there are
plenty of other folk in the neighborhood who'll recognize
her. She won't have that *devil* to run to, and once she's
locked up in Winchester jail, there'll be nothing he can do
to save her."

Lucien tugged his right earlobe. "Something happen to

rouse you, dear boy . . . Ah, Dick. Bring up another bottle of that gut-rotting brandy."

"Not sure there is any," the surly manservant muttered.

"Then go and buy some!"

"Wi' what, m'lord?" he demanded with a mock bow.

"Here." George dug a note from his pocket and handed it to him.

"Ah, good man!" Lucien approved. "Get going, then, you lazy varlet. I'm dry as a witch's tit."

Dick sniffed, pocketed the note, and disappeared.

"Impudent bugger," Lucien observed. "Only stays around because I haven't paid him in six months and he knows if he leaves before I'm dead, he won't see a penny. So," he continued with another sharp glance, "why the urgency about this abduction?"

George was not about to reveal to his malicious partner what the duke had done to him. He shrugged, controlled a wince, and said, "I've an estate to get back to. I can't hang around here much longer. But I need your help."

Lucien nodded. "And what incentive are you offering, dear boy?"

George looked startled. He'd assumed that Lucien's own desire for vengeance would be sufficient incentive. "You'll have her in your hands," he said. "You can have her first . . . for as long as you like."

He was astounded at the look of repulsion that crossed the viscount's expression.

"I want to be rid of her, man. Not *have* her," Lucien pointed out disgustedly. "I thought you understood that. You lay charges against her. I can repudiate her. Tarquin is helpless and mortified. The girl is destroyed. But I ask again, what incentives are you offering for my assistance?" His eyes narrowed.

George's puzzlement deepened. "Isn't that enough?"

Lucien chortled merrily. "Good God, no, man. I'll have a thousand guineas off you. I think that would be a reasonable remuneration. Depending, of course, on what you have in mind." He leaned back, crossing his legs with a casual grin.

George struggled with himself for barely a moment. He could lay hands on a thousand guineas, although it went against the grain to throw it down before this loathsome, grinning reptile. But he needed the viscount's help.

"I need you to help me get her out of the house," he said. "We have to go in there and winkle her out."

"Good God!" Lucien stared at him, for the first time startled out of his indolent and cynical amusement. "And just how do you propose doing that?"

"At dead of night. We go into her room. We overpower her while she's sleeping and we carry her out of there." George spoke with the flat, assertive confidence of a committed man. "You'll know where her room is. And you'll know how to get undetected into the house."

"What makes you think I can perform such miracles?" Lucien inquired with a lifted eyebrow.

"I know you can," George responded stubbornly. "You lived in the house. You probably have a key."

Lucien resumed the gentle tugging of his earlobe. He *did* have a key to the side door, as it happened. He'd had one copied several years earlier when he'd still been a lad. Tarquin had been an exasperatingly strict and watchful guardian, and Lucien had had frequent resort to subterfuge to evade both the duke's rules and his guard.

"Perhaps I do," he conceded after a minute. "Getting in might not be too difficult, but getting out again, with that red-haired virago screeching and fighting, is a different matter."

"She won't make any noise," George asserted in the same tone.

"Oh?" Lucien inclined his head inquiringly.

"I'll make sure of it."

Lucien examined his expression for a minute, then slowly nodded. "I believe you will. I almost feel sorry for my lady wife. I wonder what could have happened to arouse such vicious urgency in your breast, dear fellow."

He waited, but no explanation was forthcoming. Ridge's reticence increased his curiosity a hundredfold, but he was prepared to bide his time. "There's one other small difficulty," he continued in a musing tone. "My estimable cousin has the chamber next door to our quarry. I daresay he finds the proximity convenient."

"You know for a fact that Juliana is his mistress?" George's voice was thick. He knew it, but he wanted it confirmed.

"Why else would my cousin take such an interest in the wench?" Lucien shrugged. "I've never known him to take a woman under his roof before, either. I suspect he'll be most disconcerted to lose her." He grinned. "I think I can contrive to lure my cousin from the house tomorrow. It would be best if he was elsewhere while we're abducting his doxy. . . . Ah, at last . . . Dick with the cup that cheers. We will drink a toast to this enterprise. Set it down there, man. No need to pour it. I've strength enough for that."

George took the smudged glass handed to him by his host. He drank, his eyes for the moment turned inward on his vengeance. He was a man in the grip of madness. The Duke of Redmayne had unleashed demons when he'd set out to subdue Sir George Ridge.

The duke reined in his horses outside the house on Albermarle Street. Ted appeared as if by a wizard's conjuring, running down the steps lightly for such a big man. He'd heard the coachman's story, as had the rest of the household, and now glared at Juliana, as if personally insulted by her grim adventure.

"Take the horses, Ted." Tarquin sprang down, reaching up a hand to assist Juliana, then Lilly. He took Rosamund from Quentin so that his brother could alight unencumbered, then handed the still-limp figure back to Quentin and strode ahead of the party into the house.

"Catlett, summon the housekeeper and have these two

young women escorted to a bedchamber. Send a maid to
attend them. And ask Henny to come to Lady Edgecombe's apartment immediately."

"Oh, no!" Juliana exclaimed. "No . . . I have no need
of Henny. She must look to Rosamund. Truly I can look
after myself, but Rosamund has need of expert care."

He took her hands, turning them palm up. "You can do
nothing for yourself with your hands in this condition. If
you won't have Henny, then *I* will attend to you."

"There's no need for you to trouble yourself, sir." Her
voice was stiff. "I have no need of a nurse."

Impatience flared in his eyes. He drew a sharp breath and
said, "You will have either Henny or myself to attend to
you. Take your pick."

"You, then," she replied dully, seeing no option.
Rosamund needed all Henny's skills.

"Very well." He nodded briefly, then turned back to
Catlett. "I want a bath, hot water, salve, bandages, and lye
soap taken up to Lady Edgecombe's apartment immediately. . . . Quentin, you'll see the other two installed?"

"Of course."

"Come, Juliana." The duke took her wrist in a firm
encircling grip and set foot on the stairs. Juliana followed
him up willy-nilly.

Her bedchamber was filled with sunlight; the bowls of
roses were replenished daily, and the air was heavy with
their scent. The sight of the bed with its crisp, lavender-
fragrant sheets, the downy invitation of the feather bed and
plump pillows, drew her toward it as the nightmare images
of Bridewell became smudged by the familiar comforts of
home.

Home. This was home? It felt like home. Her own place.
The duke's voice broke into her train of thought.

"Bed will have to wait, Juliana. There's no knowing
what you might have picked up in that filthy hole. Vermin,
infection . . ."

"Vermin?" Her hands flew to her tangled hair, her eyes
widening in disgust. That was why he'd ordered lye.

"Stand still. I don't want to touch your clothes any more than I must, so I'm going to cut them off you." He went to the dresser for the pair of scissors Henny kept to make minor repairs or adjustments to Juliana's wardrobe.

Juliana stood rigid, shuddering with disgust. She remembered the woman Maggie touching her dress, tearing Rosamund's fichu, her gnarled, filthy, bleeding hands sullying as they clawed and fondled. A wave of nausea rose violent and abrupt in her throat. With an inarticulate mutter she pushed Tarquin aside as he approached with the scissors, and dived for the commode.

Tarquin put down the scissors and went over to her. His hand was warm on her neck, soothing as he rubbed her back. Distantly he realized that if anyone had told him a few weeks ago that he wouldn't think twice about ministering to a vomiting woman, he'd have laughed. But that was before Juliana had swept into his life.

"I beg your pardon," she gasped as the spasms ceased. "I don't know what came over me." She envied Rosamund Henny's calm, attentive presence. Vomiting in front of a man, even one's lover—especially one's lover—was a wretched mortification, and she cringed at the thought of what he must be thinking. But his hand on her back just then had been ineffably comforting.

"There's no need for pardon," Tarquin said gently, dampening a washcloth with water from the ewer. He wiped her mouth and brow, attentively matter-of-fact, and when she searched his face, she could see no inkling of his earlier rage. There was a rather puzzled frown in his eyes, but his mouth was relaxed. He tossed aside the cloth, picked up the scissors, and swiftly cut the laces of her bodice.

She was naked in a very few minutes, his hands moving with deft efficiency, cutting away her petticoats, her chemise, slicing through her garters. She rolled down her stockings herself, tossing them onto the heap of discarded clothing. Then she stood, awkward and uncertain, wishing for Henny, not knowing where to put her hands, wanting absurdly to cover herself with her hands, as if she'd never shared glorious intimacies with this man; as if he hadn't touched and probed every inch of her skin, every orifice of her body; as if his tongue hadn't tasted her essence; as if his hard, pursuing flesh hadn't taken and possessed her fragility; as if she hadn't, in yielding the ultimate secrets of her body, possessed his.

His gaze was not in the least desirous; in fact, he seemed to be going out of his way to be matter-of-fact about the whole business. But that made things all the more confusing. How she wanted Henny. A woman; a nursemaid. Someone whose attentions would be straightforward and uncomplicated, and she could receive them in the same way.

A bang at the door yanked her out of her reverie. She looked in panic at Tarquin, who merely handed her a wrapper and gestured toward the shadows of the bed curtains at the head of the bed. Juliana retreated, drawing the folds of the muslin wrapper tightly around her, listening as two footmen labored with a porcelain hip bath, copper jugs of steaming water; a maid followed with bandages, salve, the pungent lye soap, a heap of thick towels.

No one spoke. No one glanced toward Juliana's retreat. The duke remained perched on the windowsill, arms folded, watching the preparations. Then the entourage withdrew, the door was closed. Juliana stepped forward.

"I'll bandage your hands first." He poured hot water into the basin on the dresser.

"How can I wash myself with bandaged hands?" Juliana objected.

"You aren't going to, *mignonne*. I am doing the washing." A flickering smile played over his mouth, reminding her vividly of the last time they'd made love, when he'd looked down at her, looked into her very soul, with so much wonder and warmth. Where had his anger gone? Juliana was plunged anew into the chaos of bewilderment. What *was* he feeling?

He gestured to the dresser stool. "Sit down and give me

your hands." As deft and gentle as an expert nurse, he bathed the raw strips of flesh, smoothed on salve, then wrapped around bandages, tearing the material at the ends to make a knot. He was as surprised as Juliana at this new-found skill, and his smile deepened with an unlooked for pleasure and satisfaction.

Juliana nibbled her bottom lip. "Were you concerned for me when you heard where I was?" The question was tenta-tive, and it was only as she asked it that she realized she hadn't intended to.

"Sit in the tub," he responded. "Keep your hands well clear of the water."

"But were you?" she persisted, one foot raised to step into the hip bath. Suddenly the question was more impor-tant than any she'd ever asked.

"I wouldn't leave my worst enemy in such a place," he said flippantly. "Are you going to sit down of your own accord?"

Juliana hastily slipped into the water. It was not a satis-factory answer. She stared down at the water.

Tarquin caught her chin, bringing her face up. "I have never been more concerned in my life," he stated flatly, both expression and tone now devoid of flippancy. "You frightened the living daylights out of me, Juliana. And if you ever scare me like that again, I can safely promise that you will rue the day you were born."

Releasing her chin, he poured hot water over her hair. Juliana snuffled, impatiently pushing aside the drenched mass of curls so she could see his face again. That same luminous glow was in his eyes despite the conviction of his threat. And for some reason she found the threat as pleasing as the glow. Satisfied, she bent her head beneath his strong fingers.

Juliana grimaced at the smell of the lye as he rubbed it vigorously into her tangled hair. It reminded her of sheep dip. It was even worse when he scrubbed her body with the washcloth, leaving not an inch of skin untouched. He was not rough, but very thorough, and when he soaped her breasts, she had to force herself not to flinch at their new tenderness.

Tarquin noticed the almost imperceptible wince. He wondered how long it would be before she told him of her pregnancy. Presumably it didn't occur to her that he might have guessed for himself. There was something touchingly naive about the idea that she didn't realize he was as attuned to her bodily cycles as she was. He smiled to himself but gave no indication of his thoughts; she would tell him in her own good time.

"I think you're clean," he announced finally. "No vermin that I could find. It's to be hoped you weren't in there long enough to catch an infection either. Step out." He picked up a large towel.

Juliana stood still while he dried her as gently as if she were a china doll, attending to the most intimate parts of her body with a careful thoroughness that again was deliberately matter-of-fact. Finally he dropped her nightgown over her head.

"Now you may get into bed and tell me precisely what flight of fancy led to this latest debacle."

"Flight of fancy! Is that what you call it?" Juliana, fatigue and confusion momentarily forgotten, glared, her damp hair flying about her face. "I try to help those women see a way to gain some power over their lives, and you call it a flight of fancy!" The contempt in her eyes scorched him. "There's a world of slaves out there . . . slaves whose bodies you enjoy, of course, so it's in your interests to keep them enslaved."

She turned aside with a little gesture of defeat and climbed into bed. "You have no compassion, no soul, my lord duke. Just like the rest of your breed. If you would speak out . . . you and Lord Quentin, and others like you . . . then people would listen. If you insisted on fair treatment for the women whose bodies you use, then it would happen." She dragged the covers over her and thumped onto her side, facing away from him.

Tarquin stared at the curve of her body beneath the coverlet. Absently, he raked a hand through his hair in an uncharacteristic gesture of bewilderment. No one had ever spoken to him, looked at him, with such furious derision before. And instead of reacting with anger, he felt only dismay. A seventeen-year-old chit accused him of utter callousness in his way of life, his view of the world, and he was standing there wondering if she was right.

She was driving him to the edge of madness. When she wasn't terrifying him with her crusading adventures, she was unraveling every neat thread in the tapestry of his life, forcing him to look and see things that had never troubled him before. More than a few of those revelations concerned himself, and they were not comfortable.

He took a step toward the bed, then, with a bewildered shake of his head, left the chamber, softly closing the door behind him.

As the door closed, Juliana rolled onto her back. She gazed up at the flowered tester, her eyes fixed unseeing on a strand of ivy. She closed her lids on the tears that spilled over, telling herself she was crying only because she was fatigued. Because of reaction to what she'd endured.

Chapter 27

❧

"Mercy me, but I don't know what the world's coming to when you young things can get yourselves into this state." Henny shook her head as she untied the bandages on Juliana's ruined hands the following morning.

"How is Rosamund?" Juliana was feeling limp, filled with a deep and most unusual languor. She'd slept all day and all night and now couldn't seem to drag herself fully awake. Rain drummed against the windowpane, and her chamber was candlelit, which didn't help matters.

"She'll do. Had a nasty shock, but she's recoverin' nicely. That Mistress Dennison came and took them both home."

"Already?" Juliana winced as a strand of bandage stuck to an open cut. "Why didn't someone tell me?"

"You were sleeping, and His Grace gave order that you weren't to be disturbed until you rang." Henny dipped a cloth into a bowl of warm water. "When y'are dressed, he'd like to see you in the library. If you feel up to it, that is." She bathed Juliana's palms and patted them dry before applying fresh salve.

Juliana closed her heavy eyes, wondering if she could have unknowingly swallowed a sleeping draft. She could remember nothing after Tarquin had left her in yesterday's morning sunshine. Who had informed Mistress Dennison that Lilly and Rosamund were here? Did she bear them a grudge? It would seem not, if they were received back into the fold so quickly. Tarquin would have the answers.

Depression slopped over her as she remembered how he'd left her in anger, without saying a word to her bitter accusations. She'd most effectively doused whatever warmth he'd been feeling toward her. She didn't regret what she'd said, she'd meant every word of it, but now it seemed mean-spirited to have attacked him on the heels of his ministrations.

"I think ye'd be best off back in bed, dearie," Henny clucked, deftly retying the bandages. "I'll let His Grace know that y'are not ready to go downstairs."

"No . . . no, of course I am." Juliana forced her eyes open. She couldn't avoid seeing him for long, and, besides, she wanted answers to her questions. "I'll wash my face and drink some coffee, and then I'll be wide-awake. It's because it's raining and so close in here."

Henny tutted but made no further demur, and half an hour later Juliana surveyed herself dispiritedly in the cheval glass. Her hair was particularly unruly this morning, startlingly vivid against her face, which was even paler than usual. Her eyes seemed very large, dark shadows beneath them that she decided gave her a rather interesting look. Mysterious and haunted. The whimsical notion made her feel slightly more cheerful. Anyone less mysterious and haunted than her own ungainly, big-footed, clumsy self would be hard to find. But the pale-lavender muslin and her white-bandaged hands did give her a more delicate air than usual.

"Off you go, then. But don't stay down too long. You'll need to rest before dinner."

"You're so kind to me," Juliana said. "No one ever took care of me before or worried about me." Impulsively, she gave Henny a kiss that made the woman smile with pleasure as she shooed her away with a "Get along with you, now, m'lady."

Juliana didn't at first see Tarquin's visitor as she entered the library, her questions tumbling from her lips even before she was through the door. "Was Mistress Dennison angry with Lilly and Rosamund, sir? How did she know they were here? Are you sure she won't be unkind to them?"

"No. I told her. Yes," Tarquin replied, rising from his chair. "Take a deep breath, *mignonne*, and make your curtsy to Mr. Bonnell Thornton."

Juliana took a deep breath. To her amazement she saw that the duke was smiling, and the same warm light was still in his eyes. There was no sign of the chill she'd been expecting.

"Juliana?" he prompted, gesturing to his companion, when she didn't immediately move forward.

"I beg your pardon, sir. I didn't see you at first." Juliana recollected herself and curtsied to the tall, lean gentleman in an astonishing pink satin suit.

"I am delighted to make your acquaintance, ma'am." The gentleman bowed. "His Grace has told me all about your misadventures and their cause."

Juliana looked inquiringly toward Tarquin, unsure how to take this. He handed her a broadsheet. "Read this, and you may begin to understand that you're not the only champion of the cause, Juliana."

She had not come across the *Drury Lane Journal* before. Its subtitle, *Have at Ye* became clear as soon as she began to read. It was a scurrilous, gossipy journal, full of innuendo and supposedly truthful accounts of scandalous exploits among the members of London's fashionable and political world. It was also wickedly amusing. But Juliana was puzzled as to what Tarquin had meant. She skimmed through reviews and critiques of plays and operas and then looked up. "It's very amusing, sir, but I don't see . . ."

"In the center you'll find an article by one Roxanna Termagant," Mr. Thornton pointed out.

She went back and found the column. Her lips parted on a soundless O. Miss Termagant had given a precise description of the so-called riot at Cocksedge's, directly accusing both Mitchell and Cocksedge of orchestrating the riot and the subsequent raid in order to achieve the arrest of four women—one of whom was no whore but the wife of a viscount. The account was followed by an impassioned castigation of the authorities, who'd allowed themselves to serve the devious purposes of the bawds and had imprisoned innocent women who'd merely been gathering for a peaceful discussion on how to improve their working and living conditions.

"Who is this lady?"

Mr. Thornton bowed with a flourish. "You see her before you, ma'am." He grinned mischievously.

Maybe it explained the pink satin. However, she was still confused. "My lord duke told you all of this?"

"It's not an unusual story, my lady. Any attempt by the women to demand basic rights of their so-called employers is always defeated. However"—he took the paper from her, tapping it against the palm of his hand—"we can make life uncomfortable for them with public ridicule and public outrage. Unfortunately, it's difficult for me to find out about all the horrors that go on. I didn't know about the case of Miss Lucy Tibbet, for instance. So I have a proposition for you, Lady Edgecombe."

Juliana perched on the arm of the sofa. She glanced at Tarquin, who was leaning back in his chair, his fingers steepled against his mouth, his eyes resting on her face. "Not all members of our society close our eyes to injustice, *mignonne*. Mr. Thornton has a powerful voice in Covent Garden. I believe his methods are more effective than inciting harlots to rebellion and landing yourself in Bridewell."

"So you . . . you want to help too?" she asked with a doubtful frown. It seemed impossible to believe, but what else could he mean?

"Let's just say you've opened my eyes," he said wryly.

Juliana was so taken aback, she wasn't aware for a moment that Mr. Thornton had begun to talk again. He coughed pointedly to attract her attention and continued.

"As I was saying, Lady Edgecombe, I understand you have friends in the Garden. Women who are in a position to know what goes on. If you can encourage them to confide in you, then I will have the material to make war."

"Act as a spy, you mean?"

"An informant," Tarquin said.

"I will also hold whatever funds you're able to collect," Mr. Thornton went on, "and take responsibility for disbursing them to those women in need. Their employers may quarrel with my apparent philanthropy, but they'll have no excuse to be avenged upon the women, so no one need fear reprisals." Mr. Thornton nodded his head decisively.

"I prefer to be *doing* things," Juliana said. "Just telling tales seems a little pathetic."

"But when you *do* things, Juliana, you fall head over heels into trouble," the duke pointed out. Bonnell Thornton chuckled, and Juliana flushed but didn't attempt to deny the truth.

"Your fault, *mignonne,* lies in overestimating your abilities to change the world," continued Tarquin. "You can't do it without assistance."

"That's what I said yesterday."

"And as you see, I took it to heart."

"Yes," she agreed slowly. It was still hard to believe her words could have had such an effect. She turned back to Bonnell Thornton. "Well, if you think this will work, Mr. Thornton, then of course I'll help however I can."

"Good. You will see that we can make a difference little by little. . . . Well, I'll take my leave now. Your Grace . . ." He bowed to the duke, who rose politely and escorted him to the door. Juliana curtsied as the visitor took her bandaged hand gently and lightly kissed her fingertips. "Good day, Lady Edgecombe. I look forward to our association."

Tarquin closed the door after him, then turned back to Juliana. "I know you think it poor work, my dear, but believe me, it's the best you can do."

Juliana was not too sure about that. She could think of many ways in which she could become more actively involved in Mr. Bonnell Thornton's activities. But it would not be politic to mention them at this point. "I can't do Mr. Thornton's work without visiting my friends," she pointed out.

"No," he agreed, strolling to the sideboard to pour himself a glass of sherry. "But you won't forget to take Ted with you, will you?"

Juliana shook her head. "Why have you changed your mind?"

He set down the decanter and came across to her. Cupping her face between his hands, he brushed her eyelids with his lips. "You work the strangest magic, *mignonne*. I believe if you put your mind to it, you could melt a heart of marble." He ran his thumb over her mouth, his smile rueful. "I can't say I enjoy being the target of your reforming zeal." He kissed her as she was still searching for a response. "Go back upstairs now. You look exhausted."

She was suddenly feeling both queasy and overwhelmingly sleepy. Her brain couldn't get around his words. Were they really a declaration of some kind? A promise of some kind? She tried to find a response, but there was something in his eyes that told her he didn't want her to say anything. His hands on her shoulders were turning her toward the door. "Go to Henny, Juliana." And she went without a word.

She lay back on the chaise longue beneath the bedroom window while Henny took off her shoes and unlaced her bodice. Her hand drifted to her belly. This child would know only a guardian and an uncle. He would never know a father. All the loving tenderness in the world couldn't soften that fact. And once Tarquin knew she was carrying his child, it would no longer be exclusively hers, even in her womb. How long could she keep it to herself?

•   •   •

"Henny says Juliana can't seem to wake up today." Quentin sounded worried as he stood before the library fire, lit against the damp chill of the rainy day. "Could she have suffered more than we saw?"

"I don't believe so." Tarquin sipped his port. "I believe there's something else behind it."

"What?" Quentin reached for his own glass on the mantel.

Tarquin yawned. "It's for Juliana to say. I daresay she'll tell me in her own good time." He stretched his legs to the fire. "There are times when an evening at home is most delightful."

"Particularly listening to that." Quentin gestured to the window where the rain drummed monotonously. "It's a foul night to be abroad."

"Yes, and the thought that my troublesome *mignonne* is tucked up safely in her bed is very comforting." Tarquin yawned again.

Quentin looked into his glass. "Will you hide this liaison from Lydia when she's your wife?" His voice was stiff, his eyes strained.

Tarquin looked up, the sleepy indolence vanishing from his eyes. "What do you mean, Quentin?"

"What do you think I mean?" Quentin jumped to his feet. The agony of his frustration was suddenly no longer bearable. "You will have both Juliana and Lydia under your roof. Will you conceal your true relationship with Juliana from Lydia?"

Tarquin stared at him in astonishment. Quentin's face was pale, his lips bloodless.

"I cannot endure it, Tarquin! I cannot endure that you would treat Lydia in such fashion. I *love* her, God help me. And I will not stand by and watch you ruin both our lives." His hands twisted themselves into impossible knots, his gray eyes burning holes in his white face.

"You . . . you and Lydia!" Tarquin stuttered. "You and Lydia?"

"Yes."

"Lydia . . . Lydia knows how you feel?" He still couldn't seem to grasp this.

"Yes."

"And . . . and does she return your feelings?"

Quentin nodded.

"Dear God!" Tarquin ran a hand through his hair. "You and Lydia love each other? I know you've always had a special regard for her, but . . ."

"Sometimes, Tarquin, you are so damned blind you can't see the nose on your face!" Quentin declared, feeling suddenly purged, as if a great load had been taken from him. "It took Juliana five minutes to see—"

"Juliana!" Now he remembered her hints. "Jesus, Mary, and Joseph," he muttered.

"I will not stand by and see you insult Lydia by keeping your mistress under the same roof," Quentin reiterated, his voice now strong.

Tarquin said nothing, merely stared into the fire. He was realizing that he couldn't imagine insulting Juliana in such fashion either. What in the devil's name was happening to him?

"Do you hear me, Tarquin?"

He looked up and shook his head with a half laugh of disbelieving resignation. "Oh, yes, I hear you, brother. As clearly as I hear myself."

Quentin waited for more, but his brother turned back to the fire, twisting his port glass between his fingers. It was as if he'd put up a wall around himself. The silence lengthened and finally Quentin left the room, closing the door softly behind him. Nothing had been resolved, but he'd made his statement. The truth was in the open, and instead of feeling bad about it, he felt only an overpowering relief.

Tarquin remained immobile for a long time. Eventually he rose and refilled his port glass. His eye fell on the miniature of Lydia Melton on the mantel. Grave, composed, dignified. The perfect wife for a bishop.

Suddenly he laughed aloud. How very simple it all was if one looked at the world through Juliana's eyes.

He was still chuckling to himself when there was a
knock at the door and Catlett entered with a note on a
silver salver. "I beg your pardon, Your Grace, but a messenger has just brought this. He says it's of the utmost urgency."

Tarquin frowned, taking the wafer-sealed paper. He read
the ill-penned, ill-spelled contents, his expression darken-
ing. "Damn that degenerate, profligate fool!" He
scrunched the note and hurled it into the fire. "Have my
carriage brought around."

"You're going out, Your Grace?" Catlett's eyes darted to
the rain-blackened window.

"You may assume so from my order," the duke said
acidly. "Tell my man to bring my cloak and cane."

Damn Lucien! Lying sick unto death in a sponging
house. The note had come from the owner of the house,
presumably at Lucien's urging. A debt of five hundred
pounds to be cleared to obtain his release. Until then he
was lying in the cold and the damp, coughing his heart out,
without medicines, food, or blankets.

Tarquin didn't question the situation. It was not the first
time it had happened in the last five years. It didn't occur
to him either to abandon Lucien to his fate, despite casting
him from his door with such finality. He knew just as
Lucien had known that in extremis Tarquin would always
come to his aid. However vile and despicable Lucien had
become, Tarquin couldn't free himself from the chains of
responsibility.

He opened the strongbox in his book room and took out
five hundred pounds. It was a minute part of Lucien's overall debt, so presumably he'd been caught by one of his
minor creditors. A tailor or a hatter, probably.

His valet brought him a heavy caped cloak and his
swordstick. Tarquin turned up the deep collar, thrust his
hands into his gloves, and went out into the driving rain.
The coachman shivered on his box.

"Ludgate Hill." Tarquin didn't glance at him as he gave
the order and climbed into the coach.

The coachman cracked his whip. He was new to the duke's service and far too anxious to make a good impression to complain about turning out in the middle of such a foul night.

After the coach disappeared into the sheeting rain, George and Lucien emerged from the basement steps opposite. "Hell and the devil," grumbled Lucien, water pouring from the brim of his hat. "Why this night of all nights? It hasn't rained in a month."

George dived across the street, head down against the wall of water. He was unaware of the rain, the hot blood of vengeance warming him to his core. He was so close now. He darted around the side of the house into the alley that led to the mews and stopped, leaning against the wall, panting.

Lucien appeared beside him, a drenched wraith in comparison with his companion's bulk. "You'll owe me another five hundred for this," he said, coughing into his sleeve.

George merely gestured impatiently to the door set into the wall of the house. "Will the servants be up?"

"Not at this hour . . . unless Catlett's still roaming." Lucien hawked into the street. "The night watchman will be in his cubbyhole under the stairs, but we'll not be going anywhere near the front of the house."

"What of this Catlett?"

"He'll be in his pantry if he's not abed. I know the routine." Lucien fitted the key into the lock, and the door swung open without so much as a creak. "Well-maintained household we have here," he observed sardonically, stepping into a narrow foyer. "Now, keep your mouth shut and be light on your feet."

He opened another door, revealing a set of stairs set into the wall. It was pitch-dark, no candles in the sconces, but Lucien went up with the sure-footed tread of one who could find his way in the dark. George fumbled behind him, trying not to breathe, conscious of his rasping excitement, of a heaviness in his loins that hitherto he had associated only with carnal congress.

Lucien opened another door at the head of the stairs and peered around. The corridor was dimly lit with sconces at wide intervals along the wall. There was not a sound. He slipped into the corridor, George looming behind him, the man's shadow huge on the wall ahead.

The house was as quiet as the grave when they reached Juliana's door. Lucien stepped back, pressing himself against the wall. "She's in there. You find your own way out. I'll fetch a hackney and bring it to the street corner."

George nodded, his eyes glittering in the waxy, sweating face, his lips wet. He put a hand on the latch as Lucien flitted away to safety. The viscount had no desire to get any closer to this abduction.

George pushed the door, and it opened soundlessly. The room was in darkness, except for the faint glow of embers in the fireplace. The bed curtains were not drawn around the bed, and he had a clear view of the sleeping figure. For a minute he watched her. Watched the way the sheet lifted over her bosom with each even breath. The way her hair spread out in a rich pool against the white lawn of the pillow. He frowned at her bandaged hands, then shrugged. She wouldn't be needing them for what he had in mind.

He bent over her, his hands large, heavy, the fingers strong as any laborer's. Those fingers went around Juliana's throat and squeezed.

Her eyes shot open, filled with sleep and terror; her bandaged hands scrabbled at the fingers pressing her throat. She opened her mouth to scream, but not a sound came out. She was drowning, suffocating, and her befuddled brain didn't know whether this was real or nightmare. The face hanging over her, so intent, so closed in on its purpose, was familiar, and yet it wasn't. It was a mask . . . a mask of hideous menace . . . a mask from a nightmare. Surely only a nightmare. Please, dear God, only a nightmare. But she couldn't breathe. She struggled to wake up.

Her eyes were popping in their sockets. Her chest was col-
lapsing. A black wave rolled over her.

George released his hold as she sank limply into the pillows, her eyelids drooping over her terrorized eyes. The
marks of his fingers were shadows in the darkness on the
white of her throat. He placed his hand over her mouth.
She was still breathing, but light and shallow. He took a
thick scarf from his pocket and tied it around her mouth,
knotting it at the back of her head. Then he pulled back
the bedclothes and looked at her unconscious form, every
curve and hollow outlined beneath the thin lawn shift.

He dragged his eyes from her, conscious of the passing of
every minute, and opened the armoire. He pulled out a
thick cloak and rummaged through the dresser drawers,
finding a pair of silk stockings.

Bending over her, he bound her ankles together with
one stocking, pulled her arms in front of her, and tied her
wrists with the other; then he swaddled her still form in the
cloak, bringing the hood over her head. Her breathing was
still shallow, but it was regular. He maneuvered her over his
shoulder, took one last look around, then made for the
door. His excitement was such that it was difficult to move
slowly and cautiously along the deserted corridor. At any
moment he expected a door to open, to be accosted with a
shout of outrage. But he reached the door to the internal
staircase without mishap.

He slipped into the darkness, closing the door behind
him. The house was pitch-black and there was no Lucien
to guide him. He waited, his heart hammering, his hands
wet, until he was steady enough to step down the steep,
narrow flight, an arm encircling his burden. He could feel
the shape of her, could smell her hair and skin, could feel
her breath warm on his neck.

At the foot of the stairs he stepped into the narrow
lobby. The side door was slightly ajar, and his heart leaped.
He was a second away from success. He stepped through
the door and into the alley.

A shrill whistle made him jump. But it was Lucien,

beckoning from the end of the alley. George set off at a lumbering run, Juliana's head bumping against his back. A hackney stood in the street, Lucien already inside, shivering with cold and wet.

"Goddammit, but I'll get an ague with this night's work," he complained as George tipped Juliana off his shoulder onto the bench and clambered up after her. "So you got her." He examined his wife's unconscious body with an air of mild curiosity. "What did you do to her? She's not dead, is she?"

George loosened the cloak, tipped back the hood. Juliana's head fell back against the stained leather squabs. Lucien raised his eyebrows at the gag, then leaned over and lightly touched the bruises on her throat, observing casually, "Dear me, quite rough weren't you, dear boy?"

"I wasn't taking any chances," George replied, sitting beside Lucien, where he could see his victim as she lolled against the cushions with each jolt of the iron wheels over the cobbles. He smiled and stroked his chin.

Lucien's teeth chattered, and he fumbled for the flask of cognac in his pocket. With a shudder he put the neck to his mouth and tipped the contents down his throat. "Dear God, but I'm cold." He drank again, desperate to warm the icy void in his belly. His hands and feet were numb, his fingers blue-white, as if his blood had stopped flowing. He cursed again as his chest heaved and he was convulsed with a violent spasm of coughing.

George had never seen anyone cough with such violence. Lucien grabbed for a handkerchief and held it over his mouth. George saw the white cloth darken with blood. Instinctively, he moved a little away from him along the bench, fearing some contamination. He reached into his pocket for a small vial of smelling salts.

Lucien continued to cough, his hollow eyes blood-streaked with the strain. But he watched through the paroxysms as his companion uncorked the vial, leaned forward, and pushed it beneath Juliana's nose.

"What d'you want to wake her for?" Lucien croaked.

"Wait until we get there, you fool. You don't want her making any trouble."

"She won't," George said sullenly, but he sat back again, replacing the vial in his pocket. He wanted to be there when she came to. He wanted to see her eyes open. He wanted to see her realize what had happened to her. He wanted to see her eyes fall upon him and know that she was powerless as she felt the bonds at her wrists and ankles, the gag in her mouth. But he would wait. He turned his head to look out at the black night, and he missed the moment when Juliana's eyes fluttered, opened, then closed again.

Her throat hurt. It was agony to swallow. She couldn't move. She couldn't open her mouth. The faint stinging tang of smelling salts was in her nose. She kept her eyes shut. What had happened? The memory of the terrifying nightmare flooded back. The hands at her throat. George's face, swollen and greasy and triumphant.

No nightmare.

She kept still, trying to work out why she couldn't move; her befuddled brain took what seemed an eternity to conclude that she was gagged and bound.

"We're coming up to the Bell now."

Lucien's voice. Dear God, she had both of them to contend with. A cold sweat broke out on her back. How could they possibly have spirited her away from the house without someone's knowing? Where was Tarquin? Why hadn't he been there? Tears pricked behind her eyes, and she tried to swallow them. Her throat was agony, but she couldn't bear the idea of tears seeping down her face, into the gag, and she unable to move her hands to wipe them away.

The hackney rattled to a halt. There were noises. Running feet, shouting voices. Light shone on her closed eyelids as she was hauled up and out of the chaise, still swaddled tightly in the cloak. George hoisted her over his shoulder again. She risked opening her eyes and saw that they were in the familiar yard of the Bell of Cheapside. A postchaise stood at the door, horses in the traces, ostlers sheltering from the rain under the eaves of the inn.

She was carried across. George thrust her into the interior of the chaise and slammed the door. "The lady's sick," he told the ostlers. "Sleeping, so don't disturb her. We'll be back in a minute." To Lucien he said, "Let's get a bite of supper. I'm wet as a drowned hen, and parched as the desert."

Lucien glanced at the closed door of the chaise, then shrugged and followed George into the taproom. "What happens if someone looks in?"

"No one's business but mine," George growled into a cognac bottle. "Besides, she's not going to make a sound. She can't move. Who's to look inside?"

It wasn't his business, Lucien reflected, shivering with that bone-deep cold. He'd not been responsible for the abduction. He drank thirstily of the brandy but waved away the meat pie and bread and cheese that George was eating with greedy gusto. He felt ill and knew from experience that the ice in his marrow presaged one of his serious bouts of fever. Perhaps he should take a room there and sweat it out.

But he wanted his thousand guineas, and he wasn't prepared to leave George until he had them firmly in his hand. He understood the man couldn't lay hands on such a sum until he got home; therefore, Lucien would accompany him home. Besides, it might be amusing to see how his wife reacted when she recovered her senses.

Juliana lay in the chaise just as she'd been thrust, half on and half off the seat. She thought she could maneuver herself fully onto the bench, but if she did that, they would know she had moved. Instinctively, she knew that she must maintain her unconsciousness until they reached wherever they were going. At some point they would have to untie her. She was acutely uncomfortable, every muscle twisted and crying out for relief. She tried to take her mind off her discomfort, wondering what the time was. How close to dawn. What time had she been abducted? And where, for pity's sake, were they taking her?

George needed her dead or convicted of murder in order

to reclaim her jointure. So which of the two did he have in
mind? Neither alternative appealed.

They came back. She could smell cognac as they
breathed heavily into the cramped space, thumping down
on the bench opposite. Lucien's cough rasped, hacked. She
kept her eyes tightly closed when hands moved beneath her
legs and lifted her fully onto the seat. She was grateful for
the small mercy. A whip cracked, the chaise rattled over the
cobbles. Where in the name of pity were they taking her?

Tarquin stood in the rain, staring in disbelief at the ruined
building on Ludgate Hill. It was burned out . . . had
been for months. A roofless, blackened shell. He knew he
had the address right. There was no sponging house here.

Lucien had tricked him. Had wanted him out of the
house.

He spun on his heel. "Home!" he snapped to the
drenched coachman. "And be quick about it." He leaped
into the chaise, slamming the door shut as the horses
plunged forward under the zealous coachman's whip.

His mind was in a ferment. Whatever reason Lucien had
had for luring him away must have to do with Juliana. But
what? It was so unlike the impulsively vicious Lucien to
plan.

He was out of the carriage almost before it had halted.
"Stay here. I may need you again."

The coachman nodded miserably and pulled his hat brim
farther down.

The night porter opened the door at the duke's vigorous
banging. "Who's been here in my absence?" the duke
snapped.

The man looked alarmed, defensive, as if he were being
accused of something. "No one, Your Grace. I've been
sittin' 'ere all alone. Not a soul 'as come in or out, I'll swear
to it."

Tarquin didn't respond but raced up the stairs two at a

time. He flung open Juliana's door, knowing what he would find and yet praying that he was mistaken.

He stared at the empty bed. There were no signs of a struggle. The armoire door was ajar, the dresser drawers opened, their contents tumbled. He pulled the bell rope again and again until feet came running along the corridor. Catlett pulling on his livery, Henny bleary-eyed, Quentin in his nightshirt, eyes filled with alarm.

"Lady Edgecombe is not in the house," the duke rasped. "Henny, find out what's missing from her clothes. Catlett, ask the servants if they heard anything . . . saw anything unusual in the last two hours."

Quentin stared stupidly at the empty bed. "Where would she go on a night like this?"

"Nowhere of her own volition," Tarquin said bleakly. "Lucien has a hand in this, but how in God's name did he manage to spirit her out of here? She's stronger than he is. And even if he managed to overpower her, he couldn't possibly carry her down the stairs."

"Why would he?"

"Why does Lucien ever plot mischief? . . . Well?" he demanded of Henny, who'd finished her examination of the armoire and dresser.

"Just a heavy cloak, Your Grace, and a pair of stockings," she said. "Can't see nothin' else missing."

"No shoes?"

Henny shook her head. "Seems like she's gone in nothin' but her shift, sir."

"*George,*" said Tarquin softly, almost to himself. "*George Ridge.*" He'd miscalculated, grossly misread the man's character. Instead of intimidating him, he'd succeeded in rousing the devil. Lucien would have provided the means to get to her, George the brute force to remove her.

"What are you saying?" asked Quentin, still too shocked to absorb the situation.

"George and Lucien, the devil's partnership," Tarquin said bitterly. "God, I've been a fool." He turned as Catlett hurried in, his livery now neat, his wig straight. "Well? Anything?"

"No, Your Grace. The household's been abed since before you left. I was up myself for a short while, in my pantry, but I retired soon after your departure."

Tarquin nodded, tapping his lips with his fingertips as he thought. They all watched him, hanging on every nuance of his expression. "We have to guess," he said finally. "And God help us all if I guess wrong. Henny, pack up a cloak bag for Lady Edgecombe. Basic necessities . . . her riding habit, boots. You'll know what she needs. Catlett, tell the coachman to bring around my phaeton with the grays harnessed tandem. Quentin, do you accompany me?"

"Of course. I'll dress." Quentin didn't ask where they were going; he would know soon enough. A night drive in an open phaeton in the pouring rain was not a particularly appealing prospect, but speed was obviously of the essence, and the light vehicle would make much better time than a coach.

Chapter 28

❧

They changed horses three times before dawn. Juliana didn't move, even when a strand of hair tickled her nose and she was sure she was going to sneeze. Lucien coughed and shivered and was generally silent, taking frequent pulls from a cognac flask. George stared fixedly at the bundled figure on the opposite bench.

A gray dawn broke, the sky weeping a thin drizzle. They rattled into the yard of the Red Lion at Winchester, the horses drooping. The coachman had driven them hard, a substantial bonus resting on achieving the seventy miles to Winchester in seven hours. Twice the speed of a stagecoach. George stuck his head through the window.

"Change the horses. We'll not stop for more than that."

"Flask is empty," Lucien muttered through clenched teeth. "Get it filled." He leaned to open the door and was seized with another paroxysm, doubling over, the reddening handkerchief pressed to his mouth.

"Here, give it to me." Impatiently, George snatched the flask from his limp grasp. He left the carriage and hurried across the yard to the taproom. "Fill this, and give me three extra bottles." At the rate Lucien was drinking, he reckoned that three bottles should last for the rest of the day.

He returned to the chaise, returned to his watch on

Juliana. He couldn't understand why she hadn't regained consciousness. She was breathing. Her face was deathly white, it was true, but her complexion was always milky pale against the vivid flame of her hair. He leaned over her, touched her cheek. Her skin was reassuringly warm.

Juliana knew that she couldn't keep up the pretense for much longer. Her muscles screamed for relief, and worst of all, she had a pressing need for the privy. How she would express the need with the gag in her mouth she didn't know, but if they didn't stop soon, she was going to have to make some effort to communicate. She'd been given no clues to their destination during the changes, but she guessed from the length of the journey, and from what she knew of George, that he was taking her back to his house. To the scene of the crime. Was he going to haul her before the magistrates immediately? Or did he have a more devious plan? The chaise jolted violently in a pothole, and her discomfort magnified. She closed her mind to it, forcing herself to remember, room by room, the physical plan of the house. To envisage the windows, the doors, the outbuildings, the lane that ran behind the stables.

The chaise turned up the drive to the Ridges' squat redbrick house and came to a halt before the front door. George jumped down, reached in for Juliana, and dragged her out feet first. Her head bumped on the floor, and she opened her eyes.

"Ah, my sleeping beauty, that woke you," he said with satisfaction, toppling her forward over his shoulder again. "We're going to amuse each other, I believe." He carried her up to the door. It opened as he reached it. An elderly housekeeper curtsied, her eyes startled.

"Eh, Sir George, we wasn't expectin' ye."

He merely grunted and pushed past her. Lucien followed, hunched over the deep, deep chill in his body, teeth chattering, limbs trembling.

"See to my guest, Dolly," George ordered as he strode to the stairs. "The man needs fire, hot water, bed."

"Cognac," Lucien declared feebly, raising the flask to his lips.

The woman stared at him in horror. She knew when she looked upon the dying. "This a-way sir." She took his arm, but he shook off her hand with a curse.

"Just bring me cognac and hot water, woman." He stumbled into a room to the side of the hall, handkerchief pressed to his mouth as the bloody phlegm was dredged from his lungs.

Juliana, listening to this, felt a smidgeon of hope. Lucien was clearly too ill to be capable of serious violence. That left only George. But trussed up as she was, George was quite enough to deal with.

George kicked open a door at the head of the stairs and threw Juliana down onto the bed. "Remember this room, my dear? Your wedding chamber." He pulled the cloak loose, flinging her onto her belly as he dragged it away from her.

Juliana was conscious of her shift riding up on her thighs, the air cool on the backs of her legs. With a jerk she twisted onto her back, trying to push down her shift with her bound and bandaged hands.

George chuckled and twitched it up again. "I like it just the way it was."

She moved her hands to her mouth, trying to pluck at the gag, her eyes signaling frantically. At this point she had only one thing on her mind.

"Want to say something?" He smiled. "You'll be doing a lot of talking soon, my dear stepmother. You'll be giving me a full confession of murder. You'll write it out for me, and then we'll visit the magistrates, and you'll be able to tell them all about it, too."

Juliana heaved her legs over the side of the bed and kicked her feet backward under the bed, trying to locate the chamber pot. George looked puzzled for a minute; then he smiled again.

"Ah, I understand. Allow me to help you." Bending, he pulled the pot out and pushed it with his foot into the middle of the chamber. "There," he said solicitously. "I trust you can manage. I'll be back when I've breakfasted."

Juliana's eyes spat green fire. But at least he'd left her to struggle alone. And her hands were tied in front rather than behind. There was always something to be thankful for, she thought wryly, standing up and hopping across to the chamber pot.

She managed somehow, and with little shuffles also managed to push the pot back beneath the bed; then she hopped over to the windowsill and took stock. The gag was so tight in her mouth, she couldn't work it loose with her fingers and, with her wrists tied, couldn't get at the knot behind her head. The strips of silk stocking were tight, and she couldn't slip her bandaged hands free.

Her eyes roamed around the room, saw Sir John's razor strop hanging on the wall by the washstand. Where there was a strop, there was usually a razor. She hopped to the washstand. The straight blade lay beside the ewer and basin, waiting for Sir John, as it had every morning of his adult life. No one had touched the room since his death.

Gingerly, she picked up the blade with her fingertips and tried to balance it on its edge, the cutting blade uppermost. She slid her hands forward until the silk at her wrists was directly over the blade, then sawed the material against the edge. It was blunt, in need of the strop, but she was too impatient now to attempt to sharpen it. It fell over. Carefully, she rebalanced it, holding it steady with the tension of the silk. Began again. Little by little the thin, strong silk began to fray. Twice the blade fell over when the tension of the silk lessened. Patiently, she replaced it, her heart thudding, ears strained to catch the sound of a footstep outside, the creak of a floorboard. Her throat hurt so badly, she wasn't sure she would be able to talk even if she weren't gagged. Then the material parted, the razor clattered to the washstand.

Juliana shook out her wrists, cramps running up her arms, clawing her fingers. Then she struggled with the gag and freed her mouth. Wool stuck to her tongue and her lips, reminding her vividly of Ted's ruthless lesson in the dangers of the London streets. Sleeping in one's bed seemed to be as hazardous as anything else, she thought, slashing the razor through the bonds at her ankles.

She was free. Her hurts were forgotten under a rush of exhilaration. She had heard George turn the key in the lock of the door as he'd left. She ran to the window. It was a long drop to the soft earth of a flower bed beneath. But the ivy was strong. Or looked it, at least. Whether it would bear her weight remained to be seen. There was no other option.

She pushed up the casement. The wind blew cold and wet, pressing her thin shift against her body, but she ignored it. Twisting sideways, she dropped from the window-sill, gripping the edge with her fingers, ignoring the pain in her torn palms. Her feet scrabbled for purchase in the ivy. Found a toehold of brick. Heart in her mouth, she let go of the sill with one hand, moved it down to clutch at the creeper. It held. She brought the other hand down, and now her entire weight was supported by the ivy and the toehold. Hand over hand she inched downward, feeling the creeper pull away from the wall. But each time she managed to move her hands and feet to another site before the vine gave way.

She was concentrating so hard on her hazardous climb, she didn't hear the pounding feet in the room above. But she heard George's wild bellow. Looked up, saw his face suffused with rage, staring down at her. She let go and dropped the last ten feet to the soil. She landed awkwardly, twisting her ankle. For a fateful minute or two she sat in the soil, gasping with pain. Then she heard George's bellow again, knew he was running downstairs, would appear out of the kitchen door. She was up and running through the drizzle, ignoring the pain of her ankle, making for the driveway around the house. Instinctively seeking somewhere out in the open, where there might be other eyes to witness.

She could hear George behind her now, hear his heavy,

panting breath, imagined she could almost feel it on the back of her neck. In ordinary circumstances she could have outstripped him easily. But she was barefoot and the gravel was sharp. Her ankle turned with each step, bringing tears to her eyes. She rounded the side of the house. The gravel drive stretched ahead to the lane. If she could make it to the lane, maybe there'd be a carter passing, a farm laborer . . . someone . . . anyone.

George ate up the distance between them. His breath raged in his heaving chest, his great belly jounced, his massive hands were in fists, but he was gaining on her. She was slowing, her feet troubling her. He reached out, seized the hem of her shift, hauled her backward as she fought, kicked, scratched, hair swinging wildly.

Somehow she wrenched herself free, hearing the thin material of her shift rip as she hurled herself forward, toward the gate to the lane . . . so close . . . three more steps . . .

George's breath was on the back of her neck, his hands reaching for her. The sound of iron wheels on the lane, jouncing over the rough pebbled surface . . . With the last gasp of breath Juliana leaped into the lane, in front of a hay wagon.

The driver pulled back on the reins, staring in disbelief at the frantic figure in the path of his shire horses.

"Please . . ." Juliana struggled for sufficient breath to speak. "Please . . . help me . . . I—"

She got no further. George had seized her from behind, clamping his hand over her mouth, twisting her hair around his other hand, holding her head still. His voice was calm, sensible. Not his voice at all as he explained to the astounded farm laborer that she was deranged, was kept confined for her own safety. That she'd escaped from her chamber by attacking the servant who'd brought her food. That she was violent and dangerous.

The laborer looked at the half-naked, wild-haired, frantic figure struggling in the hands of a man who was clearly in full possession of his senses, who spoke so rationally, with such assurance. The girl gazed at him with desperate, almost feral, eyes, and he shuddered, muttering a prayer, averting his eyes from the danger of a lunatic's stare. He shook the reins urgently as George pulled the madwoman aside, and drove off, urging the horses to greater speed.

Juliana bit deep into George's palm. He bellowed and slammed his flat palm against the side of her head, dazing her. Then he hoisted her over his shoulder before the ringing in her ears had subsided and carried her back to the house.

Lucien stumbled out of the drawing room, glass in hand, as the front door shivered behind George's kick. "Good God," he slurred. "Now what?"

"Thought she could escape . . . tricky bitch," George declared. He pushed past Lucien into the drawing room and threw Juliana into a chair.

She lay still, slumped into the cushioned depths, her head numb with shock and the stinging pain of the blow. For the moment she was defeated.

George poured himself a measure of cognac, downed it, and poured another. "The sooner she's locked up in Winchester jail, the better." He drained the second glass. "Let's go."

"Go where?" Lucien lounged against the door frame. His eyes burned with fever, tremors racked his body, and he clutched the cognac glass as if it were his only connection with life.

"To the Forsetts," George said, throwing his glass down. "They'll identify this whore before a magistrate, and you'll identify her as your wife and say how and when she became so. They'll arraign her and lock her up. And then . . ." He wiped his mouth slowly, lasciviously, with the back of his hand. "And then . . . my dear stepmother . . . I shall pay you some visits in your cell."

Juliana still said nothing. She was drained of physical strength and knew she couldn't get away from George again. Not here . . . not now. Maybe the Forsetts would offer her protection. But she knew that was a fond hope.

They wouldn't want to be touched by any scandal created by the ward they'd thoroughly disliked and resented. They'd repudiate her as soon as look at her.

"Come, Edgecombe," George said brusquely. "We'll ride. I'll take the whore up with me."

Lucien shook his head, opened his mouth to speak, and was promptly engulfed in a coughing spasm worse than any Juliana had witnessed. When he could speak, he gasped, "Can't possibly, dear boy. Couldn't sit a horse like this. Stay here . . . rest a bit . . . you go about your business." He gulped at the cognac.

"Oh, no," George said with soft fervor. "You're coming, Edgecombe. I need you. You won't see a penny of that money until you've done what I need you to do."

Lucien stared at him, the realization in his eyes that he couldn't withstand this man . . . this oaf whom he'd despised and thought he was using for his own revenge. Lucien wasn't using Ridge, Lucien was being used, and George now carried himself with all the cold, calculating assertion of a man possessed.

George took a menacing step toward him, his great hands bunched into fists. Lucien shrank back, all the strength of his own malice dissolved in the face of this threat, leaving him as weak and timid as any coward facing a bully.

"All right," he croaked, pressing the bloodstained kerchief to his mouth. "All right, I'll come."

George nodded brusquely and turned back to Juliana's slumped figure. She'd closed her eyes as the easiest way to absent herself from what was happening. He hauled her to her feet and grasped her chin, his other hand again twisting in her hair. "You don't want to be hurt, do you, my dear?"

She shook her head, still keeping her eyes closed.

"Then you'll do as I bid you, won't you?"

She nodded, then felt his mouth on hers, hard, bruising, vile, pressing her lips against her teeth. He forced his tongue into her mouth so she could taste the stale sourness of his brandy breath. She gagged and went suddenly limp.

George drew back and looked down into the white, closed face. He was holding her up by her hair as she sagged against him. He smiled. "Not quite so full of your-self now, Lady Edgecombe?" he taunted. "And when you've spent a week or so in a jail cell . . ." He chuckled and spun her to face the door. "Let's go."

In the hall he paused to pull a heavy riding cloak from a hook on the wall and swathed Juliana in its thick and musty folds. She walked as if in a trance as he pushed her ahead of him out of the house and to the stables, Lucien stumbling behind. The wind still blew cold and damp from the sea, and Juliana was pathetically grateful for the cloak, even though she knew it had been provided not to lessen her miseries but to avoid drawing attention to her. Lucien shiv-ered and shook, and it seemed he had no strength left even to cough.

A groom brought two horses from the stables, saddled them, looking curiously at the trio but knowing better than to say anything in front of his master. He assisted Lucien to mount. Lucien slumped in the saddle like a sack of potatoes, feebly grasping the reins, his head drooping.

George lifted Juliana onto his horse and mounted behind her, holding her securely against him as he gathered up the reins. Juliana tried to hold herself away from the hot, sweaty, triumphant maleness of his body, but he jerked her closer and she yielded before he did anything worse.

They trotted out of the yard and took the road to Forsett Towers.

Tarquin drew up in the yard of the Rose and Crown in Winchester. Quentin stepped out of the phaeton, stretch-ing his cramped, chilled limbs in the damp morning air. "Where to now?"

Tarquin turned from giving the ostler instructions to change the horses. "I'm not certain. Let's break our fast and make some inquiries."

Quentin followed him into the inn. In a few minutes

they were ensconced in a private parlor, a maid setting light to the kindling in the hearth.

"A drop of porter for the cold, my lord?" the innkeeper suggested, casting a critical eye around the wainscoted room, checking for tarnished copper, smudged window-panes, a smear of dust.

"If you please." Tarquin peeled off his gloves. "And coffee, sirloin, and eggs." He strode to the window, peering down into the street. "Where is the nearest magistrate?"

"On Castle Street, my lord."

"Send a lad to me. I need someone to run an errand." The landlord bowed himself out.

"So?" Quentin leaned over the new flame, rubbing his hands. Rain dripped off his sodden cloak.

"So we discover if Ridge took her straightway to the magistrate," Tarquin said succinctly, discarding his own dripping cloak. "Ah, thank you." He nodded at the girl who placed two pewter tankards of porter on the table.

"Ye be wantin' an errand run, sir?" A cheerful voice spoke from the doorway, where stood a rosy-cheeked lad in a leather apron, spiky hair resisting the discipline of water and brush.

Tarquin gave him brisk instructions. He was to go to the magistrate and discover if a woman had been brought before him in the last few hours.

"And if not?" Quentin took a grateful draft of porter.

"Then we assume he took her to his own house."

"And if not?" Quentin tossed his own cloak onto a set-tle, where it steamed gently in the fire's heat.

"Forsett Towers." Tarquin drank from his own tankard. His voice was flat. "If I'm wrong, then . . . I don't know." He shrugged, but the careless gesture did nothing to conceal his bone-deep anxiety.

Breakfast arrived and they ate in silence, each distracted with his own thoughts. The lad returned. The magistrate had not yet left his bed and had spent an undisturbed night.

Tarquin nodded, gave him a coin, and summoned the landlord. "D'ye know the Ridge estate?"

"Aye, sir. Ten miles south as the crow flies." The man gave precise directions. "Big stone gateposts . . . crumblin' like, m'lord. Ye can't miss it."

"Ready, Quentin?"

"On your heels, brother." Quentin put down his tankard and followed Tarquin downstairs and out into the yard. The incessant drizzle had stopped, and there was the faintest lightning in the sky. Tarquin paid their shot as fresh horses were harnessed to the phaeton.

They turned through the crumbling stone gateposts just as a feeble ray of sun poked through the clouds. The horses splashed through puddles along the driveway where Juliana had run with such desperation an hour earlier.

The housekeeper answered the furious tolling of the bell, her expression startled, her gray hair escaping from beneath her cap. She curtsied, her eyes like those of a scared rabbit. The morning had brought too many alarums and excursions into her normally peaceful routine.

"Sir George . . . is he at home?"

Dolly gazed up at the splendid figure in the caped driving cloak. His voice was cold and haughty, but his eyes were colder and carried a fearful menace.

"No, sir . . . no. . . . 'E left . . . a short while ago. 'E and 'is visitors."

"Visitors?" Tarquin raised an inquiring eyebrow.

"Yes . . . yes, indeed, sir. A gentleman . . . mortal sick 'e was. Coughin' fit to raise the dead . . . an' a girl . . . a young woman . . . sick, too. Sir George carried 'er upstairs. Then they all left." Her scared eyes flitted sideways, found Quentin's reassuring gaze. She seemed to take courage, and her fingers loosed her apron where they'd been anxiously pleating and tucking.

"Do you know where they went?" Quentin asked gently.

She shook her head. "No, sir. But they went on 'orseback. The three of 'em on two. So they can't 'ave gone far."

"What road do we take to Forsett Towers?" Tarquin's

voice still betrayed none of his agitation. He knew now that he was within a hand's grasp of Juliana, and his rage was cold and deadly. George and Lucien would have had to hurt her to compel her thus far. And they would pay. He drowned the images of what they might have done to her in the icy certainty of their punishment.

Lucien fell just as they turned onto the gravel driveway leading to the gray stone mansion of Forsett Towers. He had been barely conscious throughout the ride, slumped over the horse's neck, the reins loose in his fingers. Every few minutes his body would be convulsed with violent spasms as he shivered and coughed into the now scarlet handkerchief. When his horse stumbled into a pothole on the drive, Lucien slipped sideways. The horse, startled, broke into a sudden trot, and his rider tumbled off the saddle.

Juliana watched in horror as the confused horse quickened his pace and Lucien, still with one foot in the stirrup, was bumped along the gravel. He was making no attempt to free his foot, just dangled inert until George managed to seize the animal's bridle and pull him to a halt.

George dismounted, hauling Juliana down with him. Still maintaining a tight grip on her wrist, he released Lucien's foot and then stared down at the still figure on the ground. Lucien had struck his head on something sharp, and blood pulsed from a gash on his forehead. His eyes were closed and he was barely breathing.

"Damn him to hell!" George declared, the calm, controlled facade cracking for the first time since he'd caught Juliana on the lane. He dragged Juliana back to his horse and pushed her up into the saddle, mounting behind her again.

"You can't just leave him." Juliana at last found her voice again. She wished Lucien to the devil, but the thought of abandoning him unconscious and bleeding was appalling.

"He's no good to me in that condition." George picked

up the reins of Lucien's horse, roughly kicked his own mount's flanks, and started off again to the house, leading the riderless animal.

Juliana twisted round to look at the figure still lying on the drive. "We should carry him into the house."

"Someone else can do it. Now, hold your tongue!" He pulled on her hair in vicious emphasis, and she fell silent again. She'd always known George was a brute and an oaf, but she hadn't understood quite how brutal he was.

At the house George sprang down, dragging Juliana with him. He held her by the hair and the nape of the neck, shoving her up the steps to the front door, where he banged the knocker as if to sound the last trump. A footman opened it, looking both outraged and alarmed at such an uncivilized summons. He stared at Juliana as if he couldn't believe his eyes. "Why, Miss Juliana . . ."

George pushed past him, thrusting Juliana ahead of him. "Where's your master?"

"In the library . . . but . . ."

George ignored him, pushing Juliana toward the library door. Before he reached it, however, it opened. Sir Brian looked at them with an expression of acute distaste.

"I see you found her." His voice expressed only annoyance.

"Yes . . . and I'll see her burn outside Winchester jail," George stated, shoving Juliana into the library. He held her by the neck and glared in triumph at Sir Brian. "And you, sir, and your lady wife will identify her before a magistrate this very day."

"Goodness me, whatever's going on?" Amelia's irritated tones came from the door. "Juliana, whatever are you doing here?"

"Nothing of my own volition, ma'am," Juliana said, recovering some of her spirit in these drearily familiar surroundings. "There's a badly injured man on the driveway. Would you send some men to carry him in?"

Amelia looked between the sweaty, glowering, triumphant George and his pale prisoner. "You were never anything but trouble," she declared. "First you bring this clod into my house . . . and now you want me to take in some accident victim. Who is he?"

"My husband, ma'am. Viscount Edgecombe." Juliana began to feel a bubble of hysterical laughter welling in her chest. It was extraordinary that they should continue to behave toward her with the same exasperation of her childhood. She was about to be arraigned on murder charges. She was half-naked, battered and bruised, in the clutches of a vicious brute, her husband was lying near death in a puddle on their driveway, and they were both blaming her for disturbing their peace, as if she'd brought mud into the house, or broken a precious dish.

Amelia sighed and turned back to the hovering footman. "Dawkins, take some men and see about it, will you?"

"Yes, my lady."

"And send someone to the nearest magistrate," George demanded belligerently. "Tell him it's a matter of murder and he should come here immediately."

Dawkins looked askance at his master. Sir Brian said shortly, "You may ignore that instruction, Dawkins. If Sir George wishes to find a magistrate, he may go in search of one himself . . . and take his prisoner with him," he added coldly.

"You would obstruct justice, sir?" George's sweaty face flushed crimson. "I tell you straight, sir, I'll lay charges against you of impeding the process—"

"Oh, hold your tongue, man," Amelia interrupted acidly. "Do you think we wish to listen to your puffing and blowing? If you have a grudge against Juliana, then you may do what you wish, but don't expect us to assist you."

Juliana was somewhat surprised. True, they weren't taking her part, but neither were they taking George's.

"A grudge!" George exclaimed. "Is that how you would describe the willful murder of my father . . . her husband. Petty treason is what it is, and I tell you—"

"You will tell us nothing," Sir Brian snapped. He turned

to his erstwhile ward and asked calmly, "Juliana, did you by any chance murder your husband?"

"No."

"That's rather what we assumed. It was just another unfortunate piece of clumsiness, I daresay."

"It was certainly very clumsy of you to run away," Amelia scolded. "I can't think what could have possessed—"

"Put him down on that settle . . . careful now. Send someone for the physician."

The crisp tones of the Duke of Redmayne came from the open doorway to the hall. Amelia stopped in mid-sentence. George inhaled sharply. Juliana wrenched her head around, ignoring the savage tug on her captured hair. Her heart thudded so loudly, it was impossible that only she could hear it. She stared at the door.

Chapter 29

I give you good morning, ma'am. Sir Brian." The duke stepped into the library. "Accept my apologies for this disturbance. I wouldn't have had it happen for the world."

"And who might you be, sir?"

"Redmayne," Tarquin said with a courteous bow. "Lady Edgecombe is in my charge during her husband's indisposition. May I introduce my brother, Lord Quentin Courtney?" He gestured to Quentin, who stood behind him. Quentin bowed in his turn and murmured a pleasant greeting.

Juliana wondered whether anyone was going to notice her as she stood silent, still held captive by her hair. The scene resembled a stage farce with this exchange of polite greetings in the stuffy formality of the library.

Then Tarquin came over to her. "Take your hands off her," he said quietly.

George recovered himself. "Don't you give me orders, Redmayne. She's my prisoner, and I'm accusing her before a magistrate of petty treason."

Tarquin shook his head. "No," he said consideringly. "No, you are not going to do any such thing. *Take your hands off her!*"

George's hands fell to his sides. He could no more have withstood the soft-voiced ferocity of the order than he could have changed the direction of the wind.

"It wasn't my fault this time," Juliana croaked through her bruised throat. "I didn't get myself into this trouble, it came and found me. I was perfectly innocently asleep in my bed—"

"I am aware," the duke interrupted, taking her hands. "Are you hurt?"

"Only my throat, and I twisted my ankle," she rasped, wishing that he would take her in his arms, wishing that he wouldn't look at her with those strangely dispassionate eyes.

Tarquin saw the bruises on her throat, and livid fire chased the dispassion from his gaze. He touched her throat. "He did this to you?"

Juliana nodded, her skin alive beneath the gentle brushing of his fingers. Surely he would take her in his arms now. But he didn't. He turned back to George, his expression once more unreadable.

"Step outside. I don't want your blood on Lady Forsett's carpet." The same cold, invincible tone. The gray eyes were as pitiless and implacable as the Last Judgment. He paid no further attention to Juliana, every fiber of his being concentrated on the annihilation of George Ridge. A wicked blade suddenly flickered at the end of the cane he held in his hand. "Step outside, sir." The blade pushed between George's fat thighs.

George could feel the sensation in his groin. His knees went to water. The pitiless eyes held him, mocking his terror. He stumbled toward the door. Quentin stood aside. Tarquin followed him out, the tip of the sword still menacing George's quivering manhood.

"Lucien?" Juliana shook her head in an effort to dispel the trancelike sensation. "Is he all right, Quentin?"

Quentin didn't answer. He crossed to her in two long strides, taking her hands in his strong grip. "My poor child," he said. "What you must have suffered."

"Not that much." She smiled a wan smile. "I'm so glad to see you."

"Did you imagine Tarquin wouldn't come for you?" Quentin sounded almost reproachful.

"Your husband is dying in my hall," Amelia announced before Juliana could respond. "I really do think it most inconsiderate of you, Juliana, to bring these people down upon us."

"I hardly think Juliana is to blame, ma'am," Quentin said. "If you'll excuse me, I'll go back to my cousin and await the physician."

Juliana followed him out to where Lucien lay on the settle, his body strangely limp, his complexion waxen. Clotted blood formed over the gash on his forehead, and blood flecked his blue lips. He didn't seem to be breathing. Juliana placed her hand lightly over his mouth and felt the faint stirring of air. "He's still alive." She kept her hand there, filled now with a perverse pity for the man who had tormented her. She glanced up and read the same emotion in Quentin's eyes.

Outside George was pinned against the stable wall with a piece of wood across his throat. He didn't know how it had happened, but one minute he'd been on his feet and the next felled with a blow to the back of his neck. He'd been hauled upright and slammed against the stable wall. The duke pressed the wood tighter. "Not a pleasant feeling, I believe," he said coolly. He dropped the wood and once again pushed his unsheathed swordstick between George's pudgy thighs. George's eyes rolled.

"Listen to me very carefully now, my friend. You are going to tell the nearest magistrate that Juliana could not have been responsible for your father's death. You will say that your father was old, had a weak heart, had been drinking heavily. You will say that you have no doubt at all that he died from excitement and overexertion, leaving his child bride blameless but alone and terrified."

George's eyes rolled again. He tried to shake his head, tried to speak, but managed only a grunt that changed to a squeak as the sword pressed upward and he could feel the blade, razor sharp against his shriveled softness.

"Let me tell you why you will do this, you dolt." Tarquin paused, glancing over his shoulder at a groom who'd sauntered into the yard and now stood staring at the tableau. The duke dismissed him from his mind and turned back to Sir George.

"If you say anything else, I will lay against you charges of assault with intent to murder Lady Edgecombe. I will lay charges of stalking, of abduction, of breaking into my house, of thievery. I will have witnesses to your every action. I will say that you are obsessed with Lady Edgecombe, that you believe she is your father's widow. I will prove beyond a shadow of a doubt that Lady Edgecombe is *not* Sir John Ridge's widow. I will say that you bear me a grudge because I had you thrashed for trying to break into my house. Believe me, I can do these things. Whom do you think a magistrate is going to believe? The Duke of Redmayne, or an ignorant dolt of a country squire?"

George stared into the cold gray eyes. He knew he had lost. He had no defense against the charges. He knew the duke would produce witnesses who would swear blind to his guilt. He knew he would be bumbling and inarticulate and the duke and his lawyers would run rings around him. They would discount anything a convicted felon said against Viscountess Edgecombe, the Duke of Redmayne's cousin by marriage. They would hang him . . . transport him if he was lucky.

"Of course, if my words aren't sufficiently persuasive, there are other ways," the duke mused. The sword moved upward. George's gut loosened; he opened his mouth on a bellow of fear, but no sound came out. "It is really very tempting," Tarquin murmured. "Emasculation seems such an apt punishment, don't you think?" George felt the sword nick his inner thigh. He couldn't believe it might happen, and yet he could believe anything of this avenging devil with his ice-cold eyes. The sword nicked his other thigh, and George groaned with terror, bitter bile filling his mouth. He retched helplessly.

Tarquin stepped away from him with a disgusted curl of his lip. "You are a fool," he said contemptuously. "Oh, you might have succeeded in intimidating Juliana if she hadn't been under my wing. She's still an innocent . . . a child in many ways. But when you crossed swords with me, my friend, you made the biggest mistake of your bumbling oafish life. If you ever come within ten miles of Juliana again, I will unman you. I suggest you believe it." He turned on his heel and left George sagging against the wall, vomiting up his breakfast.

In the hall Juliana and Quentin still stood beside Lucien. Of Sir Brian and his wife there was no sign. Tarquin came over to the settle. Juliana still had her hand over Lucien's mouth, but she didn't know why anymore. She looked up at Tarquin. "He's dying."

"He's been dying for a long time," Tarquin replied. "What happened to him?"

Juliana started to explain, then stopped as Lucien's eyes fluttered open. He stared up at them, and she shrank back from the naked malice in the rapidly glazing eyes. "God rot the lot of you!" Lucien declared. His head dropped to one side, his eyes staring sightlessly at the wall.

Juliana stepped backward, suddenly conscious of an invisible thread connecting Tarquin and Quentin. As she slipped into the library, Tarquin bent over and closed Lucien's eyes. Quentin laid his hands on his breast. They stood in silence, looking down at the dead man.

"He's dead," Juliana said flatly as she entered the library.

"Who? Your husband or that oaf Ridge?" Sir Brian asked, sounding only mildly curious.

"Edgecombe."

"Well, I never knew the man, but if he was anything like that crude ox, the world's well rid of him," declared Lady Forsett. "But I consider it in the very worst of taste to die in a stranger's hall."

"No one could ever accuse Edgecombe of having taste,

ma'am," Tarquin said ironically from the door. "But I do apologize once again for the inconvenience. It was most thoughtless of him to sully your house in such fashion."

"Well, I daresay it was not exactly your fault," Sir Brian allowed. "It was that clod Ridge who brought him here, as I understand. Or was it Juliana?"

"I didn't bring anyone here," Juliana said wearily. "I was dragged here against my will. I can assure you I would never knowingly have troubled you."

"Well, since you're now a widow again, what's to become of you?"

"After a suitable period of mourning, Juliana will become my wife."

The duke's cool statement produced a stunned silence. Sir Brian blinked; Amelia stared at Juliana as if she couldn't believe such a thing of the ugly duckling. Juliana and Quentin merely stared at the duke.

"But . . . but Lydia . . . ," Quentin finally stammered.

"She will be eloping with you, my dear." Tarquin leaned against the mantel, an enigmatic smile on his face. He was clearly enjoying the effect he was having. "It seems the only workable solution. You and Lydia will elope. I will of course be the gentleman. Suitably upset at being jilted, but very noble about relinquishing my betrothed to the man of her heart. Lord and Lady Melton will have no choice but to put a good face on it. It's hardly a bad match, dear boy."

"But . . . but an elopement! I'll be drummed out of the Church." Quentin still gaped in disbelief at this impossible scenario.

"Nonsense," Tarquin said briskly. "People will know only that a private marriage took place with the blessing of Lydia's parents. It had to be quiet because of the bereavement. I will give my blessing graciously. Your bishop will welcome your most excellent wife, and everything will be smooth as silk."

The astonishing words fell into Quentin's brain like diamonds, sharp-edged and shining with clarity. It sounded so easy. He looked at Juliana, saw the glow on her pale cheeks, the light in her eyes. He looked at Tarquin, who was smiling softly to himself, his eyes resting on Juliana. And it became clear to Quentin that it was the only possible step for any of them to take.

"You wish to marry me?" Juliana found her voice at last. She still clutched the old cloak around her shoulders.

"So it would seem."

"I have always been astonished at your energy, Juliana, but three husbands in one year is industry beyond belief," Sir Brian remarked dryly.

"But you do seem to have done remarkably well for yourself," Amelia observed. "I would never have believed you could make a duchess."

"She will make an exemplary duchess, ma'am," Quentin said with one of his rare flashes of anger. "Juliana is a very special person."

Amelia looked surprised. "Do you think so, indeed? We always found her a great trial."

"How very unfortunate and how very blind, Lady Forsett." Tarquin stepped toward Juliana and took her hands. "Those of us who know her find her only a source of delight."

Juliana flushed and her fingers fluttered in his palm. "Really?"

"Really." He bent and kissed her lightly.

"There's something I should tell you."

"There's no need." His hand moved to her belly, rested there.

"You guessed?"

"Yes, my dear. It was not difficult." He laughed at her chagrined expression. "I have known that you're my heart and soul for many weeks now, *mignonne*. There are no secrets you can keep from me."

"There are no secrets that I would wish to keep," she affirmed, lost in his gaze, in the overwhelming wonder following so hard on the heels of despair, unaware of Quentin's discreetly ushering their hosts out of the room. Unaware of anything now but the sweetness of his mouth on hers, the sudden fire as his body moved against hers. The absolute knowledge of love.

ABOUT THE AUTHOR

Jane Feather is the nationally bestselling, award-winning author of *Vanity, Vice, Violet* and many more historical romances. She was born in Cairo, Egypt, and grew up in the New Forest, in the south of England. She began her writing career after she and her family moved to Washington, D.C., in 1981. She now has over a million books in print.

Coming from Bantam Books in early 1997

THE DIAMOND SLIPPER

A breathtaking new romance
by the nationally bestselling

Jane Feather

Prologue

"No . . . please, no more." The words emerged as barely a breath through the woman's dry, cracked lips. Feebly she tried to push aside the silver chalice held to her mouth.

"You must take it, my dear. It will make you well." The man held her head in the crook of his elbow. Her eyes were closed and she was too weak to resist as he tipped the contents of the chalice down her throat. At the familiar bittersweet taste, the woman groaned faintly. Her head fell back against his arm and gently he lowered her head to the pillow. He hung over her, staring down at her beautiful white face, the skin so translucent he could almost see through to the bones of her skull. Then her eyes opened. For a moment they were as clear and brilliant as they had ever been, and in them he read her unspeakable knowledge of what he was doing to her.

For a long moment, her dying gaze held his. Then her eyelids dropped, her lips parted on a struggling sob of a breath.

The man stepped back into the shadows of the bed-curtains. He took up a glass of wine from the bedside table and sipped, his cold brown gaze never leaving the woman's face. It wouldn't be long now before Elvira paid the price for her crime.

A whimpering snuffle came from beyond the

bed-curtains. He moved them aside and stepped into the warm, firelit chamber. A nurse sat beside the fire, rocking a double cradle with her foot.

"Should I bring the babes to her, Your Highness?"

The man came over to the cradle. He looked down into two matching pairs of bright blue eyes, two sets of rosy cheeks, four dimpled fists clutched on top of the pale pink blankets.

Were they his? He would never know. And it didn't matter now. "Yes," he said. "They will bring the princess comfort, but don't let them tire her."

"No, of course not, sir." The nurse bent to scoop up the two snuffling bundles. She smiled and kissed them. "There, my pretties, your mama is waiting to see you." She moved softly with her burden toward the bed.

The prince sipped his wine and stared into the fire. The nurse returned the infants to their cradle in a very few minutes. "Her Highness is so weak. I don't believe she'll last the night," she said sadly.

The prince didn't reply. He returned to his death watch in the shadows of the bed-curtains, listening to the rattle of his wife's labored breathing. He was still there when the sound stopped.

He approached the bedside, leaned over, pressed his lips to hers, felt their cold deadness, the total absence of spirit in her body. He straightened slowly and lifted the woman's fragile right wrist. He unclasped the charm bracelet she wore, holding it up to the dim light of the lamp burning at the the bedside. The dainty charms glittered and glowed, shockingly frivolous in this dark chamber of death. He slipped the bracelet into his pocket and called for the nurse.

Chapter One

The procession of gilded coaches, plumed, gaily caparisoned horses, officers resplendent in blue and gold uniforms wound through the great gold gates of the palace, coming to a halt in the center of the massive square before the palace.

"Look at those two carriages!" a fair-haired girl hanging perilously far out of an upstairs window exclaimed to her companion leaning out beside her. "They are both to carry me into France. Which do you prefer, Cordelia? The crimson one or the blue one?"

"I can't see it makes much difference," Lady Cordelia Brandenburg responded. "Of all the ridiculous things. There's the Duc de Dufort riding into the city as if he'd just come from France, when instead he only left Vienna an hour ago."

"But it's protocol," the archduchess Maria Antonia said in shocked reproof. "It's how it has to be done. The French ambassador enters Vienna as if he's just come from Versailles. He must formally ask *Madame ma mère* for my hand in marriage on behalf of the dauphin of France, and then I will be married by proxy before I go into France."

"Anyone would think you hadn't been promised to the dauphin for the last three years," Cordelia stated. "What a stir it would cause if the empress refused the ambassador's request." She chuckled mischievously, but her companion didn't see the joke.

"Don't be absurd, Cordelia. I shan't allow you to be so impertinent when I am Queen of France." She wrinkled her pert nose.

"Considering your bridegroom is only sixteen, I imagine you'll have to wait awhile before attaining such high honor," Cordelia retorted, not in the least affected by her royal friend's castigation.

"Oh, pshaw! You're such a wet blanket! When I'm dauphine, I shall be the most popular and important lady at Versailles." Toinette twirled in a crimson swirl of silk as her hoop swung out around her. With an exuberant gesture, she began to dance around the room, her dainty slippered feet faultlessly executing the steps of a minuet.

Cordelia cast a glance over her shoulder and then turned back to the considerably more interesting scene in the court below. Toinette was a gifted dancer and never lost an opportunity to show off.

"Now, I wonder who that is?" Cordelia mused, her voice suddenly sharp with interest.

"Who? Where?" Toinette came back to the window, pushing Cordelia to one side, her fair head a startling contrast with her companion's raven black curls.

"There. Dismounting from the white stallion. A Lipizzaner, I think."

"Yes, it must be. Look at those lines." Both girls

were passionate horsewomen and for a moment the horse interested them more than its rider.

The man drew off his riding gloves and looked around the court. He was tall, slim, dressed in dark riding clothes, a short, scarlet-lined riding cape swinging from his shoulders. As if aware of the observers, he looked up at the creamy ocher facade of the palace. He stepped back, looked up again, shading his eyes with his hand.

"Come in," the archduchess said. "He's seen us."

"So what?" Lady Cordelia responded. "We're only looking. Don't you think he's handsome?" Not as handsome as Christian, of course, but quite well-looking, although she was probably too far away to be certain.

"I don't know," Toinette said with a touch of petulance. "Come away. It's shockingly bad etiquette to stare like that. What would Mama say?"

Cordelia had little difficulty imagining what the empress Maria Theresa would say if she found her daughter and her daughter's friend staring out of the window like a pair of oglers at the opera. However, something kept her at the window, even as Toinette tugged at her arm.

The man continued to look up at her. Mischievously, she waved and blew him a kiss. For a moment, he looked thoroughly taken aback, then he laughed and touched his fingers to his lips.

"Cordelia!" The archduchess was scandalized.

"I'm not going to stay in here if you're going to behave like that. You don't even know who he is."

"Oh, some equerry, I expect," Cordelia said airily. "I doubt we'll come across him again." She plucked half a dozen yellow roses from a bowl on the deep windowsill. Leaning as far out as she could, she tossed them down. They fell in a cloud around the horseman, one of them landing on his shoulder, caught in the folds of his cloak. He extricated it and carefully inserted it in the buttonhole of his coat. Then he doffed his plumed hat and bowed with a magnificent flourish, before moving out of sight as he entered the palace below the window.

Cordelia laughed and drew back from the window. "That was amusing," she said. "It is fun when people enter the spirit of the game." A contemplative little frown drew her thin arched eyebrows together. "An ordinary equerry wouldn't be riding a Lipizzaner, would he?"

"No, of course not." The archduchess was still annoyed. "You've probably been flirting with a senior official from Versailles. He must assume you're a kitchen maid, or something."

Cordelia shrugged. "I don't suppose he's important. Anyway, I'm sure he won't recognize me close-to."

"Of course he will," Toinette scoffed. "No one else has such black hair."

"Oh, well, I'll just powder it," Cordelia declared, selecting a grape from a bunch in a crystal bowl and popping it into her mouth. A silver clock on the mantel chimed prettily. "Goodness, is that the time?" she exclaimed. "I must fly, or I'll be late."

"Late for what?"

Cordelia winked. "I'll tell you before you go to France, Toinette." And she whisked herself out of the room in a cloud of primrose yellow muslin.

The archduchess pouted crossly. Cordelia didn't seem to mind that their friendship was about to come to an end. Versailles had decreed that when Maria Antonia married the dauphin and came to France she must leave behind everything that was tied to the Austrian court. She was allowed to take none of her ladies, none of her possessions, not even her clothes.

Disconsolately, she plucked grapes from the bunch, wondering what secret Cordelia was holding these days. She was even more ebullient than usual, even more mischievous, and she was always disappearing mysteriously for hours at a time.

Cordelia, well aware of her friend's disgruntled puzzlement, sped down the corridor toward the east wing of the palace. She couldn't risk telling her secret to anyone, and most particularly not Toinette. If the empress suspected anything amiss, she would soon worm the truth out of her daughter. Sometimes, Cordelia was so full of the wonderful thing that had happened to her, she thought she would burst if she couldn't tell someone. But she knew perfectly well that if her uncle suspected she was in love with Christian Percossi, the roof would fall in. A court musician, even if he was an acknowledged prodigy as a violinist and composer, was no suitable companion, let alone match, for Lady Cordelia Brandenburg. Christian was dependent upon the empress's patronage and he couldn't risk losing it, and if even a rumor of such a misalliance reached Maria Theresa's ears, he would lose his patron and be out on the streets.

Cordelia turned aside down a little-used corridor and through a massive wooden door at the end. She was in the west wing of the palace, in a long gallery lined with heavy tapestried screens. She ducked behind the third one.

"Where have you been? I've been waiting an eternity!" Christian pulled her to him, pushing up her face with his hand under her chin. His great brown eyes devoured her countenance.

"I was watching the arrival of the French wedding party in the courtyard," she said, running a finger over his lips. "Don't be cross, Christian. I'm only a very little late."

"But you don't know how dreadful it is to hide here, trembling at every mouse," he whispered fiercely, running his hands down her back.

"Oh, I do, I do," Cordelia protested. "But I'm here now and we're wasting time. Kiss me." She flung her arms around his neck, pressing her body close to his.

He groaned as he kissed her with wild passion, his hands scrabbling against her hoop as he pushed it aside, trying to feel the shape of her beneath. He moved his lips down her neck, down to the swell of her creamy white bosom rising from the low neck of her gown. His lips nuzzled, pressed, his tongue darted into the deep cleft. Cordelia moaned, caressed his bent head, holding his mouth to her breasts, wanting more and more, her loins full and aching with an indescribable need that could never be satisfied in this mad and dangerous fashion.

With another moan, she drew his head back, gazing up into the musician's hungry brown eyes, drinking in the angular beauty of his face. Her hands moved through his crisp fair curls. "I must go."

"How I wish there were another way," Christian muttered. He let his hands fall away from her and looked helplessly into her face. "All this hiding in corners, snatching moments . . . it's driving me insane, Cordelia."

"I know . . . I know," she said soothingly, touching his lips again with her finger. "And I'll think of something. I always do, don't I?"

"I don't know what we can do," he said on a despairing sigh.

"Don't be such a pessimist. Wait for five minutes before you leave." On tiptoe, she kissed him swiftly, and then was gone from behind the screen, leaving Christian with the faint fragrance of orange-flower water that she used on her hair and the lingering impression of her quicksilver personality like the diffusion of a fading rainbow.

Cordelia slipped backward into the long gallery. She smoothed down her skirts, turned to stroll casually toward the door at the far end of the gallery, and came to face to face with the man who rode the Lipizzaner.

He turned from his contemplation of a particularly bloody hunting scene on a tapestry on the far wall. He still wore his scarlet-lined riding cape, startling against the impeccable white of his ruffled shirt.

"Well, well," he said. "If it isn't the flower girl. Where did you spring from?"

Cordelia was for once in her life at a loss under the quizzical scrutiny of a pair of merry golden eyes, aglint with flecks of hazel and green. Her heart was beating very fast. She told herself it was fear that her clandestine exchange with Christian had been overheard, but for some reason she didn't seem to find that worrying. Something else was causing this tumultuous confusion, the moistening of her palms.

"Cat got your tongue?" he inquired, lifting a slender dark eyebrow.

"Behind the screen . . . I was behind the screen." Cordelia finally managed to speak. "I . . . I was adjusting my dress . . . a hook came loose." She gathered the shreds of her composure around her again and her eyes threw him a defiant challenge, daring him to question the lie.

"I see." Leo Beaumont regarded her with amused curiosity. Whatever had been going on behind the screen had had little to do with dress repairing. Hooks and eyes didn't cause such a delicious flush, or create such lusciously reddened, swollen lips. He glanced pointedly toward the screen. "I *see*," he repeated, his eyes filled with laughter. "I'm hurt. I thought your kisses were exclusively for me."

Cordelia swallowed and touched her lips with her tongue. They were still tingling, and presumably showed it. It didn't matter what he thought of her, she'd already compromised herself at the window earlier on, but she had to prevent him from looking behind the screen and identifying Christian. "Who are you?" she demanded with a rudeness that she hoped would distract him.

"Viscount Kierston at your service." He bowed solemnly, seemingly unperturbed by her lack of finesse.

An English viscount. No mere equerry, then. Cordelia nibbled her lip. His eyes continued most unnervingly to hold her own blue-gray gaze. Close-to, he fulfilled the promise of her distant window observaton. She found herself taking inventory. Tall, slender, with a broad forehead and pronounced widow's peak, his hair, almost as black as her own, confined in a bag wig at his nape. There was something disturbingly sensual about his mouth, a long upper lip above a deeply cleft chin.

Lucifer! What was she thinking? Her mind flew to Christian, cowering behind the screen, but his image seemed to blur under the English viscount's steady gaze and her own rapt bemusement.

"You now have the advantage over me," he prompted gently, noting the elegance of her gown, the silver pendant at her throat, the pearl-sewn ribbon in her hair. "I take it you're not a flower girl or a parlor maid, despite your fondness for kisses."

Cordelia flushed and said awkwardly, "I trust we'll keep that little incident between ourselves, my lord."

Again, he glanced toward the screen and his mouth quirked. "Your delightful greeting on my arrival, or some . . . some other incident?"

"It was unwise of me to throw the flowers, sir," she said stiffly, refusing to look toward the screen. "I am sometimes unwise, but it was only a game, and I intended no discourtesy, or . . . or . . ."

"Excessive familiarity," Leo supplied helpfully. "I assure you, I didn't take it in the least ill, and to prove it to you, allow me to make good a distant promise." Taking Cordelia's chin between finger and thumb, he kissed her before she fully grasped what he meant. His lips were cool and pliant, yet firm.

Her mouth still carried the memory of the fierce, moist passion of Christian's unsophisticated urgency, but instead of withdrawing in shock and outrage, she was responding, opening her lips for the strong muscular probe of his tongue, greedily inhaling the scent of his skin. His hands moved over her back, cupping her buttocks, lifting her toward him. She pressed herself into his body, her breath swift and uneven as hot waves of hungry passion broke over her. She nipped his bottom lip, her hands raking through his hair, her body totally at the mercy of this desperate craving.

Leo drew back. He stared down at her, his own passion fading slowly from his eyes. "Dear God," he said softly. "Dear God in heaven. What are you?"

Cordelia felt the color draining from her face as the wild, uncontrolled passion receded and she understood what she'd done. Understood what, but not why. Her body was still on fire, her legs shaking. With an inarticulate mumble, she turned and fled the gallery, holding up her skirts with one hand, her hoop swinging, her jeweled heels tapping on the marble floor.

Leo shook his head in bewilderment. What had started as a little playful dalliance with an appealingly mischievous young woman had taken an astounding turn. He wasn't used to losing himself in the kisses of an ingenue, but whoever she was, she weaved a powerful magic with that unbridled passion.

"An author to treasure."—*Romantic Times*

Jane Feather

VANITY

A seductive thief with a deceptive air of innocence picks
the wrong pocket. ___57248-2 $5.99/$7.99 in Canada

VALENTINE

An arrogant nobleman must marry one of four sisters if he
is to inherit his fortune. ___56470-6 $5.99/$7.99

VELVET

A daring beauty sets out to seduce England's cleverest spy . . . only
to find that seduction works both ways. ___56469-2 $5.50/$6.99

VIXEN

When a reclusive lord finds himself saddled with a beautiful ward, life
takes a dangerous and seductive turn. . . . ___56055-7 $5.99/$7.99

VIRTUE

She was a reckless beauty who played for the highest stakes: one
man's ruin and another man's heart. ___56054-9 $5.50/$6.99

VIOLET

A dazzling tale of espionage in which a beautiful bandit accepts a
mission more dangerous than she knows. ___56471-4 $5.50/$6.99

Ask for these books at your local bookstore or use this page to order.

Please send me the books I have checked above. I am enclosing $____ (add $2.50 to
cover postage and handling). Send check or money order, no cash or C.O.D.'s, please.

Name _____

Address _____

City/State/Zip _____

Send order to: Bantam Books, Dept. FN131, 2451 S. Wolf Rd., Des Plaines, IL 60018
Allow four to six weeks for delivery.

Prices and availability subject to change without notice.   FN 131 6/96

DON'T MISS THESE FABULOUS
BANTAM WOMEN'S FICTION TITLES

On Sale in May

From Jane Feather, nationally bestselling author of
Violet *and* Vanity, *comes a sinful new romance*

VICE

Juliana drew the line at becoming a harlot. After all, she had already begun the week as a bride, and ended it as a murderess. But now she's at the mercy of a powerful, handsome Duke . . . and in no position to bargain.   ___57249-0 $5.99/$7.99 in Canada

THE ENGAGEMENT
by beguiling bestseller Suzanne Robinson

An enticing Victorian tale of passion and intrigue that pits the daughter of a duke against a handsome stranger—a man who's part cowboy, part hero, and part thief . . . but altogether irresistible.   ___56346-7 $5.50/$7.50

NIGHT MOVES
by award-winning Sandra Canfield

"A master storyteller of stunning intensity." —Romantic Times

With a spellbinding mixture of passion and suspense, past lovers struggle to find a daughter who has been kidnapped . . . and the courage to reclaim love.   ___57433-7 $5.99/$7.99

SWEET LOVE, SURVIVE
by Susan Johnson

"A queen of erotic romance." —Romantic Times

In this powerful finale to the bestselling Kuzan Dynasty series begun in *Seized by Love* and *Love Storm*, a man and a woman find themselves in a desperate and passionate liaison, while the fires of a nation in revolution burn around them.   ___56329-7 $5.99/$7.99

Ask for these books at your local bookstore or use this page to order.

Please send me the books I have checked above. I am enclosing $____ (add $2.50 to cover postage and handling). Send check or money order, no cash or C.O.D.'s, please.

Name _____

Address _____

City/State/Zip _____

Send order to: Bantam Books, Dept. FN159, 2451 S. Wolf Rd., Des Plaines, IL 60018
Allow four to six weeks for delivery.

Prices and availability subject to change without notice.   FN 159 5/96